Really appreciated the
support-

A FATE
UNKNOWN

George Demarakis

ISBN: 1530388201
ISBN 13: 9781530388202

ACKNOWLEDGEMENTS

I would like to thank Colin, Greg, Ryan, and Andrew. Their kind words were beyond motivational in starting me down this path. To my loving wife, who has been by my side through this whole process, and who has also been my most valuable critic. To my family, who had the confidence in what I could achieve. And to my dad who always wanted me to finish what I started. I can finally say I did.

PROLOGUE

The obituary read,

"Charles Morgan was a loyal friend with an adventurous heart. His love for exploration led him across the globe where he engraved many marks onto this world. To those who knew him, Charles was the most selfless man who always offered a helping hand. This trait garnered him many friends from all regions of the world. He left this Earth doing what he cherished most, searching to uncover a lost treasure. He was thirty five years old when he fell to his death on an expedition in the Ningan region of China. His body was never found, but Charles would have loved it no other way. Now, he will forever be destined as the next great mystery for a future generation.

He is survived by his best friend, Jeremy Jenkins."

I finished reading the handwritten piece of paper and dropped it on the wooden table. I had to say that was beautiful—borderline poetic. It almost brought me to tears. The sad thing was that those words were written about me, and as nice as it all sounded, I was far from dead.

I cringed when I saw the photo that lay beside the paper. It was an old headshot from years ago. My fingers entangled my short brown hair. An awkward smile stretched across my face, and my one eye was clenched shut. It was a hot desert day, and the blistering sun blinded me, when my old friend Jeremy snapped that photograph.

Out of all the pictures the man had of me, this was the one he had chosen to put above my obituary? I needed to revise my *will* so when the day actually did come where I really died, they would have decency to insert a better photo than this.

Jeremy and I had been friends for seventeen years. We had been through thick and thin together. The amount of stories I had of all our adventures was nearly infinite I was positive he could have found something better than this picture.

Leaning back in the chair, I diverted my attention to the guy sitting across from me. All I could make out was the top of his bald head. He sat, hunched over on the table, snoring away in deep sleep. Beside him rest an empty bottle of bourbon.

Even from this angle, I easily made out my best pal, Jeremy Jenkins—or J.J. as I liked to call him. The stench of alcohol oozed out of his pores. This was a pale image of the usually proper, elegant, and well-kept man that I called my friend.

With the hell I'd been through over the past three months, J.J. looked a lot worse than I did—not to mention the dump of a bar that I just found him in.

The place was an old wooden shack in the middle of nowhere. The dense forests of China hid its location well. Even the dirt path that led here was barely a road. It was almost as if the owners of this *fine* establishment didn't want any customers. Be that as it may, the place was flowing with alcohol and from the looks of it, Jeremy had his fair share.

I called out his name.

Nothing.

I smacked him in the head.

Nothing.

I leaned in to do it once more when a voice spoke out from behind me. In a broken accent, the voice said, "That does not work."

A young Chinese waitress approached.

"You speak English?" I asked.

She nodded. "This man comes every night. He drinks, sleeps, and wakes up at close to go home."

It was odd to hear those words. I never considered J.J. to be a *drinking man*. The alcohol I smelled on him proved otherwise—as did the empty bottle of liquor. I glanced at the clock on the wall. "What time do you close?"

"In one hour," the waitress responded.

"It looks like I have some time then, don't I?"

"You are the man from the picture, no?" The woman pointed at the hideous photo on the table.

"Unfortunately," I commented.

"Should you not be happy? They say you were dead."

"I thought I was too."

I considered telling her that the *unfortunate* part was due to the picture itself. The being alive part was actually quite fortunate. I mean, for what I had actually lived through, I could barely believe it myself.

I reached out and grabbed the glass of liquor by Jeremy's hand. I took a sip.

The woman sat down. "He talks much about you. I believe he misses you."

"I thought you said he just drinks then sleeps?"

"That is when he talks most." She smiled.

"Well I missed him too." It was true. A lot of time passed since my supposed death. There was a moment where I thought I would never see J.J. again. It was a miracle that I found him in the first place.

"How are you back from the grave?"

"It's a long story."

"We're in no rush," the woman said.

"Well... It wasn't long ago when I first came to this neck of the woods. At the time, ironically, I was here to save *that* man from his own obituary."

PART I

The Day I Died

CHAPTER ONE

Ningan Province, China

The battered bus screeched to a halt.

Dust kicked up off the gravel road, surrounding the rusted vehicle in a blanket of smog. I sighed in relief. For eight hours, I had to listen to the chug of that whining engine scream to keep the bus moving through the humid wilderness. Like the rest of the passenger car, the engine was years beyond its lifespan.

I sat in my seat, peering out the window at our final destination. It was impossible to see anything through the filthy glass.

Large, burly men took up the other seats of the bus. Their foul odor filled the air. There was a chance that part of the vomit-inducing smell may have been coming from me since I hadn't showered for days, but I liked to give myself the benefit of the doubt.

They were all prisoners, just like me. Thieves, killers, and some simply unlucky fellas made up most of the bus. Of course, I was classified as one of the *simply unlucky fellas.*

At the front end, a Chinese man in a wrinkled police uniform ushered everyone out of their seats. Getting up, I could feel the numbness in my legs. It was a long drive. My butt ached from the spring-less chair that had been my home for the entire trip.

I filed in line with the rest of the prisoners, and their disgusting body stenches engulfed my nostrils. Yeah, now I was positive that the smell wasn't coming from me. The officer at the front barked out some more orders in his native tongue, and everyone started their way out the exit.

I reached the door. I began my way down the steps when the officer spat something out at me. A boot drilled into my lower back, launching me forward. Maintaining my balance, I stumbled out of the bus and onto the dirt road.

It was nice to see the hospitality a foreigner was given.

I guess, for what I was about to be thrust into, that was my 'Welcome to paradise.' Though, what did I expect? I was an American in the tiny Ningan Province of China who was just sentenced to five years in a laogai prison. This wasn't a vacation spot. While most people would love to feel the sun's burning rays on their body, the view of a lush forest with a mountainous backdrop, and the adventure of visiting some other country, this was not the case for me.

I was still stuck in the faded jeans and ripped gray T-shirt I'd worn for weeks. My brown hair was rustled and dirty. A thin beard had settled in from days without shaving. Grime covered my body from head to toe, and I felt the tingling desire to bathe. Don't worry, that *tingle* was partially masked by the pain of my back, numb rear, and Jell-O legs. This was not a good way to start off my morning.

Many said I was one of the unluckiest guys out there. For some reason trouble always followed me around. I guess that was an inherent job hazard in my field of work.

Being a treasure hunter put me in league with many un-friendly characters. I couldn't count the amount of times the cards had been stacked against me. From being hunted by mob bosses, getting double-crossed and left for dead, narrowly escaping elaborate traps that guarded buried treasure, and being attacked by vicious wild animals (I include some women in this category), the list went on and on.

I'd lost a number of friends along the road and killed my share of bad guys, but not enough for my hands to stop shaking every time I pulled that trigger. I'd broken dozens of bones, and scars and bullet wounds littered my body as permanent reminders of all my adventures.

Yes, it looked as if I may have been one unlucky fella, but I begged to differ.

I was more of a glass half-full kind of guy, and I'd say I was one of the luckiest guys out there. I mean yes, I got into a lot of trouble, but there was a key point to that. The fact that I survived every time was proof I had to be one lucky guy.

So, instead of looking death straight in the eye, I managed to dodge him and keep on going. And right now, being sent to this prison had to be one of my luckiest moments yet.

Why?

Because Jeremy Jenkins was an inmate at this very same prison. It also happened that he needed my help.

J.J. was the man who introduced me to the treasure hunting business. There was no real limit to what I would do for him, and there was nothing he wouldn't do for me. This crazy idea to help J.J. fell in line with the higher side of my limits.

Luckily, I knew exactly where they were holding him—in the cell block. I just needed to get there.

As my vision cleared from the bright sunlight, I took in my surroundings. Standing on a raised platform was a group of prison guards. They all looked exactly the same—short and angry. Around us were twenty foot tall concrete walls topped with barb wire. Four wooden guard towers anchored the corners of the prison, and a few large concrete compounds littered the area.

That was it.

The entire central area was an open dirt field. A solid hundred prisoners roamed the grounds. Most of them were skin and bones, hard at work in some sort of assembly line in the center of the camp.

See, laogai prison camps were more like adult sweat shops. Prisoners worked to create amenities to be sold on the market. Smart move if one thought about it—free labor to the government, and extra cash in their pockets.

Anyways, I watched in awe until someone shoved me forward. I took a few more steps and huddled around the rest of my company.

Through a megaphone, one of the guards started announcing names. After each name called, the prisoner amongst our group stepped forward. They motioned him off, and he walked on into the facility.

No check-up.

No change of clothes.

Nothing.

That's exactly what I was told to expect, and that was exactly what I wanted.

"Charles Morgan." I heard my name called out in a broken accent. I moved forward and began my march into my new home.

I navigated my way around. I kept my head down as I passed my fellow inmates. I didn't want to stir any trouble. From my periphery, I quickly realized that none of the prisoners really gave a crap about me. They were too miserable to care.

The Chinese patrols, on the other hand, did seem to care. They paced back and forth across the compound, guns by their side. They surveyed the area in broad strokes.

Being a sweat shop, the guards made extra cash if more items were shipped. This provided them with great incentive to keep things moving along. When they noticed a well-fed man strolling about, they saw an opportunity.

Without even getting a tour, and without any proper training in how the place operated, I was immediately thrust to work. The other inmates I had the pleasure of riding with on my way here joined in on the work detail as well.

There was just no escaping their awful stenches.

My job was simple. I called it *haul* duty.

Boxes of uniforms needed to transport from the assembly lines to the main garage. There, they were piled into the back of a delivery truck.

Each box was crammed with pants, shirts, belts, and socks. And each outfit looked exactly the same. The boxes were heavy, but I didn't mind. This gave me the opportunity to survey the land. Stretching my legs, I grabbed a loaded container and carried it across the open courtyard.

Inside the garage, I found a few dozen ancient military vehicles. Rust covered their metallic hulls, and countless bullet holes riddled the side panels. Like the bus that brought me here, these jeeps had seen their fair share over the course of their lifetime. A few mechanics struggled to breathe life into these crippled vehicles. Their old tools scattered about.

Passing the mechanics, I made it to the far end of the garage and reached the delivery truck. I placed my first box into the back of the truck. Setting the container down, I left the garage and went on for another.

This process continued. As I progressed back and forth across the courtyard, I further analyzed my new home.

It was pretty easy to figure out. There really wasn't much to the place. Other than the few larger concrete structures, a number of smaller ones littered the yard. Most of the prisoners sat in the large open area. They all huddled around large tables, working away.

Then there were the *cool* kids. These seemed like the notorious prisoners that no one messed with. You could tell by the permanent grumpy looks on their faces. They huddled together, glaring at the crowd. Cigarettes dangled from their lips, and somehow they were all in abnormally good shape. Muscles bulged from areas I never thought possible. It was tough to discern where their necks ended and their shoulders began. None of them spoke a word, but their eyes said enough.

The withered inmates toiling away at the assembly line were all pushing old age. I realized that my position on this so-called workforce was the best I was going to get. I already saw my future here. First, I would do manual labor. As months and years would go by, I would become weaker and step down to boxing the shipments. Finally, when I became fragile, they would put me at the start of the line sewing the outfits. It was a messed up way to look at it, but that was what I had to look forward to.

Thankfully, I wasn't planning on being a tenant here for long.

As I grabbed my next box, I passed a large wooden executioner's platform. This stage was comprised of rotted two by six planks. Large heavy timbers interconnected to form the shape of a standard swing set. It anchored on top of the platform. A single noose dangled from the main horizontal branch. A few guards were tightening the knots and checking the wooden supports.

They were preparing for today's execution.

Beyond that structure, at the far west corner of the prison stood a fairly large single story building. Periodically, a fellow inmate exited the building with a bucket. He'd walk over to a hose bib protruding from the ground and leave it there. Sometime later, another prisoner would walk by, pour water into the bucket and take it back inside.

The layout of the facility was just as I researched, and that *waterboy* job was exactly what I needed.

Not because the task looked easy. My arms might have been getting a little numb from the heavy lifting, but no, it was because I needed to get into that very building. The sole reason I wanted to get into this prison was to gain access to the lower levels of that structure—the cell block.

J.J.'s life depended on it.

Unfortunately, seeing the guards put the finishing touches on the noose, I realized my friend's time on this Earth was closing in on becoming past tense. The clock struck eleven.

I was cutting things close.

The bucket lay unattended near the water spigot. Seeing everyone else focus on the pile of boxes in the distance, I broke from the line and diverted toward the bucket.

I filled it up. None of the guards took notice as I strolled nonchalantly across the field toward the compound at the opposite end.

I reached the stainless steel door of the building and pried it open. Risking one last glance back, I disappeared into darkness.

I didn't think it possible, but the smell inside the building was worse than the suffocating stench of that bus. I sped across the corridor, scanning the cursory rooms on either side. The hall was lined with bathrooms and shower stalls that looked like they hadn't been cleaned in ages.

I pressed on. Turning left at the edge of the hall, I ran into a pair of guards heading my direction.

My heart stopped. I couldn't get busted now. All I had to do was play it cool—pretend like I belonged. The two men glared at me as our gap narrowed. The beating of my heart drowned their footsteps. They got closer and closer.

They passed by in silence.

Letting out a deep breath, I took another step forward. For as deadly as I heard this place to be, things were going a lot more smoothly than I had anticipa—

A hand burst out of one of the side rooms and yanked me toward the wall. I pried myself free of the man's grip and instantly pulled away. The man was stuck behind the bars of a prison cell. He laughed and screamed. The man grasped at thin air, still trying to grab me once again.

"Easy pal," I managed to choke out as I went by him.

I had entered the cell block. I was getting close.

At the end of the hall, stairs led deeper down into the facility. I reached the bottom landing and opened the next pair of steel doors. As I entered, I was welcomed by a few more prison guards.

They said something.

I didn't comprehend.

One of the guards raised his voice and repeated himself.

"Yes, if you speak to me louder I'll understand you," I said in an even higher tone.

I'm not sure if the man understood my sarcasm or if he didn't really care, but he smacked me on the side of the head and pointed to the ladle that hung on the wall.

He motioned me to pass out the water to the prisoners in all the cells. At least that's what I thought his hand gestures insinuated.

I grabbed the oversized spoon and moved on. The cell block was full of barred cages. Five or six prisoners sat motionless on the ground of their individual cells. Getting a closer look at each of them I could see that they, like most of the inmates upstairs, barely had any meat on their bones. It was a sad sight.

That is, until I reached the last cell.

Sitting on a stool, dressed in cargo pants, a green safari shirt, and sporting a lobster tan, was Jeremy Jenkins. Even at the age of sixty, J.J. still looked quite fit and well nourished. I flashed a smile at him and opened my mouth to say hello, but...

"What took you so long, Charles?" J.J. said dryly before I could speak.

"What took me so long? No, 'I'm so glad to see you, Charlie. Thank God you're here.' Thanks J.J."

"Well, why would I be glad to see you? I'm stuck in a crap-hole and wouldn't wish it upon anyone. You being in this hole with me isn't really cause for celebration. I should be saying, it's unfortunate to see you."

"Well seeing how burnt your bald head is looking, I can say the same for you," I quipped.

"You know, in less than an hour's time, I'm going to be departing this world."

"I know. That's why I'm here."

"Cutting it a little close, I would say."

"You should be thanking me for coming to rescue you."

"Well technically you haven't saved me yet, Charles. I'm still behind these bars, and you're simply carrying a bucket of water."

"Nice. That's how you're going to treat your savior?" I pulled out a cup of water to give him.

"Unless that's a bucket of acid to corrode these bars then the only thing you're saving me from is thirst." He grabbed the cup with his filthy hands and drank it down. "Sorry. With an hour to live, I'm a little on edge."

I glanced over my shoulder to see if anyone was watching. "What is this all about J.J.? Jenny told me you were in trouble. It didn't dawn on me as to how bad until I got here. She said something about you attacking a police officer."

"That part is true. I… wait. My daughter knows I'm here?"

Jenny was Jeremy's thirty year old daughter. I know, I know, J.J. and J.J.? Jeremy was big into initials.

"How do you think I found out you were in trouble?" I said.

"Didn't you get my letter? I sent it to you before I was incarcerated into this fine establishment."

I shook my head. "What letter? I was in the field when Jenny called."

"How did she know? Wait, she's not here is she? Charles, don't tell me you brought my daughter to this…"

I saw veins pulsating from J.J.'s forehead so quickly cut him off. "Jeremy, we don't have time for this. How and why are you getting executed?"

J.J. slowly took another sip of water. It was like he suddenly had all the time in the world. I knew my friend. He loved to tell stories. I mean, all his life as a treasure hunter gave him hundreds of tales to tell.

Even with his impending doom rushing up on him, he was still prepping to tell his latest. "A few months ago I was met by a lively old fellow with…"

"J.J. just spit out the highlights. Give me the cliff notes version."

Jenkins smiled. "You have no flare for drama, Charles." Before I could comment, J.J. continued, "To be frank, I was hired for a job out in this region. I realized things weren't as they seemed and needed a way out. Of course my client didn't like me leaving."

"And so he wanted you dead," I pieced together.

"Yes. Coming to this prison was better than my alternative."

J.J. paused a moment, then continued, "It was pretty easy to get sentenced here. I instigated a little scuffle with the local law enforcement. You are aware of that much. That was simply what led me here a month ago.

"It wasn't all bad. I actually found a few of the tenants here to be quite charming. But, last week I had a run in with some unsavory fellows. One thing led to another, and one of them pulled a knife on me. I defended myself and let's just say that the coyotes had a feast that night."

"And they're killing you for that?"

"Eye for an eye, Charles."

"What decade are these guys from?"

"It's a whole different ball game in these remote territories. For them, it's simply black and white. No trial. They just ordered me a public execution by strangulation."

"A *hanging*, I know. I saw them preparing for it outside. I thought they stopped hangings when they invented electricity."

"Actually, the United States outlawed it in 1936. Ironically, the person who was sentenced then was because of murder. It still is a standard method of execution in the eastern part of the world."

Good old Jeremy. He was a boatful of knowledge.

One of the guards tapped the metal bars to let me know he wanted me to keep on going. I moved to the next cell and fed another prisoner some water. I continued whispering to my friend. "Don't worry J.J. I'll get you out of here. We've got a plan."

J.J. plopped onto his stool as if giving up. "I hate to say it Charles, but what you typically plan, and what actually happens rarely are the same."

"Have some faith." I was getting further and further from my friend now as I fed the other prisoners.

"I'd say that your plans are more accurately described as happy accidents," J.J. added.

I gave water to the last prisoner, and the guard motioned me to leave. "Call them whatever you want J.J., we got this under control," I blurted out.

Jenkins lurched out of his seat and grabbed his bars. It was as if something suddenly dawned on him. "Charles, what do you mean *we* got this under control?"

As I was escorted out of the cell block I added with a smile, "Me and Jenny."

The door shut behind me, but I could still hear J.J. screaming through the stainless steel. Thankfully, his words were muffled. I could only imagine what sort of curses he was inventing to express his anger.

I knew he wouldn't want me to have involved his daughter in this. If anything were to ever happen to her, he would never forgive himself. I know, because I felt the same way. I had known the two of them for most of my life. Jenny was like a little sister to me, but I didn't really have a choice. Actually, SHE didn't really give me a choice.

I headed back up the stairs and out the building into the open courtyard. I searched for a little hidden corner in prison and took off my shirt. I flipped it inside out and laid it down on the dirt.

Hunching over, I scanned the fabric. Scribbled all over the shirt was a map of the whole complex. I had detailed every little piece of the puzzle onto this shirt knowing they weren't going to make me take off my clothes. This was one of the many benefits of being in a third world country.

I was going to break my friend out of prison.

I had a plan, and it was going to work.

I hoped.

CHAPTER TWO

Two weeks ago I was on a typical job in Paris, France. When I say *typical,* I mean that I found myself bound to a metal chair, wrists and ankles tied to the frame, getting tortured by a group of thugs in suits.

As for the sights? Instead of having the stellar backdrop of buildings and historical monuments, I was sitting sixty feet below street level. The room was dark. Technically, it wasn't even really a room. It was a cavern. A cavern made from walls of bones and skulls.

I sat in the center of a chamber in the catacombs of Paris. Back in the eighteenth century these catacombs were created as a burial ground for the citizens of France. With all the overcrowding up above, those who weren't wealthy enough to be properly buried would be ripped apart. Their bones were carried down and placed in this vast network of tunnels under the city.

Now it was a tourist attraction.

And from the looks of it, I was on track to be one of the new exhibits.

Weeks earlier, I had been contracted by a Mr. Theodore Riley to acquire a certain artifact. It was one the missing eight Faberge Golden Eggs that belonged to Russian jeweler, Peter Carl Faberge. There were fifty two of these eggs in total, and over time, a number of them had disappeared. Being a treasure hunter, that was how I made my living.

My client, Mr. Riley heard that one of these eggs was buried in a tomb somewhere near Boudreaux, France. I was hired to find it, retrieve it, and return it for payment. It sounded simple enough.

Of course, I performed my end of the deal, but Mr. Riley didn't. No payment waited for me. Instead, I was greeted by a bunch of goons ready to take the artifact through force. Luckily, I had ridden this rodeo enough times to know never to bring the goods to the exchange. Mr. Riley was apparently new at this.

So here we were, locked in a dungeon well below the city. The group of hired stooges were trying to get the information out of me while good old Theodore Riley waited upstairs.

A few punches to the gut from a fist made of bananas helped remind me what I ate for breakfast. I strained to break free from my binds, but the rope was thick and expertly knotted.

I gave the brute that much.

The monstrous thug demanded, "Did you really think the boss would pay you?"

Spitting out some blood, I chimed back, "Well, did Mr. Riley naively think that I was going to bring the goods?"

That earned me a few more blows to the stomach.

"Where is it?" he asked.

I said nothing.

"Tell us or else," the man yelled.

"Or else what, you're going to kill me? I find it sad that you wasted all this effort to carry me down that narrow flight of stairs with nothing to show for it. You need to get the updated rule book on how to interrogate. The promise of death won't motivate me to talk."

"No, but this might." The thug pulled out an electric Taser. Without hesitation, he zapped me.

I honestly didn't see that coming.

Apparently there was a new rule book.

The shock jolted my body instantly. I think the surprise outweighed the pain the first time. When the man struck again, I could feel my heart pumping so hard I thought it was going to tear out of my chest.

"I can do this all day, Mr. Morgan," said the henchman.

I tried to respond, but my mouth jittered in pain. My body instinctively tried to suck in air and calm back down before another bolt of electricity struck.

My mind was racing to find some way to break free. I searched wildly for some sort of help—for some sort of plan. Another shock rocketed through me. My hands clenched the steel arm rests, trying to brace the pain.

Then it hit me. The metal arm rests! When my body settled once again, I feigned to pass out.

"Hey," the man said, shaking my head. He slapped me once. It stung, but I maintained the composure of looking dead. He backhanded me again.

"You kill him?" one of the others guys weaseled.

"I don't know." The man leaned in close to my head. I could smell his cheap cologne. His heavy breathing depressed my sweaty brown hair. He was close. I sensed the shadows of his arms resting on the back of the metal chair. He braced himself as he bent closer to my face.

My fingertips stretched out, making contact with the Taser that dangled from the man's belt. They curled around the plastic casing, finally grabbing hold of the device. My hand was restrained, and I couldn't twist the handle to point it at my captor. But I wasn't planning to.

The ropes that tied me to my seat were double wrapped around my limbs. That meant my hands and ankles weren't in direct contact with the chair. If I could arch my body off the seat and have the Taser send a surge of electricity into the metal handrail, it should cause a current to conduct through the metal. And right now, the monstrosity hovering over me clasped his hands on that very metal.

In theory of course.

My body came alive, arching off the seat. I jammed the Taser against the steel and pulled the trigger. The thug screamed as the current flooded through the chair and into the man's body. My muscles ached trying to maintain my body in the awkward position. I held strong. I couldn't let go of that button.

Adrenaline flushed through my veins. Even with such focus, I could hear the feint sound of the other brutes jumping to action.

I let go of the Taser and fell back to my seat. The unconscious thug above me went limp. His full weight fell directly on top of me.

I angled my head to look past the large mass, only to see the other three thugs pull out their guns and yell, "Fire!"

Without pause, they did.

Bullets rang through the confined space as the limp body covering me was riddled with holes. The momentum of the shots tipped us backward, and we fell to the ground.

Now, I laid helpless under a two hundred and fifty pound dead guy, still tied to the metal chair.

I didn't really think that far ahead into this plan, did I?

My opposite hand came across another object that hung from the dead thug's belt. This wasn't the same Taser. It was the man's handgun. With my other three attackers marching toward me, I quickly unholstered the weapon and held it up. I wasn't the best shot but these guys were close, and I didn't really have a second chance at this.

I fired.

One by one they dropped around me. I kept firing until no bullets were left in the chamber. Luckily, no men were left standing either.

I dropped the gun and calmed down. I risked a smile at the fact that I survived, but then I realized something. Now I was stuck in a dark cavern, tied to a chair, flattened by a giant man, and I had no way out.

It took me forty minutes of rolling around the floor and searching every body, until I finally found a knife. I cut my binds free and got to my feet. What was I to do with these guys? I figured I'd leave them alone until the tour groups showed up in the morning. At least this would buy me some time to get out the country.

But the first thing on my agenda was to find Mr. Riley and get my money.

When I got back to the surface I was out of breath. I couldn't spot my client anywhere. I needed to find him. I ran to my car a few blocks away and got in.

Resting in the passenger seat was a bronze compass. I owed my life to this little object. I might not be very superstitious, but I did believe in this compass. It was my lucky rabbit's foot. I gave it a little rub and sat it back down. That's when I saw my cell phone on the armrest. A *Two New Messages* icon flashed on its screen. I clicked on my voicemail.

The first message began with, "Hello there Mr. Morgan. My name is Baron William Ruthford. I have a lucrative proposition for—"

Before the pompous voice could finish his message, I skipped it to the next one. I didn't have time for this, but as the next message began, I recognized a familiar voice.

"Hey Charlie, it's me… uh… Jenny. It's been awhile… I need your help. It's my dad, Charlie. He's in trouble. I don't know what to do. You're the only one who could help. Call me when you get your messages. Please." Then silence.

Jenny Jenkins.

Even though it had been ten years since I last saw Jenny, I had not forgotten her voice. The only difference was that this time, I could sense desperation in it.

I quickly called her back. There was so much to catch up on, but her father, my best friend, was the primary focus.

Jenny somewhat led in her father's footsteps. The last time we spoke, she was heading off to college to become an architect. Somewhere in the ten years that passed, she picked up a love for archeology, and soon after, started globetrotting from place to place. I'd say we were her influence, but thankfully her desire to find treasure was in a more structured atmosphere with a lot less danger.

I was eighteen when I first met J.J. and his daughter. She was only thirteen at the time. As my friendship with J.J. solidified, I fell into the older brother role for Jenny. It was kind of strange if you thought about it, seeing that I wasn't much of a role model. Still, this was all Jenny had, and even though years drove us apart, I would always inhabit the role.

Jenny explained that she was at an archeological dig site out in China. One night, she overheard some villagers talk about Jeremy. She continued, telling me about the stories she heard about her father.

J.J. had caused quite a scene at the local establishment. He attacked a few Chinese police officers and that got him sentenced to the laogai prison. Jenny tried to see her father a number of times, but visitors weren't allowed. The only acknowledgement she received was the confirmation that J.J. was indeed in there.

But he wasn't going to be there for long. He had been sentenced to be executed at the end of the month.

This was all the information I got. At the time, the story didn't add up. J.J. wasn't much of a fighter. I knew there needed to be a good reason for what happened. In any case, I needed to figure out what was going on.

Before I could ask about Jenny, about what she was doing out there... about anything... she cut me short. "Charlie, can you help me? I don't know where else to turn?"

"Jen, you got it. Just promise me one thing. You stay out of trouble. Your dad would kill me if I put you in harm's way."

"No, sir. I'm not a little girl anymore. This is my father. I am not sitting on the sidelines. Plus, I already got a head start on things. I called a good friend of mine to look up the plans for the prison. I'm getting a hard set of the construction documents this afternoon. Charlie, I've got to go. I'll see you soon."

The phone went dead.

Without changing out of my clothes, I kicked the engine alive and drove off toward the airport. My current vendetta to find Mr. Riley suddenly felt like a distant memory. My friend was in trouble, and I needed to figure out a plan.

CHAPTER THREE

My plan sounded simple enough.

Jenny kept up her end of things, providing me the full schematics of the facility. Those same plans and details were scribbled all over the inside of my shirt. So far, they proved to be accurate.

The cell block holding J.J. was exactly where it had been drawn.

The officer barracks was a two story concrete structure that anchored the corner of the prison. Attached to it was the garage. Rusted standing seam metal panels and large bow trusses held the building up.

My morning trek back and forth to this very garage proved that everything followed the blueprints. And just like it was shown on those prints, splitting the difference between the main building and the cell block was another small single story structure. The building was no more than twenty feet wide by fifteen feet deep. No windows. Just one door.

That was my next stop. But before going there, there was one thing I needed.

The crowd of prisoners continued their factory assembly line out in the center of the yard. I scanned passed them to the notorious group huddled away from the rest of the group. Everyone stayed clear from those guys. Every nerve in my body screamed to do the same.

Unfortunately, as I watched one of mammoths pull out a cigarette, I knew I needed their help. The man grabbed a Zippo out of his pocket, flipped it open, and ignited the flint. The flame emerged instantly, and a second later, the cigarette was puffing out smoke.

I needed that lighter.

My mind scrambled to figure out a way to steal the object. I was tight on time and had a fleeting set of options. Seeing the bucket of water I just brought back from the cell block, I got an idea.

I quickly grabbed the half empty container and marched toward the crew. As my trajectory brought me closer to the giants, the scale of their massive frames grew. Veins rippled all over their exposed muscles. They pulsated, looking like they were ready to burst. It was as if the men constantly flexed while they stood there with little to no movement.

Suddenly, they became aware I was heading their way. In unison every one of the men's eyes beamed my direction.

My heart skipped a beat.

A tingle shivered through my body. It pleaded for me to turn away. I glanced around to see if there was any other option—if there was any other person who had a lighter. Instead, I was met with the eyes of the rest of the prisoners. They stared at me. It was like they all sensed something bad was about to happen. I could feel the tension build in the prison yard.

I looked forward again and found I had reached my targets. Scooping up some water into the ladle, I extended the large spoon out to serve one of the men.

For a moment, no one reacted. The man's eyes locked with mine. His permanent angry look didn't budge. Then he shifted his attention to one of his cohorts. This seemed to be the guy in charge. I knew so because he was the largest of the crew. That, and the fact that when he gave an approving nod, the man before me leaned in for a sip.

Trembling, I moved to the next mammoth. He too, took a sip of water.

As I moved to the third man, my arm started to shake uncontrollably. I tried to calm myself, but it was no use. Extending my hand out, the ladle vibrated violently, and the water splattered all over.

More importantly, the water splashed onto the pants of the very man I was trying to serve.

The giant bellowed in anger, launching up off his stoop. He knocked the spoon out of my hand in a thunderous roar. The others stood up alongside him. Before I could react, the man swung a fist, knocking me straight in the head.

The animal packed quite a wallop. I launched backward, falling into the arms of one of the other thugs. Stumbling, I braced myself around the guy's waste. My head pounded. It took all my might to stay on my feet. Still, I held on strong and regained my balance.

It didn't last long though. The thug whose body interrupted my fall didn't like my tight grip on him. He peeled me away and threw me to the ground. My wet adversary picked me off the dirt and threw me away from the rest of the gang.

I tumbled, rolling away, and jumped back to my feet. I raised my hands saying, "I'm sorry, I'm sorry." In the same motion, I back pedaled away from the five giants.

They didn't pursue me though. They turned their attention to the bucket of water, and started to take their own sips of water.

Palming my head, I continued to back pedal away from my new enemies. As I finally turned away, I reached into my pocket and felt a little metallic object. Even with all the pain, I couldn't help but smile.

I learned a long time ago that a good thief was one who mastered the art of distraction. Being clumsy lowered people's guards and made you less threatening. What I gained from those lessons was, if I took a good beating, no one would pay attention that I stole something from them... and the goon who braced my fall was the one man who had the item I required.

The Zippo rested snuggly in my pocket. I got what I needed, and now it was onto my next stop.

Like when the final credits of a movie roll, the crowd of prisoners quickly lost interest in me. They settled back into their daily routine while I quickly made my way to the windowless building. I slipped unnoticed through the door and into the dingy interior.

Another stairwell led underground. I bolted down the steps and into a network of tunnels. A sense of déjà vu struck as I followed the map on my shirt.

At least these walls weren't lined with the bones of the dead.

When the facility was constructed, the officers built an arterial group of passages that connected most of the structures above.

Years ago, the prison tasked its reluctant tenants to fabricate the first clothes for the black market. Those clothes were housed in a building positioned right where the new wood executioner's platform stood.

One night, in an act of defiance, a prisoner snuck into the building and lit the clothes on fire. The flame grew and encompassed the entire edifice, causing the whole thing to go up in flames.

Instead of patching up the building, the warden demolished it, leaving only the foundation. He built the wood execution platform over it, and the first thing he did was execute the prisoner who started the fire. That platform became the icon of fear to all prisoners who misbehaved.

That platform, and its origin story, was also the key to my plan.

I took off my shirt and ignited my new Zippo. The small flame illuminated the markings on my shirt. Scribbled all over was the complex layout of the labyrinth of tunnels. I mapped out my path and began my way through the dimly lit tunnels. Concentrating, I counted every step. Forty paces straight... I turned left... twenty five paces... then right... another fifty paces...

This continued until finally, I reached another stairwell. Heading up it, I emerged back at the surface.

The new corridor was much more polished than the previous ones. It looked very familiar. It should though, because I was back in the large garage where I spent most of my morning. To my right sat a battered jeep. Crouching low, I ducked behind it for cover.

Up ahead, I saw a few inmates loading some boxes onto the back of the delivery truck. Nearby, the two mechanics who had been working earlier were gone. Their work on the rusted vehicle was only half finished. I assumed they were on break since their tools still spread about the floor.

Carefully, I snuck over to their work bench and nabbed a few things. More specifically, a hammer and a screwdriver. Then, I wrapped around the garage to get closer to the delivery truck. The assortment of other vehicles acted as perfect cover as I bounced by way around the room.

Finally, I was only a car length away from the delivery truck. I kept low, watching as another group of inmates dropped off some more boxes. For my plan to work, I needed to time this just right.

I waited.

The last man jumped off the truck and left the garage.

Now!

I leapt to my feet and bolted for the back of the truck. Climbing in, I ripped open one of the boxes. Perfectly folded military uniforms filled inside of the cardboard. I flipped open the Zippo and lit the flame.

I heard footsteps approaching.

Moving fast, I dropped the lighter into the pile of clothes and sealed up the box.

The footsteps grew louder.

I ran to the back of the truck, jumped off, and darted to my hiding spot. Just then another group of inmates arrived with more containers.

I exhaled in relief. The men loaded up more boxes. I didn't have time to watch anymore. I made my way back to the tunnels.

Once down, I fell back into darkness. This time, I didn't have my *lantern*. I counted my paces in reverse order as I sped through the dense network of tunnels. I was almost back when I heard a siren blare from above. It worked. The box of clothes caught fire and the smoke would have alerted the guards.

When I reached the surface to exit the building, the area was clear. All the guards had scrambled toward the garage. I saw them off in the distance rushing for the large overhead doors. Black smoke seeped out the metal roof.

Apparently, that flame worked better than I expected.

This was my chance.

With the distraction in full swing, I sprinted for the wood execution platform. The noose single wrapped over the main horizontal member. The support member hovered over twenty feet above the platform. There was a raised pedestal that a prisoner would climb onto, get the noose tightened around their throat, and then step off.

The rope of the noose was long and taut. It extended down to the base of the platform, anchoring into a threaded stake. I knelt down and loosened the knot.

I completed my task swiftly.

The clock read 11:40a.m. I still had twenty minutes.

Most of the chaos back at the garage settled down. I couldn't help but wonder what kind of damage I caused. How many boxes probably caught on fire? It wouldn't take them much longer to put out those flames though.

The prisoners used the opportunity to take a bit of a break. They just stood there, motionless, watching the Chinese guards run around frantically.

I was preparing to turn and head back to the tiny concrete structure for the last part of the plan when a fist struck me right in the cheekbone.

I tumbled.

I fell off the wood platform and onto the dirt. My head felt like it was ripped off of my body. Stars fluttered around the outskirts of my peripheral vision. While I struggled to focus on what just happened, another fist pummeled my face.

Hands grabbed my shoulders and lifted me up. I helplessly fought to break free but could feel more than one warm body tighten their hold on me. Within seconds I was thrust onto my hands and knees.

Legs attacked my ribs.

Finally, the beating stopped, allowing me to take in my surroundings. Five rugged monstrosities towered over me. My *friends* were back. Apparently, they weren't done with me. The man in charge spoke surprisingly decent English. "Do you think you are better than the rest of these men? Do you think you do not have to work?"

I found this ironic. I tried to respond only to have a boot stomp on my face. Apparently that was a rhetorical question.

"American, why are you hiding over here?"

Again, he didn't care for my answer.

The man rambled on, but all I thought about was the fact that time was running out. I needed to be somewhere. I half-expected him to ask me about the missing Zippo. In all honesty, he might have, but my head was ringing too hard.

When the men loosened their grasp on me, I used it as my time to act.

I scrunched my fists over some loose gravel. I flailed my arms, throwing the debris at my attackers' faces. It blinded them momentarily. I sprung to my feet and sprinted in the direction of the large crowd of inmates.

My only hope was to lose them.

I pushed my way through, getting deeper into the crowd. I could hear the heavy footsteps of my pursuers struggle to follow through the dense bodies. One man was easier to slither through a crowd than five. (Especially when the five men were the size of bulls.)

I pressed on, not daring a look back. Commotion spread all around. My head throbbed, but I continued to shove random bodies aside. I needed to move faster. I needed to disappear.

I mazed through the mob, and sounds around me simmered down.

I lost them.

I risked a moment's pause to catch my breath.

A man burst out of nowhere. He bull rushed me and tackled me down to the gravel.

It was the leader of the crew.

We wrestled in the dirt for some time. A circle grew around us as the other inmates started watching our fight rather than the fire that was being subdued in the garage.

Blows exchanged frequently. Still, I held my own, dodging most of his slow far stretching swings, then throwing a few jabs when the window allowed.

I wrestled many bulkier guys over my time. The key to these fights was to keep your feet planted and more importantly, stay under them. The goal was always to take out the other guy's legs so that he'd lose balance. Once on top, you could do as you pleased.

That was no different here. I dove for his legs and tightened my grip around those tree trunks for thighs. I anchored my feet and kicked my body upward off the ground.

My trajectory cut the man's legs out from under him. He fell backward. I sprung over and directly on top of his chest. As routinely as brushing my teeth, my arms wrapped around the thug's head and I put him in a chokehold. If I held on long enough, the lack of oxygen flowing to his head would eventually knock him out.

My grasp tightened. I could sense that any second, the brute would pass out when…

The deafening sound of gunfire rattled, instantaneously followed by bullets kicking up the dirt inches from our bodies. I let my grip go and rolled away. More shots dug into the ground nearby.

Everyone fell silent.

The shots came from one of the guard towers fifty feet away. Two of the Chinese patrols rushed up to hold us at gunpoint. They forced us to our feet, and a third man came to tie our hands behind our back.

With all the craziness going on in my direct environment, I failed to realize that the fire had been put out, and all the patrols were getting back to their posts.

The most devastating news was that the clock read 11:55am. Five minutes until the execution.

The first domino fell.

There was no chance for me to protest.

Fighting was not tolerated.

I was ushered off toward the cell block—the same cell block that I visited earlier as a waterboy. Now, it looked as if that was going to be my new home.

As we marched in its direction, a loud *ding* reverberated throughout the walls of the prison. Another followed. I looked up at the clock and saw why.

It was noon.

We continued our trek toward the concrete structure when the doors to the building opened and out came Jeremy Jenkins. His hands were bound, and now, in the scorching sunlight, I could see the grime that covered his body. His eyes adjusted to the brightness and the minute they did, the first image he saw was me heading his way.

I could see the happiness in his eyes, followed by sorrow when he realized why I was being escorted. As I approached, he said, "It looks as if you have been very discrete up here, Charles."

Our paths closed in on one another. "Hey, don't you worry J.J. This is all part of the plan."

"Awfully close, aren't we?"

"We are right on schedule."

"Whatever you say my young friend. It's just my life here."

We crossed each other. Jeremy was being escorted directly toward the executioner's platform. "J.J. do me a favor when you're up there."

"What's that?"

Without looking back at my old friend, all I said was, "Take a giant leap of faith. They're going to want a good show."

"Whatever you say Charles."

Jeremy's voice cut away as I was led into the cell block. The officer took me downstairs and into the same cell that Jeremy once resided.

The bars slammed shut while the other monster of a man that had instigated the fight was thrown into another nearby cell.

The guards untied us and left to head back to the surface. We remained—all alone.

Outside, I heard the chanting of the crowd. From the sounds of it, this was live entertainment for everyone. Even the cell block guards on duty left to witness the *main event.*

They were going to be very disappointed.

CHAPTER FOUR

I t was time to improvise.

I acted fast. I pulled the hammer and screwdriver out of my pant pocket. Quickly, I banged out the bolts of the hinges to my cell door. I pried the door open and snuck out. It was as easy as that.

True, my intentions for these two objects hadn't been for this, but it worked. I was free from my cell and ready to continue the next part of my plan.

The other cellmates excitedly got to their feet. I shattered their hopes as I darted past them and out the room. Their screams were drowned by the cheering that continued outside. (I didn't dare leave without giving my large adversary a wink and a smile.)

I scrambled down the corridor to the opposite end. I bolted up the stairs and back outside. Everyone crowded around the executioner's platform. With all eyes on the main stage, I snuck across the open field to the windowless building. In seconds, I was downstairs and in the familiar dark tunnels I had visited earlier.

I got back on track.

Trying to remember the markings on my shirt, I sped down the tunnel to my final stop. Fighting the darkness, I felt my way around. I cut left, then right. Pushing forward, I could hear the crowd up above.

Their chants escalated when I reached my destination. This wasn't because more people had joined in on the yelling. No, this was because I found myself directly underneath the wooden platform that housed Jeremy Jenkins's execution.

The room was a rectangle of reinforced concrete, no more than ten feet tall. Light bled through the reveals of all the wood planks that formed the platform. I saw the shadowy figures of a few Chinese guards. Then a single silhouette marched onto the stairs that led up to the noose.

That could only be J.J.

Through all the hollering, I still made out Jeremy's voice. "Charles, any time now would suffice. Any time Charles!"

He was right. I really was cutting it close. But I only needed a minute.

The floor joists that held up the perpendicular floor boards were rotted wood studs. I ran to the main headboard that the joists met at and pulled out the hammer and screw driver.

Systematically, I used the screw driver as a chisel and the hammer as a driving force to punch out the nails that held these wood elements together. Luckily, the crowd above masked my clanking.

I went from joist to joist, knocking each one free. Once I loosened the six members that aligned directly underneath the noose, I swung the hammer to break them completely away.

The first one dislodged and fell to the ground. The next one followed.

As more joists fell to the ground, I saw the floor boards start to sag. The joists were the structural support that diverted the heavy loads above. With them missing, these flimsy wooden floor boards would collapse under heavy strain—or a massive impact. All I needed to do was free one more floor joist.

"Charles they're tightening this rope around my neck!"

The last wooden joist fell, and I fled to a corner of the room. Watching through a large gap in the floor, I clearly saw J.J. He stood on the edge of a stair platform ten feet above.

Silence came over the crowd.

It was about to happen.

J.J. looked terrified. One of the officers climbed the steps and positioned himself behind my friend. For a moment, no one made a move.

That's when I heard the rumbling of a plane.

Jenny was right on time.

Up above, a single engine plane descended upon the prison. As it passed over the open field, the side doors slid open. A dozen metallic objects launched into the open air. They glistened in the sunlight as they rained down on the group of people below.

The tiny asteroids smashed into the dirt. Only these weren't asteroids. They were smoke grenades shaped like soup cans. Prisoners and guards alike dove for cover as more of these deadly objects fell from the sky.

Gunshots rattled. The tower guards fired at the aircraft. It was too late though. As quickly as the plane had appeared, it was already flying away. In its wake, it left a few things behind.

The grenades exploded on impact. Dense clouds of smoke rose from the ground, creating a veil of fog.

This was our chance.

Amongst the confusion, the executioner shoved Jeremy over the ledge and to his death. I watched as he dropped. The tension on the rope tightened, and J.J.'s neck yanked back. He choked and gagged as he dangled for a moment.

The rope unraveled at the base of the platform, and an instant later, Jeremy was falling once again.

My preparations worked just as I planned.

Suddenly, something stopped his descent. The chord tensioned once again, and Jeremy hung a few feet from the wood floor below. He kicked violently to break free. Life was quickly draining from his body.

Through the fog, I made out the executioner standing at the back edge of the platform. He held onto the rope. Rope burn dug into his bare hands, but he wasn't going to let go. My old friend had seconds to live.

In a heartbeat I was under the Chinese man. The souls of his boots spanned between floor boards as he anchored himself down to hold J.J.'s weight.

I drove the screw driver between the wood planks and directly onto the bottom of the man's shoe. With all my might, I drove the hammer into the butt of the shaft, puncturing deep into the ball of the executioner's foot.

The man lost his grasp on the rope and let out a monstrous scream. At the same time, Jeremy's body crashed through the wood floor. The boards caved under the pressure. They splintered like twigs as J.J. smashed into the basement below.

The concrete floor rushed in on him. He collapsed onto the hard surface. Jeremy screamed in agony as his body sprawled onto the floor, while the cracked wood platform buckled in the center.

Up above, confusion flooded the grounds. Smoke enveloped the area making it impossible to see. Prisoners rioted. Guards panicked. What no one saw was a man fall to his death, continue to drop through the floor, and disappear into a black hole.

Confusion would only last so long, and that smoke faded quickly.

I sprinted to my friend and flung the debris off him. I pulled him to his feet. "Come on, we've got to go!"

J.J. slowly pulled himself up, shaking his head. He was hurting, but nothing seemed broken. "THAT was your grand plan?"

I pulled him along as we sprinted through the darkness. Behind, I heard terrifying screams. Sirens roared.

That was quick.

As we sprinted through the passages, I said, "That was MY plan!"

I counted my steps as we sped along. J.J.'s complaining made it tough to concentrate. The hell breaking loose outside didn't help either. Amongst the insanity, the guards rushed into the underground passages in pursuit. The prisoners continued to fight one another. Alarms echoed throughout the entire complex.

We woke a sleeping beast. Now, all we had to do was stay out of that beast's path of destruction.

I led J.J. down the tunnels like they were my home. "How you feeling?"

"I feel like this was the dumbest plan I have ever been subject to." Jeremy massaged his neck.

"Hey, I didn't have much time to think it through. It worked didn't it?"

We approached the stairs to the exit. The tunnel shook, and debris collapsed around us.

"We're not out of here yet, Charles. You do know that during a breakout attempt the goal is to make your way toward an exit, not deeper into the enemy's stronghold. From the looks of things, we may have skipped the execution and headed straight to the burial."

"Have faith J.J." We reached the stairwell. I turned and motioned my friend up it. "Age before beauty."

"I could beat you in a—" A barrage of voices echoed and flashlights bounced around the tunnels behind us. The approaching footsteps cutoff Jeremy's attempt at a witty comeback.

"Just hurry!" I urged.

We burst through the doorway and locked it behind us. We found ourselves back in the garage. The delivery truck waited in the distance. Smoke still drifted off the back of the vehicle, and a dozen fire extinguishers spread around the floor.

I was impressed with my handiwork.

"What's next on this grand plan of yours, Charles?" J.J. asked.

I pointed to the truck.

"I need to pick something up," I said.

"What could you possibly need from there?" J.J. asked as he followed me to the truck.

I didn't bother to answer. I reached the truck and jumped in. Inside, I sifted through the mess. Everything was burnt to a crisp. Digging through all the garbage, I finally found what I needed. I pulled out the two objects and hopped back out.

"What in God's name are those?" J.J. asked.

I held up two leather belts in my hand. "This is how we escape." The rear door of the garage started banging. Gunshots penetrated through the metal door. Our pursuers had caught up to us.

Grabbing my old friend, I tugged him toward another set of doors. We stormed through them and found ourselves in the main barracks.

"This plan is getting worse by the minute," I heard J.J. grumble. But he continued to follow me along.

We sped down a hallway and up another stairwell. I could hear the echoing of footsteps hot on our trails. When we reached the top of the stair, I found a ladder. The ladder led to the roof.

I was thankful that Jenny's plans were so accurate. The layout of the facility matched perfectly to what she showed me. I climbed up the ladder and through the hatch.

J.J. reluctantly followed. Just as he popped through the opening, more bullets pinged off the metal hatch.

We were cutting it close!

I slammed the hatch shut, and locked it.

From the rooftop, the sound of the prison sirens blared even louder.

Getting to my feet, I turned to Jeremy. He stood there just shaking his head. I could see the look in his eyes. He was ready to give me another lecture about how bad this plan was.

I cut him off before he could. "Don't worry J.J., we're in the last stretch here. Take this." I handed him one of the belts.

"And what shall I do with such a lavish belt?"

"Follow me and you shall see."

We made it to the edge of the roof. There was a thirty foot gap between the edge of the structure and the perimeter wall. Beyond that was the open expanse of the forest, and beyond that, our freedom.

Still, we had a large chasm to contend with. Luckily, that's where our belts came to play. Tied directly to the nearby transformer was a power cable that extended away from the building, over the wall, and to a wooden power pole on the opposite side.

It was the perfect zip-line for an escape. And our leather belts were the perfect means of which to slide down the cable.

"You ready for this?" I asked my friend.

"Are you serious? Charles, this is the last time you are allowed to come save me. Next time, just let me perish."

"Come on J.J. Stop being so pessimistic."

The roof hatch exploded. Any second now, the roof would be flooded with Chinese soldiers. We didn't have time to quibble.

"Go!"

Without a second thought, we both slung our belts over the electric wire and jumped.

We glided across the open chasm. Air rushed past our faces as we picked up speed. Only a few more feet and we were gone.

That's when I heard a snap.

The taut cable went limp like a cooked noodle. Our forward progress turned downward as we fell out of the sky. We grabbed hold of the cable for dear life. Our bodies pendulum swung like Tarzan.

Our momentum flew us straight at the concrete wall.

The impact hit hard. It felt as if every bone in my body shattered. Our hands let go of the chord and we dropped to the ground.

Looking up at the roof, I saw one of the guards standing there, a rifle in his hands. Bullet holes sizzled the panels of the transformer. Sparks flew.

The man shot at the cable, cutting it free from its anchor. His aim wasn't the best though, because he shot up the transformer pretty well too.

The good news was that, with the transformer destroyed, the power was cut to the complex. That annoying alarm ceased. The bad news was that the escalating footsteps of the Chinese patrols were closing in on us.

CHAPTER FIVE

Our bones ached. Our heads pumped violently in pain. Our limbs exhausted. Still, with the threat of our lives at hand, Jeremy and I managed to keep our bodies moving.

We bounced to our feet. Directly ahead, hordes of men rushed our way. To our right, the garage remained wide open.

Looks like were heading back into the building.

Without exchanging words, both of us ran for the bank of parked vehicles inside the garage. Over the years Jeremy and I experienced many *odds against us* scenarios. Our history made it easy to stay on the same page.

As we approached the cars, we were greeted by two patrolmen. Machine guns dangled over their shoulders. Expressions of surprise filled their faces as they saw the two of us rushing up on them. They didn't have a chance to act. We disposed of them with a couple of blows and stole their assault rifles.

This evened the playing field a bit.

The large space was filled with trucks and jeeps. I bounced from jeep to jeep in search of keys in the ignition.

Jeremy yelled, "Charles, come here. I have an idea."

As I rounded a parked vehicle, I found J.J. already straddling a motorcycle. The rusted cycle looked more than thirty years old. A tiny sidecar mounted to the side of it. "You've got to be kidding me."

"Hop in." He motioned to the sidecar.

"Out of all the cars in here, this is what you pick?"

"This is a perfectly good vehicle. Limber. Easy to maneuver. No time to argue Charles. Get in."

"I'm the rescuer, I drive," I commanded, trying to push him off.

"Don't be a child. We all saw how your rescue attempt played out. It's my turn. They're nearly upon us."

The rear door smashed open as armed men entered.

Stubbornly, I hopped in the side car. J.J. revved the engine and twisted the throttle.

The acceleration caught me off guard. The motorcycle lurched forward. It tore across the concrete and toward the open barn doors.

The encroaching soldiers stopped in their tracks as we rushed toward them.

Like a game of chicken, we raced forward while the men dove out of our way.

The vehicle stormed the open yard. Bullets rippled past us as we sped the three wheeled cycle toward the front gate of the facility. As our gap narrowed a large truck emerged, blocking our exit.

Reinforcements arrived.

The cycle narrowly crashed as it sharply turned away from the truck.

Jeremy cut the bike and maneuvered it to thread the crowd. I fired a few rounds in the air to scare people out the way. The gun only had one clip and I didn't want to waste all the bullets.

The motorcycle circled the perimeter of the complex. Round and round we went with nowhere to go. The more we drove, the more pursuers locked onto us. We weren't going to make it that much longer. The gunshots got closer and became more plentiful.

Desperate, I got an idea. It was a stretch of one, but it could work. It all depended on how accurate Jenny's information was. So far, her plans worked perfectly. We were about to find out how perfect.

I pointed at the front doors of the main barracks and ordered J.J. to drive into the building.

"Are you nuts?"

"You got a better idea?"

Reluctantly, Jeremy drove the cycle straight for the front doors. They were wide open with a group of armed men blocking the path. I fired. (My bad aim compounded with the rickety driving of the rusted motorcycle made hitting anything nearly impossible.)

It did the job though. The soldiers dove out of the way clearing the path for us.

We jet down the corridor. Narrow walls screamed past us.

"We need to get upstairs!" I yelled.

Jeremy steered the cycle up a flight of stairs and onto the next level. My entire body rattled as the tires rolled up the treads. On the second level, I pointed to the far end of the hall and told him to floor it.

This time, J.J. didn't ask twice. Twisting the throttle to its maximum, we picked up speed. At sixty miles an hour, the walls and ceiling blurred. The end of the hall closed in, as did the large bay window that terminated it. I fired the rifle, shattering the glass window, just as the cycle burst into the opening.

The motorcycle crushed through the mullions of the frame and out into thin air. For a second it felt as if we could fly. The wheels of the cycle spun vigorously, as if still driving on land. Our momentum launched us forward through the sky.

The main barracks building anchored the north side of the prison, and the second floor windows looked out to the forest. It wasn't pretty, but it *was* an escape route.

The bike's trajectory quickly shifted angle toward the ground. Our girlish screams were all I could hear as the grassy field sped in.

We fell out of the sky, landing hard onto the earth. The motorcycle threatened to tip over as it bounced like a basketball.

Screws and bolts snapped. The strain of the impact struggled to tear the side car apart. My knuckles were dead white. My hands clenched onto the rails of the little cart.

Jeremy regained control of the motorcycle and we sped off into the forest. The laogai prison that was my home for the past four hours quickly shrunk in the distance.

After a few minutes cutting through the grass, we finally found a gravel road. Jeremy never once let up on the throttle as we drove down the winding path. Even though the prison was behind us, we weren't in the clear. Those Chinese men seemed angry from the start. Now, with two escaped convicts, blood vessels had to be bursting.

Our best bet was to get as far away as possible. Unfortunately, that was easier said than done.

"Kind of like old times, huh?" I asked. I felt like a little kid stuck in that side car.

Bullet holes dented into the rear of my crammed compartment. Looking back, two jeeps lunged out of the woods, hot in pursuit.

"NOW it's like old times," Jeremy retorted as he swerved the vehicle back and forth.

The jeeps crammed with guards, each man armed to the teeth with weapons.

I fired back at them to little avail. The jeeps were much quicker than our cycle, and they were catching up fast. Uniformed soldiers hung out of the cars, shooting wildly at us.

More holes riddled our hull. I leaned away from Jeremy. The bullets struck the area between the cycle and my sidecar. As more shells tore at the metal, the connection holding the two segments of bike together started to give way.

"Jeremy, you've got to—!"

I didn't have time to finish my statement. My sidecar ripped free from the rest of the vehicle.

Suddenly, I was careening down a bumpy road, balancing on one tire.

I adjusted my body to keep the darn thing upright. Jeremy screamed, but I heard nothing. We were rolling down a gradual slope, and the death trap that I was stuck in was gaining speed.

My muscles tensed as I struggled to balance the thing. I was a lone member of a bob sled team guiding the car through downhill curves. Jeremy followed, providing some moral support, but I was terrified.

The rushing wind caused my eyes to water.

The rattling of metal threatened to break the car apart at the seams.

The blurring greenery of trees zipped past at an alarming rate.

I was going to die.

My concentration broke as I heard the rumbling engine of one of the jeeps speed up to greet me. The road angled upward now and my cart started to lose speed. The jeep got closer and closer.

Finally, the large four-wheel vehicle pulled up directly beside me. Inside, the driver smiled. I must have looked like a sad little puppy because the other two guards that hung off the rear of the jeep had yet to act. I clenched my eyes to brace for the firing squad. I heard the rapid shots of a rifle.

But somehow I was still alive. No bullets hit me. Opening my eyes, I realized why. The gun fire didn't come from the guards hanging out of the jeep.

Jeremy miraculously appeared on the motorcycle. His fingers tightly gripped the trigger of his gun while he aimed at the pursuing jeep's tires. One of the wheels blew, and the vehicle swerved my direction.

Great!

The two gunmen stumbled back, one nearly falling off the truck.

The wall of the dwarfing vehicle rammed my tiny death-mobile. Without thinking, I reached out and grabbed hold of the ledge of the jeep. The side car kept together as I now ran parallel with my attacker.

The driver jogged the wheel back and forth in an effort to launch me off the edge of the road, but I held on tight. Jeremy fell to the rear, distracting the other jeep in pursuit.

My grip clamped. I was not going to let go of that ledge. That was, until I saw the jeep starting to veer the car to the edge of the road and into the oncoming foliage.

The side car couldn't handle the rough terrain. It shook violently. My eyes widened as another obstacle came my way.

I started to second guess my luck. Fifty feet ahead, the foliage ended and the ground dropped. The road was about to follow along a cliff edge. I couldn't tell how long the drop was, but suffice it to say there wouldn't be any road left for my little car.

I pulled myself up.

Straining my body, I lifted it out of the side car. I almost got my leg over the lip of the jeep when the cart disappeared from under me. My full hundred and seventy pounds fell upon my two hands.

I clung to the edge of the jeep, legs flapping in thin air. With adrenaline pumping, I lifted my body up and into the rear of the jeep just as it turned away from the edge.

The driver looked stunned as did the two gunmen who were now regaining their balance.

With the element of surprise, I lunged at the first attacker, pushing him over the rear of the vehicle. His body flipped over itself like a rag doll as it hit the dirt behind us. The other man bear hugged me from behind. Meanwhile, the jeep zigzagged on the road, making things even more difficult.

I planted my leg into the stern frame and shoved backward. I dug my attacker into the upper bar of the jeep, but he wouldn't let go.

We tussled.

My sandwiched hands fumbled for some sort of hope. They grabbed something and yanked it away from the attacker's belt. Before I could realize what I grabbed, the vehicle swerved.

We lost balance, and I dropped the object.

A metal clank vibrated as the object fell onto the bed of the jeep. Both my attacker and I paused a moment to look down. Our eyes nearly popped out of our faces.

The oval shaped grenade rolled along the floor. Its arming pin still dangled from my finger.

Whatever quarrel the soldier and I had with one another was instantly forgotten. We both scrambled to the ground to grab the ticking time bomb.

The soldier palmed it first and stood up. He pulled his arm back to throw it over the ledge. I turned away to shield myself from the blast when I saw a massive tree branch rushing straight for my head. I ducked as the jeep sped under a low hanging tree.

My attacker wasn't so lucky.

In the midst of throwing the grenade, the branch slammed him in the head, launching him over the ledge. His body tumbled along the gravel path, and then exploded in a ball of fire.

I only allowed myself a second to take in the disgusting sight. Then I diverted my attention to the driver. I grabbed a gun that lay on the floor and aimed it straight at the man, yelling, "Stop the car!"

He looked at me in terror. Then, he opened the side door of the jeep and jumped off. I simply watched as he rolled by.

I now rode in a driver-less jeep.

Really?

The jeep drifted without a captain. Wherever the bumps in the road led, it followed. I pulled myself to the front seat and struggled to take the wheel.

Jeremy and the other jeep lagged behind. They caught up to me as I regained control of the vehicle. The gunmen in the other jeep steadied themselves and aimed right for the motorcycle. The road wasn't wide enough for any strategic maneuvers.

So I did the only thing I could.

I slammed on the brake and prayed.

Jeremy's cycle zoomed past. The rear of my jeep clashed into the front of the pursuing one. The bumpers ripped off our vehicles upon impact. One of the gunmen standing in the rear of the jeep fell forward, firing his assault rifle.

Bullets tore into the body of the driver, and the jeep yanked right. It stormed over the cliff edge.

My car skidded to a complete stop. The death curdling screams of the Chinese men was all I heard as they fell down the wall of rock.

It was over.

J.J. pulled up next to me in the smoking motorcycle. "Well done, Charles."

"Get in," I told him.

Jeremy pet his motorcycle like it was a puppy and got in my jeep. We drove off. For a moment, we were both quiet. I finally broke the silence with, "You're welcome."

"I'm welcome? Technically, I'm the one who saved you."

"What are you talking about? The breakout was my idea."

"True Charles, but you forget the motorcycle was mine."

J.J. always loved to get a rise out of me. "Yes, but…"

"And might I add, who took out the tire to stop that jeep from turning you into road-kill?"

"Who risked their life stopping that jeep just now?"

"I had those poor men under control."

I paused. "Well who's driving? If you are being technical, I'm the one with the escape vehicle, and you are my passenger."

"A rickety vehicle at that…with one flat tire."

"That was your doing—when you supposedly saved my life. Three good tires are better than nothing though."

Jeremy pondered, then grinned. "Touché Charles. I concede. You did well, and I am extremely grateful."

Surprised, I looked at Jeremy and smiled. That was one of the first times he'd ever truly complimented me. The moment was short-lived as my old friend punched me hard in the shoulder.

I winced in pain. "Easy old man, I could just as easily take you back there."

"That was for getting my daughter involved in this. Now where is Jenny?"

CHAPTER SIX

When Jenny told me J.J. was in trouble two weeks ago, I dropped everything—literally. I booked the next ticket to China and took my seat on the airplane. All I had on me was a small bag with spare clothes, my passport, and some money. The clothes smelled like musk from months of being jammed in the nylon bag. If I would have known I'd be stuck in those dirty jeans and shirt for two weeks, I might have better prepared myself.

I also forgot how long the plane ride was going to be. I sat in my seat, fingering my palm. Thoughts brought back memories of Jenny. I had a lot on my mind. Our conversation was short, and I still had a lot of questions for her. After our call, we never spoke on the phone again. Our only exchange was an e-mail I sent her with my itinerary. She wrote back saying she would be there to pick me up. Still, I would do anything for the two J.J.'s. They were all I had.

As I mentioned, I was eighteen when I first met Jenny and Jeremy. It was a very different stage in my life. Orphaned at twelve, I spent a lot of my childhood on my own. Once I hit sixteen, I ran off to see the world. By world, I meant Chicago because that's as far as my money got me.

Being homeless, most of my time was eaten up at the library. Books and magazines were my education. I lost myself to countless hours learning about pyramids, ancient civilizations, and world cultures.

One night as I left the library, something unexpected happened.

A car accident.

I heard the crash before seeing it. Turning the corner off of Michigan Avenue, I witnessed the craziness of a seven car pile-up. Cars crumpled. People injured. Debris filled the street.

Emerging out of one of the cars was a man. He marched up to a red Honda Civic and shattered the back window. The man reached in and pulled something out of the car. Then, he yanked out a gun and pointed it at the unconscious driver.

Most people screamed in terror, but not me. The idiot that I was, I sprinted head-on toward the man, calling for him to stop.

I must have looked like a lunatic, flapping my arms and yelling at the top of my lungs. The man saw me fast approach and bolted.

As I got close, I noticed gas leaking out of the Honda. Bullet holes punctured most of the hull. Without thinking, I unlocked the side door and pulled the driver out.

That driver was Jeremy Jenkins. He had a full head of salt and pepper hair back then. As I carried him out of the car, I saw that there was a passenger in the other seat.

Jenny.

Petroleum covered the asphalt. I dragged Jeremy to safety and ran back to the Honda. Around me, pedestrians gathered, helping the other victims away. I dove into the car and hurriedly unlatched Jenny's seatbelt.

She woke up in panic.

That was the first time I saw her big blue eyes. She was so fragile and innocent. I could only imagine what ran through her head. A stranger stood above her, grabbing her body.

But I calmed her, reassuring her that everything would be all right. With the amount of gas that was pouring out onto the street, a fire was going to start any second. We needed to move fast.

Jenny grabbed onto me. We started for the exit when the area outside the car erupted into flames. We were trapped. I didn't know what to do. All sides of the vehicle were on fire. The only option was up.

I kicked out the sun roof and up we went. Carrying Jenny in my arms, I ran across the trunk. We jumped to the hood of the next crumpled box on wheels.

I didn't stop. I ran to the next car, then the next. I pushed my body to get us as far away from the Honda as possible before it blew. Finally, I leapt one last time when Jeremy's car exploded.

The pressure launched us through the sky, directly into a parked van. Instinctively, I managed to turn my body around. My back took the brunt of the damage.

I smashed into the windshield. Jenny still cradled in my arms as half of my body embedded in the shards of glass.

Then, I lost consciousness.

When I woke, I was in a hospital bed. Thirty six stitches spread across my back. Sitting on the seats next to me were the two J.J.'s.

Little Jenny's hand clutched mine.

"Thank you for saving our lives," Jeremy started. "We owe you a great debt."

I was a lost kid then. Jeremy believed that any man who would risk his own life without hesitation was a good man. He saw something more in me. Something I never did. From that day forward, he took me under his wing.

I found my family.

It wasn't much later that I realized about all the dangers of being Jeremy's friend. I sought adventure, and I got that in spades.

That memory of the Jenkins family remained front and center as my airplane landed.

The Mudanjang Airport was fairly lively for such a small place. The beautiful jungle backdrop got lost the minute I exited the main gates. I stepped out of the building to the sight of little Jenny Jenkins leaning against a car. Only she wasn't the little girl I remembered.

Jenny was tall, fit, and all grown up. A striking tan and rich blue eyes made her stick out amongst the crowd. Other than her massive blues, the only other resemblance to her younger self was in her blonde braided ponytail.

I smiled and went straight for her. Sorrow filled her eyes. I knew she was happy to see me, but I sensed her worry. "Hello Lady!" I said to help lighten the mood.

She just hugged me. "Thank you so much for coming, Charlie."

"Don't sweat it. It's not like I had anything else going on."

Speaking of sweat, only ten minutes passed after getting off the airplane, and I was already soaked.

After our loving embrace, we drove off to a nearby bar to catch up. Watching her command the wheel through the jungle was impressive. We reached a small shack, found a booth, and Jenny ordered us two drinks.

We got to work.

I had an idea for a plan. I laid out all the details, finishing with the fact that I needed some sort of distraction. Jenny was the one who came up with the smoke canisters.

"And how are you going to launch those things into the prison?" I asked.

"I dated a pilot a few years ago. We still keep in touch, and he owes me a favor. One call and he'll be here in a heartbeat."

She said it so *matter of factly*. Where was the young, shy girl I remembered? The Jenny before me was night and day from what I used to know. This girl was in the middle of nowhere, filled with an aura of confidence. I asked what my friend got herself into.

That's when she explained.

Jenny worked under the archeologist Alvin Mitchell, an Australian who made a name for himself after uncovering the sarcophagus of a nineteenth dynasty Egyptian official, Ptahmes. In the years that followed, he emerged with more discoveries. I always assumed that guys that skyrocketed to fame were typically cocky, but Jenny kept praising the man.

Jenny explained that she and Alvin were working at one of the *Makapansgat* archeological sites in the Lompopo Province of South Africa when they got a phone call.

It was a once in a lifetime opportunity, Alvin was told. A rich benefactor discovered the tomb of a shamaness, *Xi Wangmu,* at the base of the Wanda Mountains in China.

"The *Wu?*" I asked.

In ancient Chinese culture, *Wu* was used to delineate a shamaness or priestess. Over the years, history erased the strong pattern of female shaman's in Eastern Asia. What many didn't know was that females pre-dominated shamanism in Ancient China. These figures acted as deities amongst the public. They had different types of abilities. Some spoke to spirits. Others read dreams. Even others had the power to control weather. But in all the text dating back to the Shang Dynasty, all of these great *Wu* had one thing in common. They were extremely powerful.

"You know your Chinese history," Jenny said, impressed.

I knew my share. *Xi Wangmu* was a name I heard a few times before. She was a pretty famous shamaness, but I didn't know all the specifics about her. There were shaman related tombs spread all across the country. It didn't really provoke any jaw-dropping reaction.

Jenny added, "*Xi Wangmu* is basically the mother to all shamans that existed throughout the entire Chinese history. Different references call her by many names like 'Golden Mother of the Shining Lake', or 'She of the Nine Numina', or even 'Grand Marvel.' But in her Taoist title, *Yaochi Jimu*, her name literally translates to *Queen Mother*."

My face must have looked quite perplexed, because Jenny paused a moment.

"Charlie, why do you look so surprised? I may be blonde, but I'm not that blonde."

I coughed out, "No, you just remind me a lot of your father right now. You have the same excitement that he typically gets when he talks about history."

Jenny smiled. J.J. was a smart man. Putting Jenny in the same league as him was an honest compliment, and she took it as such. "What do you know about the origins of Taoism?" she asked.

"It's fairly rusty, but I know the basics. Yin and yang. The balancing of life energy. It's a Chinese philosophy."

"You're right. It looks at the Universe, and how one balances one's self within the world. In essence, its goal is to 'be one with the Earth'. This *Queen Mother* wasn't just the origin of shamans in China. She is also the originator of the Taoism belief itself."

Jenny continued to impress.

"In Taoism, it was thought that if you maintained perfect harmony with the Earth, then you could harness its full potential. At the moment of true enlightenment, you could do almost anything. You see these beliefs throughout history in hundreds of different religions. Buddhist priests. Hindu Prophets. Mayan Sorcerers. All expressed the idea to a degree.

"The one trait that was shared amongst them was the ability to see the future. A select few *Wu* were thought to possess this power. *Xi Wangmu* was one of them. Known as the shaman of the Far West, at the margin of Heaven and Earth, she harnessed the cosmic forces of the stars to give her power over seeing what lie ahead."

"So basically, you found the tomb of a glorified fortune teller."

"We haven't exactly found the tomb, just the main entrance. Actually, that's a lie. The entrance was already discovered when we arrived. What WE are doing, is trying to figure out a way to open the front gates to it."

"And this billionaire fronting the cash for this expedition is?"

"Baron William Ruthford," J.J. said, interrupting my tale about his daughter. It was as if he knew the exact words that were about to come out of my mouth.

Typical J.J.

Stealing my thunder just as I was getting to the good part of my story.

I had just finished changing the tire to the jeep. Thankfully, the spare wasn't all torn up in bullet holes like the rest of the vehicle. I hopped back in and started the engine.

"How did you know that?" I asked as we got back on the road. We sped through the hills of the Ningan Province on our way to a nearby airfield—the last part of my well executed escape plan.

"Because I was under his employment prior to my incarceration. He was the client I was escaping from. Who do your think found that tomb entrance in the Wanda Mountains? Yours truly. And, it looks as though my daughter has followed in my footsteps."

I felt J.J.'s penetrating stare as I tried to focus on the road ahead of me. "Now it's your turn to explain," I said.

And so J.J. began, "William Ruthford approached me months ago with an enticing proposal. He brought with him a parchment for me to inspect. The five pages were written in an archaic version of Ionic Greek. You know me Charles. I have a soft spot for anything related to the Ancient Greek civilization.

"The papyrus pages were only a fragment of the overall writings, and the good Baron sought my abilities to decipher them. Knowing me to be an expert in the field, I was his first stop. Or, so I was led to believe."

Jeremy paused for dramatic effect. I continued the vehicle along as he went on with his tale.

"Something struck me as odd as I analyzed the words," Jeremy said. "The prose and poetic rhythms had a distinct syntax. They formed a dactylic hexameter that was divided into uniform pauses. This was the signature to the writings of ancient Greek poet, Homer."

"The 8th century B.C. Homer? The author of The Illiad and the Odyssey?" I asked.

"That very one. When I inquired about this, Baron William congratulated me on the discovery. The old fellow shared the same passion for history as I did, and this was just his test. He explained that the pages were from one of Homer's lost poems. They chronicled an adventure out to a great treasure. The details spread across the parchment marked landmarks—signs that led to this place."

I stopped J.J., saying, "But most of Homer's writings were speeches and poems, and almost all were dedicated to the gods. The *Illiad* followed the story of Troy, and the *Odyssey*, a far-fetched tale with creatures, mermaids, and gods. None of his work ever veered outside of Greece." Being friends with J.J. meant that I had to listen to these stories over and over again.

"True. Historians always doubted the existence of Homer. Many believed the man technically wasn't just one person. He was a group of individuals that over time added their own trademarks into the stories. The *Illiad* was probably far different in its original form than the version everyone knows today. For all we know, an author under the pseudonym of Homer could have written this *lost* document."

I interrupted again. "Homer was a bigger exaggerator than you are, J.J. He was a storyteller on a grand scale, and his work was always so far-fetched. Most were proven fallacies. Why would you believe any of them?"

"Exactly. That's why William came to me. He wanted to prove history wrong. It was a chance to uncover the truths behind one of Greece's most famous poets. Without hesitation, I accepted the job."

Jeremy went onto explain the research he went through to find the locations described by those pages. His surprise came as their journey distanced themselves further from Europe, and deeper into Eastern Asia. They finally reached the end of the road, only to find a massive bronze gate blocking their way. Centuries of overgrowth buried the entrance, and everyone was puzzled to find it. Chinese characters filled the face of the giant doors, and after some analysis they realized that it was the burial tomb of *Xi Wangmu*.

"But Chinese shamans didn't first appear until hundreds of years later."

"I'm proud of you, Charles. That peaked my curiosity too. Some tales of Chinese worship did date back to the 8th century. Documentation of it can be seen in the relics from the Shang Dynasty. Was there a direct connection between Greek and Chinese mythology? Whatever lies behind those doors could provide some facts to it."

"J.J., all this sounds nice and dandy, but I still don't see the big scary part yet. What led you to attack some cops and get arrested?" Jeremy was never one for violence.

And so, my non-violent friend explained, "When we arrived, everyone was filled with excitement. We were on the brink of something extraordinary, but months went by without any progress. Things became stagnant. I worked day and night trying to figure out a way to open those doors, but they wouldn't budge. William got angry. He pushed me for answers I didn't have. I told him we couldn't have foreseen this. The gate was built sometime after the writings on Homer's papyrus. Nothing in the pages clued us in on what to do next.

"That was the first time I witnessed how angry William could become. He threatened my life, and gave me an ultimatum to find the answers within the week. I knew something was up. I should have known. I typically do my research before working with someone and truthfully, it wouldn't have taken much to find that Baron William Ruthford wasn't all that he seemed."

"Jeremy, that's rule number one. You taught me that." Even as I said it, I flashed back to my trip to Paris. I didn't follow the rule book on that one.

"No need to lecture me Charles. I was lost in the moment. That excitement disappeared with what I uncovered. The first thing that tickled my throat were the five pages of Homer's lost poem. The fifth sheet did not match the others. The writing style was different, and it was a photocopy of the original. William said that the other sheets were badly damaged and that he had a crew meticulously cleaning them to become readable. The sheets I examined looked to be in pristine condition. It didn't add up.

"Then I searched some more and found that I wasn't the first treasure hunter to be called in for help. He contacted Eric Blake first."

"That piece of work? Boy did he choose wrong. After what that guy did to you and Jenny." Eric was a rival treasure hunter. A sleazy one at that. He wasn't well versed in world history, but he made his way into the limelight by backstabbing everyone around him.

He was also the one who caused J.J.'s car crash in Chicago those many years ago. That's when he stole an artifact Jeremy had dug up for a client. Ironically, if that dirtball didn't do what he did, I would have never met my good friend.

"Charles, but Eric did find something. Something at a dig site in India."

"Wow, he's graduated to the big leagues. But India?"

"Yes. Guess who funded his operation? Our good Baron. Weeks after the discovery, they found Eric dead in his hotel."

As much as I hated the man, I never wished death upon anybody. A good beating? Yes. But not death. "An accident?"

"That's what the authorities say, but I didn't buy it. I dug deeper and found Mr. Blake was murdered. Guess who followed through on his threat? Eric was never good with Ancient Greek. The Baron demanded him to decipher those pages, and when he couldn't, he was killed."

"What did India have to do with anything?"

"I have no idea. Maybe it was a test to prove his worth. Maybe it's part of Homer's story. I didn't care. The minute I realized this, I wanted out. I finished dinner at a local establishment. On my way out, a few of William's goons entered. These were hired mercenaries—thugs working for a paycheck. According to them my time was up. I did the only thing I could to survive. I picked out two off-duty police officers having dinner. I jumped them and punched away like a lunatic. I knew that getting arrested was better than being dead."

"It kind of all makes sense," I said. We approached the dirt airfield. A lone jet positioned itself on the makeshift runway.

"I explained all this in the letter I sent you. I can't believe you never received it."

"J.J. even in these remote regions, they still have e-mail. You know I'm never home. Anyways, we have to get you long gone. Here's our escape." I pointed to the jet. Rust and cracks filled the majority of the plane. A short Asian pilot smoked a cigarette on a nearby rock.

"We can't go anywhere, Charles."

"What do you mean?"

"I can't leave my daughter with that man. Something larger is going on here. What happens when the Baron feels that her services are no longer required? We need to get her."

I tried to stop him, but Jeremy could be a tough old man. I needed to get him out of there. I promised Jenny that. So I decided to come up with a different option. "What if I go? No one knows me. Jenny should be at the dig site. I'll swing by, grab her, and get her out of there. It will be easy as pie. You can't go J.J. They'll recognize you."

Jeremy pondered the notion. It was a good idea. Actually, it was a great idea, and I needed him to accept it. I paid good money for this pilot. I couldn't let him go to waste.

"Okay. But be careful. William Ruthford is as sly as they come."

"Don't you worry, I'm always careful."

I dropped Jeremy off at the plane and drove off into the jungle. According to my map, the site was only an hour away. Maybe I'd catch everyone on their lunch break.

I realized that I had yet to bathe and still wore the same ragged clothes. Sweat now soaked through most of my shirt and jeans. I couldn't wait to get out of this country, but it looked like I was going to be here just a little bit longer.

CHAPTER SEVEN

Wanda Mountains, China

The needle of the gas tank neared empty as I finally arrived at the dig site. What I thought would take an hour took nearly three with all the winding dirt roads. The map made it look like a breeze. All I needed do was follow the Mudan River all the way there, but that was easier said than done.

Initially, the path along the river was simple. I drove along the beautiful turquoise waters of Lake Jingpo. Locals called it *Mirror Lake* because the water gave a perfect reflection of the sky and wilderness that framed it. (There wasn't much reading material on the long flight in. At least the tour guides stuffed into the back of the airplane seats provided me with some good research.)

If I had more time to take in the vista I could have embraced the beauty, but trying to make sense of the makeshift road required all my attention.

Then I saw a massive waterfall up ahead. The Diaoshuilou Falls towered up the cliff. Mist covered the base of the roaring, one hundred foot tall, waterfall. That was also the elevation change I needed to make up in order to reach my destination. Things instantly slowed down as the car zigzagged up the steep cliff.

Now, I'm not afraid of heights. I never was. But going up a narrow path carved out of the rock with no guardrail really made me clench the steering wheel.

After the climb, the rest of the way was smooth sailing. The Wanda Mountain range ran parallel to the river. I drove a ways until I found the northbound road that led to the campsite at the base of the mountain.

As I approached, massive Chinese Tallow trees lined the road. The prickly black bark trees trunks extended a distance before branches stemmed out with foliage. These must have been thousands of years old.

The late afternoon sun cast strange shadows through the foliage. I realized it was because large dark objects hovered in the branches.

I marveled up at the tree-line. I adjusted my eyes to understand what the shadows were. These impressive feats were an arrangement of wooden structures framed out of the trunks.

Single story huts extended from each Tallow tree. Angled wooden supports anchored these floating buildings back to the bark. The huts formed a village of dozens of tree houses. Rope bridges and primitive dumbwaiters tied them together. Decades, if not centuries, of wear and tear decayed most of the shells of the structures. Surprisingly, the rope bridges still looked to be in good condition. Most of their floor planks were cracked or missing, but the entire hovering village was preserved.

A floating city in the middle of nowhere.

What could possess an ancient civilization to build so high up in the trees? Was it protection from invaders? Floods? Animals? The train of thought disappeared from my mind as I exited out of the dense forest and into an open grass plain.

The plain was littered with green tents, trucks, portable generators, and large spotlights. Workers huddled around camp fires. Laughter could be heard. It was pretty standard fare for an archeological dig.

Well, except for the massive power generator and sophisticated machinery. That, and the two helicopters sitting on a landing pad. Money oozed out of the every facet of this place.

Beyond the camp rose the face of the Wanda Mountain. The mountain soared up the horizon.

With all the people scattered about, it was going to be difficult to find Jenny.

"Stop!" a voice called out. I was so distracted by the rest of the site that I neglected to see the two armed guards standing in front of me. From their black clothing, automatic weapons, and buzz cuts, I discerned that they were mercenaries—the thugs-for-hire that J.J. told me about. I found it uncanny how stereotypically similar these guys all looked.

"I'm here to see Jenny Jenkins," I said confidently, not to attract suspicion.

"Is she expecting you?" the thug asked. He pulled out his radio, prepping a call.

"No, it's a surprise. Tell her Charlie Morgan is here to see her."

I waited. The man chatted into his radio, and a moment later a voice echoed back permitting me through.

"She's in the last tent to the right," the thug added.

The two men stepped away and let me pass. Finding Jenny was going to be easier than I thought. I parked the jeep near the rest of the vehicles and hopped out.

I noticed another handful of mercenaries patrolling the perimeter. Security was fairly tight around the grounds. I was sure it was to promote the safety of the workers, but something seemed off. I couldn't put my finger on it, but from what J.J. said, I wondered if the mercenaries were protecting the people from outside threats or making sure no one had the opportunity to leave. I had the utter feeling that I just walked into another prison.

Still, I had a task at hand. The last tent on the right was my next stop.

No one harassed me as I reached the tent. Upon entering, I found a lone worker standing over a table. The blonde ponytail instantly gave Jenny away. She wore khakis and a white tank top. Most of the tank top was covered in sweat and dirt—an obvious indication of how passionate she was about her job. She pulled off the ensemble though. She looked radiant.

"Hey kiddo," I said, walking up behind her.

Jenny turned around, stunned. Her surprise swiftly turned to excitement, and she ran to me for a big hug. "Charlie! Why didn't you call? I was worried sick. Tell me you got my dad out safe."

"Yes ma'am. I sent him off on a plane a few hours ago. Your pilot friend came through." I stressed the word *friend*.

"I know. He called me after the job, freaking out. I don't think he realized the danger he got himself into. I also forgot how nervous he got under pressure. He flew out of here as quick as he did when we broke up years ago."

"You were a life saver."

Jenny blushed a bit. Then her brows rose into a questionable look. "What are you doing here?"

"I'm here for you. Rescue operation number two for the day. I talked to your dad, and he says you're in danger. He knows this Ruthford guy really well. So well, that they were working together before you got here. Your dad was the one that found this tomb.

From what J.J. told me, the Baron is not a good person to be associated with."

"Charlie, the man's harmless. If you met him you'd understand."

"It's not my job to question your father. You just have to trust him on this."

"I can't. This is my job. Alvin needs me."

"Jenny, I wasn't really asking. I promised your dad I'd get you to safety, much like I promised you I'd get him to safety."

Jenny had a lot of her father in her. I watched her eyes scanning the photos that spread across the table. The allure of uncovering a hidden treasure tempted her to stay. She closed her eyes, finally admitting, "Okay Charlie. I'll leave with you."

That was easy.

Then she added, "But we're bringing Alvin with us."

"What?"

"If William is as dangerous as you say he is, I can't leave Alvin alone. We have to tell him."

"Jenny, how well do you know this guy? It is going to be hard enough coming up with an excuse to get you out of here."

"That's my deal, Charlie. It's both of us, or none of us."

"Where's Alvin now?"

"My ears must be burning?" a voice chimed behind us. I turned to see a thin man in full safari gear. A brown fedora covered the man's dirty blonde hair. Any stereotypes of Australian outbackers were fully exemplified in good old *Crocodile Dundee*.

"You must be Alvin Mitchell," I said.

"Yes, *mate*. You've heard of me, I see." An all-star grin showcased the man's pearly whites.

"Jenny's told me a few things."

"Has she told you of my roguish good looks, or just of all thirty five discoveries that I've bloody made in the last three years."

Even with the cartoonish outfit that he was wearing, Alvin Mitchell was a good looking man. I hated to admit it. He was a lot younger than I expected too. Jenny had mentioned how down to earth the man was. She couldn't have been farther from the truth. Alvin Mitchell was one cocky fella.

"Did Jenny also tell you of all the foundations that I have started for young archeologists?"

Was he serious?

"No, she glossed over those details." I stepped forward and extended my hand. "Name's Charles—"

"Morgan. I know who you are, *mate.*" Alvin Mitchell shook my hand. Both of us sustained a firm grip. It was easy to judge a man by his handshake. Mitchell seemed to be judging me the same. His hands were rough—signs of a hard worker. Yet his nails were well manicured, signifying class.

Still clutching each other's hands, I decided to play Mitchell's game. I retorted, "I'm amazed you've heard of me. I'm not nearly as famous as you. I'm just a low treasure hunter that barely makes a living doing what I do."

"Non-sense, Charlie. Can I call you Charlie? We all share the same passion for discovery. I just make a better Quid. Jenny had plenty of things to say about you. Yet she neglected to tell me that you were stopping by. Are you here for a few lessons?"

Our hands separated. "Actually, I was just in the neighborhood. When I heard Jenny was here, I figured I'd pay her a surprise visit. It sounds as if you keep her working pretty hard."

"I'm the one having trouble peeling her away from her work. She has a keen eye for this sort of thing. She's going to surpass both of us pretty quickly one of these days."

"Yes she will," I said, glancing over at Jenny. I then added, "Mitchell, I'd love to hear about your countless expeditions, but you think I could steal your prize pupil for a few hours? I hoped to take her out for a drink or dinner and catch up."

Jenny stepped in. "Alvin, join us? You two have a lot in common. It would be nice for you to exchange some war tales."

I glared at Jenny. Her stinging stare back reminded me so much of J.J.'s. I knew I was going to lose this battle, so I easily conceded. "Yes Alvin, I'd love to hear more about the legend you are." I felt sick. Hopefully he missed my sarcastic undertone.

Before Alvin Mitchell could respond, the tent opened and in came another figure. Actually, it was more of an eclipse. The large shape of the man blotted out the sun that tried filtering between the parted canvas. As the figure stepped into the room, his features became much more apparent.

A well-groomed bull of a man stood before us. His tucked in polo and pants tightly stretched over his muscular frame. His jet white hair signified his sixty years of age, but his body looked to be in peak physical form.

This was the man Jenny called harmless?

Even without ever opening his mouth, Baron William Ruthford made his presence felt. "Mr. Mitchell, you did not inform me that we were having guests?"

Crap.

My plan of sneaking in and out unnoticed really just flew out the door. "You must be the man behind the curtain," I said politely.

"Baron William Ruthford. You are Charles Morgan, I presume," the bull said cheerfully.

"I'm surprised at how well-versed everyone here is about me," I puzzled.

"I contacted you weeks ago. I offered you an opportunity to join us on the brink of this discovery. Did you not receive my message?"

It suddenly dawned on me that I had heard of this guy's name before. The day Jenny called. I remembered the pompous voice on the voicemail, but I deleted it before hearing what it was about. "I'm a busy man, Mr. Ruthford. I apologize. In any case, it looks like you're in good hands. Based on Alvin's track record—much more capable of hands."

The Baron gave a disappointed look. "I'm starting to have doubts on that. It seems as though Mr. Mitchell's extensive resume is a tad exaggerated. He has failed to impress with any progress over the past few weeks." Ruthford then turned to me. "Nonetheless, it seems that today is a day of good fortunate. Do you believe in fate, Mr. Morgan?"

"Not really. I was never much into putting my life in the hands of a higher being."

"Well I do. I think its fate that brought you here. What are the odds that you'd be in the vicinity of this remote region of China?"

"I account it to dumb luck."

"I don't think so. How would you like to stay for a bit and take a look at our discovery? I'd be honored."

"Well you'll be doubly unsatisfied. I'm sorry I can't stay, and I wouldn't want to steal Alvin's thunder. You have a full crew of professionals more proficient in Chinese history that can help you out. I'd just embarrass myself."

"People don't say no to me, Mr. Morgan," the Baron said with a snarly grin. "I always get what I want."

"I hate to knock you down a couple of notches, but it looks like both you and Alvin are breaking your track records."

The Baron laughed. I sensed insult and anger buried under it, but he maintained his composure. "I've met many young men like you. You relish mysteries, Mr. Morgan. Come, take one glimpse of what we are searching for here. Give me one hour of your time and I will let Jennifer have the rest of the evening off."

I tried to back out. Even Jenny came to my rescue for us to leave, but nothing worked. There was no fighting it.

We stepped out of the tent to tour the site that William Ruthford deemed *the greatest discovery of all time.*

CHAPTER EIGHT

I t really was a sculpture of beauty. I gave the Baron that.
A large grass field surrounded the campsite. The field died
abruptly at the limestone wall of the Wanda Mountain. Most of
the mountain had a steep slope rising up to the clouds, but not
this area. Here the rock was smooth, shaped like a massive ninety
degree wall.

In the center, a three story bronze gate called out the entrance to the shaman tomb. The double doors were exquisite
in detail. Chinese characters and carvings filled the three sided
frame. A large circle spanned between the two butted door panels. What looked like flames, radiated around the circular shape.
On each door leaf, engraved human silhouettes filled most of
the face. Their proportions were greatly exaggerated, making
each figure over twenty feet tall.

Both figures were positioned facing each other. Their hands
extended as if holding the weight of the large circular image that
centered on the two doors.

Even more impressive were two ornately detailed totem poles that stood side by side in the middle of the grassy plain. Chinese totems were quite different than the wooden ones that Native Americans made popular. They were typically made with a mixture of bronze metal and wood. In this specific case, they were almost completely covered in bronze. They towered above us, looking like five foot diameter candles sticking out of a birthday cake.

"You weren't kidding, Ruthford. This is a thing of splendor," I said. I didn't trust the man, and even though I only just met him, I already didn't like him much. Still, it didn't negate the fact that this was an attractive find.

The Baron's eyes followed me as I surveyed the site. I saw why Jeremy was so excited about this. The meticulous detail that flooded every surface of the totems and gateway screamed something important was buried here.

Nearly ninety percent of these totems were engraved in bronze, which was rare. The Sanxingdui culture that started these rituals in ancient China typically contained minimal amounts of bronze. Poles were used to represent the dead, or in some cases, the gods. None ever had this much detail.

"Quite a *beaut*, huh?" Alvin spoke, interrupting my marvel. "How fluent are you about the Chinese culture, Charlie?"

"I know enough to see that whatever's buried here has extreme significance. The amount of bronze used—"

"Is well beyond your average totem," Mitchell cut. "We've been analyzing these two piers for some time. They date back to the early Shang Dynasty."

"I agree. It's very reminiscent to the Sanxingdui Culture from that time."

Alvin paused. I must have surprised him with my historical knowledge. The Australian then moved over to the totem. He fondled the bronze rather awkwardly—like it was his baby. "I think it's the key to opening the gate."

I looked beyond the poles to the set of grand doors. "You're telling me there is no way to simply pry those two doors open?"

The Baron responded, "Mr. Morgan, I have tried everything. I even used quantities of dynamite, but never beyond safety levels that could risk damaging whatever lies beyond those gates. Nothing has worked."

I turned back to Alvin. "And these totems are the key because?"

"Have you ever heard of *Men Shen*?" Alvin asked.

I shook my head.

"*Men Shen* are two deities who ward against evil spirits. They were depicted with faces of opposing color—one, a red face, and the other, a white face. Talk of these deities is rare, *mate*. Only a few relics proved the existence of their worship. They date back to the fifth century B.C."

Mitchell pointed to the gateway. "Look at the bronze doors. The two silhouettes stare at one another. If you inspect the faces closely you can see that the bronze is carved out, and small wooden icons are inserted. We found fragments of red and white dye in each of those heads."

Alvin said all this in grand fashion. He pulled me away from the totem to get a better angle on the two looming objects. "Look at the two faces engraved on the totems. They are the bloody same. These two totems were built to thwart enemies."

"I can't wait to see what you find in another three weeks," I said sarcastically.

Jenny gave me a stern look, then added, "Charlie, you see that circle in the center of the door? That circle is split directly in half by the crease between the two doors. It's a Taijitu—a yin-yang symbol. Together the two halves are shown in perfect harmony."

I understood what Jenny was saying, but I was distracted. Admiring the door, I noticed a Chinese character engraved all over it.

It's true I had a minimal knowledge of Chinese characters, but there are a few that I made sure to understand. The most glaring one was the character signifying the *white tiger*. And that character repeated itself all around the massive doorway.

I knew that symbol all too well. Mainly because it meant 'get the heck out of here.'

The tiger was used in Ancient Chinese lore as a protector, much like the *Men Shen*. If something was meant to stay buried, that symbol was drawn over it. From past experience, only bad things came from disregarding that warning.

Thankfully, I knew better. This was a mystery I didn't care to solve. The doors had layers upon layers of protective glyphs. Whatever lay beyond them was important. In my profession, important ran hand in hand with dangerous.

"What's going on in that head of yours?" the Baron asked.

"You truly are on the brink of something. From the looks of things, you have quite a good crew working on it."

That wasn't enough for Ruthford. He wanted more. "Do you see anything out of the ordinary? Anything from your past expeditions clue you in?"

His speech accelerated. The man was getting anxious. It was strange, seeing as I got there less than a half hour ago. He expected me to have answers that people haven't been able to figure out for months, including the man who trained me into the man I was. "Listen…"

The Baron stopped me. "Just take your time. I'm going to go get my daughter. She found a few artifacts this morning that may help."

Daughter?

Before I could respond, the Baron left.

I quickly turned to Alvin and Jenny. "Okay guys, are we ready to get out of here?"

"I understand this may be a little overwhelming for you, *mate*. It is a tough nut to crack, and this may not be your cup of tea," Alvin responded.

"Easy there, Dundee. I know my history. I just don't..." I nearly told this balloon headed Australian what was really going on, but I stopped myself. If I led on that things weren't all rainbows and butterflies, there was a good chance Mitchell would think I'm out of my mind. I couldn't risk him telling the Baron. I held back. "You know what? Let me do what I do. I work better alone."

I left Jenny and Alvin behind to do my own investigation. Jenny easily read my annoyance and let me be.

I had a half hour to spare.

The gateway grew as I paced my way to it. The bronze doors shimmered in the sunlight. I analyzed the stunning engravings. I tried to make sense of what all the symbols meant. This was one of the times I wished I really did know more about Chinese history. I wasn't about to admit that to Alvin Mitchell though. As I scanned the doorway, I started to jog my memory. What did I know?

China... Taoism... Shang Dynasty... Constellations... Shamans... Tot...

Wait—constellations. China was broken up into four quadrants based on constellations. They related the stars to animals and each quadrant identified with its own animal: Azure Dragons in the East, Vermillion Birds in the South, and Black Tortoise of the North. The West was the White Tiger. With the Wanda Mountains being on the western most portion of China, this made sense.

That went nowhere.

I thought of the shaman's many names. What did Jenny say her name translated to? Mother of the Shining Lake? Lake Jingpo was known as *Mirror Lake*. It made perfect sense being so close to *Xi Wangmu's* tomb. The lake was so calm with such clear waters, it made a perfect reflection. At night, one couldn't tell where the night sky ended, and the lake began.

Again, that led me to the stars, and for some reason constellations kept creeping up my mind. The metal, bronze, typically represented the Universe. Almost all spiritual beliefs had something to do with balance of the Universe and the sky.

Look upward? Something above?

I examined the upper portion of the doorway. Just above the frame, a series of circles were carved out of the limestone. There were ten in total. Looking closer at their arrangement, they decoratively spread across the entire head of the door frame. Could they simply be more ornamentation?

Each circle had a hole carved out in its center. Circle of life? Center of the Universe? I didn't know. I was grabbing at straws.

I gave up the train of thought and distracted myself with the rest of my surroundings. Looking back beyond the campsite, I made out the tall Tallow trees that continued off into the distance. I could barely see the hovering buildings hidden in the foliage at the tops of the trees.

To either side of the grass plain, seven foot tall wild grass followed the base of the mountain. It looked like a maze to get through. I wondered if something might have been hidden under it.

Before I could head toward the tall grass, a voice called out. It was the Baron. He returned, and now with another member for the party.

Lynea Ruthford stood ridiculously close to her father. Her twenty year old frame looked tiny next to the giant proportions of the Baron. Fear spread over her eyes as I approached.

I introduced myself but she shied away, barely shaking my extended hand. Her delicate nature either meant that she was a very sheltered child, or I made her nervous. I do have that effect on some women. I mean I couldn't blame them of course. My charm and looks typically won me access into a number of girls' hearts.

"Sorry for taking so long," the Baron said. "Have I missed anything?"

The four of us delved a little deeper into the hidden meanings of the markings spread across the gate. I didn't factor Lynea into the equation because she just stood there listening.

But then things changed.

Lynea pulled out some tiny artifacts that she picked out of the limestone near the sill of the bronze gate. There were a few circular stones with irregular edges. She cleaned them, making the marks on the rocks much more prominent.

As we rotated the objects in our hands, my mind kept thinking about the sky, and the stars, and the Universe. These rocks appeared to be miniature suns. A spade carved into the center of each of the objects. I handed them back to Lynea, commenting on their beauty.

"They were covered in mud. I found nine of them, but some were cracked. I thought they very pretty," she said softly.

That was enough for me. I glanced at my watch and said, "Well everyone, it has been enlightening. I'm sorry to be cutting out like this but it looks like our time is up."

The Baron grabbed me firmly. "Mr. Morgan, I haven't even gotten the chance to explain all of our previous discoveries. The sun will be setting soon. I'd be a horrible host not to invite you to spend the night. It's not safe to travel after dark. The authorities here are extremely ruthless."

What did he say? Did the Baron know I was on the run from the police? As much as I wondered if the man knew, something else struck me—something that I remembered learning from an old Chinese acquaintance.

I broke free of the Baron's grasp and walked over to the large bronze doors. I counted the ten circles that framed the top of the doorway. "Lynea, where did you say you found those relics?"

Lynea pointed at the base of the one door. Ten indentations depressed into the metal where the objects once were. Ten. Yet Lynea only found nine.

"What have you discovered?" the Baron asked excitedly.

Still not saying a word, I stepped back to take in the enormous doors once again. I sensed the anxiety in my immediate surroundings as the others watched. No one said a word. The more I focused on the circles up above, I started to think that maybe I might be onto something. Could it be that easy?

I knew I shouldn't have pushed forward. J.J. would have been screaming at me to get out of there, but I remained. Maybe it was my pride to show up Alvin, or maybe it was simple curiosity. (That may be the death of a cat, but they had nine lives, and I only had one.) All signs warned for me to stop.

Alvin broke the silence. "Charlie, it looks like you excel at theatrics. You want to clue us in on what you are thinking? Or is this all an act?"

Hearing his voice, I smirked. "How about I just show you."

Yup, it was all about my pride.

Years ago I heard a tale. The tale of *Yi* the Archer. It was an old Chinese story about the origin of the sun. Ten day weeks were the standard cycle used in ancient China. They believed ten suns existed for each day of the week. The suns traveled with their mother, the goddess *Xi He*, to the Valley of the Light in the East, got bathed, and one by one traveled back to Mount Yen-Tzu in the Far West. Each sun traveled alone for a day long journey.

As the story goes, one day, all the suns decided to travel back together. With them all up in the sky, the Earth started to burn.

Everything began to melt away. Humanity was being killed by the intense heat.

A brave young archer, *Yi*, with a magic bow came to the rescue. He shot down all the suns to save the Earth from devastation. One arrow missed though, and the last sun survived to finish its trek to the West. Hence the birth of our Sun.

The bronze gate was filled with Sun imagery. The most obvious was the giant circle in the middle. Looking up at the ten circles that lined the upper portion of the doorway, one of them had to be the key. Each had a small recessed hole in its center.

Only one sun technically made the full journey west, so it only made sense that the western most engraving would be the key. Or so I thought.

I marched up to the limestone wall. Scanning the surface I mapped my path up the handholds and protrusions that extended out of the rock. It was a thirty foot climb, but I'd scaled worse.

"Charlie what are you doing?" Jenny asked.

"I just got to go for a little climb."

Alvin interrupted, "You know I'm a certified mountain climber. I did it all the time in the outback. Let's not hurt yourself, *mate*. I'll do it. I insist."

I shook the man off. "Don't you worry about me, Alvin. I've done this enough times. I'll be fine."

Jenny grabbed me aside, whispering, "Charlie, you don't have to do this."

"Jen, I'm good. Trust me." I threw out my infamous grin and refocused on the task at hand.

Like any good treasure hunter, I was in the moment. My original goal to escape with Jenny fell to the wayside. My intrigue to see if I was *right* took over.

Grabbing two holds, I angled my body away from the rock. I braced my feet on an extended ledge and lunged upward.

Finding grips were easy. As I continued up the surface, I discovered that there were more than enough nooks and crannies to grab onto. The goal in any climb is to let the legs do most of the work. The hands were just the guides.

Halfway up the wall I started retelling the tale of the ten suns to my audience. I pulled myself up another few feet. Then another.

The footings were solid. I wondered if it was luck that time carved away at the beautiful limestone, or if these holds were man-made. They conveniently led me up the steep surface.

I took another step when a foothold gave way. The ledge my other foot rested on broke under the sudden pressure. My muscles tensed as my hands clenched on for dear life. I felt the pain in my forearms. My upper body carried my entire weight. Calming myself, I rubbed my legs against the surface in search of new anchors.

They found some.

For a minute there was silence. Even the wind felt obligated to stop moving. Everyone down below must have been white with fear. I, on the other hand, nearly crapped myself. I risked a glance down to see that I was almost thirty feet above the ground. A drop from here would easily break my legs.

I was only a few feet away from my destination.

I climbed over to the first engraved circle.

Now, being much closer to the object, I made out many more elaborate details carved around it. The center hole was about five inches in diameter. It was the perfect size to fit a hand. I balanced my body against the wall and extended my arm out to the small opening.

"Are you sure that's a good idea?" Jenny yelled out. "What if it's booby-trapped?"

"Leave the man be," the Baron said.

I reached into the hole. My hand got deeper and deeper. Still, there was no end to it. The further my hand got into the dark void, the tighter the hole became. I felt the rock closing in on my knuckles. Heat radiated off the stone.

Finally, my fingers touched something. They stroked over the hard object. It felt like a circular bar. Soon my entire hand clamped around the lever. I jiggled it. It wouldn't turn. I pushed it, and nothing. Finally, I tugged on it.

It shifted an inch.

I tugged again.

It moved some more.

The bar was under a lot of tension. Something was holding it in place. I braced myself once more and pulled as hard as I could.

The lever dislodged from its housing and lost all friction. It pulled out a few more inches then stopped.

In that same moment the ground quaked. I grabbed hold of the rock ledge. The earth rattled. Looking back, I saw the two bronze totem poles viciously vibrate. They started to rise out of the ground, revealing their wooden foundations.

The poles continued their vertical ascent simultaneously. After ten feet they stopped abruptly. The mini earthquake ceased along with them.

The others noticed the rising objects, and all eyes locked on the two massive totems that grew further out of the ground. At their base, four wooden bars pivoted, extending out like levers.

What looked like a quiet campsite was now filled with other researchers and alert mercenaries coming out of their tents. The large group huddled around this new discovery.

"See what I mean when I said I'll just show you?" I said.

The climb down was a little more difficult. Everyone waited for me to reach the base of the mountain. After a number of congratulatory pats on the back, William said, "Now what, Mr. Morgan? This is your show."

I walked up to the two totems. Alvin fell silent in the background. I could tell he was not too happy about what I just did. I decided to throw him a bone. "I think Alvin was right about one thing. These pillars are the key."

"How?" Lynea asked.

"By mirroring their orientation with the door," Jenny responded for me. She too was excited. "The Taoists believed self-reflection is what a person needs to fully understand themselves. A mirror shows you who you are. If we rotate these totems to face each other, they will mirror the doorway as a specular image," Jenny said lively.

She was a quick one.

I grabbed one of the levers and started to push. The totem rotated on its center. Soon, I had the one bronze *Men Shen* facing the other. Alvin grabbed the other totem and turned it. Within seconds, both statues matched the vision inscribed on the bronze gate.

The earth rumbled once again. This time no one was afraid. The three story bronze doors cringed at the joints.

Everyone stared in astonishment as the gates guarding the tomb of the legendary *Wu, Xi Wangmu,* parted for the first time in thousands of years.

CHAPTER NINE

A nti-climactic was probably an understatement.

The grand doors parted fully, revealing the entrance to the mountain. It also revealed another pair of locked doors behind them.

The large cavity carved out of rock created a vestibule—a little room that was only ten feet deep. The chamber terminated with this second pair of secure doors, preventing one from continuing on into the mountain. After all this work in figuring out how to open the bronze gate, the Baron was halted by another puzzle.

I found the revelation to be pretty darn funny.

The new doorway was very different than the first. Wooden gears and cogs covered the ceiling. The doors themselves were a more human scale. The only similarity was that the ten foot leafs had the same intricate bronze details as the exterior gates.

The creators of this temple were giving us one last chance to leave. These doors begged us to stop.

And stop I did.

The rest of the crew ran into the large vestibule while I remained behind. I watched the joy of the others slowly drop to confusion once they realized that their jobs weren't over. Ruthford approached.

"You are an astonishing individual," Baron William Ruthford commented with a congratulatory hug.

"That was one hour of my time, just imagine what I could have done with three weeks," I gloated. I sounded like Alvin Mitchell. Replaying my comment in my head, I felt gross at how cocky it came out.

"Well come on then. Let's see where this leads." The Baron's eyes lit with delight.

I paused. "No sir, my hour is up. This was a freebie. You asked for me to just take a look. I gave you more than that. Now it's time for me to leave."

The Baron hesitated. "And let's say that the fact that I didn't call the police to notify them of your location was my *freebie* to you, Mr. Morgan."

I said nothing.

"I'm not a fool. Your vehicle has Chinese military insignia all across the side panels, and it is covered in bullet holes. That's not a typical jeep rental. Even in these remote regions of the world, you would be surprised at how good of reception our radios obtain. Lynea called me over when you arrived. We received chatter about two escaped convicts from the laogai prison. It was easy to connect the dots."

That's why the girl was terrified of me. I was speechless.

"How is good old Jeremy?" The Baron came close. "Mr. Morgan, I don't know what Mr. Jenkins may have told you, but I'm not an evil man."

"Threatening to kill him is not evil?"

"It was motivation. I like to provide my employees with incentive, and I have found death to be the strongest incentive of all.

I wouldn't have killed him. He is one of the reasons we've made it this far."

"Right." I stepped back from the enormous man. "Well, I held up my end of the deal. If you're not a bad man, you would hold up yours."

"How about this? You see this through and I will let you and your friends go. All I want is to find the tomb of *Xi Wangmu.* After that, your services will no longer be needed."

"What's so important about this tomb?"

"This time, it will be my turn to show you." Ruthford tossed me a backpack. Inside were the essentials. Water, snacks, flashlights. "Now come on and show me how good you really are. If not for me, for young Jennifer."

Reluctantly, I walked forward.

I gathered with the rest of the crew. My emotions must have been leaping off my face because Jenny came straight over. Even without the exchange of words, she understood something was wrong.

Baron William hushed the crowd. He went on with a short speech as to the significance of what we were all there to find. I couldn't listen. The sound of his voice annoyed me. I was also distracted by all the mercenaries with guns that outlined the perimeter of the group. J.J. was right. This was a man you did not want to associate yourself with.

In my pride, I helped bring the man one step closer to his goal. Now, I was locked in for the long haul.

The Baron called me out of the crowd to congratulate me. It was amazing to see his tone shift from death curdling to pleasant and innocent. Looking out at the huddle of people around us, they had no clue what they got themselves into.

Out of all the faces in the crowd, it was easy to spot Alvin's. He was the only one without a smile. If there was anything good that came of this whole situation, it was that I got to see that look on Alvin Mitchell's face.

"Impress us some more, Mr. Morgan," the Baron began. "You have the honor of leading the way."

The only way to get out of here was to push forward, so that's what I did. The crowd settled, allowing me to think. With all the flashlights in the dimly lit cavern, I got a better image of what we were dealing with.

Twenty feet straight above me were a network of gears and cogs. They dangled off an intricate wooden catwalk. Interestingly, we now saw the back face of the exterior limestone wall. The holes in the center of the circles that were engraved on the exterior completely cut through the stone. Thin beams of light bled through the little portholes, partially illuminating the gears. Whatever needed to be done, those gears were the answer.

A few overly eager researchers ran to get me a ladder and propped it against the wall.

Where was that ladder ten minutes ago when I hung from the side of the mountain?

Alvin approached, saying, "Charlie, let me go on up there. You've had enough death defying feats today. You don't want to press your luck, *mate*."

The Baron held the Australian back. "No Mr. Mitchell, Morgan has earned this. It's time to suck up your pride and let the man work."

Talk about adding fuel to the fire.

Jenny handed me a two-way radio. "Keep in touch with us up there. And be careful."

I took the radio and climbed up the ladder to the wooden catwalk. It was rickety as heck. The thin wooden planks creaked with every step. Surprisingly, the rope railings were all in excellent condition.

I slowly walked across the tiny bridge and reached the gears. One by one, I inspected the connections between them all. Each hexagonal gear overlapped another. Their center rods disappeared into the limestone. I pushed and shoved with all my might, but none of the objects moved.

Down below, more words of encouragement echoed.

I searched some more.

Climbing up to another level of the catwalk, I lost sight of the others. Deep shadows lined the rocky walls. The only illumination came from the beams of light shining through the holes in the exterior rock.

"Charlie, we can't see you," muffled the radio. It was Jenny.

"I'm good. I'll keep you posted," I bounced back.

Cautiously, I moved forward in the darkness. Thin strands of light filtered through the narrow space. The beams clearly cut across the room, shining speckled dots onto the far wall. The dots created distinct circles on the smooth surface of dark rock.

Counting the dots, I realized there were only nine in total. Even though the holes in the exterior wall penetrated the surface in a straight line, the beams of light refracted into the space at different angles. None of the circular dots on the opposing wall lined up.

I turned my attention to the source. Where ten engraved stone circles lined the outside surface of the mountain, bronze circular disks matched their location on the interior. Only nine of the disks had holes. The last one—the one I stuck my hand into—had a wooden cog cover most of it.

That must have been the mechanism I unlatched to open the outer doors.

Inching closer to the other disks, I shined a light on one of them. The center hole completely cut through the rock, but the bronze disk had an arched deflector at the end. This bounced the direction of the light. No wonder none of the light beams followed the same trajectory.

But why?

I glanced back at the far wall. The lights appeared randomly arranged along a dark black surface. Entranced by the imagery, it almost looked like I was staring at the night sky blanketed by stars. I shifted my gaze back to the source once again.

I touched one of the bronze disks and found that it easily rotated. It spun until there was a click. The beam changed its trajectory. Where a circle of light once reflected off the far wall, darkness replaced it. That dot now appeared a few feet to the right. I turned the disc some more, and it clicked again. The light shifted once more on the far wall.

Interesting.

Xi Wangmu was the goddess of the Universe—Heaven and Earth. With all the symbolism to the sky, the sun, and the stars, maybe this was trying to tell me something. I grabbed the radio and pushed 'talk.' "Jenny, you there?"

Static, then a voice crackled, "Charlie?"

"Question for you. This *Wu* shamaness… you said she was one with the Universe, right?"

"Yes. Stories say she lived at the point where the sun set and night began—the moment where Heaven touched the Earth. Why?"

The night began? "Any constellations related her?"

"Um… an old oracle bone dating back to the Shang Dynasty tied her existence to Ursa Major."

"Ursa Major? You mean the Big Dipper?"

"Yeah. The most important star formation in Taoist astrology."

Astrology held that there was an astronomical relationship tying humans to the Universe. Constellations and planetary positioning were used to predict future events or even explain a person's behavior. In the Chinese philosophy, the stars tied directly to the three harmonies: Heaven, Earth, and Man. Hence the belief in the yin and yang.

Ursa Major, or the Big Dipper, was a collection of distinct stars that formed the shape of a ladle. It was probably the most identifiable constellation that one could see in the night sky, and seven stars comprised the grouping.

I looked at the far wall again. Nine beams of light. The numbers didn't add up.

The radio came alive once again. "Charlie, why do you ask?"

"Because I thought I found the key to opening this door. There are nine stars projecting into the room. They looked like an astrological grouping, but there are too many of them. The Big Dipper only had seven. Any other constellations that it might tie to?"

A moment later, another voice came on the radio. "No that's the one, *mate*." It was Alvin. He continued, "The Chinese believed the Dipper had nine stars. Other than the seven visible ones, two invisible stars existed on either side of the star *Alkaid*. They used to be lit centuries ago, but faded away."

That was actually surprisingly helpful. This may work.

"Okay, give me a second." I pocketed the radio and got to work.

Walking across the catwalk to each bronze disk, I twisted and turned until each one locked into proper position. The dots of light along the opposing rock began moving into place. Soon, I arranged seven speckles into a perfect representation of the Big Dipper.

I went to the last two holes and angled their light to fall on either side of the third star in the ladle.

The last light fell onto its mark.

The wooden gears kick-started.

One by one, they turned, like an assembly line.

The deafening sounds reverberated between the narrow walls. The rickety bridge quivered furiously as I clung to the ropes. I could hear radio chatter from my pocket, but the loud grinding of all the gears stifled the sounds.

Just as quickly as the gears started, they came to a stop.

Empty silence filled the air.

Then I heard the faint sounds of cheering. Jenny's voice came through the radio. "Charlie!"

"What happened?" My heart was still racing.

"You are not going to believe this," her voice said.

CHAPTER TEN

J enny was right.

When I returned back to the vestibule chamber, everyone was gone. This time they didn't wait for me. The second pair of doors stood propped apart. Voices rang from beyond the newly opened gates.

Past the doors, a new chamber waited. Actually, I would call it more of an arena. The roof of the monstrous space disappeared in darkness. Everyone looked like ants compared to the scale of it all.

The floor of the chamber consisted of individual square stones laid in a waffle pattern. A small gap separated each rock. Reddish light radiated through the grid arrangement in the floor.

Cautiously stepping into the monumental room, I felt the heat rise out of the ground. I flashed my light around to survey these new surroundings. Nine tall statues carved out of the walls. The statues were meticulously sculptured, and each one looked unique. Focusing on the depicted faces, I didn't know what any of them meant.

My knowledge of Chinese history was maxed out.

What interested me instead were the gaping passageways cut into the base of each statue. Peering into some of the holes, all I saw was a dark oblivion.

Which of the nine pathways led the right way? More importantly, what lay at the end of them?

The others followed suit, lighting up flares and bringing spotlights into the chamber. The red glow from the floor may have dimly lit the room, but within minutes, the entire space came to life in harsh fluorescence.

The Baron spoke out, "Exquisite."

"But what is it? I asked.

The Baron smiled. "The mythological Mount Kunlun."

I didn't bother asking what the heck that meant. Ruthford answered my thought for me.

"Mr. Morgan, Mount Kunlun is one of the Axis Mundi, points on the globe that are thought to be gateways to the heavens. There are only a few known locations on this planet that hold this status. They are described as the points where the *Earth meets the Heavens.*"

The bullish man continued, "Of course, our Shamaness, *Xi Wangmu*—the Queen Mother of the West—was believed to live in this mythological Mount Kunlun. It was a perfect and complete paradise. A mountain range north of here bears the same name. Many thought it to be where her palace resided. They were wrong."

"The Chinese had a very different perception of paradise," I thought out loud. It was more like hell. I felt like I already lost ten pounds in this sauna.

The Baron continued, "It was the meeting place for Chinese deities and a cosmic pillar for communication between these gods and humans. Look at the statues. Nine gods made up Queen Mother's circle. These are their spiritual incarnations. Mr. Morgan, this isn't just the tomb of *Xi Wangmu*, this is her temple. Her paradise."

"Interesting lesson, Baron," I said. The man was ecstatic. His daughter, on the other hand, just stood beside Ruthford with a blank face. I nearly forgot she was even here.

I circled the perimeter of the room. Jenny came up beside me. "You did some amazing work back there," she complimented.

"I think I made your boyfriend jealous." I motioned to Alvin who stood angrily in the corner.

"He's not my boyfriend, Charlie." Then Jenny got serious. "What happened earlier with the William? You looked worried."

"Oh nothing, he just wanted to toot my horn a bit," I lied. "If you keep feeding my ego, I may start to float away."

"Oh stop. I can easily deflate your bubble. Remember the time I caught you searching through elephant dung because my dad told you there was treasure buried in it? You dove right in."

"Yeah, well J.J. had a unique sense of humor."

"Or, he just wanted you out of his way because you kept harassing him."

I laughed, recalling the incident. "I was a young kid then." As if that justified anything.

"A smelly one at that," Jenny quipped back, smiling.

Out of embarrassment, I changed the subject. I knelt down to brush my hand over the light permeating from the rock. "You feel that heat?"

"Yeah," Jenny said. "Wanda Mountain is a dormant volcano. That light must be coming from an open fissure of lava somewhere below the Earth's crust."

"Looks like this isn't so dormant after all," I responded.

"The last time this volcano erupted was centuries ago. That eruption was what formed the Mudan River south of here."

I sniffed, smelling gaseous vapors.

"Ethylene gas," the Baron said nearby. "It's common in volcanoes. Inhaling enough vapors can give a person hallucinations. Some even say that is where shamans got their power."

"You're chockfull of information, Baron. Is that why we're here? So we can get high and see some visions?"

"No Mr. Morgan. You will see shortly."

"I'm not sure how shortly. We have a one in nine shot of finding the right way, unless all these tunnels lead to the same location. Speaking from past experiences, I highly doubt that."

"Ah, but we do know where to go. You never let me finish about Mount Kunlun."

The Baron led us back to the center of the room. Now fully lit, we easily made out the tall figures lining the walls of the chamber. He then began, "These nine statues are larger than life—a typical representation of deities. It explains the considerable doorways. In ancient times, when people erected statues or temples for the gods, they constructed enormously tall structures. In their eyes, the gods were much bigger than the average man. A standard doorway could not fit the body of a divine being.

"The Acropolis in Greece is a perfect example. Each building, from the Parthenon to the Erechtheum, had such a doorway. The Erechtheum functioned as a treasury. Every year citizens brought monetary offerings to the gods, and that chamber housed those treasures. The exaggerated gateway to the vault was designed for the gods to retrieve their offerings. This seems no different. *Xi Wangmu* had her own followers and deities, hence the gateway."

"That still doesn't tell us which way to go," I interrupted.

"Yes, it does. Look at all the faces on these statues. All are human in complexion and body, but each has an animalistic trait. During the Zhou Dynasty, our shamaness was referenced as a goddess. Writings described her to have teeth of a tiger. Pay close attention to the fourth statue."

Looking closely at the illuminated statue, I saw a tall slender shape of a woman. A flowing robe ran over her shoulders. Her hands looked soft and delicate. In her arms, she carried a basket of fruit. Her hair pulled up in an elegant weave. Nothing screamed *tiger.*

Then I saw her mouth. It was subtle, but two fangs extended out. "The teeth?"

"Exactly."

It was a stretch, but the Baron seemed convinced.

"Let me educate you some more. In *Xi Wangmu's* paradise, paintings described an orchard of peach trees—the fruits of life. You see the fruit basket extending out of the statues arms? It's fairly obvious. That is the correct way."

Alvin stepped up, planting a seed of doubt in the Baron's theory. He recommended we investigate each tunnel, one by one. Ruthford quickly shot him down. He was betting all his marbles on that single route.

I agreed with Alvin though. So much so, that I told the Baron to explore that path while Jenny and I looked into the others.

The Baron just smirked. "Nice try Mr. Morgan. I want you close to me."

Ruthford did somewhat listen though. He split the rest of the mercenaries and researchers into eight groups. Each was to explore a different path while the Baron, his daughter, Alvin, Jenny and I followed this lead.

One big happy family.

I threw my backpack over my shoulder and slouched along. It was no use to argue. Too many guys with guns. I figured the quicker we got through this, the faster we'd get out of here.

The tunnels were tight to say the least. Mind you I'm an average sized male, and I had some troubles getting through. The only entertainment I got was in watching Baron William Ruthford squeeze his abnormally large frame through the narrow openings.

The limestone was exceptionally smooth. It formed a winding path through the depths of the mountain. Pockets of light continued to radiate through holes in the walls. They were a clear trail of breadcrumbs through an otherwise pitch black tunnel.

We started off cautious, constantly flooding our road ahead with light on every surface before proceeding. We didn't want any surprises. The path continued on a gradual ascent, but there were no signs of an end to the tunnel. Luckily, there were no options on which way to go. We were linearly guided along.

Jenny and I hung back. "Your dad is going to kill me when he finds out about this," I said.

"If we get out of this alive, then we can keep it our little secret," Jenny responded.

Alvin fell in line with us. "Charlie, I have to say, you've surprised me."

"I find that if you set the bar low enough, you can surprise anybody," I said.

"No honestly. You did bloody well back there. I hate to admit it, but it's true. Kudos to you, *mate*."

This sudden shift in tone was strange. Maybe this guys was halfway decent. I decided to play nice. "Listen Alvin, I got lucky. You came to the rescue with the Big Dipper solution. You would have figured it all out sooner or later."

For the moment, we were at a truce.

We continued on, traversing further and further into the belly of the mountain. Periodically, calls came in from the other teams. One by one, each group phoned in their failure.

Dead ends terminated five of the tunnels.

Our path, on the other hand, opened up to another cavernous chamber. A stone bridge led across the room to another passageway. A series of stone tiger heads stamped out of the rock on either side of the bridge. Out of their open jaws, constant streams of molten lava poured out like water spigots.

The waterfalls fell to a pool of lava a hundred feet under. Taking a gander over the ledge, I watched the glowing liquid flow like a river in a large channel. Red magma stretched as far as my eyes could see. "It seems we're on the right track," I said.

The Baron thought so too. "What are we waiting for, come on." He ushered us forward.

"I'm tired," Lynea said. "Can we take a break?"

"We'll break when we're done," William said.

The imagery was lost as we crossed the bridge and disappeared once again into darkness.

Jenny's radio roared.

"We're...attack...cl...men...robes...ah..."

It was one of the groups. The voices sounded frantic. Static crackled, covering up most of the transmission.

Jenny spoke into the radio, "Repeat. We missed what you said. Is everything okay?"

Static... then the voice, "Help... We..." A thump, and then the radio when silent.

Jenny worried. "Come in. Repeat."

She paced back and forth with the radio in hand. She raised it up to get better reception. "What the heck?" she asked.

The rest of us paused. I followed Jenny with my beam of light as she sped away from us. In the darkness I could barely make out her figure.

"Hey slow down," I said trying to catch up.

She stopped and turned to me. "Charlie, something bad happened. Did you hear their voices? We need to go back."

I didn't answer. None of us did. None of us could.

Our flashlights illuminated Jenny's figure, but they also drowned her backdrop. A dark silhouette stood directly behind her. As more light found the figure, we made out the full outline of a body.

A body veiled by a black hooded robe.

CHAPTER ELEVEN

"Um, Jen?" I said.

Before Jenny could react, the mysterious figure sprung to action. Swiftly, the man wrapped his arm around her neck while pulling out a large blade in his other hand. He held the sharp tip inches from her face.

My heart leapt out of my body. I skipped a step forward, but the man jerked Jenny back, threatening to kill.

"Wait!" I exclaimed.

Everyone paralyzed. Jenny stood under the spotlight, helpless. I was only a few feet away. Any sudden movements could kill her. Should I back away? Should I hold my ground?

A black hood covered the man's entire face. My flashlight brushed past his head, revealing a glimmer of white eyes but no other features. He didn't say a word. He didn't move.

I needed to act, but somebody else acted for me.

No, not Alvin.

Not the Baron.

Not even Lynea.

In the face of death, Jenny stomped her right heel into her assailant's foot. I watched her fist follow suit, pummeling the man's crotch. (At least I hoped he was a man.) The hooded attacker's grasp loosened. With her free hand, Jenny peeled the man's arm away from her and twisted her body under his grip. She spun around in the same motion and kicked her enemy square in the chest. The man stumbled back while Jenny brought her arms up in a boxing stance.

My jaw dropped.

Then my ears erupted in pain as a gunshot rang through the confined tunnel. The hooded figure was flung off his feet and to the ground—dead.

Covering my ears, I yelled, "Are you crazy!"

The Baron stood with his revolver in hand. Smoke drifted off the barrel of the gun. Where did he pull that out of?

"You could have shot her!"

"Mr. Morgan, I am an excellent marksman. I've trained with guns since I was a boy. You had nothing to fear."

I ran to Jenny. "Are you okay?"

"Yeah. I'm fine." She still held onto her neck.

In awe, I added, "Where did you learn those moves?"

"I lived with a cop for a year. He taught me a thing or two in self-defense."

Another guy she dated?

As things settled, we turned to the dead body on the floor. Alvin was already hovering over the man. He felt for a pulse. "Bloody dead," he confirmed. He sounded quite sad about it. Peeling the hood back, we took in the man's full complexion.

He appeared to be of Chinese descent. His face was painted completely white with fangs drawn on either side of his mouth. Black outlines rounded his eyelids. He actually had a good resemblance to a tiger. Was this what the symbols on the door meant? The white tiger protecting the temple?

"How did he get in here?" Lynea spoke up.

"I don't know," I stated. "But I think we've worn out our welcome."

"No, we must press on," Ruthford commanded.

I got to my feet. "Who knows how many more of these clowns are hiding in the shadows. I think it's about time we…"

My eyes glossed past the intimidating Baron. They adjusted, making out three more silhouettes positioned a few feet behind the bullish man.

I didn't have to warn Ruthford. My sudden trail of speech was enough to alert him of trouble. With lightening reflexes, the Baron spun around and fired his weapon.

The three figures darted out of the way, disappearing into the shadows.

Gunshots bounced off the walls, creating another painfully loud echo. I mumbled, "You're going to cause a cave-in."

I spoke too soon.

If there was one thing I learned in my many adventures, it was to never make loud noises in confined ancient temples. Old architecture never bode well to vibrations. Flimsy wooden structures or crumbled concrete walls, collapsed under such pressures easily. Deep in the belly of this giant volcano, it would be even worse.

And worse it was.

The walls of the tunnel rattled. The floor shook. My flashlight followed a thin crack branch up the wall and into the ceiling. It veined its way above our heads toward the path we once came. Debris sprinkled over our heads as the compressed rock above slid out of place.

The tunnel started to cave in on itself. Heavy boulders fell away, smashing into the ground.

"Everybody move!" I yelled.

There was no turning back. Our only way was forward. Without arguing, everyone sprinted blindly down the tunnel.

Our flashlights flickered around the walls as our panicked hands struggled to illuminate the road ahead.

No one dared to stop.

The earth violently racketed as more boulders crashed behind us. The smooth stone turned a lot more slippery the further we ran. The path steepened.

It felt like ages before the commotion settled down.

We all slowed to catch our breath. Bracing myself at the knees, I looked at the blocked passageway to our rear. "There goes our way out."

"That was a sign, Mr. Morgan. A sign for us to push forward," the Baron said.

"No, that was a sign that we've just become permanent residents," I rebutted.

Lynea spoke up. "Those other men found a way in here somehow, maybe there's a way out for us."

"First, your father's got to put that gun away before he causes more damage," I demanded.

"This gun is what saved your little friend's life, Mr. Morgan. You should be thanking me right now." Ruthford holstered his weapon.

I marched up to the man, ready to give him a piece of my mind when Jenny interrupted. "Guys?"

Turning around, I saw Jenny looking off into the distance. Her body glistened in a faint reddish light. My eyes tracked her gaze. The stone path ahead was lined by lava. The lava spread out to form the largest lake of red I had ever seen. The walls of the Wanda Mountain rose endlessly, disappearing into the cavernous abyss.

Directly in front of us, our stone path terminated at a grand flight of stairs. The steps climbed up above the pool of magma in a straight twenty story ascent. A stairwell to Heaven. Or more accurately, a stairwell to Hell.

At the top, the stairs passed through a large statue of a tiger's mouth. The fangs dropped on either side of the path, creating the walls of the opening.

"I think we're here," Jenny finished.

"Time for me to show you what this is all about, Mr. Morgan." The Baron shoved past me and began his climb up the stairs. Lynea was a step behind. Within seconds, the rest of us did the same.

About halfway up, my legs started to numb. The volcanic fumes made me light-headed, and the lack of a guardrail really got me nervous. Baron William Ruthford barreled along without any signs of slowing down.

Jenny and Alvin kept up a brisk pace as well. Thankfully, the sound of spewing lava below masked my heavy breathing.

We were almost there.

I couldn't wait to see what all this fuss was about. What kind of treasure would be waiting for us at the top?

My imagination didn't have to wonder long as we finally reached the landing.

The large platform was fairly barren. An ornately decorated coffin planted itself at the center of a circular bronze floor. Nine totems stemmed religiously along the far wall, and two statues were erected on either side of the enormous tomb.

It wasn't much.

A grin stretched across the Baron's cheeks as he walked to the stone sarcophagus. His hands brushed the top of the box. "This is it." He tried shoving the top lid off the tomb. It didn't budge. "Don't just stand there, help me with this."

With everyone pushing, the lid reluctantly slid off the stone coffin.

We all gazed into the bowels of the casket. The skeletal remains of the shamaness, *Xi Wangmu*, lay peacefully within the box. Her arms crossed over her chest, cradling a cloth wrapped object.

Really? There was so much build up to this moment. The promise of something amazing. The thought of an abundance of treasure. The hope of some sort of epiphany.

No.

All we got was the decayed skeleton of a female shaman. They really dropped the ball on the pay off.

I opened my mouth readying some sort of witty remark, but nothing came to mind.

Luckily, Jenny thought of one for me. "At least we know what we'll look like after a few years trapped down here."

The Baron reached into the coffin. He pushed the bones aside as if they were inconsequential. He grabbed the cloth covered object. "This, Mr. Morgan, is what we are after." He carefully unraveled it.

"And that is?"

"A piece to a bigger puzzle. This is the key."

"The key to what?"

"The key to the future." The Baron continued pulling away layer after layer of the fabric. "Our dear *Xi Wangmu* was just a stepping stone. A means to an end. The end is something much more luxurious."

The last piece of the wrapping fell away, revealing the object the Baron so desperately sought.

It was a half-moon stone tablet inscribed from top to bottom with text. Getting a better angle on it, I made out line after line of writing. The characters instantly became apparent. They weren't Chinese. They were written in a different language—a language I easily recognized.

Ancient Greek.

Was this what J.J. was talking about? The connection between Chinese and Greek culture? Could this be part of Homer's poem? But how? How did this shamaness tie to the Greek legend? Questions whirled through my head. For once I wish I knew how to read Ancient Greek. Jeremy would be in Heaven right now, no pun intended.

I noticed something else. The text seemed to cut off at the edge of the tablet. "Baron, it looks like you only got part of your key. Half of that tablet is missing," I commented.

The Baron realized it as well. "This can't be." He handed the artifact to his daughter and reached back into the tomb.

I had to give it to those Chinese, they really loved that Tatisu symbol—the idea of two halves making a whole. They purposely split whatever this key was in two.

The Baron turned frantic. He climbed into the open sarcophagus. Hollering, he threw the bones around in search of the other half of the tablet. "This can't be. The other one wasn't like this."

The other one? What was he talking about? I didn't have time to ask. As the Baron had his childish tantrum, the ground began to quake.

The walls of the dormant volcano pulsated. A blood curdling groan bellowed from its depths. The stone shook violently.

I struggled to maintain balance.

The volcano wasn't happy. Looking over to the Baron, I could see why. He was defiling the precious remains of the goddess of the mountain. The more remains William flung out of the casket, the more the earth rumbled.

"Uh, I think you're pissing somebody off," I said.

A large rock crashed nearby.

"Yeah, you definitely did."

The Baron halted. He jumped out of the coffin. "I can't believe this." He looked defeated.

"Dad, what do we do?" Lynea trembled.

A boulder came barreling down on us. I grabbed the Baron and pulled him out of the way just as the rock smashed onto the casket. The sarcophagus crumbled under the weight.

"Charlie, which way?" Jenny panicked.

I searched. The platform extended off in two directions.

Alvin spoke out of nowhere. "That way," he said, pointing randomly. With the ground vibrating more and more, he rushed off.

It was better than nothing.

The Baron stormed away from the tomb, following the Australian. Jenny did the same.

The platform became unsteady.

I heard a scream.

Lynea stumbled to the ground behind me. I ran to her. Getting her to her feet, I turned back to the others. They were far ahead.

I tried to lift the poor girl up. She couldn't budge. Her foot was stuck.

"Mr. Morgan?" she pleaded.

"Don't worry." I pulled at her ankle. Just as I dislodged her foot, more boulders tumbled down the interior of the cavern.

The earthquake multiplied in magnitude. A crack exploded up above. My eyes followed the sound's origin only to see an enormous boulder scream out of the darkness. It was on a crash course with the path between us and Jenny.

We weren't going to make it.

The boulder crashed into the ground in front of us.

Our way was blocked, and Lynea and I were stranded.

CHAPTER TWELVE

My world fell apart.

Monstrous rocks collapsed, smashing into the ground. The earth shook violently. Thick layers of ash and fumes blanketed the innards of the cavern. I heard the blood curdling bubbles of magma rise from the depths below. Chaos filled the air at an alarming rate...

...And I was separated from the one person I was there to save—Jenny Jenkins.

Instantly, my pulse quickened. I was stranded at the shaman pedestal with Lynea. The once dormant volcano was now alive and extremely angry. A deafening hiss boomed from the base of the mountain. It was building up pressure to blow.

My flashlight searched, but the dense fog of ash blocked my vision. I felt a trembling body. Lynea was at my side, holding on from behind. Terror filled her eyes.

"Don't worry," I assured.

We braced ourselves for the worst. Then suddenly, everything simmered. The ground eased up. The hissing softened. Only the blinding fog remained.

Jenny shouted through the radio, "Charlie, are you there?"

"More or less," I blurted back.

"Good to hear."

"It looks like we woke up Ruthford's dormant volcano," I commented.

"Hopefully it was just a bad nightmare. I don't want to be here when it rolls out of bed. You see a way around this thing?"

I felt around the boulder that separated us. It was jammed in place. "I got nothing. How's everyone else? All of their limbs still intact?"

"Yeah, we're—"

Jenny's voice was cut off by another. It was the Baron's. "Morgan! Is my daughter safe?"

Was that genuine compassion?

"She's fine. Don't you worry." I tripped over something. Shining my flashlight down, I saw the outline of the half-moon stone disk resting on the floor. I picked it up. "Looks like I also found the infamous shaman artifact you so desperately wanted."

"Thank God!" The jury was out on if William was more thankful that his daughter was all right or that I found his precious relic. I slipped the object into my backpack. This could be a good bargaining chip when we got out of this.

If we got out.

Jenny's voice came back. She said that they saw daylight coming from a hole nearby. She was going to head that way with Alvin and Ruthford to find a way out. I assured her that there had to be a way for us to get out as well. We figured we'd backtrack the way we came. Time was of the essence.

Lynea was rattled, but she silently obeyed my every move. The hibernating mountain calmly swayed around us. The ash slowly rose upward, giving us a little breathing room to navigate the dark interior.

We followed the narrow stairwell back down the way we came. Maybe the quakes opened up a new path? After a few dozen steps, we came to an abrupt halt. The earthquake crumbled a large portion of the stair. A massive chasm remained.

There went option A.

We returned to *Xi Wangmu's* tomb to find another route. A small path led toward the outside wall of the mountain. It looked to follow the perimeter into the distance. The route was narrow, but it was better than nothing. Our bodies hugged the rock as we slowly walked along the stone.

I glanced down. A steep drop loomed below. Hot red magma flowed like a river current throughout the dyke of the volcano. A grouping of arterial veins of lava met at one end on their way toward the center conduit of the beast. That central core was building up pressure. Unfortunately, there was no turning this thing off. Our only hope was to be long gone before it erupted.

Lynea trailed my gaze. I heard her yelp in fear. I felt it just as much. Her hand nearly cut off circulation to my arm.

"Don't look down," I soothed.

"That's a little easier said than done." My face must not have been hiding my own fear as Lynea added, "And, you should take your own advice."

I smiled. Maybe this girl was a little tougher than she looked.

We pressed on.

We finally reached the end of our little path. It died to nothing but an open crevice. We were stranded once again.

Across the crevice was another rocky path. It was as much of a fall as it was distant, but with the clouds of fog dissipating, I made out a distinct pathway.

I went first.

I propped myself on whatever little ground I had available and propelled forward. I landed on the balls of my feet, feeling the pain surge up my shins and into my torso. I rolled on the ground to break the shock. Dusting myself off, I turned back to Lynea. "Come on!" I yelled.

She was reluctant. It was a far jump.

"Don't worry, I'll catch you," I guaranteed.

"I don't know," she said.

"Trust me, I've done this a gazillion times." That was the truth. "I'll count to three. Ready? One…"

Before I could say *two*, Lynea leapt. She flew through the air and landed square on her feet. Her body arched up as she stood, fully erect.

"Impressive," I added.

She risked a faint grin.

Suddenly, the ground shook. Another earthquake. Lynea lost her footing, and her brief triumph of courage faded to panic. She reached out for help, and I lunged forward to grab her. Our finger tips just missed.

Lynea slipped over the ledge and fell backward to the lava abyss.

I dove to the ground, scrambling for the ledge. As Lynea tipped over, head first, I locked my hands around her ankles. The rumbling of the earth tried its best to shake me off, but I sprawled my body flat on the floor. Lynea's tiny hundred pound frame strained at my wrists.

Still, I held on.

The quakes accelerated. Lynea's screams heightened. She hung upside down, pleading for help.

"I got you," I grunted. The stress in my voice was probably not comforting. A rock smashed inches from my head. We needed to move. Sweat trickled down my forehead as I pulled Lynea back up to the surface.

"Oh my God, thank you!" she said hugging me. The minute was short lived when the platform we stood on cracked. Its foundation started to crumble. We dove to the side just as the floor broke free and fell into the lava pit.

Quickly getting to our feet, the ground once again began to break away.

"Run!" I yelled.

We sprinted along the pathway, blind to our final destination. We didn't care. We couldn't care. Following hot on our heels, the ground collapsed, fading away into the melting liquid below. It was like a game of dominos. Once one fell, the cascading drop of the others systematically followed suit.

I didn't dare look back. I clenched Lynea's hand as I led us down a random path. My head was dizzy. All of the methane fumes were taking effect. Would I soon hallucinate like the old shamans?

I needed to maintain focus.

The heat from the rising lava started to suffocate the cave. Time was running out.

The radio suddenly came alive with Jenny's voice, "Charlie, we made it. How about you two?"

I grabbed the radio in stride, saying, "Still working on it!"

"Things are crazy out here. You better hurry."

Thanks for painting the obvious.

Directly ahead, I saw a raised platform. I hurled my body toward it, going into a full blown sprint. The sound of lava hissing upward, compounded with the crashing of stone on stone, propelled me onward.

Surprisingly, Lynea kept up. The ground behind us continued to fall away, closing the gap on our heels by the second.

We reached the platform, and I lifted Lynea onto it. The ground disintegrated just as I finished hauling her over the ledge.

And, I dropped.

I braced myself on a hand hold just as I lost my footing. The drop nearly jolted my shoulder out of its socket. This mountain was not making this easy. I searched for another hold. Nothing. The rock I tightly held onto began cracking free of the wall. I felt it dislodge an inch. Then another.

Frantic, my free arm felt around for some life-saving grip.

It dislodged some more.

A hand wrapped my wrists.

Above me, I saw Lynea. My vision blurred by all the vibrations, but I knew it was her. Miraculously, my guardian angel pulled me up onto the ledge.

"Wow, remind me never to arm wrestle you," I said in hopes of a laugh. Where did that superhuman power come from?

Winded, she just smiled. Her body trembled. I commended the young girl for mustering up the courage. I could only imagine how afraid she must have been.

We perched ourselves on the small platform. It cantilevered from the wall of the mountain. Around us, any viable route crumbled away. All that remained was a pool of lava, and it was catching up fast.

The earthquakes continued. Black smoke covered the sauna filled room. I searched for some way out, another path, an exit, anything. I found nothing.

Lynea was the first to see it.

A faint glimmer of daylight filtered through the heavy fog twenty feet above. The wall was littered with holes and protrusions.

This could work.

"You up for a little climb?"

Lynea shook her head. "Can I have a minute?"

"Yeah no problem. I have nowhere to be," I said. Then I looked back and saw that the molten lava was only a few feet below us. A bubble of liquid burst, and burning magma splattered onto the platform. The rock sizzled. "On second thought, maybe we should move now."

Up we went.

Lynea went first. The air was difficult to breath. I started to feel more light-headed the higher we climbed. My only driving force was to reach that daylight. Within minutes we got to our destination.

A small light filtered into the volcano. Getting close, I saw that the rock was thin there. Parts had already cracked away. The hole was roughly a foot in diameter.

Big, but not big enough.

I used my flashlight as a hammer and whacked away. Little by little, I chipped apart the rock. The opening grew.

As if retaliating, the mountain shook more violently. Both of us held on tight. I thrust again.

Lava fast approached.

I swung once more. The bulb shattered within the flashlight. Its plastic frame deformed under the pressure.

But the hole got bigger.

Another bubble burst and I felt my ankle singe in pain. My jeans caught fire. I shook my leg, and clanked it against the rock to put out the flame. My ankle throbbed.

"Charlie faster!" Lynea screamed.

I banged the rock one last time, and a large segment of the wall broke free. Fresh air rushed into our confined tomb. "Go!"

We broke out into the open. The blistering sun was now covered in a large cloud of ash. Below, I saw that we were still pretty high up from the base of the mountain. A steep decline led down the mountain face. At the bottom, the tall grass lined the camp grounds. From our angle, the mountain blocked our view of the rest of the camp.

Up above, Wanda Mountain was smoking out of its ridge. Hail of rocks rained all around. Ash particles flew with the wind, getting denser as the current circled over us. Then I saw a more immediate threat.

Lava fissured out of the walls of the mountain. It poured down the rock like melted hot fudge on ice cream. Everything in its path disintegrated away. Cracks in the surface oozed the liquid out of every orifice. And that liquid flowed directly toward us.

"Charlie?" Lynea said, staring at our latest terror.

"I know," was all I could mumble.

We turned and bolted down the mountain. The seismic activity made it tough to maintain balance, as did the forty degree decline. Somehow we stayed on our feet.

Dodging downed tree trunks and rocks, we raced down the mountain. Pressure built up under the surface, launching segments of earth into the air. Geysers of lava spewed out of holes in the rock. We cut left as a rain of spraying magma fell nearby.

A tree snapped in half, narrowly flattening Lynea. Her pace quickened to keep up.

We continued on. Behind us, the lava crept down the mountain as if having a mind of its own. We remained silent, focused on staying alive.

Almost there.

The rumbling earth cracked along a fault line. Rock heaved upward causing me to lose balance. Still holding Lynea's hand, I pulled her down with me.

We tumbled.

The path got steeper. I struggled to regain balance, but my body kept on rolling.

Each flip racked my bones. My head throbbed as it slammed the ground. Lynea's screams were masked by the blows to my ribs and back. I toppled the rest of the way down the mountain.

In the dizzying whirlwind that flashed over my eyes, I saw us rolling to an abrupt end of the mountain. The rock simply dropped away.

I tried to slow down, but our momentum kept barreling us forward. My hands reached for a safety net. There was nothing to grab onto.

It was too late. I launched over the edge, followed by Lynea.

The ground was only ten feet under us. As my body landed on the thick bed of grass, I sprawled out, exhausted.

"Ah!" I heard as Lynea twisted her ankle on her fall.

My moment to catch my breath was short-lived. I jumped back to action. Lynea held her leg in pain.

"I think I sprained it."

"We can't stop. You have to be strong." I looked around. The base of the mountain was behind us, but it was nearly impossible to see what was ahead. The tall grass rose over our heads, and it was so thickly planted I couldn't see two feet in front of me. It was like being stuck in the middle of a dense corn maze. At least those had pre-defined paths. Lava crept down the wall to our backs. Whichever way we went, I knew exactly what I wanted to get away from.

Lynea winced in pain, but she fought through it. Hand in hand, we limped our way along. I pushed past the blades of grass. My mind raced. The crackling sounds of the volcano rang. Meteor rocks large and small continued to fall out of the sky. Chaos enveloped me, and I had no compass to guide us.

I could have used my lucky rabbit's foot in that moment.

It started to rain. The heavy drops of water pelted our bodies.

Great, what else could go wrong?

Then, I heard a thundering.

Did I have to ask?

The thundering turned into a consistent thumping. I tried to make sense of it, but I kept getting whacked in the face by the grass. I resented opening that gate now. We made it some distance into the grass field while the thumping grew in volume.

My radio sounded.

"Charlie, Charlie! I see you!" It was difficult to hear, but I recognized Jenny's voice.

"What?" I barked back into the speaker.

"Look up."

Above us, a helicopter hovered. The spinning blades cut through the wind. The roaring engine chugged constantly.

I found the origin of that thumping.

The side door of the helicopter propped open, and Jenny's body appeared. She waved down. "You see me?"

"You're about all I see."

"The grass is too thick. We can't touch down. You're going to have to get over to the open field. Charlie, we don't have much time."

"You're telling me. We're kind of blind down here."

"It's okay. I'll guide you to..." Jenny stopped talking. She looked beyond us, at the field of grass. I waited.

"You know, typically when someone says they'll guide you, they provide some direction."

Jenny came back on. "Um... Charlie, you need to move."

"Obviously."

"Something's coming your way. Actually a lot of somethings. Like eight of them. I can't tell what they are, but they're cutting through the grass pretty fast from all directions. And from the way the grass is collapsing around them, they're big. They're closing in on you."

I jerked Lynea forward. "You're our eyes Jen. Which way?"

"Charlie, run. Forward!"

Lynea couldn't move. Either from the pain, or paralyzed in fright, she stood still. I tossed her over my shoulder. My body was exhausted, but I was not about to leave this poor girl behind.

I ran.

Jenny's voice led me along while I cut through the tall grass. The stiff blades stung as they continuously smacked my body.

My heart pounded. I concentrated on Jenny's voice. Up in the helicopter, she had a clear view on our direction, and on whatever was chasing us. She told me to veer right. I did. Then left, and I blindly followed.

The fear in her voice must have meant that our pursuers were catching up. The growls and heavy breathing coming from the grass reassured that notion. What seemed like hundreds of footsteps stampeded the ground behind us.

The smell of wet fur slowly crept up on my nostrils.

These were definitely creatures.

"Go straight! You're almost there!" Jenny yelled. The helicopter disappeared off in front of us.

Lynea remained silent.

My thighs burned as I bolted through the thick grass.

Suddenly, the grass disappeared. I broke free into the open plain of the campsite. Fires burned. Cars were toppled. Other researchers scrambled to get the last remains of their discoveries and escape. Directly ahead of us, Jenny's helicopter touched ground. She motioned us over. She didn't have to ask twice.

I darted.

Lynea screamed. Straddled over my shoulder she was watching our backs. And she was the first to see what our pursuers were. I glanced back and saw them.

Out of the grass emerged eight new guests. They stood on all fours. Their bodies lean in muscle and covered in fur. Their narrow ears perched up alert. Salivating fangs glistened in their open mouths, and their blood colored eyes locked onto us.

Siberian White Tigers.

Having signs of tigers on walls, I understood. Men painted as these animals, that was a little over the top. Actual Siberian

Tigers? I mean, come on! It was just my luck that, of all the times, this time the ancient Chinese took the symbols literally.

I asked what else could go wrong, and my answer was delivered in spades.

The tigers growled.

It didn't stop me though. Within a few strides, I reached the helicopter. Jenny and Mitchell were propped on the seats, waiting with open arms. I hurled Lynea into the compartment.

Large debris rocketed down on the dirt around the helicopter. Segments of rock clanked off the rudder of the flying machine. Alert signals boomed, and the pilot pulled back on the controls. The helicopter lurched off the ground, trying to dodge the falling asteroids.

I nearly lost my stability as I grabbed onto the handle of the sliding door. My legs propped on the side supports. Jenny held onto to me by the shirt. My body hung from the side of the helicopter as it began to rise off the terrain.

Then I felt a tug.

It was more like whiplash. A Siberian Tiger leapt out of the sky clenching its jaws on my backpack. With the nylon straps securely wrapped over my shoulders, I was jerked back.

I pulled away, tearing free from the side of the copter. The twirling rudders got further away, while I fell to the earth.

I crashed to the ground along with the tiger. My bag still scrunched between the beast's mouth.

The tiger jogged its head back and forth flopping my body around. Then it threw me to the grass.

I heard Jenny's voice arguing with the pilot on the radio. The pilot wouldn't come back down to get me. It was too dangerous.

I lay slumped on the floor, free of the tiger's hold. The helicopter's engines got quieter as it rose.

Getting to my feet, I dusted the ash off my body. My vision extended away from the floor to come face to face with the tiger that ripped me from my freedom. The creature stood only a few feet away.

The other creatures circled me. I was stuck in the center of the arena with no way out.

In unison, the tigers pounced.

CHAPTER THIRTEEN

Like any normal man would do in a situation like this, I closed my eyes, covered my face, and braced for the inevitable.

The inevitable never came.

Instead, a loud boom sounded. I opened my eyes to see the leading tiger collapse to the ground, only a few feet away. A large needle with a red tassel stuck out of its neck. I recognized the object.

It was a tranquilizer dart.

The dart lodged into the animal's neck, instantly putting the beast to sleep. It lay limp on the grass. The other tigers stopped in their tracks. Their attention veered to someone above me.

Baron William Ruthford hung out of a second helicopter, a sniper rifle in hand. Another shot rang out, and another tiger fell to sleep. The animals retreated. Confusion spread across their faces.

"Now would be your cue to run," the Baron's calm voice came through my radio.

Things never ceased to surprise me.

Ruthford was right, but where did I run to?

Past all the chaos, I made out the Tallow trees.

The wooden village!

I dashed toward the forest. More tigers emerged out of the grass fields, and the Baron picked them off one by one. The man wasn't kidding when he said he was a heck of a shot.

The gunfire stopped. In the midst of my scramble, I heard Ruthford's voice on the radio. "I'm sorry Mr. Morgan, but I'm out of ammunition."

Halfway there.

It took the tigers a minute to regroup. In a snap, they switched from cautious to full blown predator mode. Their angry growls now sounded like screams as they roared after me.

Out of breath, I reached the forest. With the tigers on my tail I jumped at the first tree. My arms and legs wrapped around the massive trunk of bark. I had only seen this done in movies, but I clung my body to the bark. I wiggled my way up the tree.

Little by little, I got higher up the Tallow. A tiger with an impressive vertical leap nearly caught my pant leg. I felt the hot breath of the beast flare near my butt. This motivated me even more.

I kept climbing.

Years ago, I earned the nickname *Curious George*. Obviously, it wasn't for my name, nor was it because I was curious. It was because the unoriginal man who made it up likened me to a monkey climbing walls.

At the time, I thought the name was childish, but right now, it felt earned. My climbing skills were keeping me from being an animal's dinner.

Claws scratched at the base of the tree while I scoured upward. A few more feet above started the base of a wooden platform. I reached up and climbed on board.

The fog made it close to impossible to see much this high up in the tree. I faintly discerned the silhouettes of dozens of huts suspended from tree branches. Rope bridges tied the huts together.

This ancient civilization built within the treescape was going to be my escape.

"Charlie, Charlie! Are you alive?" It was Jenny.

"Yeah, just taking the scenic route," I said into the radio. My heavy panting lessened the impact of my sarcasm.

"Thank God. Where are you exactly?"

"In that old village built up in the trees. Now I know why they built so high up—to survive these dang tigers." I peered down at the ever growing posse waiting for me.

"Charlie, the debris is making it tough for the pilot to get close to you. Can you make it to the cliff at the other end of the forest?"

I could barely see anything. "The cliff that drops down to the river? Yeah sure. I think I can manage."

"Okay, we'll wait for you there. With the weather getting this bad, you're going to need to move fast."

"Going as fast as I can Jen." I sat on the platform, leaning against the tree.

"We are not leaving you," she added.

"I hope not."

I pocketed the radio. The volcano was now covered with molten lava. At the top of the mountain, tremendous amounts of smoke exhausted.

The fog lightened up a bit as the wind pushed it along.

The wooden village looked surprisingly sturdy. Each hut was roughly the same size, mounted at different elevations. Bamboo formed the roofs of each building. The openings to each structure filled with darkness—a deep black that kind of creeped me out.

One of the black holes of a neighboring hut looked different. I made out two small white circles hovering in the sea of darkness. The circles blinked. My eyes adjusted, and I saw the outline of a body standing in the doorway to the hut.

The figure stepped out of the structure. Dressed in a black hooded robe, all I saw were his white eyes under the hood. Give me a break. Another one of these guys?

He looked just like the man that tried killing Jenny, except for the fact that *this* man was armed with a bow and arrow. That bow was armed and pointed directly at me.

I rolled. An arrow zipped past my head, digging into the bark of the tree.

Crap!

I sprang to my feet and sprinted across one of the rope bridges to the next hut. The ropes squealed under the strain of my weight. I just prayed that they stuck together. Arrows continued to zoom past as my attacker pulled more out of his quiver.

One skimmed my sleeve, grazing my skin. (That lit a fire in my step.) I reached the other end of the bridge and dove into a building for cover.

The darkness consumed me. I sprawled on the floor.

An arrow sunk into the wall of the hut, partially penetrating the wood. The deadly sharp tip protruded out the plank, inches from my head.

When would this stop? From volcanoes to tigers to crazy men with bows, it was not my day. I popped my head above the window sill, and my attacker fired another arrow.

It missed, narrowly.

I needed to do something. Staying here would be my funeral. Either the volcano was going to kill me, or this guy.

That's when I heard breathing. I didn't once stop to think if this hooded attacker was not alone.

Slowly, I turned around to the sight of another hooded man towering over me. A large blade glistened in his hands.

The blade thrashed down.

I rolled out of the way as the man dug the sharp sword into the floorboard. Instinctively, I kicked, taking out the man's left shin.

He dropped to his knee, while I threw a wide punch. I nailed the man square in the jaw, but there wasn't much power to it.

We both got to our feet and circled one another.

The hooded assassin lunged with his blade. I dodged.

With the man off balance, I swung at him, but all I caught was air. He quickly spun out of the way.

The chess match continued, yet I felt like this guy was just playing with me. His moves were too fast.

More arrows shot through the window, missing their mark.

Couldn't I have the luxury of fighting one battle at a time?

Our dance went on. Finally, the assassin stormed me, sword held high.

When I was young, I used to duck and curl into a ball when I was afraid. Through, years of experience, I molded that into a legitimate move of self-defense. Holding onto the notion, I did exactly that.

As the man rushed at me, I dove to the ground and cuddled my knees up to my chest. My attacker was caught off guard, tripping over my body. He stumbled to the ground, dropping his sword.

This was my chance.

I bounced onto the man, ready to attack. Before I could get my hands around him, he slithered out of the way and spun on top of me. His knees pinched my chest down to the ground.

Rough, burly hands tightened around my esophagus. As the grip strengthened, I gasped for air.

My head dazed.

Life slowly sucked out of me. I had one last chance.

I thought of Jenny. I took a page out of her book and thrust my knee into my hooded attacker's groin. He yelped.

Fast, I whipped him over my body and into the wall. I grabbed the sword and turned to thrust the blade, only to find the man limp on the floor. I gave a little shove, but the body didn't move. The man's head rest snug against the wooden wall.

Leaning in, I pulled back the hood. The arrow that nearly took my head off earlier by piercing through the wood plank was now jammed into my attacker's skull. Luck was still on my side.

One down.

I peered out the window. Where one robed *Robin Hood* once stood, four joined him. All of them bore bows and arrows, and I was their number one target.

They fired.

I dropped back to the floor for cover. Searching the dead body in front of me, I found that he too carried a quiver of arrows on his back. I crawled around the room until I found the man's bow. Returning to the window, I armed it.

It had been years since I fired one of these, but it was like riding a bike, right? I readied the bow, tensioned back the chord, took a deep breath, and popped up.

Aiming at the closest figure, I let go. The arrow jet across the sky, missing wildly. A tight grouping of arrows answered my attack, zipping by. I ducked back down.

Apparently it wasn't like riding a bike at all.

I tried again. There were only a few arrows left in the quiver. I took one, aimed, and risked another shot. This time, my arrow was much closer to its target.

The third time was the charm.

I fired.

As the arrow flung across the way, it dug into the shoulder of one of the men. The impact launched him over the edge and to the earth way down below.

The White Siberian Tigers instantly feasted.

My other attackers stepped back for shelter. This was my opportunity.

I bolted out of the shack, and onto another bridge. Scrambling, I focused on each of the floor planks. I couldn't afford a missed step. Within seconds I was across the way to the next building.

I zigzagged between the hovering structures. The blood thirsty tigers followed down below. Hooded attackers silently trailed in pursuit.

An arrow struck me from behind. I stumbled and smashed through a door to one of the buildings. I rolled over in pain. The agony fleetingly dissipated. Feeling my back, I found that the arrow sunk into my nylon bag. Something blocked it from fully penetrating the pack.

The arrow wedged into the stone artifact I carried.

Thank God.

I yanked the arrow out, and I shouldered the pack.

Exiting the hut, I saw that my assailants had grown in numbers. Now over a dozen of them were rushing my way. With the arrow still in hand, I struck the tip against one of the rope supports to the bridge I just crossed. If I could cut the line free, I could hold off these clowns.

The first strap ripped. Two of the pursuers boarded the bridge, coming right for me. I sawed away at the next rope. The men neared. Their swords whirled above their heads.

My arrow cut through the last strand.

The bridge fell away, the two men with it.

A smile dared creep up my face.

I looked onward. I was almost there.

A hundred feet away, the forest ended. The earth ended. Everything ended. A rocky cliff dropped straight down to the Mudan River. Framed by the Tallow trees, I saw my escape.

Hovering at the edge of the cliff was Jenny's helicopter. A rope ladder dangled from the open door—the carrot at the end of my trail. It was only a few feet away from the cliff. All I needed to do was make it to that ladder.

I darted across the connecting link, then another. I was on the home stretch. My pursuers were well behind now. The tigers had zero shot of reaching me. I was golden.

I spoke too soon.

As I sprinted across a bridge, something caught my eye. Shooting a glance over, three of the hooded attackers swung through the trees from ropes. They glided, swiftly landing on the platform at the end of my path.

Seriously?

Two more swung to the platform behind me.

I stopped in my tracks. Stranded in the middle of the link between two huts, I had no idea where to go. Unfortunately, my assailants to my rear made the decision for me.

They pulled out their blades and sliced the rope holding my bridge up. The floor disappeared, and I fell.

I clung to the loose floor boards of the falling bridge as I pendulum swung toward its anchored tree. I slammed right into the bark of the large Tallow. Somehow, I managed to hold on.

Dangling ten feet above the grassy earth, I clung to the remains of a once sturdy bridge. The tigers barreled toward me. Thankfully, they couldn't reach me. I was too high up.

That changed with a snap.

A snap of the rope.

The other two attackers up above cut the cord on the fixed end.

I dropped once again.

I landed on the grass with a thump. I could hear Jenny pleading through the radio for me to run. I heard the galloping thunder of the tigers rushing at me. I even felt the wind sizzle as an arrow shot past.

These guys were not giving me a break.

I saw the helicopter. Adrenaline surged. Amongst all the pain, I kicked my legs one after the other.

I ran as fast as I could, B-lining it straight for the floating ladder.

The cliff edge closed in fast. I was nearly there. I was going to make it.

Another step.

Push!

I reached the ledge and leapt.

I felt like a bird soaring through the sky. I grabbed hold of one of the rungs of the ladder, and my hands clamped shut. There was no way I was going to let go.

The helicopter pulled up, away from the forest. I finally let my body loosen.

Wanda Mountain was barely visible amongst all the black smoke. Fires loomed off in the distance. The Mudan River streamed by below. I marveled at the sight. The tigers and hooded figures looked like ants as we rose away from the cliff.

I climbed the ladder to the top. As I reached the opening, I was welcomed by Alvin Mitchell. "You're like the Energizer Bunny, *mate*. That was bloody amazing."

Still pulling myself into the open compartment, I said, "You can't get rid of me that easily."

"You have the artifact?" he asked.

I removed the backpack, handing it over to him. "There it is. I hope this was all worth it."

My eyes shifted past Alvin to Jenny. She was seated next to Lynea. I gave her a wink. She blushed back.

I tried to step further into the helicopter, but Mitchell's body blocked me. He moved in close and whispered, "I'm truly sorry *mate*, but the Baron says your services are no longer required."

Everything happened at once.

Alvin shoved me back. I flung out of the helicopter.

I heard Jenny scream.

Lynea's voice followed.

I felt the wind flap at my skin.

I fell.

I reached out for some sort of safety net. The rope ladder was just out of my grasp. My arms flailed like a bird trying to fly me back to the copter. It was useless. My body continued to drop fast out of the sky.

Arching, I looked down at the river screaming toward me. My descent sped up. The Mudan River was coming up fast.

I was about to die.

It all happened so fast.

The water slapped me like a wall as I crashed into the river. Every bone in my body felt like it shattered to pieces. I got sucked under.

Somehow I managed to remain conscious. Through all the pain, I was still alive. The frigid current pulled me deeper into the depths of the water. It flipped me over and over, disorienting me.

I fought my way back to the surface. Exploding out of the river, I inhaled deeply before being yanked back underneath.

The current whipped me around. My muscles strained as I kicked and swam. I felt my body pulled further down the river.

I reached the surface once again, gasping for air. I kept myself afloat under the chaotic waves crashing all over.

The river carried me along. Its current was picking up speed. My mind raced, but I fell upon one thought. Alvin Mitchell screwed me over—Jenny's good friend. More importantly, Baron William Ruthford won.

But I survived.

That's when I saw it. Directly ahead the river came to an abrupt end. It dropped away to nothing. I was fast approaching the Diaoshuilou Waterfall, a one hundred foot drop into the Jingpo Lake.

Oh crap.

Before I could act, the river launched me over the edge. Water pelted me like a fire hose as I washed away down the falls. Everything slowed to crawl. For a second, I felt like I was floating in zero gravity. The sounds of the world drained away to silence. My beating heart pounded through my body.

Then reality sped back up.

And I dropped fast.

I crashed into the lake below. The rapids vacuumed me under the turquoise surface.

They say that life flashes before one's eyes before they die. Whoever said that lied. For me, everything just faded to black.

PART II

The Day I Got My Revenge

CHAPTER FOURTEEN

I may have used the term *died* a little loosely. For all intents and purposes, everyone thought I was dead. I sure thought so. My body even told me so. Once I passed out under the current, darkness engulfed me. It seemed like the blackness lasted forever. Like I was in a dark void of nothingness.

But then, I opened my eyes.

My vision was blurred. Everything felt hazy. The images around me warped in and out like I was in some sort of carnival house of mirrors.

What's weird was that, even though everything spun around, the room felt familiar. Bookshelves lined the walls from floor to ceiling. Thick curtains covered large windows. Hints of daylight filtered through creases in the fabric.

The room wasn't large, but I quickly made sense of all the picture frames and leather chairs spread about. Oh I knew this room all right. Its familiarity made me believe that I truly was dead. I had to be...

…Because I found myself in my parent's house—a house I hadn't been to since I was twelve years old.

How could this be?

Confused, I looked down to find that my body was scrawny. It was like I inhabited the body of my twelve year old self. My little hands clenched onto a large hardcover book.

Without reading the cover, I knew exactly what book it was. It was the same book I always grabbed in my father's study. It was the biography of Ferdinand Magellan, the man who circumnavigated the globe. At the ripe age of twelve, *that* man was my hero—a true adventurer. It was the first thing my father gave me to read, and it was always my go-to book when I was in his library.

As I tried to make sense of it all, my only logical answer was that this really was Heaven.

I mean I was back in a time when I was a happy kid. I had my favorite book, and I sat nestled up on a couch without a care in the world.

My mind somehow grasped this weird reality with ease. I felt my body relax into the chair. The serenity of it all was soothing. I clenched the book tight to my chest and leaned deeper into my seat.

The smell of leather books and dusty pages filled my nostrils. I couldn't help but smile. I was home.

Silence filled the room. But it was a comforting silence. The sun's rays radiated through the thick curtains, warming up the space. All the chaos that had just unfolded felt like a distant memory.

Oddly, it felt like it truly was ages ago. The tigers; the hooded assassins; the volcano; even Jeremy and Jenny felt like long lost images in my mind.

Was this death?

Whatever it was, it was peaceful. Cuddled up on the couch, all I wanted to do was sleep. Even though my eyelids had just parted, they wanted to shut again—to fade away within the comfort of this dream world.

My body started to lose itself in the moment. My eyelids drifted to a close. I was in a happy place.

But, suddenly I sat back up, alert. Something felt *off*. Energy flowed back through me. My inquisitive nature needed to know what was going on. I wasn't content with the idea that I was in Heaven. So I hopped off the couch. My bare feet hustled over the wood floor as I marched toward the closed doors of the library.

Turning the handle, I opened the door and entered the foyer. The layout was exactly as I remembered it. A large stairwell spiraled up the center. Framed openings led to the rest of the rooms of our old home.

Yet the complete silence continued. The quietness flipped from soothing to creepy. Was I alone?

A thought came to me. If this was my very own Heaven, then my parents should be around somewhere. Instantly, I went searching the house. I went from one room to the next, but no one was there.

I searched the basement.

Nothing.

The garage.

Nothing.

The kitchen.

Same result.

Finally, I plopped on a couch wondering where they were. Maybe I wasn't in Heaven. Maybe this was all a tease. Maybe this was Hell.

I wondered about my sanity. How did my mind grasp this weird reality so easily? Was I going to be stuck in this limbo alone?

As my heart settled, my entire body calmed down once again. My fears disappeared. My eyelids weighed heavily. All the questions juggling around in my head slipped away.

Sleep enveloped me.

The comfort of the couch sucked me in.

And my eyes closed.

Darkness returned.

I awoke with a startle.

A cloudless blue sky spanned across my vision. A soft wind brushed over my face, and the distant rustling of trees was the only noise I heard.

Was my parent's house all a dream? Was this still a dream? I was completely confused.

My eyes struggled to focus. Footsteps pattered around me. The floor felt hard as a rock. The muscles in my body strained in pain. I tried to move.

My body wouldn't...

...Or it couldn't.

My once familiar surrounding instantly disappeared to something totally foreign.

Turning my head, I rapidly searched the area. Where the heck was I? When the heck was I? Most importantly, why couldn't I move?

Disoriented, my mind raced. It struggled to catch up. Dizziness fogged up my head. I needed to focus on calming myself down.

Take a few breaths!

I slowed my pulse. The bombardment of images started to ground into reality.

Now, I didn't know what to expect. I had my share of close calls over the years, but never had I been knocked out like this.

A number of guys approached. As they neared, I made out some details. First, they were all bald. Second, they all wore similar red robes. Their bare feet rattled along a dirt path.

More objects came to attention.

Large Chinese Pagodas spread across a bed of rock. Their tiered wooden structures and gabled roofs looked like layered wedding cakes. Lush gardens spread out between the various buildings and stone pathways connected them. A vertical face of rock extended up one side of the village. More and more bald men milled about, doing some chores. No one seemed to pay attention to me, except for the four characters walking my way.

My vision fully cleared, but my body still couldn't move. As much as I told myself to sit up, my stomach muscles never got the message.

Why?

Then I made out the characteristics on one of the approaching faces. He was Asian, with a deep tan.

Asian? Chinese...China...J.J.!

My memories flooded in like a raging river. I remembered breaking J.J. out of jail, followed by the rescue operation of his daughter. I had vivid visions of Baron William Ruthford and Lynea, and our discovery of the temple of *Xi Wangmu*. Everything dawned at once, including Alvin Mitchell.

I tensed up.

This was reality.

I laid on a large white table cloth draped over a stone platform. My environment painted the image of a typical Chinese Monastery. Bamboo posts framed out bridges and roofs. Wooden totems sporadically grew out of the earth. Everything seemed serene.

I suddenly wished I was back in my dream.

With all my will, I arched my neck to look at the rest of my body. A traditional robe covered my torso and legs. From what I could see of my exposed arms, I had a number of healed scars. Thin lines spread over my skin—markings to remind me of my narrow escape from an erupting volcano.

The markings were fully mended though. How long was I here? That question didn't linger long as the four monks arrived.

"Where am I?" were the first words to come out of my mouth.

The four men just stared in silence without a single expression.

"Do you speak English?" I asked.

Nothing. We just sat in an awkward stillness.

"Why can't I move?" My tone escalated.

Finally, one of the men spoke. "Rest. Answers shall come in time."

I couldn't rest though. "It seems like I've already rested for quite awhile. Please, answer me. How long have I been here?"

The man hunched down, now only inches from my head. "Two months."

My world flipped upside down. How was I out for two months? My head ached as the monks caught me up to speed. Or should I say, the one monk. He was the only one who spoke English—and he spoke it surprisingly well.

"You are safe here," the monk began. "Do not worry, we mean you no harm."

I figured as much from all my healed scars. The monk continued.

"You lie within the walls of our sacred temple, Xuankong. You are the first foreigner to have been welcomed to our home."

"Thank you," I managed to say. When the monk mentioned Xuankong Temple, something registered in my brain. I had heard of this place before. It dawned on me that I read about it in one of the travel magazines on the flight to China.

Proud of my photographic memory, I said, "Xuankong? The *hanging temple?*"

"Why, yes."

Quoting the tagline from the magazine almost verbatim, I said, "A temple that's built off the cliffs of the Hunyuan County in the Shanxi Province?" Even though I stated a fact, I said it like a question as if not believing it. I remembered pictures from the magazine. The entire village cantilevered directly out of a rocky cliff, a hundred feet above the forest.

"I am impressed," the monk said. "We live here in the sky to be one with the heavens. It allows us to practice our beliefs."

"Taoism?" I half-stated, half-asked.

The monk nodded.

It sounded like everywhere I went, people had this screaming desire to reach the heavens. It dawned on me though that, as I mentally painted the map of where the Shanxi Province was, it was thirty miles away from the original location of my disappearance.

My throat ached. "How did I get here?"

"I found you," the monk began. As he told me about my discovery, I realized I truly was the luckiest man alive.

It just so happened that this monk and his friends were bathing in the waters of Lake Jingpo when they saw me fly over the waterfall like a ragdoll. They watched me crash into the water and disappear. When I never re-surfaced, the monk dove into the lake and miraculously found me.

Of course I was unconscious while they carried me back to their monastery.

"Weren't you a little far from home?" I asked.

"The lake is our ritual grounds. We use the waters as a birth into the heavens. It is our dedication to the Grandfather Sun, Tai Yang Gong. The journey is such that every one of us must take to remain in good standing with the Sun God."

I cringed at the mention of the *Sun God*.

"What's your name?" I asked.

"Lei-Phong," the monk responded. "What do they call you?"

"Charlie...Charlie Morgan. Well Lei-Phong, I owe you my life." Straining to move, I added, "What's left of it."

"Your body has not moved in two months. Time shall cure you, and we shall help speed up your recovery." The monk helped me to sit upright.

Even though my scars had healed, they still killed like a son of a gun. Speeding up the process sounded good to me. I had some friends that were probably worried sick. I could only imagine what J.J. was going through...

...Or even Jenny. I left her with some horrible company. As I reflected on it, I began to wonder if finding J.J. was a bad idea. He'd probably murder me for putting his daughter in danger.

"You must be hungry. I will bring you some food," Lei-Phong said, motioning to one of his fellow monks. The man ran off without a word.

My thoughts meandered to the fact that I was naked under foreign clothing. My face was cleanly shaven, and my hair groomed. What else did these guys do while I laid here like sleeping beauty?

"How did I get the luxury of such hospitality?" I coughed.

"It is in our beliefs, Charlie Morgan. Our ways embrace that of harmony. Harmony within one's soul, and harmony with the earth. When we watched you descend from the heavens, we knew that it was a sign from the stars."

The foundations of Taoist philosophy was in compassion and humility. It also focused on simplicity. Listening to the monk, it was nice to hear his good hearted nature. I felt a sort of security.

"We are a people of peace. Like I said, you have nothing to fear from us," Lei-Phong said.

I asked, "Has anyone tried looking for me?"

"We have had no other visitors. I am sorry," the monk responded.

"How do you speak English so well?" I decided to ask. Even though the man had an accent, he spoke the language flawlessly.

"I was not always a monk," Lei-Phong said with a straight face. He went onto explain that all the people here had grown up in neighboring villages. Everyone who lived in this temple did so on their own accord. They chose the life of solitude and simplicity.

Looking out at the hanging structures beyond, I made out at least fifty or so other men. Some young, some old. All of them wore the same garments.

Lei-Phong walked up to one of the pillars holding up our shelter. Sculptures of various animals carved out of the wood. Bronze accents called out the teeth and eyes. The artistic detail was astounding. The more I looked at it, the more the pillars resembled the totems back at the *Xi Wangmu* dig site.

After a brief pause, Lei-Phong continued, "Charlie Morgan, our people look to the stars for guidance. The stars paint the story of our world. We honor them by creating the animals that watch over us from above."

The conversation felt like *deja vu*. Just over two months ago, I was having almost the exact same conversation with Jenny. I remembered the excitement in her face as she described Taoism to me—how excited she was at the discovery of *Xi Wangmu's* temple.

My mind diverted to the puzzle I solved at the temple's entrance. How constellations were the answer—the Big Dipper. I heard Alvin's voice echo through my head as he provided me that solution.

God, I hated that guy.

I almost told the monk that constellations were what led me to solve the Baron's riddle months ago. And in turn cause the volcanic eruption. Instead, I said nothing. I simply let the man continue his lesson.

It was amazing how important constellations were to the foundation of Taoism. The animals this monk was mentioning were the twelve zodiac signs that molded people's characteristics.

Each animal represented a different behavior, and together the mix created balance in the Universe.

The monk continued, "Finding you was a sign. We will guide you to good health and then let you be on your way."

I asked, "What ended up happening with the volcano? Was the eruption part of your so-called harmony?"

"It was part of our balance, yes," Lei began. "Wood, earth, metal, water and fire. These elements harmoniously work together to maintain a constant balance. They are the yin and yang—opposing extremes that constantly play against and with each other.

"The Earth erupted that day to bring stability to the world. It deemed it necessary to be cleansed. The river soothed its temper and brought back balance."

"And a whole lot of destruction," I commented.

"The forest grew tall and old. Now life can start anew."

I realized that even if I did tell this man that I caused all the destruction, he would have probably said it was all *meant to be.* It was interesting to see how different people viewed the same scenario. Where I saw destruction, Lei-Phong saw hope.

"Charlie Morgan, we believe that the world is in a constant process of recreation. The basics of our religion were started many years ago by a legendary *Wu.*"

The urge to tell him I knew that all too well came again. I wanted to tell him that his *Wu,* or shamaness, was what led me here in the first place. But again, I bit my tongue. Mainly because the other monk had returned with food.

My stomach groaned in hunger. Painfully, I moved my arms to grab the bowl out of the man's hands. Inside was pure liquid. Hot liquid.

"What's this?" I asked, confused.

"It is Life," Lei said. "Everything that exists was condensed to form life. If one diluted life, then he could reach his full potential. We call this your *Qi*."

I took a sip. This tea was a way for me to dilute my inner self, and speed up my healing. It all seemed like mumbo jumbo to me, but it did taste delicious. As I kept drinking the tea, it instantly began to sooth my pain. It was strange, but it worked.

I started chugging the cup. I needed to get better fast. Two months was an eternity. I could only imagine what had happened in my absence. I asked, "How long do you think it will take for me to get back to normal?"

"It all depends on the strength of your desire," Lei-Phong said.

"In that case it should be fast," I said in a matter-of-fact tone. I had places to be and people to see. Determined, I needed to get better fast. I polished off my cup and handed it to the monk.

"Can I have some more?"

CHAPTER FIFTEEN

Four weeks.

Apparently that's how strong my desire was.

After four weeks of painful rehabilitation, I was back to my limber self. I had to give it to those monks, they were great. So was that tea they fed me. During the month that I was there, these men helped push my body back to par.

It was slow at first. The minute my hand/eye coordination returned, things picked up steam. Walking flowed right into running, lifting to climbing. By the end of the fourth week, I almost felt stronger than I was before.

But as my body returned to normal, it also meant my brief time with the monks had come to an end. All I wanted to do was find a phone, call J.J. and get back to reality.

On my last day in the monastery, Lei-Phong led me to a large pagoda. We entered a large space covered in mosaics.

Phong guided me to a box in the corner. He opened it, revealing my jeans and shirt. They had been cleaned and neatly folded. On top was a gold necklace. A circular bronze pendant dangled from its end.

Their hospitality was endless.

Lei picked up the pendant. "Charlie Morgan," he began. "It has been a pleasure to learn and teach you at the same time. Take this as a symbol of our friendship, and as a token to help protect you along your way."

I grabbed the necklace. Detailed engravings covered the small object. A fierce dragon arched over one half of the circle, while a timid goat hunched on the opposite end. "Uh, thanks Lei. But, it looks like the poor animal is about to get executed by an angry dragon."

"Quite the opposite. The dragon is your protector. It is a sign of good fortune and of a free spirit. It symbolizes your positive energy. The sheep is the negative energy."

"I would have figured the opposite."

"Why?" Lei looked genuinely puzzled by my comment.

I could have said it was because, typically, when you show an angry fire breathing animal ready to strike an innocent little one you look at the beast as the bad guy, but I didn't. Instead, I just shrugged.

"As in the yin and yang, everything needs balance. Astrologically, the dragon falls in the fifth phase of our Universe, and it is greatly adorned by the other zodiac animals."

My brain struggled to figure out the right thing to say in response. It was still catching up, trying to understand what Lei was even saying. In the end, the only thing I could do was be grateful. "I truly appreciate it Lei," I said. I clasped the chain around my neck.

"We have also prepared your clothes for your long journey home."

"Again, I thank you," I said.

Then Lei-Phong turned serious—or at least more serious than normal. "Where will your journey take you now, Charlie Morgan?"

"I don't know, Lei. I'll find my friends, get some lunch, take a shower, followed by a quick stop for a bit of revenge...maybe not in that exact order."

"And how do you propose to get this revenge?"

"I don't know. I haven't thought that far ahead," I said.

Lei-Phong moved away, toward the far wall.

He said, "I wish you luck on your journey. Your story shall be painted on these walls. This room is the way we remember those who have come before. Bringing a foreigner into our home is a tale that will never be forgotten."

I turned to the walls and realized they were covered from top to bottom in paintings. Beautiful paintings to be more precise.

I admired them closely, saying, "I am honored Lei. I wish I..." my speech stopped mid-sentence. My eyes locked on one of the images on the wall.

A mural depicted nine suns spread over a sky. Beneath them were large deities standing atop a mountain. The mountain was bright red. Buried below was another figure.

Xi Wangmu!

I stepped away from the painting to take in more of the image. Constellations covered the upper portion as a pathway to the sky—the pathway to the heavens. At the top, a clear depiction of the circular stone tablet was drawn, or at least the half of one.

Was this mural re-imagining the temple we discovered months ago?

Another path stemmed from the stone tablet, it led off to the next wall. I followed it until it terminated. I focused on the painted object. Extending out of a tall plain of grass was a massive tree. Piles of fruit lay on the ground. Twelve branches expanded out of the enormous trunk, disappearing into a night sky of stars.

Positioned at the top of the tree was my biggest exclamation point. It was a drawing of the other half of the stone tablet.

"Lei, what is this? Who drew it?"

He approached. "That is the Peach Tree. The tree of life and immortality. It is said to grow in the paradise of..."

"...*Xi Wangmu*," I finished his thought.

"Yes. How did you know this?" Lei-Phong asked, perplexed.

"Because I met the lady."

I kept searching for other clues. "Where is this tree? Does it really exist?"

"Yes. Why do you seek it?"

"Because now I know how I'm going to get my revenge."

It looked as if revenge became first on my to-do list. I'd been missing for three months. One more day wouldn't hurt.

I spent the next hour further investigating the mural. Many of the same symbols that were engraved in the bronze gate leading into *Xi Wangmu's* temple appeared here as well.

More importantly, at the base of the mountain, drawn on the first wall, black figures were shown on the one side. On the opposite, stood red figures. Were these the hooded assassins that attacked me?

"Those are the *Men Shen*," Lei-Phong explained. "They are the guardians of the tomb."

Oh I knew those guys. The scars on my body were proof.

Excitement crept up. "How far away is this place?" I asked, putting on my jeans and shirt.

"A half day's walk. I must warn you Charlie Morgan, it is not safe to travel there. Many have never returned. Those who have, come back empty handed."

"I'm not planning on bringing anything back with me, Lei. I'm planning on destroying whatever is there." I had a plan, or at least a seed of one.

"If this is what you wish, then let us go. We will arrive by nightfall."

"Wait, you will take me?" I asked.

"It will be difficult to navigate on your own. You will need my guidance. Once there, we shall part ways," Phong said.

"You're a good man Lei." I tapped him on the shoulder, and off we went.

The trek was long and bumpy. I didn't realize how high up the mountain we were until I actually had to climb down. I also didn't realize how sore I'd be, going down the winding tunnels. I was tired before our journey even technically began.

When we exited out into open terrain, the sun had already started to descend. Luckily, my motivation pushed me along.

We passed through a dense bamboo forest. Tall, thin, rods of vegetation punched out of the earth like straws. For as flimsy as they looked, the trunks were solid. Even with their hollow core, the bamboo stood stiff and upright as we passed through the makeshift path.

The road was fairly flat. Even so, Lei moved like a machine. Not once did he slow down, nor need rest. I, on the other hand, struggled to keep up. Even at a hundred percent, I was exhausted.

Still, I painfully kept up the pace.

Within hours, my entire shirt was soaked, my legs felt wobbly, and exhaustion threatened to make me faint. Fighting my pride, I finally told Lei, "Can we take a break? I don't think I'm built like the terminator."

"No need, we are here."

Breaking free from the forest, the landscape revealed an expansive field of grass. The setting sun smeared a soft orange glow over the scene. I'm not quite sure what I expected to find, but what Lei showed me was not even close.

In the mural, a massive tree with large branches towered over an open field. Being the *tree of life* I thought I would find some exaggerated shrub to the same degree. Surprisingly, I got the opposite.

Resting in the center of the open field was a small stubby totem pole. It was actually more of a stone platform with a ten foot radius. It rose out of the ground about three feet.

That was it.

Engravings surrounded the perimeter of the totem.

Honestly though, my eyes were instantly distracted the minute we stepped out of the forest. The stone pedestal may have been a bit underwhelming, but what I found more intriguing was what lay beyond.

Positioned about a hundred feet away from the pedestal was a large grouping of green tents. Jeeps and helicopters parked at the one end, and a single generator ran power to flood lights around the camp.

Men dressed in black, and carrying assault rifles, patrolled about. Seeing their dirty mugs and square jaws, I instantly recognized the good Baron's mercenaries.

Baron William Ruthford was here.

In the three months I had been away, the billionaire continued his pursuit for the second part of that ancient tablet.

Looking at how undisturbed the dig site was, my guess was that he didn't have much luck. He probably regretted ordering my death. I couldn't wait to see the look on his face when he saw I was alive and kicking.

"Those men have been here for over a month," Lei whispered.

Huddling up behind a tree, I added, "Wait, you knew they were here? Why didn't you say anything?"

"Why do you think I said it was dangerous?" I couldn't tell from Lei's expressionless face if that was a joke. He then asked, "Do you know these men?"

Squinting, I tried to recognize some of the researchers faces as they sat around a camp fire. "I know their type."

Diverting my attention back to the *tree of life*, I added, "Doesn't really look like much."

"It is a sacred stone, Charlie Morgan. It is the point where the world was created. One of the pillars of our faith."

I scanned the area some more. If the Baron's men were here, did it mean Jenny was too? Or Alvin? I needed to know.

"What is your plan?" Lei-Phong asked.

"I don't know. I typically make it up as I go." I pointed off to the campsite. "First stop, I need to see what's going on over there."

"Then this is where we part ways, Charlie Morgan." Lei got up. "I wish you luck on your endeavor. Please remember that this place is our sacred ground. My people have learned to believe in the ways of this tree.

"It holds many treasures that we have yet to uncover, but our beliefs have sufficed for us to never seek more. I hope your desire shall guide you on the right path."

I embraced my new friend. "And I thank you Lei—for saving me and for bringing me here. I owe you much."

Lei-Phong unhinged from our grasp and simply walked away. No other farewell, no look back. He just disappeared into the darkness of bamboo.

The man exited from my life as quickly as he entered it. I doubted I'd ever see him again.

I was now on my own.

CHAPTER SIXTEEN

Returning my focus to the campsite, I quickly made my way to it. Still crouched, I used the grass as cover. The last beams of sunlight barely reached the camp, creating deep shadows in the landscape.

Now, I know it was a stupid idea—going into a fortified camp with dozens of bad guys armed with guns. I admit it. But I couldn't help myself. There was an off chance that my friends were there. Plus, I needed to know what was going on.

I stealthily crept around.

Keeping to the shadows, I went from tent to tent. I dodged patrols and researchers as I scanned each area for familiar faces. Security was fairly light, which was surprising after what happened months ago.

Rounding a corner, I soon overheard two thugs talking.

"You see Jenkins anywhere?" the one bullish man asked. His silhouette framed out of the campfire beyond.

Did he say Jenkins? Was Jenny actually here? My ears perked up.

"The old man? Nah, he's probably drunk. It's after five. He's usually at the bar by now. I don't know why Ruthford wanted this guy out here. He hasn't done squat," the other responded.

Were they talking about J.J.? I never associated Jeremy and drunk in the same sentence. The conversation continued.

"But at least he's not as annoying as the Australian. That one was cocky."

"Yeah he was. Still, the outbacker's got it better than us. We're stuck in this dump, sweating our butts off, while he's babysitting that hot little blonde with the boss."

It was as if these two clowns were intentionally giving me just the exposition I needed. My luck was getting better by the minute.

I assumed that the Australian they mentioned could only be one man, Alvin Mitchell. What did they mean by *babysitting*? Was he with Jenny? I churned for answers.

"Still, I'd rather be looking at that blonde rather than her old man," the thug added. "I got to give it to the boss though. Using her as collateral got that old man working."

"Maybe that's why he's so miserable."

"If you ask me, I say they should have never offed that one fella."

"Which one?"

"The one that figured everything out three months ago. If he were here, I'm sure we would be done by now."

Now the information was flowing way too easily. I almost wanted to thank these guys. Plus, I couldn't help pat myself on my back. It was hard not to feel good when a compliment was thrown my way, even if it was from a pair of monkeys.

The two men continued to toot my horn, but I got distracted. Mainly because they steered their way toward me.

I flattened back against the face of a tent. They neared.

My heart began thumping away. I couldn't get caught now. Inching along the face of the tent, I slowly crept around the corner. This only bought me a few seconds.

The voices got louder.

Quickly, I darted through the parted tarp and into the tent. Closing the two pieces of canvas, I held them firm as the two shadows passed by.

The men paused a moment in silence. Then, their footsteps began once again, getting quieter as they got further away.

Letting out a deep breath, I turned around.

The tent was lit by a few electric lanterns. The inside was spacious. A small mattress with rustled blankets lay off to the side. A folded table with a single chair positioned at the far end. A clothesline dangled over the table, and large white pieces of paper were clipped from it.

Instantly, I knew where I was.

I stood in Jeremy's tent.

My luck continued getting better and better.

The pages were his giveaway. As I marched up to them, I made out the charcoal rubbings drawn all over the sheets.

The table was filled with these as well, along with photographs and notes. All of the images were taken straight from the stone totem which sat in the middle of the field.

Examining a few photos, I read the notes scribbled over them. Jeremy was actually trying to figure out how to open the *tree of life*.

Years ago, Jeremy first showed me how to do a proper charcoal rubbing. He stressed the delicate nature of it all, and always said that they were better than a photograph because it was as if you were drawing the picture yourself. "It's in the details, Charles," he'd always say.

The charcoal rubbings here were of various animal heads. The images had been taken from the carvings around the face of the totem. A total of twelve animals were shown: a rat, ox, tiger, hare, dragon, snake, horse, sheep, monkey, rooster, dog, and boar.

The twelve zodiac signs of Chinese Astrology.

I thought of the monks I spent the last few months with. I was amazed at how literal they believed in the constellations. Just like *Xi Wangmu's* temple up at the Wanda Mountain, looking up at the stars was the key.

It also seemed to correlate to the mural painted back at the monastery. There, twelve branches of the *tree of life* stemmed out into the starry night.

J.J. was on the right track.

On the table, a photo lay front and center. Chinese characters covered most of it, and below, Jeremy had written a rough translation.

Illuminating the creator of the world, is the key to finding those that follow. And in the footsteps of his followers, balance shall be fulfilled. Only when harmony is restored will your eyes be opened to the path of the light.

I grabbed the sheet. Beside the table was an open backpack. I noticed another map protruded out of the unzipped bag. I pulled it out and laid it across the table.

A number of concentric circles scribbled over the map of the area. 'Where are you Charles?' was written in a corner.

J.J. was looking for me, but his search zones weren't even close to where I spent my time.

I reached back into the bag. It was filled with a slew of items, from charcoal and pads of blank white paper, to flashlights and survival essentials. I stuffed the translation into the backpack and slung the bag over my shoulder. J.J. wouldn't miss it much.

Plus, I had an idea. I was going to do my friend's job for him. Well, kind of.

Footsteps crunched the gravel outside.

"Who's in there?" a voice called.

Instinctively, I ducked down. The light emanating from the lanterns must have given me away. I listened to the footsteps round the tent.

Crawling along the dirt, I sped to a corner. One by one, I yanked out the stakes holding down the end of the tent. The canvas loosened at its base. I pulled out a few more, making the opening bigger.

I was running out of time.

Glancing back, I saw a silhouette at the entrance. I returned my focus to the loosened canvas. Without checking to see what was on the other side, I crawled under the slivered opening.

I pressed my belly onto the ground and slithered through to the other side. Scrambling to my feet, I darted away from the tent.

Like always, it was a close call. I needed to get away from the camp.

So I ran toward my next stop, the *tree of life*.

It seemed like most of the other workers quit for the night. With the sun now fully set, a blanket of darkness covered a majority of the open field. The campsite was a lone beacon with flood lights and lanterns littering the area. The further away I got, the darker it became.

I walked out toward the stumpy totem.

Caution crept up my body as I progressed. The bristling of grass swayed in the soft breeze. My mind teleported back to the tiger incident, and the hairs on my arms perked up.

Alert, I continued.

Within minutes, I was up close and personal with the stone platform they called the *tree of life*. For as tiny as it looked in the expansive field, it felt much bigger when I neared.

In the dark, I did one quick lap around the frumpy stone. At its base, the totem looked as if the immaculately carved rock disappeared into the earth.

Climbing onto the platform, I marveled at how smooth and level it was. Clean lines cut across the stone from end to end, terminating at little bowls carved into the rock. In total, twelve bowls lined the perimeter in a clock arrangement.

Rubbing the inside of one of them, black ash wiped onto my skin. I sniffed it.

No odor.

I hopped back off the platform to digest the scene. Glancing back, the campsite looked far away. No one was going to find me out here in the dark. I had all the time in the world.

That is, until the sun came up.

It was time to get to work.

The monks gave me a head start. Jeremy, helped me with the groundwork. Now all I needed to do was figure out how they all fit together. I recollected my Chinese knowledge.

The first things that came to mind were the zodiac signs. All the animals that represented the zodiac were engraved around the face of the totem. What did they have in common? Why would they all be inscribed on the stone?

I pulled out J.J.'s translation. *Illuminating the creator of the world, is the key to finding those that follow…*

Staring back at the animal faces on the stone totem, I wondered what that meant. *The creator of the world.* The beginning of the Universe.

Xi Wangmu's temple was said to be at the point where Heaven and Earth met. Mount Kunlun was a part of the Axis Mundi, one of the few locations where one could access the heavens. Still, it wasn't the start of the world.

Animals…constellations…zodiacs…

I kept coming back to the zodiacs. I knew these signs had to play into the equation. In Taoist beliefs, the twelve signs fell within the twelve months of the year.

Numbers remained a constant backbone to the interpretation of the stars. More importantly, the Universe.

Zero symbolized the void, or non-being. *One*, meant isolation. *Two*, a pairing. *Three* signified the Holy Triad, where the world came full circle.

The thing is, these numbers had multi-faceted meanings. Not only did *one* mean isolation, but it also denoted the idea of masculinity. *Two* stood for feminity. The layers of meanings upon meanings were numerous.

Annoying, I know. It hurt my head to think about it.

Compound that with the fact that different religions had different beliefs for the same numbers, made analyzing them nearly impossible.

Luckily, these twelve numbers had a distinct pattern. They were arranged in perfect order to their twelve cycles of the Chinese zodiac.

In Chinese astrology, each animal was selected by its living habits. The same correlation was made with time. Every animal took up a quadrant of time in a day based on their daily routines. Somehow, the circular arrangement of these images, and their order, had to play off each other.

I thought of the clock configuration.

The tiger had one o'clock because that was when it hunted. The dragons had five o'clock since that was believed to be the time they hovered in the sky. The rat...

The rat!

My mind diverged. The rat had a specific role in Chinese mythology. It didn't have to do with the time of day, but more importantly, the beginning of time.

Every religion had its own crazy idea of how the world was created. In Chinese mythology, the origin of the world was thought to have started in darkness. Its walls acted like the shell of an egg, blocking its view from the rest of the Universe.

The rat was said to have bit into the egg, cracking it open an allowing air to enter. In turn, this act created the Earth and separated the heavens, hence the start of the world.

Could it be?

If so, how did I illuminate it?

I ran with the notion. I searched around the stone walls until I found the symbol for the rat. On top of it, the bowl carved into the rock was empty. If it needed something, maybe a simple flame would do the trick?

Reaching into the backpack, I searched for some sort of match. Luckily, a lighter was wedged in one of the side pockets. I then pulled out a small piece of paper. Crumpling it up, I placed the ball of paper into the bowl.

Igniting the flint, I held the flame near the base of the wad. Within seconds, the paper caught fire and a small flame began. Risking a second glance back, I hoped that the little light emanating from the bowl wouldn't attract the others.

My focus returned to the fire. I didn't see anything out of the ordinary. I angled my vision around the rat face but couldn't see any sign that I was on the right track.

Then my eye caught a faint glimmer from the top of the stone platform. I climbed back onto the smooth surface. One of the engraved lines that stemmed away from the fire-lit bowl glowed red. The soft shimmer followed along a path directly to the center of the platform.

The glow disappeared as the paper disintegrated.

It was a faint sign, but it was enough. I thought back to the rest of the translation.

And in the footsteps of his followers, balance shall be achieved...

Was it talking about the other animals that followed the rat in the calendar months? Or maybe it meant lighting the rest of the animals in a clockwise manner, starting with the rat? I tried lighting up a few more wads of paper into the other bowls. Nothing happened.

Round after round I came up with the same results.

Nothing.

My brain struggled as it tried to piece together the rest of the puzzle. I thought back to Lei-Phong and his beliefs in harmony and balance. He said that everything was balanced off one another. It brought forth one's Qi. The yin and the yang created the perfect harmony. Half and half. Was I supposed to light half of the bowls to create a balance of light and dark?

But which ones?

I concentrated on the zodiac symbols. There needed to be a relationship here. What did they have in common with the rat?

I lit papers in half of the bowls, but still, nothing happened. Then I lit every other bowl with fire, starting with the rat.

Still, nothing. Looking back at the backpack I realized I was running out of material to burn.

I had to make things count. I started to get nervous. Maybe this was why J.J. hadn't figured the puzzle out. I'm sure he tried everything I had done. That's why there was black ash in all of the bowls.

I had to be overlooking something.

My fingers anxiously fondled over the pendant that dangled from my neck. They rubbed the engraving back and forth as I concentrated on the puzzle at hand.

That's when it dawned on me.

The toes!

In one of Lei's ramblings, he mentioned the significance of even and odd numbers and their relationship to positive and negative forces. It had to do with the number of toes an animal had.

The pendant he gave me was my answer. The dragon, being my protector, had five toes signifying the positive yang energy.

The rat may have been the originator of the world, but it also had five toes. The tiger had five toes too, as did the monkey and dog. All the others had even numbered toes.

I started to get excited. I was onto something. Counting up the animals, I found that only five of the twelve animals had five toes per foot. I was off by one to create that perfect balance. Racing around the large rock, I tried to spark anything I could be missing.

My pulse quickened. I was on the brink of solving this. I just needed to find one more animal.

Then, I passed the horse.

I paused.

Horses only had one toe per hoof. An odd number is what enabled the yang. It didn't necessarily require the animal to have five toes. Could that be it?

Running low on paper I ripped out a bunch of grass and laid them in the designated bowls. I climbed on top of the stone circle and, one by one, lit each. The small flames glowed in the dark sky. As I enflamed the last one I stepped away to the center of the platform.

All six flames flickered in the wind. I was testing my luck. Someone was going to see this soon, and if so, my—

The earth rumbled. I nearly lost my footing at the rattling of the ground. Bracing myself, I held strong as the ground shook more violently.

Here we went again.

The platform I stood on suddenly rose upward. It continued to rise higher as I sprawled to the ground. The smooth surface was like an ice rink, threatening to slide me off the ledge.

I struggled to hang on but couldn't help but wonder what kind of geared mechanism buried down below could cause this to happen. Grumbling and cracking rock echoed through the wind, pushing the platform upward.

I was on a one-way elevator to God knows where. It felt like I rose forever. The platform continued higher and higher.

Somehow, I managed to hang on until, abruptly, the earthquake subsided and the platform stopped.

Everything returned to silence.

For a second, I didn't move. Fear engulfed me. How high up was I? The darkness made it difficult to see anything but the faint outlines of clouds. Finally mustering up the courage to move, I crawled to the edge of the platform.

I peered over the edge. I was over fifty feet above the grass field below. The once stumpy little decorated stone now towered over the grass. This revealed the rest of the markings engraved all over its body. Bronze ornaments ran up its walls like branches. This wasn't a simple little totem, this was an enormous one. And I could only imagine how much of a massive monument it looked like from down below.

This was the *tree of life*.

Unfortunately, now that I got my wish in revealing this massive totem, all my stealth efforts were just thrown out the window. I just woke up the entire campsite.

And, I was stranded with nowhere to go.

CHAPTER SEVENTEEN

Before I could panic and plan my next move, the ground rumbled once again. Looking over the ledge, a strange chaos unfolded.

Parts of the grassy field began to sink into the ground, while other parts rose up. Like an ocean ripple around the totem, the ground kept alternating higher and lower. Soon, new earth formations emerged, radiating around the *tree of life*.

It continued systematically.

As more areas sunk downward, they disappeared into deep blackness. It was juxtaposed by adjacent landforms raising over ten feet above grade level. The forms started to take shape, and my eyes focused on what spread out before me.

The earth transformed into a series of rings accentuated by massive circular wall formations. When the dust settled and the ground stopped vibrating, the rings perfectly wrapped around the base of the totem over and over again.

Way down below, a circular labyrinth of dirt and rock was formed—the totem pole at its center. At the far end of the outer ring of the labyrinth, an area rose up higher than the rest. Flames vented out of the top of the dirt pile.

I just cracked the egg, and brought life to the *tree of life*. On top of it all, I was stranded.

Voices rang out in the distance. The camp of researchers and mercenaries roared. Over by the tents, movements scurried about. The flood lights turned their angles toward the totem, and more importantly, me.

I spoke too soon about my good luck.

I scrambled to my feet. I searched for some means of escape. Anything.

A climb down the face of the totem pole would be nearly impossible. I was good, but not that good.

Squinting in the dark, I tried to find some switch or lever. The flames in the six ritual bowls dwindled to smoke, making it even harder to see. Finally, the last flame flickered out, and I was lost to darkness.

Luckily, the extinguished fires also triggered my escape.

The center portion of the platform dislodged and began to descend. It sped down a shaft of rock as the perimeter of the totem remained. I rode a makeshift elevator. On its way down, loud cranks reverberated along the smooth tunnel-like walls. Steam filled the shaft, bleeding out the creases of the elevator.

I didn't have time to react. I didn't even question it. Whatever was happening, I was on an express elevator straight back to the base of the *tree of life*. Seconds later, the platform stopped. The steam settled away, clearing the view.

I was at the ground level.

Pulling a flashlight out of J.J.'s bag, I flicked it on. All around, monstrous walls of rock towered above. The dirt walls felt claustrophobic.

I shined the beam of light to my left seeing a path disappear on a curve. Panning the other way, I found the same result. I was at the start of a maze, with a group of armed thugs rushing to my destination.

I didn't have much time.

I picked a direction and ran. I followed the path for some time before reaching a fork in the road. From here, it was a guessing game. I chose a route and went with it.

I had been through mazes dozens of times before. Most I enjoyed, but right now, I was not having fun. Countless times I reached a dead end. Backtracking, I tried once again along another path.

Screams of joy got louder as my enemies closed in on my location.

I started to resent these puzzles. Thankfully, there were no traps—at least, not yet.

I scrambled down another path that led to an open area. Four paths branched off in diverging directions. This was going to take forever. There needed to be a sign, some sort of clue to guide me the right way.

I searched the openings with my flashlight. There were no distinctions between each route. All I noticed was that one path was dense with weeds and roots stemming out of the rock.

My light paused on the weeds.

As Lei-Phong taught me, Taoism ran deep with five foundations; earth, water, wood, fire, and metal. Could the weeds signify earth?

Fire was used to light the way. Water, or more specifically, steam operated the ancient elevator. Wood and metal gears probably made up the operating mechanism of the massive totem. All that was left was *earth*.

It was a longshot, but I didn't have any better logic.

I jet into the weed covered pathway.

A second sound started to creep through my eardrums, almost like a whispering—as if a bunch of people were quietly talking through the walls.

This pushed me faster through the corridors. Looking back, I made out the black silhouette of the totem pole getting further away. I was making progress.

The whispers grew.

Entering another branch-way, I followed the same routine. This time, leaves and vines framed one opening. I sped through the hole without hesitation.

My mind kept on praying that there were no tigers hiding in the shadows. I'd rather have *Men Shen* warriors over the tigers.

The whispers turned to a deafening hiss.

Whatever lived within the walls of this labyrinth was getting close, and as I entered the next hallway my flashlight spread over the sound's origin.

This was worse than traps.

Filling the floor of corridor, from wall to wall, was a full sea of rats. They hissed and squirmed over each other as more kept fumbling out of pores in the walls. The sea of tiny animals went on as far as I could see.

These *Xi Wangmu* worshipers really took things too literally. First, I had the tigers, and now I was met with the literal interpretation of the guys that created the Universe. I had to give it to them though. When they went big, they followed through with it.

A voice yelled, "How do we get in there?"

The researchers had reached the outside wall of the maze. It was only a matter of time before they found an entrance.

Taking a deep breath, I mustered up all the courage I had and ran straight into the rat filled street. I felt my feet wobble as they stepped over the mushy ground of living animals. Squeals shrieked at every footstep. I prayed that I didn't get bit by one of these rabid rats. I hoped to God that none of them had any disease.

I couldn't stop. Even if I started to second guess my motivations, I had gone too far to turn back.

I pressed on.

My flashlight bounced around as I stumbled my way through the corridor. I wrapped around the last curve and saw my goal.

Less than fifty feet ahead emerged a stairwell. The earth rose up around the stair, creating a dark tunnel. Flames erupted out of the top of the mound, calling out the entrance.

I was nearly there. Focused on the shifting terrain, I didn't think about what laid in the darkness beyond. I reached the steps, bolted up them, and ran straight through the opening. I disappeared into the black void. The rats didn't follow. I was alone in a sea of darkness.

At least I finally stood on solid ground.

The tight tunnel continued. Dirt crumbled from the ceiling. The earth seemed to strain under pressure, but the cave held. Moving through the confined space, I prayed I wouldn't have to delve too deep.

Luckily, I didn't.

Within a few dozen feet of the entry, the cave opened up to a chamber. In the center of the chamber stood a stone pedestal, and on top of it, the thing I was looking for—the other half of *Xi Wangmu's* stone tablet.

I found it.

Running up to the tablet, I inspected the glyphs drawn over the stone. Just like the other one we discovered months ago, this tablet shared the same Greek text. My artificial light glossed over the words.

Jeremy would have been in Heaven. More importantly, the Baron would have probably kissed me—followed by shooting me dead. Of course, at the end of the day, once he found out what I was about to do, he'd definitely want me dead—again.

I didn't pick the tablet up. The last time we did that we caused a natural disaster. I needed to figure out a way to destroy it. It was the only way to stop the Baron. With a defiled tablet, there would be no way for him to continue.

Destroying the artifact was against everything I believed in as a treasure hunter.

But this was my plan.

First thing was first, I needed some collateral. If this didn't work, I was going to need some sort of back-up plan. So I prepared a plan B. From my bag, I pulled out one of the last sheets of paper and a stick of charcoal.

Flawlessly, I spread the paper over the tablet and began rubbing the charcoal on it. As if magic, the charcoal slid over the various indentations on the stone. With each passing stroke, the indentations were highlighted in black powder on the white sheet. Soon, the once clean paper was covered in multiple shades of black and gray.

When I finished, the entire inscription was clearly transposed onto my sheet.

Quickly, I folded the paper and placed it back in the bag. I then grabbed a loose rock. Rough edges protruded from one side. Pulling my arm back, I prepped to strike the tablet and deface the inscriptions.

I swung violently.

The rock chipped away at the stone. I cringed with every strike. Little by little, the raised Greek letters that spread over the tablet broke off.

I didn't stop. I continued to strike at the rock until most of the written words became unreadable.

Taking a break, I admired my work. The entire tablet was now covered in scratches and dents. There was no way Ruthford could decipher it. It was useless.

My revenge was complete.

"Stop right there!" a voice exclaimed in the dark.

I forgot about my assailants.

The sound of a gun being cocked tensed my body. "Easy fellas," I said calmly, slowly raising my hands.

"I said don't move," the thug's voice screamed out.

"Actually, you said, *stop right there*," I mumbled, but obliged the man's second request.

"Turn around," another voice said.

I could have commented on the fact that turning technically negated his *no moving* requirement, but I remained quiet. Turning, I came face to face with two burly men. Their blinding flashlights made it difficult to see. That, and the large assault rifles that were pointed at my face made it tough to look at anything else.

"What were you doing there?"

"Your job," I lied. "I was sent by Mr. Ruthford to help find the tablet. You didn't get the message?" Mercenaries are some of the dumbest guys.

"No he didn't. I talked to him an hour ago. I recognize your face. You're that Morgan character."

Of course, I had to get the brightest and most observant of the bunch. I decided to play stupid. "What Morgan character? Call Jeremy Jenkins. He'll explain everything."

The men inched closer. They didn't seem to let their guards down.

A glimmer of light glistened in the darkness behind the two thugs. Focusing on the backdrop, I made out two hooded figures with bows. Bronze arrow tips were readied at the base of the bows' arches. They sparkled under the dim light.

Great, more party-crashers who want me dead.

Men Shen warriors must have been camped out here, just like they were back at the Wanda Mountain.

Like my luck couldn't get any worse. Not only did I have to figure a way out of my current dilemma, but these assassins were a whole other story.

"Drop the bag," one of the mercenaries ordered.

Taking my time, I searched for escape ideas. I stood at the end of a dead-end corridor. All I had for cover was a small stone pedestal. The only way out was blocked by two men with guns, followed by two men with arrows.

I was dead meat.

That's when a surprising turn of events occurred.

The *Men Shen* soldiers tensioned the cable of their bows and released. Two arrows silently cut through the air, slicing into their targets—those targets being the heads of the two men standing before me.

The thugs collapsed to the ground, dead.

As if in a single motion, the hooded figures pulled out another arrow and, in unison, armed their bows once again.

My heart skipped a beat. Everything was silent.

Without hesitation, I raised my arms higher up in the air, saying, "I give up. I'm sorry. The tablet's all yours."

The men didn't fire.

Outside screams blared. The two warriors turned and fired their arrows at another mercenary who rushed into the cave. The thug had no chance. His body flung backward, landing on the dry dirt.

The *Men Shen* ran out the cave and disappeared from sight.

What the heck just happened?

Apparently a lot must have occurred in the past three months. Back then, these guys couldn't wait to chop my head off. Now, they saved my life.

I didn't have time to question it. I just needed to be gone.

I bolted out of the cave and back into the labyrinth.

Off to my left, a rope ladder dangled off the top of the wall of the maze. It lapped over the top ledge.

That was how the thugs got here so fast. That was probably a lot easier than the route I took. I would have liked to see them deal with the rats.

More screams echoed off in the distance. Gun fire rattled. Those hooded assassins proved to be a great distraction.

I darted up the ladder and over the wall. Landing back onto the open field of grass, I sprinted toward the camp. With all the action going on, I doubted any of the Baron's men would notice if I borrowed one of their jeeps.

Then I wondered if there would even be anyone left to notice.

The screams faded as I ran toward the camp. My mission was over. Now all I needed to do was find my old friend, Jeremy. Based on what those thugs said, he wasn't too far.

CHAPTER EIGHTEEN

The Chinese shack of a bar was silent. The only sound came from my drunken friend Jeremy Jenkins as he sat, face down, at the table, snoring away.

Taking another sip from J.J.'s half empty glass, I watched the waitress's stunned expression. I finished telling her the story of my supposed death and realized we had an audience. All the other patrons of the bar now stood behind her. My tale must have sparked their interest, because every one of them listened intently.

Now, they waited with baited breath to hear what was next.

"So what are you going to do?" the woman asked, finally breaking the silence.

"Have a drink with my friend."

Seeing them on the edge of their seat made me realize just how good of a storyteller I was. J.J. would have been proud.

A cell phone rang. The ringtone jolted everyone in alarm.

Oh they were on the edge of their seats all right.

The phone continued to ring. Glancing over, I saw it came from the pocket of J.J.'s hunched torso. The phone blared for a few more seconds then went silent.

Jeremy adjusted his body, as if getting ready to wake up, but fell back into his deep slumber. The phone rang again.

J.J.'s facial expression shifted from peaceful to angry. His eyebrows tightened downward, while his eyelids clenched shut. The ringtone seemed to annoy him, threatening to interrupt his beauty sleep.

The phone silenced.

The third time the phone rang, I watched Jeremy move. With his eyes still shut, he answered the cell. He mumbled and slurred his words slowly. "Tell me there is a strong urgency to this call."

A faint voice muttered on the other end. The tone sounded frantic and excited, but I couldn't make out any words.

Then J.J. spoke out again. "Slow down, you are not making any sense. What do you mean *you found it?*"

The other voice muffled.

"Who found it? How do you not know who found it? Don't give me this non-sense." My old friend still rested his head on the table, listening to the voice on the line. Every time his mouth opened, the stench of alcohol suffocated my nostrils. For a guy who didn't drink, it smelled like he truly had his share.

It had been months since I had heard his voice. Still, the raspy growl that resonated under his tone didn't seem like the light-hearted man I always looked up to. I chalked it up to the alcohol.

Finally, J.J. cut the voice off saying, "All right, I'll be right there, but I am telling you, there is no way you found it."

Jeremy hung up his phone and sat upright. With his eyes still closed, he yawned, *"Check please,"* in perfect Chinese.

No one responded. I leaned back in my chair, giving my friend time to fully wake. I couldn't wait to see the look on his face.

That wait was short-lived as Jeremy opened his eyes to the sight of me sitting across from him. He rubbed his eyelids and looked again. Then he noticed all the others sitting around me.

He stared at me like deer in headlights. Dead silence cut through the room. It felt like minutes had gone by before Jeremy finally spoke.

"What took you so long?" he thought aloud.

"That's all you're going to say?" I snarled back, smiling.

"You look like hell, Charles."

"I can say the same for you." I jiggled the bottle of nearly empty liquor. "You've graduated to the big leagues. I remember you to be a lightweight when it came to alcohol."

"I've had months of practice. The last few haven't been so kind."

I poured some of the last remaining drops into the cup. "It looks like yours were just as eventful as mine."

Jeremy stumbled out of his chair to hug me. We embraced. "I knew you weren't dead," my old friend said, not letting go. As the hug became uncomfortably long, J.J. finally released. "I searched everywhere. I can't believe I've found you?" he said cheerfully.

"Actually, J.J., I found you."

"We're arguing semantics here, Charles," Jeremy said.

"No, I'm just stating a fact."

Smiles were exchanged. Jeremy finally conceded. "Very well. Now tell me, where did you detour off to these past few months?"

"A group of monks found me in the river and took me in. They nurtured me back to health. It's a long story. More importantly, what are you still doing here?"

I only knew parts of the answer to this question.

J.J. sobered up miraculously fast as he filled in the blanks. "Charles, after you fell to your supposed death. I took the news rather harshly. I blamed myself for your disappearance. Unfortunately, I didn't have much time to mourn. William contacted me only days later. He informed me of the tablet he acquired, and explained that he needed my help.

"I turned him down of course, but William then broke the news that he held my daughter ransom. With you gone, he needed another expert."

"What about Alvin?"

"Oh that young man was useless. I'm surprised he's lasted this long."

"Why didn't you just go rescue her?" ·

"Because of you, Charles. I used this as an opportunity to find you. Returning back to China, I was determined. By day, I led the team of researchers to the new dig site. Honestly, it wasn't too difficult to find. You should see it. The *tree of life* is such beauty."

"You didn't see the half of it," I mumbled to myself.

"What did you say?" Jeremy asked.

"Nothing. Seeing that you're still here, I'm guessing that your search for the other segment of *Xi Wangmu's* tablet was just as good as your search for me."

"I've just been working at a snail's pace so as to buy myself more time in the area. It's been fairly easy with all the buffoons working over there. Unfortunately, one of those fellows at the dig site just called to inform me they uncovered the tablet. I highly doubt it. Most of the Baron's best researchers died three months ago. These morons don't know how to tie their own shoes."

"Well they didn't find it."

"I assume so too."

I reached into my pocket and pulled out a piece of paper. I laid it on the table and slowly unfolded it. Flattening the paper out, most of it was covered in a charcoal rubbing. Letters were easily visible in the charcoal outlines, and they were all written in Ancient Greek.

"J.J. your colleagues really do have the tablet, but they didn't find it."

Jeremy stared at the markings.

"I did."

"I used your old charcoal technique," I said as I finished retelling my story.

The Chinese bar was way past closing time, but my audience of drunks remained huddled around, listening to my tale once again.

My good friend sat upright, opposite me. His eyes studied the paper spread out over the table.

"Charles, this is magnificent," J.J. let out under his breath. "Look at the clarity in the text. It matches the same Greek dialect of the other stone tablet." He fingered the charcoal rubbing. "Your transcription work is not too shabby either, I might add."

"J.J., it looks like you're more excited about that, than learning your best friend is alive."

Jeremy looked back at me. "Of course you were alive. I knew it all along, Charles. My depression was only due to the lack of not finding you. I would have been angry if you went out so easily." A smirk developed over his face.

Now that was the J.J. I knew. "Oh really, old man? There is no way you would have survived half of what I went through."

"Charles, I wouldn't have had to. I would have been smarter than to have unlocked the gate and help William. Your job was simply to grab my daughter and leave."

"Thanks J.J. It was easier said than done."

"It always is. Like I said, I knew you weren't dead."

"That obituary you wrote sure made it sound like I was dead."

"Non-sense. I just wrote that to pass the time."

"And that hideous picture you chose? Honestly, J.J. out of all the photos we took over the years, that was what you picked?"

"How can you say such a thing, Charles? That was one our most memorable moments—when you discovered your first sarcophagus in Egypt. Remember how proud you were? I thought it fitting to have your happiest moment be the way we remembered you."

"I looked like crap."

"The camera can only do so much, Charles."

"Funny," I said. Jeremy's spark was back, and I was happy to see my old friend.

J.J.'s eyes locked with the charcoal rubbings once again. His hand delicately caressed the paper. He was entranced by the discovery. I also knew that it ate him up inside that he wasn't there to find it.

"Fire was the key, wasn't it?" J.J. asked.

"Yes."

"And the zodiac signs?"

"The rat led the way," I smiled.

Jeremy was as giddy as a boy eating ice cream. "Followed by the dragon and other animals making up the positive *Qi*, correct?"

"Yes sir. I found your tent. It pretty much solved the riddle for me."

"Well done Charles, but now you once again assisted William in achieving his ultimate goal." There was J.J.'s standard backhanded compliment.

"No, J.J., I destroyed the face of the tablet. He'll never be able to read the thing."

"You'd be surprised at his level of resourcefulness."

"It's nearly impossible. Don't worry."

J.J.'s phone rang once again. He glanced down at the caller I.D. saying, "Those amateurs are calling." He silenced the phone, adding, "We need to plan our next step, Charles."

"I was thinking the same thing."

Jeremy thought a moment. I watched, taking another sip from his glass of whiskey.

He finally spoke, "William is under the assumption you are dead. In all honesty, everyone is under such assumption. We can use this to our advantage. Currently, he resides at his home in Russia, high up the Caucasus Mountains."

"The Caucasus Mountains? That's a dangerous place for a wealthy man. It's like the Wild West over there," I exclaimed.

When I said Wild West, I meant it. The Caucasus Mountain range met at the intersection of the Black Sea and the Caspian Sea in the southern tip of Russia. It also met at the intersection of a gazillion different warring factions. From Chechnya and Azerbaijan crime families, to Muslim and Turkic terrorists, the region housed the worst of the worst. Years of civil war and violence painted the area's history.

Unfortunately, I learned this firsthand years ago when J.J. and I traveled the waters of the Black Sea. My first memorable discovery may have been in Egypt in my early twenties, but this Black Sea trip was more memorable for other reasons. That was when I was brought face to face with some Persian terrorists who wanted nothing more than to feed us to their livestock.

There were no laws, no mercy, no happiness. Being at the center of a number of countries, there was no safe zone.

A lot of illegal trafficking happened through those waters, and foreigners didn't really sit well with the natives. During our boat ride years ago, I was confined to the bowels of the cargo ship.

While traveling, we passed a series of checkpoints run by various bad guys. They all seemed the same, with the only difference being nationalities. They all yelled when they spoke. Each had guns strapped over bigger guns, over explosives, over knives. None of them had proper hygiene, and all of them were angry, all the time.

It was surprising because of how beautiful the mountains were. From snowy cliffs, lush forests, and expansive desserts, every different climate came together at one point. Taking in that scenery nearly cost us our lives.

During our trek down the river, I watched the passing landscape out of a porthole. At a checkpoint, one of these unwieldy characters saw me hidden in the bowels of the cargo ship. The men stormed the boat and found us concealed amongst the animals.

J.J. managed to smooth talk our way out of the predicament, and we continued on, unscathed. I had no idea what he said to get us out of it. My sole attention was taken up by the toothless man with a machete pointed at my neck.

Thank God for my good friend.

Why would a billionaire ever decide to buy a house in such a dangerous place?

"The Baron's home is more of a fortress," Jeremy began. "The residence retains a flare of Old Victorian architecture with steep gabled roofs and brick and stone veneers, but don't let that façade fool you. Surrounding it is a perimeter of reinforced concrete walls. Located high up the mountain, it makes it difficult for anyone to reach the compound unnoticed."

Jeremy revealed a few aerial photographs of the mountain range.

"It also provides him with a never-ending pool of bad guys for hire," I said.

"You never want to affiliate yourself with such animals, Charles."

I flipped through the photos of the Baron's mansion. "It seems like you know the place well."

"Not only have I been searching for you for the past three months, but I have also been planning my rescue operation for my daughter."

Jenny. "Have you seen her? How is she holding up?"

"She's a strong woman. Under the circumstances, she's doing fine."

"J.J. I'm sorry I didn't do a better job saving her."

"You did the best you could, Charles."

Jenny's blue eyes and long ponytail popped to mind. I hoped she was okay. "So what do you think?" I asked.

J.J.'s phone rang. He silenced it. "I don't know, but I have to get out to the site. I can't dodge these calls much longer before they figure something is aloof."

"What about me?" I asked.

J.J. got to his feet and started to compose himself. "You, my young friend, can relax for the night. I will call..." Jeremy's speech cut short as he fondled something in his pocket. His face instantly turned to a look of puzzlement. Then a grin spread from cheek to cheek.

When he pulled his hand out of his pocket, I caught a glimpse of some shiny metal clenched between his fingers. "I forgot I had this, Charles. I believe this is yours."

J.J. dropped the small object on the table.

I recognized it instantly. Picking it up, I flipped the circular object open. It was my lucky compass! "I thought I lost this," I blurted. "Where did you find it?"

"When you first disappeared, I naturally traced your steps. My search led me to the hotel room you were checked in at. I found it amongst your things. I knew how much it meant to you, so I thought I would hold onto it for safe keeping—until you were found."

That little object meant the world to me. Glancing back at my old friend, I said, "Thanks J.J."

"It was nothing. Now go get some rest. You will need it," Jeremy stated and gave me a tap on the shoulder.

"Sounds good. I need some beauty sleep. Today's been a long day, and what more can really happen in one night?"

CHAPTER NINETEEN

Caucasus Mountain, Russia

Apparently, a lot more could happen in one night.

Less than fifteen hours later I found myself in a cozy hotel room in the Caucasus Mountains in Russia. Brick framed all four walls. Splintered wood boards comprised the floor. Two cobwebbed pendant lights hung from the ceiling, flickering on and off. A battered up bed stationed itself in one corner and a small kitchen in the other.

This was a step up from China.

I went from torturous heat, to freezing cold in a matter of hours. Outside, snow covered the rocky terrain as far as the eye could see.

I honestly thought anywhere I could have gone would have been better than my previous lodging.

I collapsed in the bed, exhausted.

The pillow was hard as a rock, but I didn't care. I needed sleep. Jeremy never gave me that luxury when he left me in that bar in China.

When J.J. took off for the dig site, the lady bartender (whose name I never knew) was kind enough to offer up her place for the night. I gladly accepted. Unfortunately, I didn't get to enjoy it long. By the time we walked over to her home, one of the drunken patrons came running toward us. He had a message from Jeremy.

J.J. arrived at the site only to find the group of researchers already packing up their gear. Baron William Ruthford contacted the crew, telling them to take the tablet and deliver it to him at his home in Russia—immediately.

The mercenaries ordered Jeremy to board a helicopter and take off with the tablet. He barely got a message out to the bar before he was rushed into the vehicle.

J.J. said for me to get to the Mudanjang Airport. Not having a passport or money, it would be difficult for me to make it far in this region of China.

My head never got to touch the pillow as the lady bartender whisked me away in a barely functioning car. The road was bumpy, and the car squealed in agony the entire way. A throbbing headache pulsated through my skull by the time we reached the airport.

Jeremy met me off one side of the building. He took me to the rear of the plane. I was given money and directed to find the Krasnodar Hotel when I got to our final destination. It was one of the few safe locations in the area. I needed to check in and wait for J.J.

While Jeremy distracted the workers, I climbed through the side hatch and into the luggage hold. I found a dark corner to hide.

Cuddled in a ball, I tried to calm my nerves and relax. The blaring engines and vibrating metal hull didn't give me the indulgence. With the luggage fully loaded, the cargo hold door shut, and I was lost in blackness once again.

The flight was long and cranky. The hull moaned as the air pressure threatened to tear the ancient plane to shreds. Disgusting odors filled the compartment, and the crammed space forced my body to arch in very uncomfortable ways.

Needless to say, I didn't get any sleep.

Now, finally lying in a lump of a bed, I passed out.

It felt like the minute my eyelids touched, I blinked back awake. Only, I wasn't really awake. I knew it because I found myself back in my parent's house.

Maybe it was due to my exhaustion, or maybe it was my short stint in a coma, but my dreams kept bringing me back to this same place. Everything around me felt so real. It was funny how dreams had the habit of doing that.

I rested in a nice comfy bed. My sheets smelled like fabric softener. The room was warm and cozy...

...And I was twelve years old, once again.

This time, it was Christmas. I could tell by the snow outside, and by the fact that my mom and dad hovered over me, anxiously waiting for me to wake up. Their faces were clear as day. My mom in her flannel pajamas and my dad in a bright red robe.

For a moment, I took the sight in. It had been years since I had seen them, and my memory painted them in such a perfect light. The happiness on their faces. The smell of my mom's perfume. It made me hope to never wake up.

The last time I dreamt of this place, I was alone, searching for my parents. This time, it seemed my subconscious was giving me my wish. As I stared up at them, it dawned on me that this wasn't a full dream. It was a memory. This exact moment in particular was a memory that would forever be embedded into my head.

This was the year my parents gave me my lucky charm. Next to my bed was a small wrapped present. It sat on top of my night stand.

Like any twelve year old kid, I was a brat. I was an annoying one at that. I looked at the holiday through a very different lens than other kids. I saw it as a mystery that needed solving. My mission was to figure out what every present was under the tree before Christmas Day came. My mother hated it, but my father commended me for my resourcefulness.

As the years went on, my father's joy at my discoveries turned to innocent frustration. Year after year, I snooped out where every present was hidden and what it was.

True, it made the day when Christmas morning came a little anti-climactic because I knew exactly what rested in each and every box, but I got the biggest excitement in figuring it out. These were my first mini adventures.

My twelfth Christmas was different.

For the first time, there was one present under the tree that I didn't know. That's why that morning, both of my parents waited for me to wake.

My mother said, "Charlie, time to rise."

Followed by my father, "Come on buddy, you have some surprises to open. Or should I say, your one surprise."

Their voices sounded like echoes. Still stunned by my dream, I watched my father grab the present. I shot up in my bed. I snatched the box from him in the same motion.

"Easy now, little buddy. It's fragile," my dad said.

My body was on autopilot. It was as if I was an audience member watching a movie.

In seconds, my fingers sped over the wrapping paper, tearing away. What was left was a small leather container. I opened it.

Resting in the center was a circular brass object. It lay in a cushion of cloth. The object was no bigger than the palm of my hand. Pulling it out, I brushed my hands over the cold surface.

A small clip protruded on the one side. I pressed it and the metallic object split apart revealing an antique compass. It was the coolest thing I had ever seen.

My dad interrupted my joy. "That, my young man, is the original compass that belonged to Ferdinand Magellan, the Portuguese navigator that—"

"Led the first expedition to sail across the globe. He died in 1510 on his return trip home!" My voice rambled with immense speed. I couldn't believe it. I continued to quote text from the Magellan book I had read over and over again in the study.

My dad had watched me read through that book day after day. I couldn't believe he actually found something left behind by the man.

My mother grabbed my shoulder. "Merry Christmas honey. Now you can use this as a compass to guide you on your many adventures."

I was lost in the moment, mesmerized by the glistening object. It was beautiful.

In all my excitement, I didn't even hear the doorbell ring. My dad disappeared to go answer it. My mother gave me a kiss and followed suit. As she left the room, she said, "Now brush your teeth and come down to open the rest of your presents. Oh, and make it fast, you have no excuses for getting lost."

I woke up to the sound of clatter. It took a second to remember where I was. The lumpy bed was my first reminder—a chilling breeze, my second.

Russia.

The shutters of the hotel room window slapped the walls outside. It was getting windy out there. The cold breeze seeped through the cracked glass.

I instinctively reached for my pocket. My lucky compass buried itself there—a friendly reminder of my dead parents and my lucky charm. I gave it a little caress as I adjusted back to reality.

It was still night outside. I wondered how long I had been out. I looked at the clock and found that I slept through the entire day. It was already six o'clock.

With no sign of J.J., I rolled out of bed and decided to take a shower. It had been months since I bathed normally. The water pressure barely spit out lukewarm liquid. Calling it water would be giving the slimy fluid too much credit. It may not have been five-star quality, but it felt good.

Taking my time, I shaved, brushed my teeth, and washed my face.

The nap helped tremendously.

As I finished, I heard a knock outside my room. With a towel wrapped around my waist, I opened the door.

Jeremy stood before me, decked out in a black three piece suit. A white button up shirt and a dark red bow tie rounded out the ensemble.

"This is a rarity," I said, seeing Jeremy all groomed up. "First, you're drinking alcohol, now you're dressed like a butler. Where DID my old friend go?"

"I appreciate your humor, Charles." J.J. pushed past me into my room. Another suit hung in his hand. He laid it on the bed, adding, "But I'm not the only one who must dress for the occasion."

"Hold on a second J.J. You know me. I'm not much of a suit guy."

"Well, it's time to play the part. You need to clean up if you hope to get to my daughter."

"What's that supposed to mean? Where've you been all day?"

Jeremy pulled the suit off the hanger. "I was up at Willam's home. He was ecstatic about our discovery—or your discovery, I should say. So much so that he arranged a private function tonight to show off his new prized possession."

"To whom? There are a bunch of derelicts that live out here."

"Investors—existing and prospective."

"Investors? I was under the impression the Baron was loaded."

"I was not given the opportunity to inquire on the matter. William was fairly adamant about hosting the event. It seems like everything was already prepared for this day. The entire house is decorated for the occasion."

"Thanks for giving me the heads up. How much time do I have?"

Jeremy dropped an envelope on the bed beside my suit. "There is your invitation. The bus shall arrive for the guests at eight o'clock sharp. Make sure you're there."

Examining the invitation, I saw that J.J. wasn't kidding. The Baron really did have the event all planned out. The card was elegantly written in formal calligraphy on exquisite letterhead.

"Jeremy, you expect me to ride a bus with a bunch of other fellas who can probably recognize me?"

"Non-sense, Charles. Everyone believes you're dead. And these men most likely have no idea who you are. They won't even know who I am."

"You don't sound too confident. How does a bus get up the mountain anyways? I thought this place was located pretty high up there?"

"Well it's not technically a bus. It's a hovercraft transport. It's really quite beautiful. The craft makes it easy to climb the steep and vigorous terrain."

"Oh great. And what do we do when we get up there?"

"As I mentioned, the mansion is fortified extremely well, and the Baron has even enlisted a number of unsavory fellows to patrol the perimeter."

"Of course he has. They're a dime a dozen out here," I said under my breath.

"This event will be our most viable opportunity. Under the veil of a prospective investor, you can get down to the dungeon and grab my daughter while I monitor the party upstairs."

"Dungeon? This place sounds like something out of medieval times."

"Charles..." Jeremy's voice trailed off. I sensed the desperation in my old friend.

"Okay J.J. It sounds simple enough, but what about the escape? We're going to be thousands of feet up a snowy mountain."

Jeremy smiled at me. "Leave that part up to me, Charles. Now hurry up. We don't have much time, and I know how long it takes you to pretty your hair."

I marched over to grab my suit, smirking, "At least I have hair, old man."

"After all the stress you and my daughter put me through, why do you think I've lost it all," Jeremy joked. "Just wait until you're my age."

I grabbed the suit and headed toward the bathroom. "It's understandable to be jealous of my good looks J.J." In all honesty, I just hoped I would live long enough to be Jeremy's age. I knew that one day, my luck would run out. That was the nature of my profession. I just didn't want it to happen for many more years.

"Move along," Jeremy managed to squeeze out as I shut the bathroom door. "My daughter doesn't have all day, and I'd like to get out of this filthy region as soon as possible."

CHAPTER TWENTY

My evening started off typically enough—with me, surrounded by a bunch of deadly men. We sat inside one of the most unique transports I had ever been on. I didn't even really know what to call the thing. It was a hovercraft, but felt more like a cruise ship.

The engines of the massive craft roared through the harsh winds. Its black steel frame camouflaged itself in the night sky. Two circular propellers spun viciously at its rear. A metal platform rested on a balloon of inflated nylon. The air-filled cushion stretched out like a pancake over the rough surface. This cushion was what reduced the impact of the terrain.

A two-story passenger compartment anchored to the metal base. It looked as if the wheels of a double decker bus were torn off, and the entire hull was mounted directly to the craft. Inside, rows upon rows of seats lined the aisles, and at the front end was the cockpit.

The seats filled to the brim with almost a hundred filthy and slimy guests. Of course, I snuggled into a corner chair amongst these brutes. No one spoke. Everyone sat silently in their seats, gazing out the portholes of the craft.

Snow zoomed by as our transport headed up the mountain. The ride was loud. The deafening sound of the diesel engines hummed through the interior. Even the freezing temperatures bled into the compartment.

Adjusting my rigid tie, I tried to make the best of my current situation. All that separated my body from the leather seat was my thin suit. It did nothing to protect me from the cold. Shivering, I thought of J.J. The man prided himself on thinking of every little piece of his plans. Would it have been too much to ask for a coat to wear over this thing?

It didn't help that my tight collar felt like a noose around my neck, and my leather shoes were soaked in snow.

I hated suits.

I was the best dressed man on the craft. A few of the others dressed the part, but most of them garbed for the weather. By *weather*, I meant armed with weapons, bags of more weapons, and bodyguards strapped with weapons.

Still, I hunched down in my seat. I didn't need to call attention to myself. I needed to remain hidden.

At least the ride was smooth. It was more than I could say to the way my night started off.

Before boarding the hovercraft, I waited inside loading dock. J.J. confidently told me that I wouldn't know anyone attending the party.

He was mistaken.

At first, I concentrated on the various faces. I didn't recognize anyone. I snaked around the crowd, catching snippets of conversations. Different dialects fluttered through my ears, and I strained to pick up on a few topics.

A conversation suddenly peaked my interest. I stopped to listen. The topic seemed drab, but that wasn't what caught my attention. It was the voice. It belonged to a man I thought I wouldn't run into again. A man I had completely forgotten about.

Glancing over, I recognized the distinct features of my old benefactor, Mr. Theodore Riley. It felt like ages since I last saw him. In truth, it wasn't too long ago at all. The Paris job was only weeks before my prison break, and how could I forget his double cross.

Instinctively, I lost myself in the crowd. I couldn't help but wonder what he was doing here? Did the Baron send an invite to all the evil rich guys in the world? It didn't matter. I just knew I needed to stay far away from the man.

Now, I sat in my chair, on the opposite level from the one man who could recognize me. Watching the crowd of passengers, I remembered my short stint in the laogai prison months earlier. That bus was crammed with animals and murderers. This group seemed the same.

The only difference was that the security patrols running the transport were not short like the Chinese guards. They looked just as angry though. Trying to keep myself warm, I stared out the window at the blazing terrain.

This was the second time I set off into the unknown to save Jenny Jenkins. Hopefully this time would turn out better than the last.

The hovercraft made easy progress up the steep face of the northern Caucasus Mountain. It glided swiftly over the rocks, shrubs, and snowy hills as it climbed the angled terrain.

Nausea crept up my throat as the craft got higher and higher. The weather seemed to get worse the further up we progressed. Nearly an hour went by as the large craft continued its ascent.

This gave me time to muster up a lot of questions.

Why did Ruthford find the need to associate himself with such characters? He supposedly had billions of dollars. What would he need investors for?

And, why was he searching for these *Xi Wangmu* tablets? It couldn't be for monetary reasons. Was it fame? These thoughts rattled my brain. (It also distracted me from my jittering body.)

As the hovercraft broke through a dense pine tree forest, a beacon of light emerged in the distance. The Baron's gigantic Old Victorian home was all I could see through the night sky.

The house was over twenty thousand square feet. It stood at the edge of a cliff. We neared the building, passing the gated entrance to the property. Once through the front gate, the hovercraft slowed down, coming to a stop outside the main doors.

My body shivered as the compartment doors opened. The freezing winds rushed in. I was already an icicle, but now my teeth clattered back and forth, nearly breaking off.

The other guests systematically stood up and began funneling out of the vehicle. I snuck in line with the others and marched out of the craft.

Outside, I got a better lay of the land.

The house was enormous. Jeremy's pictures didn't do it justice. Brick and stone decoratively ran up the façade of the building. Steep gabled roofs accentuated the ins and outs of the home.

To the left was a parking lot of vehicles, but these vehicles were not cars. They were a mixture of small hovercrafts, snowmobiles, and helicopters. Turret guns mounted to the tops of them all.

J.J. was right. This place was a military compound.

To my right, the snowy mountain simply dropped away.

My quick survey of the land didn't last long. The group was ushered forward and in through the mahogany double doors.

The interior of the mansion transported me into another world. Gone was the harsh weather... the cold surfaces... the grays and blacks of the hovercraft... the angry patrolmen with guns... the rundown dirty nature of the village way below. In its place was the warmly lit interior of the foyer.

Ornate chandeliers hung from the ceiling. Animal tusks intertwined in a decorative pattern around each circular chandelier. Immaculate wainscot finishes ran up the walls, followed by vivid paint colors and wallpaper. Countless picture frames and paintings littered the walls. The largest rug I had ever seen spread over the wood flooring. Detailed mosaics trimmed out the tops of the space, leading into an exposed wood roof structure.

It was incredible.

Marble statues lined the hall. A number of displays were spaced sporadically around the room. From ancient pottery to delicate engravings, they ranged in culture and era. Glistening gold artifacts rested on other displays. These items easily made up millions of dollars' worth of discovery.

My nose led me elsewhere, though. Waiters with food-filled plates made their way to greet us. I was starving for some normal food. As nice as my stay with the monks was, the non-orthodox meals served there never really satisfied the appetite.

I picked up a few bites and made my way around the central hall.

Everyone admired the showcased artifacts. I, on the other hand, made note of the security cameras positioned around the hall. A second floor balcony looped around the great space. Suited guards with assault rifles strapped over their shoulders patrolled from above. Doors leading to adjacent rooms were all locked.

The Baron obviously didn't want guests roaming around his home.

At the far end of the room, a guard stationed himself in front of a pair of stainless steel doors. A security card reader mounted to the wall beside the doors, and a camera angled in its direction.

The dungeon's access.

This was going to be tricky.

Nonchalantly making my way to the doors, I paid closer attention to the guard. An ear piece hung from his lapel. It would be difficult to take him out silently without the others noticing.

I needed to find some other way to—

The steel doors suddenly parted. My train of thought stalled in its tracks. As the doors opened, two figures emerged out of the doorway.

My face whitened.

Standing within the framed opening were Baron William Ruthford and Alvin Mitchell.

My body screamed to lunge forward and attack, but I couldn't. Jenny sprung to mind. Charging the host of the party in plain view of everyone would only get me killed.

The two men looked happy. They didn't seem to have a care in the world. Like politicians, they waved to the crowd.

Everyone's attention turned to the two men. Mine was already locked on them.

Alvin looked my way.

I quickly turned and darted from the scene. I prayed he didn't recognize me. With the rest of the party huddling forward to see their host, I sped in the opposite direction. Shoving people out of my path, I bolted toward the rear of the hall.

I needed to hide. How dumb was I to stand there gazing at them. I was like a girl admiring a crush—eyes wide and jaw dropped. How could I have been so obvious?

I was going to ruin this rescue attempt before it even began.

I noticed the doors to the toilet room a few feet away. The perfect hiding spot.

I shuffled my way there and disappeared into the room. I held the door shut, waiting in silence. My back pressed hard against the solid wood. I expected Alvin outside, barking orders for the guards to tear down the door.

I heard nothing but my beating heart. Maybe he didn't see me. I doubt he would have believed it even if he did. I'm sure I was the farthest thing from his mind.

After a minute, my muscles loosened, and I stepped away from the door. The coast was clear.

Heading to the sink, I turned the faucet on to wash my hands.

What was I doing? I needed to be smart. I was much better at treasure hunting than sneaking around.

I was so close though. I needed to rescue Jenny Jenkins.

Keeping that thought in my mind, my pulse settled. I splashed some water on my face assuring myself, "Keep it together buddy."

I pulled out my lucky compass and caressed the metal.

I felt better.

This was going to work. I just needed to find J.J. and see what the next step was going to be. From there I would—

A toilet flushed.

I wasn't alone.

The door to the stall behind me opened. Through the mirror, I watched a man exit out of the stall. I instantly recognized his face.

Theodore Riley's eyes widened as they locked with mine.

My anger flushed back through my veins.

I acted fast.

I charged Riley.

His hand rose in defense, but he was a second too slow. My elbow rammed deep into the man's nose, instantly breaking it. Blood splattered across his face.

The sudden surge of pain would easily daze him. In the confusion, I wrapped my arms around his head and threw him into a sleeper hold.

Riley kicked and strained. He pried at my forearms, but my hands were clamped tightly around his esophagus. It wouldn't take long now.

Holding on tight, I felt Theodore's body weaken. My one hand still clenched my lucky charm, and I wondered it had just brought me good luck or bad. Within a minute Riley's body went limp. He was fast asleep. Of course I was stuck under the slumbering man.

Sweat trickled down my forehead.

It was a close call.

At least I took out the one guy who could recognize me. Selfishly, it also granted me some satisfaction. Pushing at the unconscious body, I wondered what I was going to do with him. Where would I hide him from the rest of the party?

Just then, the door to the toilet room opened and I heard the footsteps of another guest enter.

CHAPTER TWENTY ONE

"Lying around on the job now are we?" said my new guest. My sprawled body lay covered under a blanket of another man's frame. I was frozen. Looking past the unconscious body, I saw my friend, Jeremy Jenkins. "You scared the crap out of me," I said, pushing Theodore Riley off.

"Are you trying to make things more difficult?"

Jeremy helped me up to my feet.

"I didn't have much of a choice. What are you doing in here?" I dusted myself off while J.J. momentarily propped a garbage can in front of the toilet room door.

"I saw you run in here, pale as a ghost."

Wiping off the sweat stains, I said, "Yeah well maybe it's because this plan of yours is looking worse by the minute. Did you see the guard and the locked doors?"

Jeremy dropped a plastic key card on the counter followed by a small earpiece. "This will help you with the door, and it will gain you access to the lower levels via the elevator. Don't worry about the cameras. I have already handled the men in the security room. I've also taken the liberty of relieving them of their communication devices. We can maintain contact once you are down in the dungeons."

"J.J., I have to say that my breakout attempt back in China is looking a hundred times better than your plan."

"Maybe it's because you've already started a bodycount before my plan has even begun. Now help me with this poor fellow."

"This *poor fellow* got what he deserved. He screwed me out of a good paycheck a few months ago," I said, grabbing one arm.

"Are you proud of fulfilling your personal vendetta now, Charles?" Jeremy grunted as we lifted the body. "I hope no one will miss him."

"It's just a busted nose. He'll be fine. Plus, he's the only other guy here who could recognize me. You can say I did you a favor. And you said no one would know who I was."

We sat the unconscious Theodore Riley on the toilet seat. We propped his body upright and closed the stall door from the outside. Jeremy broke the metal handle, locking the fella in the tiny compartment. He then turned back to me and adjusted my tie.

"You clean up rather nicely, Charles."

"No need to brown nose, J.J."

Jeremy smiled. "I do appreciate it, my young friend. Now, our good Baron will be making a welcoming speech momentarily. That will be your best opportunity. I'll have to remain up on stage to field questions. You head downstairs and grab my daughter. Meet me in the parking lot where I'll have an escape vehicle ready for departure. It's as simple as that."

"It never is—especially with the fact that a guard is stationed right outside the elevator doors. How does your master plan account for that?" I remarked.

"I thought you'd never ask?" Jeremy pulled another object out of his pocket. It was a small black dart. A tiny tube of liquid projected out of the dart's rear.

He handed it to me. "Here's a tranquilizer."

"Where did you get this?" I stared at the object, dumbfounded.

"Charles, the Baron enjoys the sport of hunting. He has a chamber full of various rifles and ammunition. I'm positive, he will not notice if some of it has gone missing."

I recalled the Baron's sharpshooting back in China. The same tranquilizers saved me from ferocious White Siberian Tigers back then.

"This is an animal tranquilizer."

"Yes, but don't worry, it works on humans," J.J. said confidently.

"Do I need to ask how you know?"

"How do you think I took care of the men in the security room?"

I shook my head. Truthfully, the guests in the other room were more animals than men anyways. "And what do you expect me to do with it exactly?"

"You pride yourself on your creativity. I have full faith that you can come up with something." J.J. slid the garbage can and opened the door. "After you."

I found myself back in the main hall.

The other guests huddled around our hosts. The Baron's bullish figure towered over everyone. He gracefully waded through the crowd. Like a politician, he smiled and shook every hand he passed.

The sleazy Alvin Mitchell camouflaged himself beside his employer. The Australian's black suit and tie was a far cry from his outback gear I remembered so vividly. The clothes looked foreign on him.

William Ruthford, on the other hand, wore the suit like it was a natural extension of his body. The outfit looked perfectly tailored to fit his maniacal frame. His shoes glistened under the incandescent lights.

His outfit probably cost more than my entire wardrobe back home.

The two men continued to greet the guests while I ducked to the rear of the room. I needed to figure out a way past the mercenary guarding the elevator. He stood at attention, not moving a muscle.

The tranquilizer dart remained clenched in my fist. How did J.J. think I was going to get past him with this? Even if I got close to the guard, and even if I somehow managed to stab him with the dart, the point of the dart was to knock someone out. The man would collapse in front of everyone. That was the opposite of being discreet.

Plus, I doubted the man would even let me get close.

Up above, the other patrols surveyed the area. There was no way they wouldn't notice me. After this was all over, Jeremy and I were going to have a candid talk about his plan making.

I needed some sort of distraction—something to pull the guard away from his post.

I searched for an idea.

As I scanned the foyer, another guest caught my eye. While everyone else gravitated to the front of the room, one grungy looking fella hung back. His back was up against one of the displays.

Intrigue took over. Why was the man standing there? Even as I asked myself the question, I knew the answer.

Without looking, the man reached his hands behind his back. He grabbed the expensive looking artifact that rested on top of the display. In a flash, the gold trinket disappeared under the man's overly big coat.

I couldn't believe it. I thought it was risky for the Baron to have all these expensive items on display so openly. And I wouldn't put it past one of the guests to take something, but watching it happened still amazed me.

It took a lot of guts to do what he was doing. I could have warned the thief that stealing from the Baron was probably not a good idea, but who was I to lecture.

What else was crammed under that jacket?

The frumpy little man regrouped with the others at the front of the room. A light bulb suddenly went off in my head.

I found my distraction.

Creeping forward, I casually made my way toward the thief. Before I got close, William Ruthford and Alvin Mitchell took up the center stage. J.J. emerged alongside them. The Baron ordered some of his henchmen off the stage. Seconds later they returned, wheeling two large carts out onto the platform. The carts were set to one side, and the Baron motioned everyone to gather round.

Everyone settled down, and all attention now focused on Baron William Ruthford. I pretended to care, while nonchalantly nearing my unsuspecting target.

"Welcome," the Baron began. "I thank you all for your prompt responses. I understand it may have been difficult for some of you to arrange travel with such short notice. I also appreciate your patience through all the unsavory amenities this region offers. Being such an isolated area, it is difficult to facilitate the appropriate environment to entertain guests. I hope you find my hospitality gracious and welcoming.

"You have all traversed this treacherous mountain for a reason. It is not to fabricate new communal bond with one another. Nor is it to expand your realms. It is not even for fame and glory. No. Nearly one year ago I brought you all here with a promise.

"I promised you something much bigger than any monetary treasure. It was something that couldn't garner any measurable value."

The Baron took a long pause, and then continued. "I promised you a vision."

I stood directly behind my thieving friend. I gripped the dart, ready to act. Everyone seemed mesmerized by the Baron's words. Either that or they were still trying to make sense of the man's educated vocabulary. No one would notice what I was about to do.

I needed to time this perfectly.

"You took my vision on faith," Ruthford said. "Your unified desires helped cultivate a single man's belief into a collective dream. It was in its infancy at the time. The little amount of proof I had should not have been enough to earn your trust, but I forever thank you for believing.

"Over the year, I have kept you up to speed on our discoveries. Your funding made it possible to find the first clue in India. That fed fuel to our mission."

Alvin stepped forth. With a push of a button, the covered pedestal beside him split open. Inside, it revealed a large stone tablet.

Everyone *oohed* and *aahed* at the artifact. While they stared in amazement, I jammed the tip of the dart into the coat in front of me. I pricked through the cloth until I felt resistance. The needle made contact with skin. The minute it made contact, I instantly removed the dart.

I didn't want to inject too much of the anesthetic into my target. I needed the effects to take time. The man didn't even notice that I pricked him. My motions took less than a second.

Pocketing the tranquilizer, I casually stepped back.

Now, all I had to do was wait.

My gaze returned to the presentation at hand. The stone tablet on display shared similarities with the *Xi Wangmu* version we found in China. The main difference was that this one was a complete whole. Greek characters covered the stone. At the base of the pedestal, a small white card read *Tablet of Sanskrit- Found in Mount Mandara, India.*

My Chinese lore may have been rusty, but my Indian history was much stronger. I couldn't count how many treasures I sought out in that region. And luckily, I knew of *Sanskirt.*

Sanskrit was a shamanic priestess that worshipped the Buddhist goddess, *Shiva*. Many archeological digs found iconography of both the goddess and the female shaman, but *Mandara* was no real mountain range in India.

I did know the name though. It was the name of a mystical mountain dedicated to the god *Krishna*. According to legends, this eight thousand foot tall hill was located on the state highway between Bhagalpur and Dumka. The region fell well within the borders of Goa, an area along the southern tip of India.

The legend of mount *Mandara*, much like mount Kunlun in China, was another Axis Mundi—a point where Heaven and Earth met. The Goa region in India bled with prehistoric tales of shamanistic practice. Petroglyphs were found of exquisitely carved ocular labyrinths. These markings all depicted the same circular mazes.

Come to think of it, those markings seemed to match the traits of the *tree of life* maze I navigated the day before.

The pieces slowly fell into place. It seemed that both locations housed tablets written in Ancient Greek. Both locations were known Axis Mundi. And both locations were the homes of female shamans.

The parallels between the Chinese and Indian lore were astounding. Now, not only were we exploring the connection between Greek and Chinese mythology, but Indian myths fell into the mix.

How did all this tie together? What did it all mean? And how did the Baron get on this track in the first place? India was such a distant connection to China. I could only imagine what they must have gone through to get the first tablet. That took place well before Jeremy was hired.

I recalled J.J.'s tale of his distrust in the Baron. When Jeremy had his doubts, he investigated the man. It was then that he first discovered things weren't right. I remember the key to that resolution was the murder of a fellow treasure hunter...

...Eric Blake!

Blake had to have been the hunter contracted in India. Now, I saw what he found—another circular tablet with Greek engravings. Even with our rough history, I felt bad for Blake. I mean the guy never found anything, and upon making his first big breakthrough, he was murdered. What a horrible way to go out.

I too was the one of the Baron's victims, only I got lucky. I didn't die so easily.

The thief started to sway back and forth. The anesthetic was kicking in. (Either that, or the Baron's speech was boring the man.) Soon, he would pass out. I distanced myself even more from my *distraction*. My plan was working perfectly.

William Ruthford went on.

"This tablet gave us a fragment of the information we needed to achieve our goal. We needed another. If you recollect, the parchment I uncovered years ago painted a map. The map was veiled under the ruse of a simple poem. A poem by the famous Greek scholar, Homer.

"The tale detailed a great journey through many foreign lands. Homer left signs of this journey along the way—breadcrumbs to follow, if you wished to reach the final destination. This tablet was our first proof to that story."

Homer's tale led J.J. and his crew to China. Homer may have paved a road map for them to follow, but to what? What could be so important that all these men and women were throwing their money at Ruthford?

"Through the pages of this lost poem, we discerned that three tablets were needed to guide us to our journey's end. Following the clues, we can finally say we have found the second."

The Baron motioned Alvin to unveil the next pedestal. This new display opened up, exposing two half-moon fragments of stone. Pushed up against one another, they formed a concentric circle.

Xi Wangmu's tablet.

Half of the tablet was scarred and impossible to read, while the other half clearly showed the engravings that covered the stone. Murmurs fluttered through the crowd. Excitement bled through their veins. Even the Baron's voice rose with the heightened mood.

"I brought you all here tonight to reassure you that we are nearly there my friends. I promised you that within a year we would reach our goal. That year is almost upon us. I just require a little more time. My expert team of researchers are hard at work analyzing this tablet. Once we understand the text written across both artifacts, we will be on our way to our final location and the promise of immortality."

Immortality? Did he just say immortality? I stood dumbfounded while the rest of the guests hollered in joy. This guy was crazier than I thought. I dealt with many lunatics through my years in this business. Ruthford didn't seem that *out there* in China. Here, on the other hand, he might as well have had a long villainous mustache twirling in his fingers.

I found myself in the back of the crowd. The thief was a ticking time bomb of a distraction, and I needed to be as far from him as possible.

Everyone continued to holler with joy. Fading deeper into the background, it was nearly time to make my exit.

Suddenly, there was a loud thump from the center of the crowd, followed by a metallic clank.

Just in time.

All eyes turned toward the thief in the middle of the room. The man had collapsed to the floor, unconscious. His coat draped the ground like a blanket. All of the stolen objects hidden underneath rattled as they hit the wooden floor.

A number of objects rolled out from the jacket. One of those objects was the gold trinket that I watched the man steal. I was impressed by the quantity of other objects that fell out as well. The guy really did have guts.

Joyous screams instantly switched into angry roars as everyone focused on the little man. The crowd blocked most of my view, but I didn't care. I was more interested in the patrolling guards.

In a heartbeat, all the patrols on the balcony aimed their weapons at the thief. The roaring guests started to agitate. Their restlessness triggered the Baron to raise his voice. "Calm down." He tried to defuse the situation.

More angry men pointed at the thief.

The man guarding the elevator sprinted into action. He rushed the bandit, yelling for him to stand up.

The thief snored in response.

My distraction was working just as planned. J.J. would have been proud.

All eyes centered on the commotion. With the guard gone, I had a straight shot to the elevator.

This was going to be easier than I thought.

I felt invisible.

This was going to work.

"Mr. Morgan?" a voice called out from behind me.

I spoke too soon.

CRAP.

CHAPTER TWENTY TWO

"Mr. Morgan?"

The voice echoed.

It's tone was soft.

It was nervous.

It was familiar.

Whirling around, I met eyes with its origin. Standing amongst the crowd, little Lynea Ruthford stuck out like a sore thumb. Her elegant red dress, trim figure, and flowing hair instantly put her out of place. Her childish features and excited look still revealed her young age.

"Surprise?" was all I said. I was ready for our rescue plan to fail miserably. I waited for her to scream for help—to tell her dad an intruder was here.

Instead, Lynea rushed me, wrapping her arms around my body. Her bear hug got tighter, nearly suffocating my lungs.

"I can't believe it. You're alive!"

She didn't let go.

I think I may have been more surprised than she was.

Tears washed away her makeup as Lynea sobbed, "Charlie, I never got to thank you. I'm so sorry for what happened."

Other eyes started to lock onto us. The guards were taking the thief away, and all the commotion had already begun to settle. A beautiful young girl in a bright red dress would be the next best attraction.

My chameleon approach was falling apart. First, I had my old benefactor, and now the daughter of my enemy. I could only picture J.J. up on stage. He probably flipped from proud to angry.

I pried Lynea off me. "Easy there. It takes more than a fall into a raging river...or a volcanic eruption...or rabid tigers...or crazy men with bows and arrows, to take me down." A small grin flickered across my face.

Lynea smiled back. "Or crazy billionaire dad."

"Yeah, well *crazy* is a bit of an understatement."

"What are you doing here?" Lynea asked.

"How could I pass up such a show? I mean, I did help your father find part of this major discovery."

Lynea's excitement quickly shifted to concern. "Charlie, it's not safe."

"If I could survive all those other things, what's there to fear in a mansion located all the way up a mountainside, filled with angry men and freezing temperatures?"

"My father. He's going to kill you."

"He tried that once—well, technically it was Alvin who tried."

"Yeah, but now there are dozens of other guys who do this for a living."

In the distance, the Baron urged everyone to settle down. With the thief taken care of, he reeled the party back on track. The audience devoted their attention to the stone tablets on display.

A frantic guard took all the stolen merchandise away. Back at the elevator doors, the main guard already returned to his position.

I had lost my opportunity.

I pulled Lynea off to a corner. The Baron still hadn't noticed me, but it was only a matter of time.

My only shot at getting to the dungeon was blown. Now what was I going to do?

Up on stage, the Baron answered enthusiastic questions from the guests. With J.J. and company tangled up with the crowd, and with my failed attempt at a distraction, I needed a new avenue for help.

"Lynea, I'm actually here to find Jenny. Have you seen her?"

Lynea sunk deeper into sadness. "She's locked up in the dungeons. My dad didn't let her to join the party."

"But why? He's got his tablet. Isn't it over?"

The shy girl shook her head. Her frail voice seemed desperate.

"Not at all, Charlie. My dad is on a mission. This is just another stop in his search. You heard him. There's one more tablet."

"Yeah, I heard him. What's he searching for exactly?"

"I don't know. Some sort of snake. A *python*, I think. He keeps saying that all the time. All I know is that he thinks it will change the world."

"I heard his madness."

"And I'm part of his plan."

"What do you mean?"

"It's all written in that poem. There's some sort of sacrifice that needs to be made—something about the blood of a young girl. Charlie, my dad just told me about it. He said my blood will open the *Gates to Heaven*."

"Sacrifice? Why a young girl?" Reading Lynea's face I realized she was just embarrassed to say what the real reason was. Her dad needed pure blood, a.k.a. a virgin. Like every other ancient ritual, they always seemed to tie virgins into the proceedings.

Very original.

But it did make some sense. All myths about female shamans typically tied things back to the purity of the chosen woman. The purer the blood, the stronger the powers would be.

"Charlie, I don't want to be here anymore. I don't want to die."

One of the Baron's patrols passed by. It was too dangerous to stay here.

Lynea noticed it too. Her hands trembled. She guided me away from the crowd and unlocked a nearby door. She then pulled me into an adjoining room, closing the door behind us.

Books covered the walls from floor to ceiling. The aroma of dusty pages filled the expansive room. Tall bay windows lined the exterior wall, and a number of leather couches rested over elegant rugs.

The young girl brought me into the library.

"Lynea, I promise I will help you. First, I need to find Jenny. Is there a way for me to get down into the dungeons?"

"The only way down is through those doors outside. Those lead to the elevator." Lynea thought a moment. I watched her eyes scan the room. Her focus settled on one of the bay windows.

"The window!" she said excitedly. "It is directly above the storage chamber down below. If you climb down the wall from the outside, you can make it there."

I marched over to the window and propped it open. Lynea was right. Nearly forty feet below was another window directly in line with this one. Of course we found ourselves on the side of the house that butt up against the cliff face of the mountain.

That was just my luck.

The face of the mansion fell away into darkness with a straight drop thousands of feet down. A sudden draft of frigid wind stormed through the open window. My body shivered.

"This is going to be a tough climb," I said, turning back to Lynea.

"Not with this," she said. Lynea unraveled a rope from a nearby closet.

"Should I even ask?" I wondered aloud.

"My dad uses this to tie down the furniture when we're gone for long periods of time. There are a lot of earthquakes out here."

The young girl impressed me with her resourcefulness.

I grabbed the threaded rope and knotted it around a support column. Tossing the loose end out the window, it fell down the side of the house.

"Nice thinking," I said as I secured the rope.

She smiled.

Making sure the rope was taut, I climbed out the open window. The cold rattled my body. My exposed fingers instantly numbed. I started to wonder if this was such a good idea.

Anchoring my feet against the brick wall, I positioned my body away from the window sill. The angle propped me up as if I was standing sideways on the wall. Gripping the rope tightly, I gave one last look at Lynea.

"Be careful Charlie," she said.

"You know me," I quipped back. "I'll be back for you, I promise," I added, then leapt away from the wall.

The rope remained rigid, holding my body weight easily. Every jump away from the wall slid me down the exterior face of the building. As I arched back to the brick face, my leather sole shoes anchored back against the wall.

Little by little, I loosened my grip to allow my body to descend. Halfway down, I started to get the hang of it. A few minutes later, I reached the window to the storage room.

That was pretty easy.

But, then I looked at the window.

It was locked shut.

Worse yet, behind the glass, I saw wrought iron bars. It would be impossible to squeeze through.

I spoke too soon.

This wasn't working at all according to plan. Looking back up, I saw the faint silhouette of Lynea watching me dangle out in the open.

Another surge of wind flapped over my body. Shivers tingled up my spine. My muscles were already aching. Now I had to climb all the way back up.

Suddenly, a window to my right shattered.

Someone's head was thrust through the glass. I recognized the head, as well as the rest of the body that was shoved through the glass. It was the thief—the man I used as a distraction.

The thief was tugged back into the room. Angry voices bellowed through the broken window. Instinctively, I flattened my body against the brick wall. Holding my breath, I didn't dare move.

"You think you could steel from the Baron!" a voice demanded.

"I didn't take anything," another whiny voice pleaded.

"Because we caught you!" the first voice answered.

My heart skipped a beat. I stared at the open window. The voices echoed through the wind. My eyes widened. The argument continued while I remained perfectly still.

My arms weakened by the moment.

"Please, just let me go," the voice pleaded once again.

"We will let you go all right. We'll give you the express train out of here," the mercenary replied.

The thief's upper torso was shoved through the open window, breaking the rest of the wood frame in the process. Other hands forced the rest of the body through the opening. The supposed thief squirreled to get back inside while his attackers continued to push him out the window.

In his fight for survival, the thief screamed for help. His body hung upside down. He flailed his arms.

My skin paled instantly. One simple glance over, and these buffoons would see me. I hugged the wall even more and prayed that they didn't turn my way.

The thief's screams miraculously silenced. His arms dangled limp.

The man must have been so terrified, he fainted.

The mercenaries laughed through the window. "Did he pass out?" one asked.

"I bet he soiled himself too," the other commented.

Still laughing, the men pulled the body back inside. "This guy has a knack for sleep."

The first time the thief fell unconscious, it was my fault. This time, he did it all on his own.

"What do we do now?" the one mercenary asked.

"I'll take him to a cell. You fix the window."

"I'll do it later. That was totally worth it."

The guards' footsteps and laughter faded away. I let out a sigh of relief. I was back alone—hanging from a rope—locked out of the building.

Luck was back on my side though. One door may have been shut, but another just opened. Even with the cold chills up my body, I couldn't help but smile.

The broken window was my entry. My *distraction* actually did work out for me. He just worked a little differently than intended.

I swung my body back into action—literally.

The window was only a few feet away. If I could swing my torso over, I could easily grab the ledge.

I just knew I had to act quickly.

I wrapped the rope around my waist to free my hands.

Propping my body away from the wall, I hopped to my right. Then I hopped left. As I built momentum, my movements grew.

A few more leaps and I would perfectly swing to the open window.

Lynea's faint voice rang out up above. I was so deep in concentration that I couldn't make out her words. I didn't have the luxury to stop. Focused, I swung one final time.

I reached the window. My free hands clasped onto the stone ledge. Just then I heard a snap, and my full weight fell upon my arms.

They nearly ripped out of their sockets. The rope holding me up flapped in the wind and fell by. I clung onto the ledge.

The end of the rope flew past, and I saw the frayed end. The rope must have torn while grinding back and forth on the ledge up above.

My skin paled even more at the thought that I was hanging on by a single thread. I pulled myself up and through the window.

Collapsing to the ground, I let out another sigh of relief.

When blood flow circulated back into my arms, I got to my feet. Unraveling the rope around my waist, I tossed it out the window.

I made it.

I brought my attention back to my new surroundings. I was back in the comfort of the warm mansion, but this room was much different than the luxurious level upstairs. The walls, floors, and ceilings were all made of concrete. Boxes of guns stacked everywhere. This was like an armory. The Baron had enough guns to equip a small militia. Fondling the weapons, I found a small handgun. I pocketed it and made my way to the door.

"Charles, where are you?" Jeremy's voice whispered into my earpiece.

"In the dungeons," I responded, slowly opening the door.

"How did you already find a way down?"

"You sound a little too surprised J.J. Where's your confidence in me?"

"No, I just didn't have a visual on you, and the guard seems to have abandoned his post."

"I took the express route down. I'll update you when I find Jenny."

J.J. sounded intrigued. I could tell he wanted to hear about how I pulled off the miracle. I figured I'd let him sweat it out a bit. Plus, I was still trying to figure out how I even pulled it off.

After shushing my friend, I told him to remain quiet until I called for him. I had no idea what I was about to walk into.

Back in silence, I snuck out into the hallway. The hall matched the same cold concrete feel of the previous room. I stealthily made my way down the corridor. Dodging the Baron's goons was easy. Finding the right path, on the other hand, was a little more difficult.

The lower levels of the mansion were a maze of corridors. Blue fluorescent lights exuded a sickly tint to the passages, and a number of doors lined the walls.

After checking a dozen of them, each led to a dead end. I started to wonder if I was in the right area. There was only so long I would be able to dodge the patrols.

I had a few close calls. I wondered if it would be easier to just steal a uniform and walk freely. The goons probably wouldn't notice.

But then I heard Jenny's muffled voice in the distance. The voice grew as I reached another pair of steel doors.

I pried them open and entered. The next room was a long stretch of prison cells. Barred cages lined each side of a narrow hall. At my end, a small console operated the locks. A single guard stood outside one of the cells with a tray of food. He argued with a prisoner.

That prisoner was Jenny Jenkins.

"Let me out of here," Jenny demanded.

"Stop your complaining. You're giving me a headache," the guard said.

"I'll give you more than a headache when I get out of here," Jenny bellowed back.

The guard slid the tray of food under the locked gate. "Shut up and eat already."

As the two of them continued to argue, I crept over to the security console. Learning the controls, I found the lock mechanism for Jenny's cell.

"You're lucky I'm locked behind bars," Jenny yelled. I forgot how tough she was. Just like her father.

"Sweetheart, what do you think you could do to me?"

Jenny's cell door suddenly came to life, sliding to one side. My finger remained pressed on the *Unlock* button. It opened completely, and nothing now stood between Jenny and her captor.

The guard had no chance. Jenny pounced with rapid fire movements. She planted a number of hits, finally landing a punch across the man's jaw. His body went limp as he toppled over, hitting the ground with a hard thump.

"I hate to say he kind of asked for it," I said as I emerged out of my hiding spot.

Like everyone's reaction when they first saw me, Jenny was in awe. Her pause only lasted a moment before she, like Lynea before her, ran in for a hug. With all this affection, I could get used to faking my death more often.

"I see you haven't lost your touch," I said.

Jenny smiled. Tears formed at the base of her eyelids. She didn't say a word. Instead, her hug tightened.

"It was all my fault," she finally mumbled.

"Jen, it was no one's fault. I was the idiot that opened the gateway," I assured her. "But if you keep hugging me like this, my death will be your fault."

She let go. I wiped her tears away, adding, "Technically, I should apologize because I didn't finish the job your dad sent me out to do in the first place."

"I know. I've been waiting," Jenny quipped back. "What took you so long?"

She truly was her father's daughter.

Even locked up in a dungeon for a few months, Jenny looked radiant. Her blue eyes sparkled and her blonde hair looked perfect.

"I assume that, like J.J., you knew I wasn't dead." I said, entranced by her gaze.

"Alvin assured me. He said that you would survive."

"Alvin? The guy who kicked me out to my death?"

"Charlie, he said he had to. William ordered him to kill you when you boarded the helicopter. He didn't know what to do and figured you had a better chance surviving the fall rather than have to kill you."

"Or maybe he didn't have the guts to kill me with his bare hands, so he let Mother Nature do it."

"Charlie?" Jenny caressed my cheek. "What happened?"

A groan answered for me.

I looked over and saw the thief sleeping in one of the prison cells. He slowly awoke from his short nap. Our eyes locked. I saw the surprise on the man's face, followed by a dropped jaw. "Help!" the thief screamed.

"Once second," I paused Jenny's question.

The man screamed from the top of his lungs. He grasped his prison bars tightly. I had to shut him up. Marching up to the panicked thief, I pulled out the tranquilizer from my pocket.

I jammed it in the man's chest. In an instant, the short man collapsed to the ground, right back to sleep. This was quickly becoming the norm for the guy.

My focus returned to Jenny. "Where were we?" I asked.

"You were about to tell me about your three month vacation," she smiled.

I sped through my story as I carried the unconscious guard into a cell. I locked him up. After catching her up to speed, I said, "That about sums it all up. Now, we've got to get out of here. This time, I'm not failing."

"We need to help Alvin."

"Not again Jen. I'm sorry, but this time it's only you."

She didn't second guess me. "Is my dad here?" She asked.

"Yeah he's upstairs. Don't worry, we have a plan."

"I've heard that before," Jenny said, smiling.

I propped open the door and tugged her back out into the corridor. Holding Jenny's hand brought back memories of the old days. Her soft skin wrapped in my grasp as I led her along.

I shook my head to regain focus.

"J.J., I found your daughter. We're heading to the elevator now," I spoke into my earpiece.

"Good work, Charles," Jeremy muffled back.

"We'll be up shortly. Now's the time for your escape plan," I commented.

"I'm already on it. I'll see you upstairs," J.J. said.

Rounding a corner, we entered another long hall. We dodged some more patrols until finally, the elevator was in sight. Unfortunately, so were two guards. With their backs to us, they seemed to follow a standard route. Quickly, we cut into a side room and closed the door.

It was going to be difficult to get past them unnoticed. "Any ideas?" I asked.

Jenny didn't respond. She seemed distracted.

Turning around, I saw why. Resting on a table was an ancient leather bound book. Delicate pages filled the bindings. A large map mounted to the far wall with pictures and notes pinned up around it.

We found ourselves in the Baron's study, and smack dab in the middle of the room was the poem by the famous Greek poet, Homer.

CHAPTER TWENTY THREE

The magnetic desire for archeology sucked Jenny to the ancient artifact. The Baron had mentioned the importance of Homer's book, but this was our first chance at seeing it in person. J.J.'s daughter couldn't resist.

Within seconds she began reading the pages. It was as if she was entranced. The urgency of our escape drifted away.

"We don't have time for this, Jenny," I said. Who was I kidding though? I too drifted toward the book.

"Charlie, this is what started all this—what the Baron has been looking for. Aren't you the least bit intrigued?" Jenny's eyes sparkled with excitement.

The delicate pages were filled with Greek letters. Nearly a hundred sheets lined the bindings of the leather book.

"You read Ancient Greek?" I asked.

"Most kids learned Spanish or French in high school. My dad thought it more pertinent to learn an ancient language that wasn't used in modern society," she mocked and continued flipping through the book. "Of course, I never really paid attention."

I looked confused.

"I dated a Greek guy for a while. It reignited my interest," Jenny said. I could have done without knowing another one of her ex-boyfriends.

I diverted toward the map on the wall. Photographs were pinned up all around it. Taking a closer look, I saw an array of photos of a mountain. Multiple stone ruins littered the landscape. The images were instantly recognizable.

"Jen, that's Delphi."

Delphi stood as a famous archeological dig site in Greece. Located in the southwest side of Mount Parnassus, in the valley of Phocis, it was a major tourist attraction and syllabus material J.J. required me to know in order to graduate to treasure hunter status. Jenny and I spent many hours walking through the site when we were younger.

Looking at the pictures now, I made out the distinct terraces that formed the ancient pavilion as well as the center sanctuary dedicated to the Greek god Apollo—a sanctuary that now lay in rubble. Apollo, the son of Zeus, was one of the famous Olympian deities of ancient Greece.

Greek deities were rich with history. My fondest memories during my stint as a homeless boy, were the days I spent at the library reading the stories of Hercules, Daedalus, and other Greek myths. These massive adventures had everything from half human, half animal Centaurs, to legends of the evil Medusa who could turn one to stone with her gaze. The Greek gods were larger than life, and in a nutshell, each harnessed a distinct trait.

Zeus, the king of all the gods, wielded the power of lightening. Poseidon controlled the ocean. Other gods possessed powers ranging from human emotion such as love to the more dangerous ones like the underworld and war.

Apollo controlled one of the most important elements—the power of Light and Sun. He had also been known to have the power of truth, prophecy, poetry, and healing.

Jenny stepped over to the map, acknowledging, "You're right." She brushed one of the photos. We had fond memories playing hide and seek within the various ruins. Jenny's favorite area was the center sanctuary. Even amongst all the dilapidated structures, it was still a beautiful sight.

Scanning pictures, each brought back more memories. Every structure was exactly as I remembered it. Even though many years had passed, not a single thing had changed.

Everything was familiar...until suddenly, it wasn't.

Jenny saw it first. She pointed to a photograph. "This is new."

I paused on the same image. It was a dark chamber. I had never seen it before. "Where is that?"

Jenny thought a moment, then wondered, "Could it be the inner hearth?"

The inner hearth was an area believed to be located in the center of Apollo's sanctuary. According to myth, that was where an eternal flame burned. (They were fairly literal about the whole *god of light*) With the temple in ruins, not much evidence was left of the chamber.

Inspecting the image, we distinguished that the room was located underneath the main sanctuary. Spotlights illuminated the stone-walled room. At the far end rested a small stone statue.

"That's interesting," I thought out loud.

"What?" Jenny asked.

"That statue is of a Delphic Sibyl. It represented Pythia, the Oracle of Delphi. You remember her right?"

As if insulted, Jenny responded, "Charlie, you mean Pythia, the oracle dedicated to Apollo?"

The legend went like this...

Apollo slew Python, a dragon that lived beneath Delphi. The dragon protected the core of the Earth. When it was slain, its body disintegrated into a spring that ran up to the surface. The Oracle was the priestess who drank from the spring and suddenly gained the power to see the future. She was named Pythia, after the Python, but was later known as Apollo's Oracle. She was quite possibly the most powerful priestess known to man.

"Yeah, and who was the first person to ever write about this myth?" I said with a grin.

An exclamation point went off in Jenny's head. "Homer!"

"Doesn't the story of the Oracle sound somewhat familiar?"

Jenny stepped away from the photographs. "*Xi Wangmu* had the same power."

"Yes ma'am. Upstairs, Lynea told me her father needed to sacrifice her to a python. She thought it was a snake, but in reality it was Pythia. She just didn't fully understand what her father was saying."

I examined another photo. Positioned under the sibyl statue was Homer's leather book. "This is where the Baron found his first clue."

"But clue to what? Pythia's treasure?" Countless stories alluded to kings from across the land seeking the Oracle's council. They brought their most valuable treasures to the Oracle in return for glimpses of the future, of outcomes of wars, of hopes to survive winters.

Jenny turned back to the book at hand. "I have no idea, but I'm sure Homer's book gives a good reason." She scanned through a few pages while I continued to study the images.

I saw a picture of Eric Blake in India. There were shots of their discovery. One photo showed a full image of the stone tablet they found. I yanked it to get a better look. Another photo showed the first half of *Xi Wangmu's* tablet. I grabbed that as well.

I wondered how the two pieces related. Why would they go to all this trouble to create a map and separate it into pieces? Through my history, when all these hoops created such difficulties, it either led to something evil, or to very anti-climactic dead ends.

More often than not, they were the *evil* dead end kind.

My wonder ceased when Jenny Jenkins muttered, "Oh my God!"

I darted back to Jenny. Her mouth lip synced the words scribed on the written page.

"You find something?"

"Charlie, I found what this is all about."

That was quick.

Jenny continued, "My Ancient Greek is a little rusty, but I think I got the gist. Homer details a journey across the lands. He started in Delphi, the center of the Earth."

In ancient times, the Greeks believed that Mount Parnassus was the middle of the world. Gaia, the Mother Earth, was located deep below the mountain. Gaia was the strongest power in the world, giving life to everything. This desire for power was what led Apollo down the mountain. His search for Gaia led to his confrontation with the Python. Her destruction marked the creation of Delphi which earned the label *omphalos*, or naval, of the Earth.

"This wasn't just a journey, it was a funeral procession."

"For whom?" I asked.

"The Oracle herself." Jenny flipped to the next page. "Homer detailed an expedition to carry the body of Pythia to her final resting ground. Many believed she was buried at Delphi in Greece, but apparently that is not true.

"A group who labeled themselves the *Sons of Apollo* carried the epitaph. Her resting place was to be guarded in secret. Only those worthy would be able to find it." Jenny read some more, "It details the grave's location on three stone tablets. Together they mark the final location of Pythia's temple."

"So, just like I said months ago, the Baron is searching for a dead fortune teller."

"Charlie, she wasn't just a fortune teller. She was THE fortune teller. These *Sons of Apollo* carried her casket to the far reaches of the globe to teach other cultures of her power. If this is true, then you could say the Oracle of Delphi was the originator of all these other shamanistic beliefs."

I pondered this for a moment, then had a revelation. "Ruthford isn't looking for immortality at all. He thinks that if he finds the burial place of Pythia, he can harness her power."

Jenny was quiet. She was deep into deciphering a line of text. Quietly, she said, "Yes Charlie. There is a detailed ritual of how the process works. Some of the words I can't comprehend, but it has something to do with a sacrifice."

"Lynea," I whispered to myself.

"But William only has two of the three stones."

I investigated the pictures in my hand. "Homer couldn't make it easy. He always felt the need for symbolism," I said.

"What?"

Jenny stepped in close. It was as if the rest of the world came to a halt. Like the olden times with her father, we had enveloped ourselves with the hunt. We sat on the edge of a mystery.

"Jen, the Holy Trinity," I began. "In Greek religion, they believe that God is made up of three people—the father, the son, and the Holy Spirit. Each person is united to the other. The father creates the son, and the Holy Spirit proceeds him. Together the three make up one's existence. Because of that, Greek theology uses the symbolism of the number *three* in everything."

Jenny agreed, saying, "In every Greek wedding I've ever been to, they did everything three times. They did their crosses three times, walked around the altar three times, and even exchanged their wedding bands three times."

"Yes, that number has great significance in their culture. It's a powerful bond that is reflected in all Greek ceremonies. The Holy Trinity brings everything full circle."

"And you think the reason there are three stones is because of religious rituals?" Jenny interjected.

"Hey, the tablets are circular. Apollo is the god of the sun. Holy Trinity is a circular symbol. I mean, the shoe fits," I finished.

"And the Baron wants to wear it."

My earpiece came alive. It was J.J. "Charles, where are you two?"

As if kicking us back to reality, I said, "We're just reminiscing about your old history lessons."

"No time for foolish antics. William and Mr. Mitchell are heading your direction. They just entered the elevator."

It was time to go. I ripped a few more photos off the wall and pocketed them. Grabbing Jenny, we ran out of the room and back into the corridor.

We didn't get far.

Entering the hallway, I stumbled upon the patrol which happened to be passing by. The two men didn't hesitate to pull out their weapons.

Jenny acted first, attacking the closer of the two men. Her motion sprung me to action. I rushed the second.

I was surprised at the clumsiness of the guards. They put up very little fight. Within a few seconds, we subdued the two men and left them on the floor. Jenny held her own, which was impressive. She feared nothing.

We grabbed our fallen assailants' rifles.

"Charlie, this is your rescue, so where to?" Jenny asked.

"Nowhere," another soldier barked from behind us.

Our fun was over.

Raising my hands, I turned to face the man. His gun pointed right at me. I whispered into my microphone, "J.J. it looks like we could use some help."

"I assumed you would. I've already begun mobilizing a distraction. Give me a few moments," Jeremy responded.

"I'm not sure if we have that long."

This wasn't good.

A *ding* rang and the nearby elevator parted its doors. The Baron and Alvin exited.

"Mr. Mitchell, it looks like we have some surprise visitors," William Ruthford bellowed, half laughing.

Things just got worse.

"I believe I owe you many thanks, Mr. Morgan," the Baron said.

My mind raced. Confronted by the two men who tried to kill me, I wanted to lunge at them. The thug with the gun behind me made that impossible.

So I did what I did best, I stalled. "Why do you say that?"

"I am not a fool. You have proven to be a rather resourceful individual. I know you were the one who found the second half of my precious tablet. The men I stationed there couldn't hold a candle to your capabilities."

"And you bet on the wrong man." I motioned to Alvin.

Ruthford glanced over to his associate. "Mr. Mitchell has other talents," the Baron said. "But let us not sway our focus from you. I am enamored to see you alive and well."

I wondered what Alvin's *other* talents might be. "Thank you for your high praise...and you're welcome. I seem to be doing your job for you. Again, I helped you on your little fortune telling expedition."

"Not quite, Mr. Morgan. You see the second half of the tablet is scarred rather badly. I assume that was your handy work."

"You give me too much credit." I played stupid.

"Please, Mr. Morgan. Let us not forget, I saved your life from those tigers."

"Because I still had your precious treasure," I said.

Ruthford got back on track. "I know what you did—defiling that stone. But I also know what kind of man you are. I read it the day you helped me open the front gates to our Shaman's temple. You seek out adventure. It is in your blood. I know you couldn't have destroyed such a remarkable discovery without making some sort of copy."

"Then you don't know me well enough."

The Baron smiled. It was a mischievous grin, as if he hid something. "Mr. Morgan, then explain this. Why were there traces of charcoal on the floor of the pedestal where the tablet stood?" The Baron paused for dramatic effect, then he continued, "I'm sure you wondered why I hosted a party this evening? Why I brought all these hardened criminals to my home."

"I assumed your kind all hang out together—share tales about the hard lives you lead; the people you've killed. Things like that."

"There is that sly humor. No Mr. Morgan, this was all for you. I knew you were alive, and I was overjoyed when our cameras picked you up at the docking station at the base of the mountain. You have a keen desire to always help people. There is no way you would leave young Ms. Jenkins alone with me."

I looked over at Jenny.

"Don't worry, Mr. Morgan," Ruthford said. "She was treated like a princess."

"Locked away in a dungeon?" I pointed out.

"Isn't that how princesses always live in fairy tales? Ms. Jenkins has a knack for starting trouble during these types of gatherings. It was an unfortunate circumstance that I am not proud of."

"Well thank you for taking care of her," I said dryly.

The Baron nodded in acknowledgement. "I'm glad you two are finally reunited, but I was more intrigued by your reunion with my daughter. From your short time together, the poor girl has developed such a crush on you."

"That *poor* girl is your daughter. A daughter that you plan on killing."

"A sacrifice for the greater good, Mr. Morgan. I don't expect you to understand what I am hoping to achieve. Nevertheless, I do require your assistance. I held this event tonight to bring you here, so you can provide me with the final text written on that stone tablet."

"I'm sorry to be the bearer of bad news, but you're out of luck, Ruthford."

"Please Mr. Morgan. You have helped us tremendously up to this point. Don't ruin the good relationship we have established. All I ask is for one last little item, and you and Ms. Jenkins are free to go."

"You know how many times I've heard that line before? I learned my lesson the first time I believed it," I said.

The Baron's tone escalated. His smile disappeared, and his mood turned fierce. "Listen Mr. Morgan. You will give me the answers or else. Do not presume that I will not resort to violent measures."

"I'm sorry Mr. Ruthford, but I don't trust you. Your track record doesn't paint a good history either. I'll have to decline."

"I beg that you reconsider, Mr. Morgan. You will be part of the greatest discovery man will ever see." The Baron's tone remained harsh.

"You think finding Pythia will give you the power to see the future? You're more psychotic than I thought. But, if you do truly believe that, then you need me more than I need you, pal. Those so-called guests upstairs funded your little expedition and will soon want something in return. When you can't provide it, I think you'll have bigger worries on your plate than me and my friends."

"Just give it to him, Charlie," Alvin chimed in.

"Don't get me started with you," I cut the Australian off.

Ruthford spoke, "I am extremely disappointed, Mr. Morgan. I do not wish to hurt you, but my guests upstairs specialize in getting information out of people."

"I can hold my own."

"What about your *friends?* These men are savages. They do not draw moral boundaries." The Baron paused for a moment. He took a long breath, then calmly said, "It is a shame you are forcing me to go this route. There is no way out of here."

"Like you said earlier, I am a resourceful man," I said stubbornly. Even as I uttered the words, my eyes searched the hallway for some form of escape. My mind raced with ideas, but each one came to a dead end.

I glanced back at the soldier standing behind us. I whispered into my microphone once again, "J.J., status update?"

Jeremy instantly responded, "Working on it. How far away from the elevator would you say you are right now?"

I redirected my attention to the bullish man in front of us. "You know Baron, another fifty feet and we would have been long gone in that elevator."

"Perfect," I heard Jeremy say.

In the same turn, Ruthford responded, "Then it is fortunate that Mr. Mitchell and I came when we did. Now come, Mr. Morgan. Heed my request. I know you will do the right thing. In the end you do not want anyone to get hurt. You always want to play hero. Just like you did with your parents?"

The Baron hit a chord. My body tensed up. Did he know about my parents? Jenny grabbed my arm to hold me from attacking the ginormous man. I was so focused I forgot she was there. Easing down, I glanced back at her. She signaled caution.

Whispering into my microphone, I said, "J.J. now's about the time for your little distraction."

"Easy Charles. Just a moment longer."

The Baron pulled out a gun. He handed it over to Alvin saying, "Mr. Mitchell, please shoot young Ms. Jenkins in the leg."

Alvin grabbed the handgun. He aimed it at Jenny's still body. His hands trembled. "Is this truly necessary?" he pleaded.

"Unfortunately, unless Mr. Morgan cooperates, yes," Ruthford commanded.

I spoke a little louder into my microphone, "J.J. you better do it now!"

"Brace yourselves!" Jeremy yelled back through the earpiece.

Suddenly, an explosion roared from up above. The entire foundation of the house shook violently. Concrete crumbled from the ceiling. Reinforced walls chipped away under the pressure.

Another explosion vibrated above.

I grabbed Jenny and dove back as the ceiling around us collapsed.

Clouds of smoke instantly funneled through the narrow corridors while sirens blared alive.

And then there was darkness.

CHAPTER TWENTY FOUR

E mergency lights flickered. Dust and debris fogged up the dimly lit corridor. Screams rang through the halls.

And Jenny lay trapped under my protective body. "Are you okay?" I asked.

"What was that?" she coughed.

"Your dad's distraction." I got to my feet. A large cave-in of concrete separated us from Ruthford and Mitchell. More importantly, it separated us from our elevator getaway.

"Charlie, did it work?" Jeremy screamed into my ear.

"DID it work? What the heck did you do?" I asked. My vibrating head slowly churned to take in all the wreckage. The guard behind us was on the ground, dazed. I didn't give him a chance to orient himself. With a quick jab, I knocked the man out.

"I obtained some C4 from one of the attendees. I didn't really have many options," Jeremy's voice rang back into my throbbing head.

"And you thought blowing up the building was the most viable solution?"

"Sorry, Charles. I wasn't awarded much time. Based on a quick structural analysis, and knowing your distance from the elevator, I easily determined which structural member to destroy."

"What?" I asked, dumbfounded.

"It doesn't matter now. How is my daughter?" Jeremy's voice switched to concern.

"She's fine. But we're stuck. How do we get up to you?"

"There must be a stairwell. Such a large facility should have ample paths of egress," J.J. said. "Just follow the screams."

J.J. was right. Others down in the dungeons scrambled for exits.

Lifting Jenny to her feet, we bulleted down the corridor. Soon we found a slew of men screaming like little girls. No one seemed to care who we were. They just fled for their lives.

We followed a group of mercenaries through one of the random doors. Inside, a metal stairwell led up to the first floor.

Sprinting up forty feet of stairs numbed by limbs. As we neared the top, I snidely commented, "How come every time I see you, we're always running from something?"

"Listen mister, I was sitting comfortably in a quiet little cell until you came along," Jenny breathlessly retorted.

"I can always put you back there," I said.

"Or you and my father could have come up with a better plan."

"I can't be held accountable. This was all his idea."

We reached the first floor and burst into the main corridor. Pausing for a moment to catch our breath, we stood amongst the other tired men.

Our moment to relax was broken as a radio chimed with the Baron's voice. "To all men. I order you to bring me Charles Morgan, ALIVE! As incentive, I offer you a one million dollar reward for his capture."

I stared at the radio dangling from one of the soldiers' belts. All the exhausted henchmen heard it. That's when they noticed me. I stood in the middle of the crew.

My luck flipped instantly.

I yanked Jenny and sprinted in the opposite direction of our attackers. They fumbled after us, readying their weapons in the same motion. We cut into a side room and slammed the door shut. With the force of a battering ram, the horde of men pounded at the door.

Wood splintered as I struggled to keep it closed. "A little help here?" I quipped.

Bullets tore through the wooden door.

"I thought these guys wanted you alive?" Jenny asked.

"They're not the brightest bunch," I said as another ram dug the door into my back. Jenny disappeared behind a dresser. "Anytime now, Jen."

Jenny shoved at the dresser, adding, "I never remembered you being this demanding." Straining, she tipped the heavy object over. "Watch out!" she yelled and I moved out of the way. The mahogany casework crashed onto the ground, blocking the doorway. "How is that?"

The door was covered by the heavy object. The banging from the other end didn't cease, but the object held the door shut.

"Not bad," I acknowledged.

We found ourselves in a large ballroom. Fire crept up the far wall of the room. Expensive furniture went up in flames. The marble floor cracked and skewed all around.

That explosion really took its toll on the building. The entire place was going up in smoke.

We needed a way out.

The far end of the ballroom led to an adjoining space. Before we could bolt toward it, the windows against the outer wall shattered. Mercenaries stormed into the ballroom, guns blazing.

We dove for cover behind a couch. Bullets blasted around us.

"Yup, these guys didn't get the *alive* memo either," I said, pulling out my hand gun.

Jenny nodded.

I checked the magazine. Two bullets left.

I fired a shot wide.

The mercenaries responded tenfold.

The door behind us cracked ajar an inch. Our other pursuers were hot on our tracks.

"J.J. any way you can provide some more of your assistance?" I screamed into my earpiece.

"Where are you Charles?" He asked.

Risking a glance over the bullet riddled couch, I fired my last shot. The bad guys ducked behind their own protection. That would only hold them back another moment or two.

Out the shattered windows, I saw headlights dance around in the darkness. Engines rumbled. The ballroom was next to the parking lot—the one filled with snowmobiles and hovercrafts.

"We're in the ballroom on the west side of the house," I said to J.J.

"In that case, I couldn't have planned this better myself," J.J.'s voice rang back. "Stay down," he added.

"Planned what better yourself?" I retorted. Another explosion rocked the mansion. The blast came from the outside parking lot.

A great ball of yellowish red light filled the voids of the shattered windows. The ball of fire blinded us, followed by a massive tidal wave of pressure. Flames bulldozed through the windows.

Instinctively, my body flung over Jenny's. A momentous force stormed the ballroom. As if coming from a dragon's mouth, narrow spears of fire pulsated through the windows and into the grand room. All of our attackers were engulfed in fire. They ran around in panic, then dove out the windows to roll in the snow.

Again, I found myself on top of Jenny. "I typically have a lot better moves than this," I said trying to lighten the mood.

"I doubt it. Don't get used to it," she said smiling. In all the chaos, I could see a hint of excitement in her eyes. She truly was her father's daughter.

"If your dad keeps this up, neither of us will," I added.

J.J.'s voice came alive once again, "Charles, I incapacitated a few of William's vehicles outside."

"A few?" I chimed back. "How much of that C4 did you get?"

"Quite a bit. Don't forget the company we are in. I was in the process of masking our escape, but it worked better than I expected."

I took in all the destruction. It sure did work well.

J.J.'s voice came back once again. "I'm outside the main entrance. Now, come meet me there. I believe we have overstayed our welcome."

Getting to our feet, I saw an opening across the ballroom. It was clear, minus the fires, shards of glass scattered over the floor, and crumbled ceilings. The door behind us cracked wider. Our previous pursuers continued their efforts.

We bolted across the ballroom and into another hall. On the way, I grabbed a weapon or two from our fallen victims.

My heart pounded. Scorching hot flames made it difficult to breathe. We zig-zagged around the corridors until we reached the main foyer.

The room was deserted. Most of the guests had already escaped in the chaos. All that remained were a few dead bodies. The front doors were wide open. "Come on!" I yelled, pulling Jenny forward.

Halfway to the doors, we stopped in our tracks. A man dressed in full body armor strutted his way through the front door. Another soldier stood behind him. The armored man held what looked like the biggest Gatling gun I had ever seen. Six barrels radiated in a circle with rows of ammunition hanging from the gun.

Without saying a word, he fired.

The six barrels spun as shells were fed into each chamber. They ejected each cartridge in rapid succession.

Bullets tore up the floor in a constant stream. Walls splintered and glass exploded as the path of destruction headed our way. I helplessly fired a round or two, but Jenny tugged me away.

We sped across the open floor and crashed into another side room. We narrowly escaped the path of fire.

"Now it's official. The Baron does not want me alive," I said, rolling on the floor.

"Where does he find these guys?" Jenny retorted.

"More importantly, where does he find those weapons?" I added.

A stream of bullets exploded through the wall and cut over our heads. A clanking sound echoed around us. Looking over, I realized why.

We were in the main kitchen. Bullets pinged off the hanging pots and pans.

Crawling on our hands and knees, we sped across the floor. Bullets continued to destroy everything in sight. Stoves and ovens were still on, overcooking whatever was inside. Smoke made it nearly impossible to see. We reached a far door and propped it open.

Blazing fires filled the next room. Slamming the door shut, I searched the kitchen for another route.

Jenny frantically checked the windows. Of course, luck would have it that we were on the cliff side of the building.

"Any bright ideas?" Jenny asked.

More gunshots tore through the ceramic tile and across the room. With all the smoke, my eyes started to water. The soldier was closing in on us, and we were trapped. I could hear muffled voices outside.

Then I saw it.

Nearby, there was a small dark square on the wall. Crawling to it, I got a better view. It was a dumbwaiter built into the wall. Prying its doors open, I found a miniature elevator platform inside. The narrow shaft led straight up to the second floor, and down to the basement. This was what they used to deliver food to the other levels. It was also going to be our escape.

"You think you can fit?" I asked.

Jenny gave me a dirty look and squished herself into the small opening. "Do you think YOU can?" she asked back.

"We'll find out soon enough." I shut the elevator doors.

"Charlie?" Jenny muffled through the metal door.

"Don't worry, I'll see you in a second."

I pushed the *up* button, and the elevator started its ascent. Jenny disappeared into darkness.

With all my focus on Jenny and the dumbwaiter, it suddenly dawned on me that things were quiet. I mean yes, there was still the clatter of pans swaying back and forth, fires burning, and water boiling—even an entire building was burning down—but in a scenario where bullets continued to buzz past us at a steady rate, when they suddenly stop, you really notice.

I spun around.

A mercenary greeted me.

Before I could speak, the man swung his weapon. The butt of the gun slammed into my head, tumbling me backward. I raised my arms to defend myself, but another slug from the weapon knocked me off balance.

I dropped my gun.

As I regained my footing, I reached out for any kind of rescue.

My fingers touched something. Something mushy. Without hesitating, I grabbed the object and swirled it at my assailant.

The slimy fish clutched in my hand smacked the man. It folded easily under the pressure, barely making any sort of impact.

He laughed.

I swung the fish again, but it innocently smacked the large mercenary once more.

Another barrage of bullets sliced through the room causing us to duck. My attacker's trigger happy friend with the Gatling gun was still outside. He didn't seem to care that his buddy was in here.

At least the gunshots wiped that grin of my attacker's face. In its place was an angry scowl. He dove toward me. I didn't even get a chance to dodge. The large figure shoved me to the ground.

I struggled a moment, but the man's legs pinned me down hard.

"Easy now tough guy," the soldier growled. "I need you alive for my reward."

"That's easy for you to say," I barely exhaled. "Your friends didn't seem to care."

The soldier smiled. He pulled out his radio.

I, on the other hand, still clenched onto the dead fish. While the man called in for back-up, I dug my fist into the flesh of the animal. I slowly wrapped my fingers around the prickly spine of the fish. Even though it wasn't too rough, I hoped the sharp ribs would be enough to cause some sort of damage.

I hoped.

As the man re-directed his attention toward me, I pulled my hand free of the slimy animal. The bloody spine clenched in my fist. Holding the bones like they were brass knuckles, I thrust at the bully's face.

The impact caught him off guard. Bone sliced deep into his skin, instantly flushing his cheeks red. Punching again, I gashed his nose. The mercenary arched back in pain.

That was my chance.

I slid out from under his legs and crawled toward my rifle. It lay a few feet away. I scrambled as fast as I could...

...But the mercenary was quicker. The man leapt back on top of me. Screams of anger filled the foggy room.

The gun was just out of reach. The heavy body on top of me started pulling me back. Thinking fast, I switched to plan B. Next to me, the oven door was shut. Feeling the heat, I reached out and yanked the door down.

A heavy black cloud of smoke sucked out into the room blinding both of us. The mercenary coughed while I slipped back out of his grasp. I slid away and picked up my rifle.

The soldier stood five feet away. Through the haze, I fired.

Tick, tick, tick, was all I heard.

Of course, the magazine was empty.

The man charged.

Using the rifle like a bat, I swung at a heavy pot of boiling water. The pot tipped over the stove, drenching the lower half of my attacker's body.

In the same instant, I kicked the man to the ground and raced for the dumbwaiter. It had to be down by now.

And it was.

While the mercenary rolled on the floor, hunched in pain, I climbed into the small box. Back-up would arrive any minute. I didn't have much time.

I slid the door shut. The platform strained upward, while I crammed into the tiny little elevator cart. The gears ground, struggling to pull my heavy weight.

The dark metal shaft seemed to continue on endlessly. Up above, I saw Jenny's silhouette. She was screaming, "Charlie, what's taking so long?"

"I had a lunch date," I quipped. I was nearly there.

Suddenly, there was a jolt.

The cables hoisting the food cart strained under my weight. They began to tear. My cart dropped an inch, but continued to rise.

The entire platform rattled. I could see Jenny's face closing in. Just a little bit farther.

Another snap and another jostle in the cart.

Reaching up, my fingertips grazed the ledge of the opening above.

A final crack echoed through the shaft as the hoist mechanism above completely crumpled from my weight.

My hands latched onto the ledge just as the cart fell. My contorted body yanked on my wrists as my firm grip kept me from falling.

Gears and pulleys ricocheted down the metal walls of the shaft, hitting me in the head. It wasn't enough that my head was already throbbing from all the explosions.

But I was still alive, and I was still dangling below the second floor opening of the dumbwaiter. Pulling myself up, Jenny helped me into the floor above.

I collapsed to the ground, exhausted. "Thanks," I panted.

"It was nothing," Jenny said. "But Charlie, you are not going to believe this."

"Believe what?" I said, opening my eyes.

"Look," was all Jenny Jenkins said.

I followed her gaze to take in the full extents of our surroundings.

I was speechless.

CHAPTER TWENTY FIVE

I was transported to another world.

Stark white walls surrounded us. Medical monitors and equipment filled the room. They beeped and chirped in a constant rhythm. A hospital bed positioned itself in the center of the space. Tables full of vials, test tubes, and microscopes lined the perimeter shelving.

I was in the twilight zone. Somehow, I had teleported into a hospital room.

"Where are we?" Jenny asked.

"I honestly have no idea," I commented. Taking in the sight for another moment, I got to my feet. I marched over to the hospital bed. The sheets were crumpled. The pillow indented as if a body recently laid in the bed.

I smelled a faint scent of perfume.

"Was the Baron performing some sort of experiments in here?" I wondered aloud.

Jenny took a closer look at the vials along the wall. "I don't know, but there are a bunch of shattered blood samples on the floor." She picked one up. Dried blood surrounded the shattered glass. "The same initials are written on all of these vials. L.R."

"Lynea Ruthford?" I asked. Nothing was making any sense.

The floor pulsated below us. Another explosion could be felt from outside. Our immediate threat instantly resurfaced. "We have to go," I said. I grabbed Jenny's hand. "We'll figure out all of this craziness some other time."

We fled to the end of the room and opened the door. Familiarity returned. We exited onto the upper balcony over-looking the main foyer. The mezzanine level wrapped around the entire foyer. Large timber trusses spanned the room. The structural members were charred and on fire. Chandeliers swayed back and forth as the ground shook. A dead mercenary was hunched on the floor beside us.

Now we were back in reality. J.J.'s distraction worked a little too well.

I stole the rifle from the man's lifeless grip. It felt good to have a weapon again.

Across the way, a grand stairwell led down to the lobby. Miraculously, it was still standing. That was our escape.

J.J. called in. "Where are you two, taking the scenic route?"

"Keep your pants on J.J. we're almost there," I retorted.

"If you haven't noticed, the building is about to collapse. Now hurry, I'm outside," my friend added.

"You don't say?" I mumbled. We ran toward the stairs.

Jenny yanked back on my arm and stopped me in my tracks. Looking back, I realized why.

Down below, the armored titan with the monster Gatling gun was still guarding the front doors. The worst part was that he saw us. The mercenary tightened his grip around the trigger.

The deafening rattle came first, followed by a rain of bullets dancing all around us. We planted ourselves on the floor as the walls splintered.

Canvases ripped to shreds. Wall sconces shattered to pieces. This guy was really getting on my nerves.

Jenny's eyes showed their first hints of panic. I needed to figure a way out of this. Looking up at the rafters, I scanned for an answer. I found one.

It came in the shape of a chandelier. The three chandeliers that dangled in the center of the room were massive. Antlers and husks decoratively extended out of all sides. What was originally intended to be a beautiful piece of artwork, was going to be our savior.

The farthest chandelier dangled from support cables. The cables spread to all of the structural beams. A number of them had already snapped free due to the explosions. The chandelier was hanging on by a single thread.

I peeked over the railing to take another look at our attacker. He hadn't moved. He stood right at the doorway blocking our exit.

I glanced back at the dangling chandelier. "This could work," I thought out loud.

"What could?" Jenny asked.

I smirked. "Ready to be impressed?"

I pulled out the rifle. The last support cable anchored back to the wall on the opposite side of the room. I took aim at the anchor, and I fired away.

Bullet holes dug into the walls around the anchor. Each missed its mark. I continued to fire, but I missed the cable every time.

"I'm still waiting to be impressed," Jenny observed. At least she was making light of our current predicament.

I calmed down. Focusing my aim once again, I eased my breathing. I pulled the trigger.

The bullet barely grazed the cable. Like the other shots, it dug into the drywall beyond. But that slight graze did the trick.

A thread in the cable partially tore. The extreme tension from the chandelier did the rest. In a second, the entire cable snapped.

Suddenly, the weight of the massive chandelier caused it to fall out of the sky. The momentum tugged the other two lights loose as well. They were all tied together by a single chord. Now the only cable left anchored was the one over the main entrance.

As it went taut, the three circular balls of light bulbs, metal, and animal husks, swung through the air. Like wrecking balls, they flew toward the armored mammoth with the gun. The sharp antlers rammed into the man's body, launching him off the ground.

He flung off his feet and into the far wall of the foyer. The last cable snapped free and all three chandelier came crashing down on the lifeless body.

"Now THAT worked better than I thought," I said triumphantly.

Jenny gave me an approving smile.

We jumped to our feet and sped around the balcony. Smoke started to fill the room. It was difficult to breathe.

We made it though. Through the dense fog, we sped down the stairs and to the front doors.

The innards of the once lush lobby now looked like a skeleton of its former self. Walls and structures collapsed. This whole place was coming down fast. Nature was getting ready to reclaim its territory.

Holding my breath, I made my way toward the front doors with Jenny by my side.

We were getting out of here.

The entire Mansion engulfed itself in flames. Red hot fires erupted out of the windows. Black clouds blocked the view of anything above the second floor. High winds funneled the smoke in swirls of blinding fog.

I burst out of the doors coughing—my lungs desperate for air. Taking in a deep breath, I checked on Jenny. She too was sucking in the fresh air. We were finally clear from the burning building.

Chaos still ensued. Vehicle engines roared in the distance. Screaming guests and servants ran, searching for any means of escape. Mercenaries were gunning people down like animals.

And, our savior was nowhere in sight. Instead, we were greeted by two thugs with assault rifles.

We were out of the frying pan, but still deep in the fire.

A blaring horn rang, and beams of light blurred into view. The distracted henchmen looked over just in time to see a black mechanical beast plow through them.

Actually, it was more like, over them.

The double decker hovercraft screeched to a halt a few feet away. The side door popped open revealing Jeremy Jenkins at the helm. "You ready to go, Charles?" he yelled over the rumbling engines.

I had to give it to the man. J.J. always picked unique getaway vehicles.

Bullets rippled into the snow behind me as more soldiers zeroed in on our location. I bolted for the hovercraft. I lifted Jenny onto the metal platform and then followed suit.

Before I could even get my bearings, Jeremy floored the gas pedal, lurching the monstrous vehicle forward. It spun in place, finally orienting itself to the path that led away from the crumbling Victorian estate.

The hovercraft launched, speeding away from the insanity. My body nearly sucked off the vehicle as I crossed the platform and entered the main compartment. Jenny was steps ahead, already inside.

"You sure know how to make an entrance J.J.," I said marching up to him.

"I told you I had a plan. It worked like a charm."

"I'd say you just dethroned my prison break in the *crazy* department," I quipped. The fires shrunk in the distance.

Jeremy piloted the craft down the mountain as if he'd done it a thousand times. The craft glided over the snow like a speed boat through water, expertly navigating its way through the terrain.

"How you holding up Jenny?" I said.

"When my dad told me stories of all your near death experiences together, I always thought he exaggerated. The last two times I've been with you have proven otherwise. Do you always leave these wakes of destruction?"

"More or less," I said smiling.

Jeremy interrupted, "Now you know why I never wanted this life for you, Jennifer."

Jenny's eyes didn't show fear though. They twinkled with excitement. As much as J.J. never wanted his daughter to follow in his footsteps, it seemed the apple didn't fall too far from the tree.

I added, "Jenny, this went a lot smoother than normal. Typically we don't get away that easily."

An explosion sounded outside, and the hull suddenly shook violently. The glass windows of the narrow compartment shattered into pieces as bullets penetrated the metal hull. Deafening winds cut through the inner compartment, instantly dropping the temperature.

"I believe you spoke too soon, Charles," Jeremy said, struggling to maintain control.

Hot in pursuit, five smaller hovercrafts circled ours. The Baron's mercenaries manned rooftop machine guns on each of the vehicles. They fired away at our enormous target.

J.J. switched to evasive maneuvers, using the large tank of a craft to ram the other vehicles. The smaller machines were a lot more agile though. Their pilots easily cut back on the throttle and pulled behind us.

We were bombarded with another round of fire.

"We won't last long like this," Jenny cried.

She was right. I scrambled back to the rear of the bus and propped open the door. I stepped out to the open platform. The wind smacked me like a wall. It nearly knocked me to the ground. Planting my feet, I scrunched my body low and walked along the platform.

The metal landing around the main compartment was large. It was shaped as a rectangular plate which rested on top of the inflated nylon pancake.

I rounded the main propellers to get a better view of our attackers. Two of the hovercrafts were right on our tail. Bullets pinged around me.

I ducked for cover. Pulling out my gun, I aimed and shot back. Bullets wildly flew in every direction. None near their targets. Another barrage of gunfire dinged around me.

This was a stupid idea. J.J. voiced the same concern through my earpiece. I rolled out of cover and fired some more.

The exchange continued.

On the opposite end of our hovercraft, one of the other pursuing vehicles ran alongside. It positioned itself inches away from our platform. Three mercenaries leapt and boarded our escape vehicle.

I scrambled to my feet and sprinted toward them. Cutting through the central compartment, I dove through a broken glass window and onto the opposite side of the platform. I tackled one of the thugs to the ground, quickly rolling off him.

The other men had just gained their balance. Jeremy rocked the vehicle, causing them to tumble. In a single motion I brought my knees to my chest and kicked outward. Each foot landed right in the arch of each man's back.

They launched off the side of the platform, bounced over the edge of the air filled cushion, and disappeared in the thick snow that rushed by.

Adrenaline coursed through my veins. I felt unstoppable. That feeling was quickly knocked out of my head—literally.

A fist smashed into my side temple. The other mercenary had gotten back to his feet and came on the offensive. I rolled out of the way just as the man's iron fist smashed down on the metal landing. The pain jolted through his body giving me a window to attack.

Still on my back, I thrust my legs at the man's side, pushing him away. I rolled back up.

My attacker took out his assault rifle. Jeremy didn't give him a chance to fire as he swerved the hovercraft back and forth.

Using this opportunity, I charged the man, tackling him to the floor once again.

We rolled over one another, getting closer to the rear propellers. Their deafening spins made it nearly impossible to hear anything. As we got closer, I felt the hair on my head vacuum up in the suction. Any closer and the blades would most definitely suck me in.

A few more punches drilled into my gut. Wincing in pain, I fought hard to regain control. The thug was much bigger than me, and he straddled me like a horse. Pinned down, I became his punching bag.

Our bodies slowly slid toward the twirling blades.

"Turn up the engines!" I screamed into my microphone. The mercenary looked confused.

Jeremy complied. The hovercraft picked up speed, and the blades spun faster. My assailant's body started to feel lighter on top of mine. He was being drawn toward the propellers.

This could work.

But, the man realized what was happening. Pulling out a commando knife, it looked like he was going to kill me before I had enough time for my plan to follow through. Still pinned down, I was helpless. The knife raised up for the attack.

I raised my hands in protest.

But instead of feeling a sharp blade pierce through my chest, I watched Jenny's fist fly out of nowhere. She punched the mercenary square in the jaw. The man rolled off of me. In a swift motion, Jenny kicked him in the chest. The man launched over the ledge of the hovercraft. He disappeared in the blanket of snow.

Breathless, I feigned a smile of gratitude.

"Wow, that hurt," she said, shaking her hand. Jenny helped me to my feet.

"You two better get back in here," J.J. calmly said in my ear. How was he so nonchalant about this?

We ran back to the inside of the double decker. Jeremy kicked the engines back to full throttle.

"That was too close," Jenny said alongside me. "Are you okay?"

Winded, I simply nodded. Two more hovercrafts pulled up beside ours.

This wasn't over yet?

This time J.J. took care of it. He thrust our beastly machine into the two crafts. They bounced of our hull and flew over the cliff edge of the mountain.

Jeremy then slammed on the break and the two hovercrafts behind us swerved to dodge. They crashed into a rock formation, exploding into balls of fire. The explosion shook the entire mountain.

"Now that's how it's done, Charles," Jeremy stated victoriously.

"Show off," I exhaled, looking at the destruction behind us.

I noticed a black cloud storming toward us from up the mountain.

The large blanket of darkness seemed to blot out the entire mountain. It ate up everything in sight.

The ground trembled. As the black wall neared, vibrations grew. My mouth dropped when I realized what it was.

"I think you were a little too good there, J.J.," I blurted.

"How so?" He asked. His eyes still focused on the road ahead.

"Because you just brought a new friend to the party, and you're not going to like him."

Jenny came to my side to see what I was looking at. Her reaction matched mine—eyes wide and jaw dropped.

The explosion must have triggered it.

Roaring down the mountain face was an avalanche of snow. As it sped down the slopes it picked up speed, and more importantly, it was coming our way.

Jenny finally spoke, "I now regret saying anything earlier about you two and your exaggerated stories."

I glanced over at her. "We're just giving you your money's worth."

The avalanche bellowed as the snow churned into a massive tsunami of rubble. Winds grew heavy.

Jeremy gunned the craft down the mountain.

"J.J., does this thing go any faster?" I asked.

J.J. was focused. "No time for backseat driving, Charles. You two buckle up."

We complied silently.

The avalanche grew.

J.J. guided the machine down the mountain. Behind us, the tumbling snow sucked everything up in its devastating path.

We sped back and forth down the snowy wilderness. Trees flashed by. As fast as our craft went, the zigzagging nature of the pathway slowed our progress. The churning avalanche was growing closer and closer by the second.

My grip tightened around my arm rests. I felt like I was going to tear them from their steel supports. I stared straight ahead, watching J.J. navigate the large hovercraft like a pro.

I didn't dare say a word. It wouldn't have mattered anyways. Sounds of the rapidly approaching avalanche howled through the shattered windows. No one could have heard me. The harsh winds slapped my body. I was an icicle.

Our roaring giant plowed after us. We weren't going to make it.

My eyes widened.

Looking ahead, I watched J.J. steer the craft off course. It diverted off the designated road and onto the soft snow. It sped along, heading straight for a cliff edge.

My friend was crazier than I thought. The craft picked up speed as it quickly approached the cliff. My body clenched.

What was he thinking?

We launched over the cliff.

The trees ended. The snow ended. Everything ended. All I could see was the night sky. Stars filled the black canvas.

My stomach flipped on itself. I could feel all the food I just ate reverse its way back up my throat. I struggled to not throw up.

For a second, I was weightless. The entire hovercraft flew through the air. Then it nosedived out of the sky.

As it pitched forward, I saw the trees come back to view. The snowy terrain returned too. We crashed back onto the ground.

This time the terrain was much steeper than before. On an eighty degree decline, the hovercraft sped along.

We barreled down the mountain. It felt like the first drop of a rollercoaster.

I swore the entire machine was going to flip on itself, but miraculously, it didn't. It continued to speed forward. We entered the express lane down the mountain. Trees screamed by now.

How did J.J. know this was a safe route?

Suddenly, the hovercraft bounced off a massive tree. We spun out of control, still careening down the mountain. Everything swirled around me. Dizziness blurred my vision.

Vomit inched higher up my throat. Every time we spun backward, I saw the massive wall of snow rushing toward us. I closed my eyes. We weren't going to make it.

But then, somehow, J.J. regained control.

The hovercraft oriented itself down the steep path once again. The area opened wide. We sped down the path even faster than before.

The base of the mountain quickly approached. Soon the terrain gradually evened out. The roaring avalanche continued, but, with the obstacles out of the way, my old friend easily guided the craft along.

I had to give it to the old man, he did well.

As we reached the mountain base, Jeremy steered the hovercraft toward the Black Sea. The good thing about these vehicles was that they functioned on both land and water. Right now, the water was the best route in getting us far from danger.

Still, my death grip didn't let up. My body remained tense as we fled away from the mountain. The avalanche continued to pour down the mountain as Jeremy, Jenny, and I sped to safety.

Once clear from the chaos, I allowed my body to loosen. The calm sea spread out before us. I exhaled a sigh of relief.

It was all over.

CHAPTER TWENTY SIX

My body shivered. Even around the burning fireplace of my tiny hotel room, I was still cold. Jenny sat in a nearby chair, taking in the warmth from the fire. It had been one heck of a night.

Our return back to the hotel was fairly quiet. Ditching the hovercraft a few miles down the river, Jeremy stole us another vehicle. He took us back to the hotel to relax. We were silent the entire trip. I was exhausted. My limbs ached, and my skin felt like ice.

Now, sitting at the fire, I couldn't wait to go to bed.

The smell of some good cooking filtered through the cramped room. J.J. stood in the kitchen, happy as can be. He gloated that his plan actually worked, but I knew that he was happier at the fact that both Jenny and I were safe.

I leaned deeper into my chair. In my hand, I held my lucky compass. I rubbed the bronze back and forth.

"You still have that thing?" Jenny said, breaking the silence.

"I rarely leave home without it," I said. "It's my good luck charm."

"You probably could have used it back in China," she quipped.

"I know. I'm amazed I made it out in one piece." Looking at the massive bruise on my shoulder, I added, "Or at least most of one piece."

"Well I'm glad you're *mostly* okay Charlie," Jenny added.

"How are you feeling?" I muttered out.

"A little cold. You at least had a suit jacket to protect you from the weather," she smiled while rubbing her own shoulders.

"Hey I would have been a gentleman and given you my jacket if I wasn't distracted with saving your life."

I stretched my toes out in the fire. We both laughed.

"You can just hold off on that move until you ask me out on a date," Jenny said.

One—thankfully the blistering cold made my face red, so Jenny couldn't tell if I was blushing. And Two—thank God J.J. finished cooking dinner because he called us over at that exact moment.

The table was covered from end to end with food. I was starving. Sitting down, I didn't even wait for the others. I simply dug in.

"Charles, it's like you haven't eaten in months," J.J. said in a failed attempt at a joke. He ran back to the kitchen to grab some more platters.

Jenny sat down, her eyes locked on me. "Charlie," she began, "I wanted to say thanks again for coming to my rescue."

"Hey, it was nothing. It's what I do."

"I know, but I should have listened to you months ago."

"Jen, you can't blame yourself. None of us knew the extent of danger we were in. Neither of us could have imagined what a lunatic the Baron was."

Jenny gave me a kiss on the cheek as Jeremy entered back into the room.

"Well the good Baron did get away," J.J. said, setting down another platter of food.

"How do you know?" I asked.

"I saw him, his daughter, and Alvin take off in one of the helicopters when I was accruing our escape vehicle."

Alvin Mitchell. Anger coursed through my veins at the thought of the man. Then Lynea came to mind—the pour innocent girl who was trapped in all of this.

I remembered the white medical room we saw in the Baron's mansion. I thought of the fear in Lynea's eyes when she told me her dad was going to sacrifice her. Homer's tale confirmed her fears. I couldn't believe that the Baron would kill his own daughter.

Years of experience with these types of characters taught me otherwise. It taught me never to be surprised by what people were capable of.

Jenny must have read my pondering facial expression. She changed the subject. "Tonight, how about we enjoy our small little victory." She poured me a glass of wine.

For the next hour, we ate. We exchanged stories about the past few months. Jenny explained how she didn't have much contact with anyone while she was locked up in the dungeons. Ruthford was always distracted with other things. Alvin was too scared to talk to her. She was alone.

J.J. didn't have any good stories either. All of his tales involved drinking. The fact that he had a glass of wine at our table meant that it was a habit he wouldn't be quitting anytime soon.

My tales were the most intriguing of all. Jenny and her father had me elaborate on my short stint with the monks. I gave all the details about the teachings, the food, and even how lucky I was in finding the mural inscribed on their wall. Without that mural, I would have never found the *tree of life*.

As we finished dinner, J.J. held up his glass. "Cheers to living another day."

"And to the end of a fun little adventure," Jenny added.

We clanked our glasses while I said, "Well, my adventure isn't quite over."

Jenny looked puzzled.

"I made a promise to the Baron's daughter. Knowing that she escaped, she's next on my to-do list." I realized too late, the unintended pun of that statement.

Jenny's mood instantly shifted. "What are you talking about Charlie? You don't have to save that girl."

"Actually I do. I gave her my word, Jen. If it wasn't for her, there was no way I would have made it down to the dungeons. You should have seen her. She was terrified."

"Still, why you? Why do you have to do it?"

"You saw that hospital room. You read about the sacrifice," I pointed out.

Jeremy entered the argument, "Charles, I understand your desire to help people, but do you believe it best to…"

I cut my friend off, "J.J. I have to do this. I can't knowingly sit back and let a man kill his own daughter."

"But you destroyed the tablet," Jenny said. "There's no way he'll find what he's looking for."

"He'll find a way. He's smarter than he looks. If not, you know he'll come looking for us. We're not safe either."

Jenny turned away in her chair, frustrated.

"Why are you getting so upset?" I asked.

"Charlie, I saw Mr. Ruthford's true colors over the past few months. He's not a guy you want to mess with. I…we almost lost you once. Why do you have this noble desire to always save someone?"

I didn't know what to say. I saw the concern in Jenny's eyes. I opened my mouth to speak, but J.J. answered for me.

"Because Charles, my young Jennifer, couldn't let a person die. Not like he did with his parents," was all he said.

Stunned, I looked over at my friend. How did he know about my past? I hated to admit it, but J.J. was right.

My twelfth Christmas was memorable for many reasons. I got the coolest gift in the form of Ferdinand Magellan's compass. It was the first year I had a surprise present to open. And, it was also the day I let my parents die.

My last dream came to mind. The day I received my lucky compass.

I was in my bedroom. After opening my present, I marveled at the compass in my hand. I was mesmerized by it. It didn't dawn on me that the doorbell rang. My father disappeared out of the room, followed by my mother. Everything seemed perfectly normal.

While I investigated the tiny object, I heard voices downstairs. Then a scream.

I leapt out of bed and raced to my bedroom door. Creeping around the corner, I stood at the top of the stairs of our foyer. Down below, I saw my parents kneeling on the ground. They faced my direction. My mom was crying, and my dad had a bloody gash across his forehead. Our front doors propped wide open.

Two other figures stood with their backs to me. They dressed dirty, and by the looks of the shotguns in their hands, dangerous.

I froze.

My brain screamed for me to run down the stairs and attack these crazy strangers, but my body couldn't move. I just watched in horror.

These two characters yelled at my folks. I was in such a daze, I couldn't hear a word. I simply trembled, staring at my father.

We made eye contact, and I saw his lips move. He was telling me something.

'Call Nine-One-One'.

I couldn't though. I was too scared. The man smacked my dad again and dragged him into the next room. When the stranger returned, he grabbed my mother. That's when I heard him say, "Go upstairs and make sure no one else is around."

Somehow I managed to kick my body in motion. I ran down the hall and into the laundry room. Terrified, I climbed into the one hiding spot I always went to—the hamper. I closed the lid and remained quiet.

I thought I was an adventurer. I thought nothing scared me. But in the moment of true danger, I was a coward.

I didn't know how long I stayed hidden in the crammed compartment. I didn't dare crawl out. Even after I heard two of the loudest *bangs* from downstairs, I still didn't move.

Hours went by. Silence filled the air. Then I heard the sound of sirens. A number of voices followed.

My hamper lid finally opened.

An old cop towered over me. I didn't realize that I was crying. Through my watery eyes, I looked up at the man. A sad expression covered his face.

All I remember him saying was, "I'm sorry, kid."

My parents were dead.

"How did you know that?" I asked J.J. I never told anyone what happened to my parents.

"Charles, I didn't just welcome you into my home those many years ago without doing my research." Jeremy put his hand on my shoulder.

Jenny came up and sat beside me. "I'm sorry Charlie. I never knew."

J.J. pulled a piece of paper out of his pocket. "After learning the truth about your past, I understood what motivated you to pull Jenny and me out of a burning vehicle. I comprehended your desire to always help." He threw the piece of paper on the table. "But it doesn't mean you have to do it alone."

A series of sentences scribbled all over the paper. J.J. dropped a photograph next to it. The picture was of *Xi Wangmu's* circular tablet.

"J.J. what is this?" I asked.

"You didn't think it took me that long to cook our meal did you? I couldn't help myself. You know me, Charles, I have a soft spot for Greek history. I deciphered the inscriptions on the tablet. If you plan to stop the Baron and save his daughter, following the trail makes the most logical sense."

I began reading through the text as J.J. narrated his opinion.

"Charles, the translation was fairly simple. It details a point at the center of the world. There, the last piece of the puzzle resides under the *rock of God*. It continues, explaining that one must pass through the *hall of the dead* and into the *holiest of holies*, where only the purest soul will find the key to one's own fate. It was fairly obvious."

"The center of the world? The Oracle of Delphi in Greece? But the Baron was already there," I said confused.

"No, no, Charles. It's true that the Greeks believed that Mount Pyrannus, the current site of Delphi, was the center of the Earth. On the other hand, the rest of the world during the 8th century gave that label to Jerusalem. More appropriately, the *Dome of the Rock.*"

The temple J.J. mentioned was an ancient structure built in the capital of Israel. It was an icon that I had visited a few times in my past.

Jeremy continued, "The dome was built on the Temple Mount, a sacred location at the center of the old city of Jerusalem. Until the discovery of the Americas, this domed structure was known as the true *Center of the World.*"

"J.J., the dome wasn't built until many centuries later. If I recall correctly, it's a shrine built for the Muslim prophet Muhammad. The temple was dedicated to his *night journey* into the heavens," I shattered my old friend's theory.

"Yes Charles, but the site where the Dome was built upon had significance well before that building's erection. Underneath that temple is the foundation stone, or *the rock*. It is the holiest site in Judaism, and it is the reason why the dome was located there. That rock also has a small hole in the corner of it that enters a cavern beneath it. If you remember your history, the cavern has a name."

"The Well of Souls," I mouthed.

"Correct. In Jewish tradition, the well is looked as the spiritual junction of Heaven and Earth."

"Just like the Axis Mundi," I whispered.

"Precisely. And, in the 8th century another building was constructed on that very ground. Well before the *Dome of the Rock* was ever built, King Solomon built his own temple in the exact same location."

Jenny and I listened intently. Like the old days, we leaned forward in our seats, watching J.J. speak.

"The Hebrew Bible credited King Solomon as the builder of this First Temple in Jerusalem. Crusaders destroyed it, and in later years, all of its remains disappeared. Still, as legend has it, the King built this structure as a vault for his most prized possessions. And guess what that vault was called?"

"The Holiest of Holies," I said, remembering my history.

I started following J.J.'s logic. Solomon, according to the Qur'an and other religious text of Islam, was once the King of Israel. He was also one of the forty-eight prophets of Islam.

The idea of prophets and shamans fell in line with the similar traits of the other two tablet locations. Solomon came to be known as a magician, with numerous amulets and medallion seals dating back to the Hellenistic period.

"And Charles, if you look further into the translation, it distinctly mentions a rock, and a cavern beneath it. Under the foundation stone in the dome, in the Well of Souls, there is believed to have been a doorway.

"A doorway to a chamber. A chamber leading to the Holiest of Holies, the vault created by King Solomon—a vault hiding such magnificent treasures such as the Arc of the Covenant. If this is true, then who knows what else may lie buried away within its walls."

"So, Jerusalem is our next stop?" I said.

"If I were a betting man, yes. There, we will find the last piece of the *Trinity* of tablets. With all three together, we should have all the information needed to find the final resting place of the Oracle of Delphi."

"And get the upper hand over the Baron," I added.

Jenny didn't seem as enthusiastic as us.

She interrupted, "I can't believe you guys are really entertaining all this." She stormed off and slammed the door to the bedroom.

J.J. and I looked at each other. Neither of us spoke.

The door opened back up, and out came Jenny. "Okay, so I was going to pack our bags and dramatically storm back out here saying 'What are we waiting for' but then I realized we don't have any luggage."

She smiled.

"Guys, you don't have to come with me."

Jenny came up close. "Charlie, yes we do. You may have lost your parents, but it doesn't mean you don't have a family."

PART III

The Day I Was Double-Crossed

CHAPTER TWENTY SEVEN

Jerusalem, Istanbul

Burt and Berta Traijan were twins. One wouldn't have guessed it from their looks though.

Burt was a heavy set Armenian. Hair covered most of his body, making him look more *bear* than *man*. Always dressed in a wrinkled suit and wearing a number of gold chains, everything about him appeared sloppy.

Berta, on the other hand, had an athletic build, model quality features, and stood a good foot taller than her twin brother. Everything she wore elegantly draped over her exquisite curves and long legs.

But that was about the extents of their differences.

When it came to their personalities, it was as if they were a single-minded individual—a ruthless one at that. These twins were known to be a dangerous duo who loved treasure and money, and their methods were barbaric.

They were also my friends.

Lucky me.

Their methods helped them accrue a vast amount of wealth and with that money, came power. Soon, they moved to the Judean Mountains, between the Mediterranean Sea and the Dead Sea. To be more exact, they built a palace in one of the biggest cities in the world...

Jerusalem.

Being the capital of Israel, Jerusalem had a long history. It was destroyed twice, attacked, captured and recaptured more times than I had fingers and toes to count. It was the holiest city in the Jewish tradition.

And for those reasons, the siblings loved the location. A past full of wars and historic battles oozed out of every pore of its streets. The rich and diverse culture gave them plenty of opportunities to explore, and a playground for them to enjoy.

Over time, Burt and Berta created a dense underground black market in the city. They were never ones for the spotlight but enjoyed playing the puppeteers, hidden in the shadows—the great and powerful Oz, as they liked to say.

On the surface, the city streets were calm. The average day functioned normally. Behind the scenes, every import and export, every piece of gossip, every exchange of money, was monitored by them. At least this is the way they believed the city worked.

They were some of the craziest people I knew, and everyone feared them—including me.

Thankfully, I was on their good side, and they owed me a favor.

"How do you know these people?" Jenny asked as our plane descended upon a small airstrip in the outskirts of Jerusalem.

"We have a complicated history," I said looking out the window. I watched the desert sand blaze by as our plane roared down the asphalt runway. The wing flaps adjusted, cutting at the wind and slowing the mechanical beast.

J.J. and his daughter sat in the seats beside me. Or I should say, Miguel and Helga, as it stated on their fake passports.

After realizing where our next destination was, the Traijan twins were the first people I called. They were the only ones I knew that could get us fake identification, money, and transport fast.

"Charlie, this seems off. Your *friends* were a little too enthusiastic about helping us," Jenny added.

"Listen Helga," I said, pushing Jenny's buttons. Her piercing glare acknowledged that it worked. "That's just how they are. You'll see when you meet them. Trust me."

"Like I trusted you in coming up with our fake names. Helga? Really?"

"Helga is a perfectly good name. It's nurturing and elegant," Jeremy chimed into the conversation with a faint grin.

"Yeah, for an old woman with a hairy mole on her lip and massive child-bearing hips," Jenny added. "Do you really want to get involved in this conversation dad? Or Miguel?"

"*I like to embrace my Spanish heritage. Plus, I speak the language fluently, my dear,*" Jeremy said in perfect Spanish.

Of course J.J. was the whitest man I knew.

I never fully understood women and was surprised by the little things that bothered them. During the fabrication of Jenny's new identity, I thought I was being kind, adding an inch to her height and guessing a good number of pounds under her actual weight. Did she thank me for those nice gestures? No, instead she lashed out over a good... proper... motherly name.

I couldn't help but laugh.

Jenny's concerns about my friends were valid though. Burt and Berta Traijan were eager to help. Having conducted business with the twins enough times, I knew that they couldn't resist the prospect of uncovering some major discovery right under their noses. Even though the siblings were tough as nails, they had a soft spot for this sort of thing.

Plus, Burt held a man's honor very dearly. As luck would have it, I was an honorable man.

Five years ago, I sat at a café in the Piazza San Marco, in Venice, Italy.

A noon sun positioned high over the large plaza. The rectangular area consisted of marble walkways, detailed structures, and long exaggerated arcades. The church of Saint Marcos dominated the eastern end. Romanesque carvings and great arches filled its elegant façade.

Tourist shops and restaurants flanked the plaza. A lone pianist played in a corner, while in the opposite end, another musician played a cello. Pedestrians roamed the area, going from shop to shop.

This was the principal public square of Venice and a massive social center for the city. Like everything in Italy, the sight was beautiful.

Sipping my espresso at the edge of the piazza, I took in the beauty.

I sat below the tall brick clock tower that terminated the end of the plaza. It opened up to the southern strip leading to the lagoon. Dozens of gondolas lined the dock, ready to take couples on romantic trips through the lush water canals.

It amazed me that an entire city could be constructed over water. Networks of waterways made up the main roads through the city. In lieu of cars, people either crossed bridges, or took boats.

Still, with every sight being more beautiful than the last, my eyes were locked on one image—the long brown hair of a woman sitting at a nearby table. I'm not sure why I was entranced by her. I mean she faced the opposite direction, so I couldn't see any of her facial features. All I saw was her arched figure, dark brown tan, and long legs.

She sat alone, just like me.

I didn't mean to stare. She just happened to be in my field of vision. Originally, I was gazing beyond her figure, at the second floor of the old procuracies—former homes of the procurators of Saint Marco's Basilica.

Those homes used to house the high officers of state in the days of the republic of Venice. During World War II, Adolf Hitler used those rooms for his residing army.

Hitler was also known as a huge collector of antiquities. Many long lost treasures were accounted to his regime.

I had reason to believe that a hidden passage in one of those housing units led to a storage room where good old Hitler hid some of these valuables. Where the other tourists marveled at the history of this romantic city, I was scoping out my current job.

And somehow, my plan shifted to scoping out this female work of art. I assumed that, based on the exquisite nature of her features, she had to have something wrong with her.

I figured it must be a hideous face.

That thought was immediately extinguished when the woman finally turned around. She caught me staring right at her. She was even more beautiful than I imagined.

The woman smiled, and I nodded in response.

A few minutes later, and a few more casual glances at one another, the woman came to my table.

"*May I sit?*" she said in Italian.

"*Si,*" I acknowledged.

I must have looked out of place because she asked, "*You speak the language?*" She gracefully sat down.

"*Only a little, but I share many traits with the Italians, including their passion for beauty.*" That was what I meant to say, unfortunately, I'm not sure what my broken Italian really translated to.

"Well how about English?" she then said.

"Much better," I replied. "What's your name, if I may ask?"

"Berta Traijan."

That was the first time I met Berta, and one of the only times she was without her brother.

"Charlie Morgan," I replied.

"And what brings you to this wonderful city?" Berta asked.

"A little sightseeing. A little business. What about you?"

Berta's smile disappeared. "Oh, I'm here in search of Nazi treasure." She pointed to the procuracies. "I believe there is a chamber hiding an assortment of Adolf Hitler's gold. I've been sitting here scanning the security of the area to see when the best time would be to break in."

I was dumbfounded. I played stupid. "You have quite an imagination."

"Do I? Are you not here for the same reason? Isn't that your *little business* that you are here for?"

I was speechless.

"Mr. Morgan, I like to be in the *know*, and you, my cute little treasure hunter, have been on my list for some time. You are here for similar reasons. I know this. Your reputation precedes you."

It was no use hiding it. "Apparently, but I know little about you."

"And that is the way I like it. Now, seeing that we both seek the same place, how about we help each other?" She leaned in, flashing her large chest. Sweat dribbled down her collarbone.

It didn't take much convincing. There was no hiding my secret. Berta already seemed to know everything. I figured, if there was a treasure to be found, all I needed was one little object. I could let her have the rest.

Plus, she pulled out a gold key with engravings on top. It seemed that the key was needed to unlock the door to the secret chamber. It was the first I had heard of it, but the woman looked fairly knowledgeable. What did I have to lose?

Our conversation remained playful, but both of us kept our guards up. It was pointless to hide our obvious intentions. We still managed to protect our specific agendas.

My agenda was art related.

I was contracted to find an old painting. *The Trial of Saint Stephen* by Vittore Carpaccio. It was one of a series of canvases missing since 1806. Some of my contacts traced it to this area. The paintings were dedicated to *Scuola di San Stefano*, in Venice, so the dots started to connect. The item was also not something I believed many people sought.

As our conversation continued, Berta and I strategized a plan of attack.

That night, we followed through with it.

Under the veil of darkness, we snuck into the small compartments, searching them one by one. Finally, we discovered the secret passage which led down to a crammed room—the hidden chamber created by Hitler's gestapo to hide his most prized possessions.

Berta's key worked like a charm. I started thinking I was lucky to have met the woman.

We headed in.

The room contained dozens of paintings and other treasures. Using my flashlight, I quickly scanned for my prize. Berta did the same.

Our beams of light both fell upon the same object, a small square painting propped up against a wall. It was frameless, and the corners of the canvas curled up toward its center. We glanced at each other.

"This is what I'm looking for," we said in unison.

I grabbed at the painting. Berta did the same. We each held onto opposing ends. Pulling, I said, "Listen sweetheart, this is my job. My employer is paying good money for this."

She tugged back, saying, "And I need to get this to save my brother."

"What?"

"My twin brother. He was taken prisoner by a lunatic whose only wish is to have this painting. If I don't get it to him, my brother is dead."

"Nice try," I said. I yanked it out of her hands.

"Please, Charlie, I beg of you," Berta pleaded.

My flashlight shined over her desperate face. She could have been lying. She could have been playing me for a fool. But the tremble in her voice said otherwise. Calmly, I handed her the painting. "Take it."

"Are you sure?"

"I don't need the money that bad. Maybe I'll just sell one of these other ones," I smirked.

Suddenly, outside our hidden room, we heard a ruckus. Whistles blew. I'm not sure how, but the police were alerted.

"We've got to go," I said.

"I'm sorry Charlie, but someone needs to take the fall for this. It's a shame, because you are cute." The woman's tone instantly switched from desperate to cold.

Before I could respond, Berta's fist smacked me across the face. I stumbled in the dark, crashing to the ground. The next thing I knew, a black boot stomped on my forehead, instantly knocking me unconscious.

When I came to, I was in a prison cell. A few straggling drunks sat on the benches. Vomit and feces stunk up the tight space. My head felt like it had been run over by a semi-truck.

Berta was one heck of an actress.

And, more importantly, I got beat up by a woman.

Sitting up, I studied my surroundings. How was I going to explain to the authorities why I broke into a government building and tried to steal government property? Property they didn't even know they had? I needed J.J. I wondered if I still got one phone call, and if so, would I be able to dial internationally?

I doubted it.

The cell doors opened, and two officers came in. They motioned me to my feet. I obliged. They escorted me out of the cell. We marched down a long corridor to the rear end of the police station. One guard propped the exit door open, and the other kicked me through it.

They slammed the door shut behind me without following outside. I was left alone in a back alley of the station.

I was still in a daze as to what was happening.

It took a moment for my eyes to adjust to the blinding sun. As they began to focus, I made out a short, round figure standing before me.

When I finally became accustomed to the bright light, I clearly made out the image of a dark, hairy man in a wrinkled suit. A big grin stretched across his face.

"I take it, you are my gracious savior?" I managed to say.

"No, Mr. Morgan, you are mine." The man wrapped his massive paws around me. "I owe you my life."

Confused, I then heard a second pair of footsteps approach. Glancing over, I saw Berta in a tiny little skirt and tank-top. Her high heels echoed over the stone after every step.

"You must be the brother," I said to the round man.

He let go of me. With a burly laugh he said, "My name is Burt Traijan. My sister told me how you helped her."

Rubbing my head, I said, "Your sister is something else."

Berta finally reached us. In her hand was a rolled up painting. "No hard feelings, Charlie." She handed me the roll. "I'm sorry, if I hurt you."

"Nothing permanent. Just my pride."

Burt patted me on the shoulder. "This is my gift to you, Mr. Morgan."

I unraveled the painting. It was *The Trial of Saint Stephen*. "I don't understand."

Burt explained. "My sister showed up early this morning with the painting. She paid off my kidnappers, and they freed me. Shortly thereafter, I returned to their hideout and killed every last one of them. They did not understand who they were dealing with. It was meaningless to leave such a valuable treasure, seeing that there was no one left to relish its beauty. So I bring you this gift."

"Thank you?" I questioned, taking the painting.

"No, thank you, Mr. Morgan. You are a good, honorable man," Burt said. He clasped my shoulder.

That was my first experience with the Traijan family.

"Jen, I don't blame you for not trusting these two, but we didn't have many options, " I said as we got up from our seats. "They hold a lot of power in this neck of the woods."

The plane had officially landed, and the few passengers on board began grabbing their bags.

"I know, Charlie," she said.

Jeremy stretched his legs. He peered out the window saying, "Ah, Israel, it has been too long. Did I ever tell you two about the time I was stranded with a camel in—"

"Yes," we both cut him off.

"Very well then," he said, stepping aside.

We marched off the plane and out into the desert heat. The scorching sun hit us like a wall of bricks. Instantly, pores opened, and my body began to perspire through my shirt.

A barren field stretched out beyond. Small rocky hills punched out of the beige sand. The bright, cloudless sky reflected off the sandy grains, making them sparkle like an ocean.

Then I saw the city of Jerusalem. Perched on a raised mound of earth, the massive city stood alone amongst the sea of sand. It looked breathtaking.

We marched down the mobile stairwell and onto the landing strip. A single bus rounded up the other passengers to take them to the main airport terminal.

We, on the other hand, had a different trajectory. Off to the left of the bus was a black Hummer. The giant vehicle looked like a tank next to the beat down old passenger bus. Leaning against the hood of the Hummer were two individuals.

One, a woman. Tall, and slender, just as I remembered. Her hair waved in the breeze.

The other, a robust little man. Even in the immense heat, he still wore a suit.

There stood my friends—Burt and Berta.

CHAPTER TWENTY EIGHT

"Welcome to my city," Burt said as he wrapped his hot soaked body around mine. "So good to see you my friend!"

Burt always looked at Jerusalem as *his*. He had this naïve perception that he and his sister ran everything in the town. It was true that they had a tremendous amount of influence in the black market, but that was only a small portion of the lifeblood of the city.

Berta felt the same way—as if she was a queen. In all honesty, a common passerby would think so. A caravan of black vehicles were stationed in the distance. They strategically planted themselves as security detail. Tinted windows covered each car, and men with guns perched the grounds in constant surveillance. Anyone would believe that someone extremely important was on site.

Berta elegantly strolled up, giving me a hug as well. "You haven't lost any of your cute looks, Charlie," she said, smiling. Her lips delicately caressed my cheek. "It's been too long."

Jenny coughed.

Her expression either hinted jealousy, or annoyance at my lack of introductions.

"Thanks for helping us out. You two are life savers," I said. I then introduced everyone.

Burt didn't seem to care much for familiarities. He grabbed Jenny's hand and kissed it. The act was chivalrous, but the beads of sweat dripping off his nose and onto her wrist were a little disgusting. "Charlie always had an eye for beautiful women."

"I'm not his...," Jenny began, paused, then just stated, "... Thank you."

"And you, Mr. Jenkins. I have heard many good things." Berta followed her brother's cordiality, politely shaking J.J.'s hand.

"Like Charles said, we too are very appreciative of your generosity," J.J. acknowledged.

"For all Charlie has done for us, it is the least we could do."

I knew better though. Burt and Berta's love for money and power would easily sway them to help anybody. If I didn't tease them about the grandness of what we were hot on the tails of, they wouldn't have lifted a finger.

Not all friends were good ones.

Burt glossed over the small talk and quickly cut to the chase. "So what have you discovered about my city?"

"All in good time," I teased. "The only thing you need to know is that it will be very lucrative."

Burt giggled like a school girl. He whisked us away into the Hummer and ordered the driver to go.

It sounded easier than it really played out.

The driver radioed into the bodyguards. They sent a car out ahead to make sure the path was clear. The rest of the crew boarded their respective vehicles, and then all the cars started down the road.

Inside, Berta offered up some glasses of wine. The large Hummer was decked to the brim with luxurious beverages and state of the art technologies.

"You guys are doing extremely well for yourselves," I mentioned.

"Yes we are," Berta said, flashing a smile. "But we could always be doing better."

"Tell us, Charlie," Burt began. "What exactly has led you to believe something may be buried under the *Dome of the Rock?*"

The vehicles began their long road toward the heart of Istanbul's capital.

I slowly peeled back the layers of our journey. I fed the twins just enough information for them to know that we needed access to the Well of Souls under the *Dome of the Rock*.

…And beyond that, King Solomon's vault, the *Holiest of Holies*.

The search for such a chamber beneath the temple had sparked centuries of wars in the city. The Qur'an detailed its location within its writings, while multiple bibles and poems provided different facts to back up its existence.

Still, little truth was really known. Most stories embellished that a wealth of caverns, cisterns, and chambers existed under the dome. More specifically, under the foundation stone at the center of the temple.

In the Jewish writing, Talmud, it was said that the large stone covered the abyss. Raging waters flowed through the open chasm, creating a river of paradise.

Other writings expressed the vast amount of treasure buried within these chambers, with the most prominent location being the *Holiest of Holies*.

Burt's eyes lit up at the sound of this.

We had the clues to access this secret mystery.

"All we need is one small object in the vault, and the rest is yours," I told him.

"We've played that game once before," Berta said. "What is that object?"

"Don't you worry about it," I retorted. "There will be plenty for you guys in the end."

Burt took a sip of his wine. "And where exactly is the entrance to this hidden chamber that no one has ever been able to find, Charlie?"

"Under the foundation stone," I said bluntly.

Burt laughed. "No one has been able to find anything down there."

J.J. spoke up. "Actually, you are mistaken, Mr. Taijan. There is no living being today who has ever been allowed to explore the cavern beneath the foundation stone. The last known archeologists to search the dome were British explorers, Charles Wilson and Sir Charles Warren. This was many, many years ago. Political issues have prevented anyone from being allowed down there for further exploration."

"And what did they find?" Berta asked intrigued.

"Not much, it seems. Just a few tunnels around the temple, according to records," J.J. said. "But you must not forget, this area has seen its share of devastation. The Crusaders disfigured part of the foundation stone back in the year 1,099 C.E."

J.J. continued his lesson. "In that era, they converted the temple to a church, and labeled it *Templum Domini*. They destroyed part of the foundation stone and created a set of sixteen marble steps down to the holy chamber beneath it. This provided easy access to the small room below. You must also remember, even before the *Dome of the Rock* was ever built, two other temples existed on the same grounds."

"Mr. Jenkins, your knowledge is impeccable," Berta said. "Your reputation certainly precedes you."

The Temple Mount, where the dome was constructed, stood as the holiest part of the city. With all the overlapping architecture erected on the mound, the *Holiest of Holies* could easily lie somewhere beneath the building.

If *Xi Wangmu's* tablet was right, then we needed to find that access point. It was just our luck that the temple was a shrine to the Hebrew religion. Hebrews and Muslims were very protective of the site.

Guards patrolled the area, and surveillance ran 24/7 to make sure no one defiled such an important attraction. It was going to be difficult to gain entry.

This was the second reason I contacted my twin friends. With their connections, the Traijans easily closed off the temple from the public.

Roped off and shut down, the *Dome of the Rock* was vacant for the entire day. We had all the time in the world to explore the building.

"This wasn't an easy task," Burt said, exaggerating the difficulty it took.

"Really? I would have thought the most powerful man in this city would have little problem getting such a task done," I commented.

"Charlie, your *task* cost us a lot of favors and money," Burt said.

Berta leaned in, touching my thigh. "I'm sure whatever Charlie finds down there will more than happily cover our expenses."

I nodded.

I hoped.

The Hummers continued down the road to the ancient city of Jerusalem. As we neared, the quiet sands faded away to small greenery and modern day amenities. The dry climate provided an airy atmosphere to the architecture and vegetation.

We passed through the outer wall of the city, and into the claustrophobic streets. The roads were dense with pedestrians and vehicles going about their business.

Through the tinted windows, I watched everyday life commence around us. The cars zoomed past fruit markets, parks, and residential districts. History bled out of every crevice of every building.

The capital stood as a lone beacon in the middle of nowhere. Short structures made up the majority of the city, with a handful of towering skyscrapers sticking out like sore thumbs in a field of beige. Crammed networks of roads seemed nearly impossible to navigate, but our driver easily made sense of the chaos.

Still, for such a prize city which consisted of years of Israeli-Palestinian conflict, it didn't seem much different than any other town in the region...

...Except for the large bronze dome that glistened in the high sun. That dome stood on an octagonal structure, which in turn was erected in the center of a large platform known as the Temple Mount. That beautiful element belonged to one of the holiest locations in the world.

The *Dome of the Rock.*

"We have taken the liberty of closing down all the neighboring areas as well. This will prevent any distractions or witnesses," Burt said, pointing ahead of our vehicle.

Caution tape ran across a number of alleyways. Construction barricades blocked others. Contractors milled about, pretending to work. I had to give it to the Traijans, they knew how to get things done.

"How did you close down the whole area, let alone the historical monument?" Jenny said, amazed.

Berta brushed off her question as if insulted.

Burt responded instead, "We claimed that there was a dangerous sewer leak. By roping off the entire vicinity, we can minimize suspicions. You will have no problems entering the temple at your leisure."

I leaned in, whispering, "I told you, my friends have some good connections."

Jenny came in close, replying, "This must have cost a fortune. With all the religious conflicts going on, I'm sure it isn't sitting well with some sects out here."

"I agree Charles," J.J. said. "There will most likely be a lot of people angered by this. We must tread cautiously."

"There is no need to worry Mr. and Ms. Jenkins. We have everything under control. We have security all over the complex. There is nothing we wouldn't do for Charlie." Berta stared at me.

Jenny whispered, "I thought you told me you helped get them out of a jam. Why do they feel like they owe you so much? From the sounds of it, you three should be even."

"You remember that painting I was searching for in Italy?" I began. Jenny nodded. "Well, after I gave it to my benefactor, I was approached by the twins. They found that there was more to the *Trial of Saint Stephen*. Apparently, there was a map inscribed on the back.

"I double-crossed the guy who hired me, and told Burt and Berta who he was. They stole the painting back, and went off to hunt for the treasure. It's what kickstarted their fortune," I finished.

"You get any of that money?"

I frowned. "Why do you think they owe me?"

Jenny shook her head. She turned back to look out the window.

The caravan drove down the final stretch of road. Ahead, a stone wall blotted out our vision of anything. The stone extended in either direction, creating a massive platform. It rose to form a mound which acted as the foundation for the large temple situated at its center.

We had arrived at the Temple Mount, and more importantly, our final destination.

CHAPTER TWENTY NINE

The *Dome of the Rock* was a thing of beauty. From the outside, the temple stood as a marvel in iconography, mosaics, and exquisite architecture.

Its structure framed out in the shape of an octagon. A series of columns and archways bordered the entrances. Porcelain walls lined the perimeter, and dozens of windows provided an abundance of natural daylight into the temple.

We all admired its splendor.

Burt's phone suddenly came alive. He answered. On his end, all we heard were a few acknowledging gestures. The voice on the other end muffled away.

Burt's excited facial expression instantly shifted to anger. His voice rose as he spoke in his native tongue. None of us understood what he was saying—except his sister of course.

Berta motioned us out of the car. "Don't mind his rudeness, go on."

Stepping out of the vehicle, J.J., Jenny, and I continued to stare at the towering structure. The sixty foot diameter main dome topped the building like a cap. Its smooth bronze finish was blinding to stare at directly.

Burt and Berta remained in the comfortably conditioned Hummer. We heard soft whispers coming from the open door of the large vehicle.

Finally, the door shut.

Berta rolled down the window, saying, "Charlie, there has been an unexpected emergency. We need to attend to this matter in a timely fashion. Feel free to do as you wish until we get back. Our men shall provide any assistance you may require."

"Thank you again, to the both of you," I said.

Burt remained on the phone arguing. The caravan of cars turned and drove away.

We were left alone.

Minus all the men with guns that roamed the holy grounds.

"That was odd," Jenny said.

"And what might be so odd, sweetheart?" J.J. asked. His eyes still locked onto the temple.

"Those two seemed so excited to find King Solomon's vault only to rush out of here so quickly."

I strolled past her. "You don't know them well enough, Jen. That is what they do. They don't have the patience to sit around and wait. They'll make us do all the heavy lifting, then swoop in at the end to reap the rewards."

"You have some good friends, Charlie," Jenny replied.

I didn't argue.

We decided to get to work.

J.J.'s translation of the second *Trinity* tablet (J.J.'s nickname for the stones left behind by Homer) pointed us to this location. Still, it didn't give us much to go on. Telling the Traijan siblings that we found the access point kind of stretched the truth. We were heading into this blind.

But we were determined. A young girl's life depended on it. If the Baron was as resourceful as J.J. believed, he would eventually figure out the puzzle. We didn't have that much time.

We needed a place to start. We quickly split up to see what we could find.

The Temple Mount housing this massive dome had many other structures littered about. The three of us did a cursory lap to analyze what we were getting ourselves into.

"Charles," J.J. began. "Do you see all the openings around the perimeter of the Temple Mount?"

A series of arched doorways flanked the walls. Most of them had crumbled in upon themselves, blocking any point of entry.

J.J. continued, "Those lead to a number of cisterns under the temple. Through the few that are still functional, there are remains from the old temple."

"You think one of those cisterns may lead to the vault?" I asked sadly. It would be near impossible to search every one of those tunnels, let alone blow them open in the first place. Plus, making that kind of noise would certainly attract attention.

"No, from my understanding, none of these caves head anywhere, and based off of Homer's tablet, the Well of Souls is the doorway."

"Great, then I think it's about time we check this *well* out?" I said.

We marched up a set of stairs and to the main interior.

We stepped into an open space. Daylight flooded through all the large windows. For as voluminous as the room was, it was fairly simple.

A circle of twenty four columns held up the main dome. The walls were smooth and covered in mosaic tiles. Still, there weren't many other intricacies. It stood as a tall dome on stilts, with flat walls all around.

We passed under the low ceiling space, through a pair of columns, and into the tall arched central chamber. Our eyes marveled at the details, but soon fixated on the ground in the middle of the temple.

Marble flooring gave way, providing a circular frame to a large irregularly shaped rock that covered most of the sixty foot radius. The rock rose slightly above the finished floor.

A few rough corners and dents protruded out of the natural stone. Other than that, it was perfectly smooth. A single pierced hole penetrated the one corner of the rock.

The way the ground disappeared around it, it was as if the entire thing hovered in space.

This is what the natives worshiped. This was the natural phenomenon that civilizations fought over. This was the Foundation Stone that was said to float over the earth.

The open cavity beneath the rock was where we would find the Well of Souls.

"She is beautiful," Jenny said, brushing her hand over the stone.

"What makes it a *she?*" I asked.

"She's too beautiful to be a *he.* Women were God's miracle, Charlie. Seeing this, it definitely falls into miracle territory."

I took a closer look at the rock. It was true. The entire thing did look as if it floated in space. How could nature have done this?

J.J. answered my thoughts. "This was where the prophet Muhammad transcended to the heavens. According to medieval Islamic tradition, the rock rose from the ground to follow Muhammad's ascension. Archangel Gabriel restrained the stone from rising as the prophet continued his ascent to the heavens. You can see the angel's hand print embedded into the stone there."

I saw the faint indentations. Then I noticed the breakaway in the stone. Parts of it were carved out, creating a winding path of marble stairs down to the Well of Souls. This was the mark left by the crusaders—defiling part of the holy ground to give them access to the cavern under the stone.

"You guys ready do head down the rabbit hole?" I asked.

We marched down the stairs and into the cave.

Unfortunately, our travels ended fairly quickly.

The place was made for midgets.

The ceiling of the cavern was barely six feet tall. It was a small square space that outlined the same shape of the foundation stone above. A niche in one corner formed the shrine of King Solomon. Another shrine carved out of the opposing end. The rest of the space was bare.

That was it.

My hair frizzled under the rocky ceiling as I calmly walked around the crammed room. "Wow, this isn't quite what I expected."

Jenny's eyes were wide. "Are you serious? This place is beautiful."

Faint daylight crept into the chamber. Another solid bead of light spotlighted through the pierced hole in the corner of the rock. It laser pointed a bright spot on the ground. I approached it.

"Jen, don't get me wrong, it is a marvel, but this isn't really giving us many stones to turn over."

Pun intended.

I knelt down by the lit area and washed my hand over it.

Nothing.

Glancing around the room, there wasn't a single loose surface or mark hinting to any point of access to the *Holiest of Holies*.

This might be a short trip.

J.J. made his way around the walls. "Charles, there's a reason the tablet led us here. Have faith. Now, make yourself useful, and start looking around."

I did.

In the center, the stone ceiling opened up to another circular hole. This was much larger than the pierced hole. Looking through it, it seemed more like a circular shaft up to the surface. The opening allowed for a good amount of daylight to enter the small chamber.

"A natural skylight," I commented out loud.

Jenny stood near King Solomon's shrine. She felt along the walls, searching for signs. "These walls are so smooth. How could they have done this?"

"Water of course," J.J. began. "This chamber must have been filled with water at some point. Typically, a constant stream could smooth the surface of its entrapping walls."

"Hence the name Well of Souls," I said ironically.

I glanced back up the circular opening in the center. "If this chamber acted like a literal well, this opening must have been the area where the bucket was lowered to retrieve water."

"That is an Islamic theory, but look at the walls of the opening. They too are smooth. There are no rope burns that are typical of wells. If it were the case, then the lowered bucket would usually scratch the walls of this shaft."

Jenny entered the discussion. "Still, where would the water have come from?"

Good point.

The chamber was enclosed by walls on all four sides. There was no tunnel leading anywhere, but the fact that water ran to this location meant that there did need to be an opening somewhere.

I got excited.

In silence, we continued to feel around the room. It was no use. Every wall, ceiling, and floor was solid.

I paused a moment to think.

There had to be something we were missing.

That's when I felt it.

The soles of my shoes felt soft vibrations. It was barely noticeable, but it was just enough.

"You guys feel that?" I asked.

I dropped to my knees and put my ear to the ground. Pressing hard against the rocky surface, I strained to listen. Faint sounds echoed below. It was the sounds of running water. There was some sort of river flowing beneath us. I could feel the water current pulsate its rocky walls.

"J.J. there's a river below us," I said. I knocked on the ground and heard the hollow thump.

There was definitely a cavern below our feet.

J.J. did the same. "Charles, the writings in the *Talmun* were correct. They detailed an abyss below the well, where a river of paradise existed."

We were onto something.

"J.J., this is great and all, but we still don't know how to get down there. Do we blow the floor?"

"We can't do that," Jenny chimed in. "This is holy ground."

We felt around. There needed to be some loose surface. Suddenly, J.J.'s eyes lit up. He jumped to his feet, stepping away from us.

Confused, I followed suit. "J.J. what's wrong?"

I watched my old friend pace back and forth in silence. I knew this look. His brain was churning. He was onto something. I had seen it many times before.

"Dad, what are you thinking?" Jenny asked.

J.J. smiled at her, yet still said nothing.

"Okay old man, no need for your theatrics. You figured it out, didn't you?" I said.

J.J. nodded. "Oh, but Charles, you two were the ones who figured it out. I was just smart enough to put it all together."

"Well, how about you spell it out for us plain folk."

J.J. started toward the stairs. "I believe it will be easier to show you. Are you ready for a little history lesson?"

Great.

Every time J.J. made a discovery, he always felt the need to relish in the moment. I guess I took after him to some extent, but he was much more over the top.

Jeremy rushed up the marble steps. Jenny and I followed, eagerly wanting to see what J.J. had uncovered. My old friend was walking fast now. He sped out the building and back to the expansive Temple Mount.

As I tried to keep up, I said, "J.J. I thought the entry point was the Well of Souls? Aren't we going in the opposite direction?"

"No, my good Charles. The tablet was correct in where we needed to go. It is us who are in the wrong location."

Standing at the southern edge of the stone platform that housed the *Dome of the Rock*, J.J. looked off in the distance. He squinted in the sunlight trying to find something. Jenny and I stood behind him, wondering what he was searching for.

Finally, my friend's smile returned. "There."

He pointed.

Following his finger, I looked off in the distance. No more than a football field away, J.J. pointed at a small outcropping of bushes.

"Uh, J.J., I'm not sure if we're looking at the same thing," I said.

"Yes, Charles we are. Those bushes surround the Gihon Spring. The spring was the source of water to the old city of Jerusalem—back when it was known as the City of David. Now, most of it has bled dry."

Jenny didn't understand. Neither of us did. She asked, "Yeah, but what does that have to do with the dome?"

"Nothing," Jeremy stated bluntly.

We remained silent.

"You two are forgetting that the dome was built much later than Homer's poem. He mentioned King Solomon and his first temple."

"The first temple was destroyed, and a second temple was built on top of it," I said recalling my limited history.

"Yes, but there were never any remains found of the original temple. Only of the second one. We base all our knowledge of King Solomon's first temple solely through the Qur'an."

"I'm still not following," I said.

"There are many theories of where the First Temple was located. Many believed it to be here, at the Temple Mount, but there are conflicting geographical facts about its true location. Different Islamic dialogues detailed that the temple was built over an enormous spring.

"The spring was a holy place, hence the name Well of Souls. And in the 10th century, when it was built, the Gihon Spring was the only functioning well."

I started to follow. "You think that the Well of Souls was a literal well—the Gihon Spring."

"Precisely. An old archeological dig, from years ago, uncovered two columns at the base of the spring which had inscriptions dating back to the 10th century.

"Jenny stated that this was holy ground. It wouldn't have been back then though. The holiest ground was the area that gave life to the world. And what was a better source of life than the waters of a spring?"

Jenny smiled at her father's acknowledgement.

"And Charles," J.J. continued, "You heard the running of water beneath the surface. You found that caverns ran under the Temple Mount. The only place that could lead to tunnels of water, is the only place to have ever had running water."

"The washed up, Gihon Spring," I whispered. My brain made the connection. J.J. was a genius. "Sometimes, J.J. you impress me."

"Sometimes? Charles, I believe I impress people more times than not."

"You're giving yourself too much credit," I said walking away.

"Where are you going?" Jeremy asked.

"To the spring." I pointed to the bushes in the distance. "We're not going to just stand here are we?"

Excited, we began our trek down the flight of stairs. We headed toward our next location. None of us noticed that all the other bodyguards hired by Burt and Berta were all missing.

CHAPTER THIRTY

Calling the Gihon Spring a well was a bit of an overstatement. As we made our trek to the open mouth of the spring, we were instead welcomed by a cavernous tunnel of dry rock.

Not a single drop of water lay at the bottom.

The cave carved out of a rocky hill. It opened up to an empty river bed. Two stone columns flanked the opening—remnants of the once grand spring.

"This is it?" Jenny asked, a little confused.

"You don't seem excited," I said dryly, stepping down into the cave.

"It's just a cave."

"It seems like this is a recurring theme for us. At least there's no gated puzzle," I said.

"You may be speaking too soon," Jenny commented. She pointed to words inscribed in the stone pillars that framed the opening.

J.J. translated one of the engravings. "It says, *only under God's name shall you be granted passage.*"

I shined my flashlight into the tunnel. The light reflected off of the jagged surfaces, disappearing into darkness. A haunting howl echoed out of the tunnel.

Then, a breeze breathed out of the opening. The hair on my arms stood upright.

"After you," I said, motioning J.J. forward. "This is your theory."

J.J. remained still. "Maybe I was mistaken. You're the one following an old man's advice. You should lead the way." J.J. smiled.

Jenny interrupted, "How about I lead." She stole my flashlight and marched on into the tunnel.

Glancing behind us, I made sure we weren't followed. I then entered the dark cave.

The interior of the Gihon Spring was damp. Mildew odors filled the path. The misshapen walls formed a distinct route deeper into the channel.

I wondered how far the tunnel ran. With the amount of water that once ran through the spring, we could be wandering through these channels for miles.

Luckily, the path was fairly linear. If this was as bad as the labyrinth I navigated back in China, we'd be stuck in here for ages.

Jenny marked the wall with a small pocket knife.

"Well done," J.J. said, congratulating his daughter.

Jenny was leaving a bread crumb trail for us, just in case the arterial passage started to split apart. This way we'd be able to find our way back.

J.J. pushed faster. His initial fear of the unknown melted away. He illuminated his flashlight and marched ahead of us.

"Easy there, J.J. You're going to hurt yourself at that pace," I joked.

"Charles, we are on the brink of something."

My friend was right. All I wanted to do was stop the Baron and save his daughter, but the treasure hunter inside of me was excited at the prospect of what we were potentially about to uncover.

I soon followed suit, matching Jeremy's pace.

Jenny, too, seemed excited. Her regret for wanting to continue the journey faded away as adrenaline propelled her. "Charlie, you think the Arc of the Covenant will be there?"

I forgot about that.

We were searching for King Solomon's vault, the *Holiest of Holies*. Our reason was for a missing tablet, but legends told of many other treasures hidden in the aforementioned vault. The most famous of them being the Arc of the Covenant—the casket that housed the Ten Commandments.

"I don't know, but it won't hurt to check while we're there, right?" I grinned back.

"How about we focus on finding the entrance to the vault before we jump to any conclusions," J.J. knocked us back to reality.

As we continued moving through the stone passageway, the walls began to narrow. Our feet splattered in puddles of water, and the temperature dropped a solid ten degrees.

Our journey was taking us deeper underground, and no signs confirmed we were on the right track. J.J. didn't lose steam though. He hated being proven wrong. He was determined to find the entrance.

In the midst of complete darkness, our first sign finally came.

The river tunnel split like a fork in the road. Both paths led in opposite directions. I directed my light down one path, then the other. Each seemed exactly the same.

"Which way?" Jenny asked.

I scanned the perimeter of the two openings, and instantly found my answer.

"Left," I said confidently.

The other two looked puzzled, but as their eyes followed my flashlight, they too saw the answer.

Engraved in the top of the one cave opening was the symbol of the sun. A distinct circle with flames radiating from it.

The sign of Apollo, the Sun God. Our symbol for Pythia.

In China, the sun led the way. From *Xi Wangmu's* cave entrance, to the labyrinth of the *tree of life.*

With the trinity tablets, each stone was shaped like the hot star.

If it worked once, I looked at it as unique. Twice, coincidence. After that, it was a legitimate sign. There was no need to question it.

In silence, we continued further into the cave. We were stopped by a few more branching paths. Again, we followed the same methodology. Like clockwork, each time we discovered one circular symbol leading the right way.

For some odd reason, none of us feared the darkness. We had been underground for nearly an hour, and we did not look back once. There was an easy answer why. With every sign we found inscribed on the wall, it fueled our passion.

Soon, we were nearly running through the slick tunnels. The walls became smoother. More water splashed at our feet.

Finally our scenery abruptly shifted.

Passing through a marked opening, we did not enter another stretch of caves. We stepped into a large chamber.

We had arrived.

It was a little early to say we arrived at King Solomon's vault, but we DID enter a different room that looked to be the entrance to it. A flat ceiling rose fifteen feet above us. The walls were straight and smooth, creating a perfectly square chamber. The most intriguing point of interest covered the far wall of the room.

Spanning nearly the entire length of wall, a series of square stones sequentially stacked over one another in a uniform pattern. Getting a better look at them, each stone had a unique Hebrew letter engraved on it.

The wall was a life size ancient keyboard.

"Stunning, absolutely stunning," J.J. said, walking up close to the stone covered wall.

Jenny too was mesmerized. "Look at the floor," she said pointing to a symbol of three concentric circles drawn over the rock.

"Whoever said, 'X' marks the spot was wrong," I snidely commented.

Shining my light up, I noticed that the stone ceiling was perforated with a series of small holes. Venting perhaps? The room was much colder than the caves we just exited.

"Charles, come take a look," Jeremy ordered.

I abided.

J.J. stood, touching one of the stone squares. "The full Hebrew alphabet is carved into these stones. More importantly, watch this." Jeremy pushed on one of the stones.

"I'm not sure you should be doing that," I thought aloud.

The individual stone depressed a few inches. When Jeremy released it, it maintained that position for a few seconds, then automatically ground its way back to its original position. A soft clattering of gears cranked behind the wall.

"It is some sort of machine," J.J. said.

"I see that. It looks like a typewriter. Plug in the correct letters and *open says me.*" I felt a few other stones.

"But what is the magic word?" Jenny asked.

We searched around the room for clues. Other than the circles in the floor, there was no evidence of any other signs. I brushed my fingers over the stones hoping to notice any irregularities. There weren't any. J.J. sat in the center of the room pondering.

I stepped up beside him. "What are you thinking?" I asked.

"I'm trying to recollect any other clues given to us up to this point. The tablet never provided any insight to this riddle. Perhaps Homer's tale has the clue."

"Unfortunately, we don't have that information," I said.

Jenny soon chimed in. "What if Homer has nothing to do with it."

We both looked at her.

Jenny continued, "Back at *Xi Wangmu's* temple, there were two totems which opened the gate. When we first entered the spring, two columns flanked the opening.

"Dad, as you said, those columns were uncovered during an archeological dig of the well. They date back to the 8th century. What if those were the same keys to opening this gate?"

She had a point, I gave her that. "So you're saying we need to head all the way back?" I asked.

"No, my dad translated a portion of it when we first entered. What was it again? *Only under God's name shall you be granted passage?*"

J.J. stood up. "You are correct, honey." Jeremy turned to face the stone wall.

If Jenny was right, then *God's name* was the answer. In the Islamic bible, there was one true God. Writings of that century described him as *El.* But, in the Qur'an, he was known by one name. A name that continued on until today.

"Yahweh," J.J. said.

The National God of Israel.

"It's worth a shot," I replied.

Jeremy marched up to the life-size keyboard and began punching in the letters.

Y-A-H-W-E-H.

The last 'H' depressed into the wall.

We waited with baited breath. Nothing happened. It seemed like hours passed. In actuality, it was merely seconds.

As the stone returned to its original position, there was a loud snap from somewhere behind the wall. Sounds of gears cranked. We had released something.

"I think you did it," I said, stunned.

J.J. did something all right. Unfortunately, it wasn't a *good* something. The opening we first came through suddenly closed on itself. A massive stone wall rose out of the ground sealing us in.

The floor rumbled alive. The vibration wasn't tremendous, but it was enough to feel the ground strain.

Dust particles fell from above. The rumbling grew, and the cranking mechanisms behind the walls rose in volume.

Shining my light upward, I realized why.

The entire perforated stone ceiling began to lower. It moved at a constant speed on a direct trajectory toward the floor.

In the process, it would squish anything separating it from its target. We were the only things standing in the way.

"I'm guessing that wasn't the right name," I commented.

Frantic, Jenny scrambled to the closed opening. She tried pushing the stone wall blocking our path. "We need to get out of here."

J.J. and I raced over to help.

The ceiling inched downward.

Pushing my muscles as hard as I could, it did little to move the stone out of our path.

We tried again to no avail.

Sweating, I stepped away. "It's no use. That thing won't budge."

The ceiling lowered two feet already. At this rate, we were in for a slow death.

"It's going to flatten us like a pancake," Jenny yelled.

The confines of the room were increasingly getting shorter. My eyes searched for another escape. My beating heart pounded through my earlobes. Panic enveloped.

Then, my sight returned to the stone keyboard. "What if we try another name?"

"Charles, but what?" J.J. asked. "What is another name for God?"

Think!

With the deafening sounds of our impending doom, my head ached. I struggled to concentrate.

"Charlie?" Jenny said.

"Give me a second," I thought. I recollected my Islamic history. Yahweh, was the name for God. Everyone knew this. In the Hebrew language, it was written just as Jeremy typed. It even—

It dawned on me.

"Guys, biblical Hebrew never used vowels. Every word was written in consonants. That means that Yahweh would have been spelled YHWH."

As if lighting a spark, J.J. jumped alive. "Well done, Charles! How did I miss such an obvious fact?"

The ceiling lowered another foot.

We darted across the chamber to the keyboard. Quickly, I typed in the four letters.

Y-H-W-H.

Was it that simple?

Suddenly, the ceiling stopped. The cranks ceased in the backdrop. Silence filled the room. We let out a victorious laugh. We did it!

I sighed in relief, but I realized something.

No door opened.

As if on cue, a high pitched screech blared. Covering our ears, our faces tightened in reaction to the bloodcurdling sound. It was as if nails scratched the surface of a chalkboard.

The noise stopped abruptly.

"What was that?" Jenny asked.

I shined my light up at the ceiling just in time to see a series of metal spikes protrude out of the perforated holes in the ceiling. Each spike extended a foot out of the stone. In seconds, the entire surface was covered in sharp blades.

The cranks came back to life, and the ceiling continued its descent once again, this time at a faster pace.

"It looks like we were wrong," I said.

My heart beat quicker. Jenny and J.J. scrambled back to the stone doorway, desperately trying to pry it loose. I didn't move. I simply watched my friends struggle to stay alive. Our room quickly closed in on itself, ready to kill us in a matter of minutes.

I looked back at the keyboard. What the heck did it want us to type? What was *God's name?* Did we even read the clues right?

Soon, it wasn't going to make a difference. We'd be dead.

My head throbbed as I strained to jog my memory. My mind flashed over every history book and every story I had ever heard. I thought of J.J.'s long lessons on religion and God.

I thought of my parents—of their death, and of my anger when I let them die. I remembered wishing I could bring them back.

Back then, I looked into many religions. I wanted to know what happened to people after death. Did they go to Heaven? Would I see them again? Those were the first days I remembered learning about the Greek gods, Yahweh, and all the other religious beings. I needed to find proof of life after death. I needed...

...My train of thought instantly stopped.

All the other religious beings.

Islam was a monotheistic religion. It believed in one true God. But this wasn't always the case.

In ancient times, the nation was a polytheistic religion, much like the ancient Greeks. They believed in multiple gods—and goddesses.

There was one more name that could work.

Excited, I ran over to the stone wall. Jenny screamed at me to help, but I ignored her. The ceiling was just under eight feet now. We didn't have time.

I reached the wall and quickly punched in a seven letter combination. As I pressed the last stone, I stepped back. The tips of blades scratched the top of my hair.

I ducked down, praying.

A quiet click released behind the wall.

The ceiling stopped in its tracks. The blades sucked back into their homes within the perforated openings, and the ceiling began to return to its original position.

Then there was a moment of surreal silence. None of us moved.

The stone slab blocking the entrance suddenly slid back out of the way. A number of the square stones lining the keyboard wall depressed inward. They disappeared into darkness. As more stones disappeared, a new opening revealed itself. Soon, a rectangular doorway framed out of the wall.

We had opened the gate to the *Holiest of Holies.*

Jeremy ran up to me. "Charles, you did it! I can't believe it." He hugged me in excitement.

I let out a deep breath. I couldn't believe it either.

Jenny rushed me for an embrace too. The Jenkins family jumped for joy.

"What did you type?" Jenny asked.

"Asherah," I said, in a *matter of fact* tone.

"Asherah?" Jenny asked, confused.

But J.J. had a grin from ear to ear. He understood. "You are a genius," he said, kissing me on the cheek.

I explained to our young apprentice. "J.J. read the stone pillar, saying, *Only under God's name shall you be granted passage,* but it never specified which one. Back in the 8th century, Yahweh wasn't the only god the natives believed in. He had himself a partner."

I paused for effect, then said, "A goddess, if you will. Many believed her to be his consort, but over time, history removed her from the religion."

"How did you know that?" Jenny wondered.

"I did my share of research on gods back in the day. And as I thought of *Asherah*, I remembered that she had a nickname— Queen of Heaven."

Jenny's brain caught up. "Just like *Xi Wangmu*, and the Oracle of Delphi."

"Exactly. Homer's story circled around women, so it only made sense that it continued the trend," I confirmed.

"Charles, I have to say, hats off to you," Jeremy said patting my shoulder.

This was the second time in three months I got a concrete compliment from my old friend. It felt good. Secretly, I was sure J.J. was disappointed he didn't figure it out. Now, having found the opening, it did validate his theory on the Gihon Spring.

We all turned to the dark tunnel that led ahead. We were the first people in history to enter King Solomon's vault. In such a momentous discovery, none of us moved.

"You may do the honors," Jeremy said to me.

I stepped through the hole in the wall, around the depressed stones, and into the next chamber.

Nothing could have prepared me for what my eyes were about to see.

CHAPTER THIRTY ONE

This was not King Solomon's vault. It was not our final destination. It wasn't even any kind of chamber.

It was a stone ledge.

The ledge overlooked a flowing river that ran down a massive underground tunnel. The path disappeared in darkness.

Water currents churned with power, crashing against the stone walls with frightening force. Falling into the rapids would easily suck a person under.

But that wasn't the awe inspiring discovery that stopped me in my tracks.

What stunned me was proof that we weren't the first people to enter this cave.

"Jeremy, you need to see this," I said, staring straight ahead.

J.J. and Jenny came through the opening to meet me. "Charles, what could you possibly have…"

J.J.'s voice trailed off as he looked at what lay before us.

A series of bronze rails hovered in the air. The metal rails ran like train tracks over the roaring water—two rods, parallel to one another. They extended down the tunnel and into the darkness.

The rods ran by in both directions. Horizontal bars connected them together, truly making them look like full blown train tracks. And our ledge was the train station.

Vertical support members disappeared under the water, most likely anchoring to the rock below. Those supports were all that held up the tracks.

Another series of tracks ran beside the first set. They followed the same route.

These modern structures could only have been built much later than the 8th century. Another sign that confirmed this theory was the large platform resting on the rails.

The platform was shaped like an open train car. In lieu of wheels, expertly carved rocks tied the car to the metal rails. And on top of the platform, a distinct set of piloting controls framed out of the front end.

Throttles, speedometers, electrical wiring, and exposed machinery proved that this car was built within the last hundred years.

"This is impeccable," Jeremy said astonished.

I walked up to the train car. The ledge we stood on molded into a perfect loading platform. It naturally led to the boarding plane of the vehicle.

Testing one foot on the metal train car, I exerted some pressure. The car didn't budge.

I peered under the machine to get a closer look at the rocks that tied to the makeshift railroad.

"How is this possible? The rock is somehow hovering over the rail, but not touching it," I said.

Jeremy leaned in to touch the rock. "This is a rare earth rock. It is magnetized, and in direct opposite polarization. That is why it pushes away from the bronze rail."

"How do you know that?" I asked.

"Because it is commonly used on engine motors these days, from small machinery to large turbines. Sustainability has led environmentalists to use these rare earth stones in compressive generators. You can run engines at a lower speed, and by having these stones operate the receiving end, the motor can multiply its efficiency tenfold."

Jenny stepped onto the train car. Even with her full weight, the car still remained hovering over the metal rails.

"I think I'm more scared now than I was when I thought this was an ancient ruin," I said, stepping on board.

"Why is that?" Jenny asked.

"Ancient mysteries, I'm good with. Finding modern technology in a place it's not supposed to be? That freaks me out."

I scanned the controls. One lever seemed to operate the acceleration. Another acted as the break.

I then walked along the entire train car. It was only twenty feet long by seven feet wide. I reached the rear of the car in a matter of steps.

Looking at the butt of the vehicle, I saw a steam engine. This seemed to power the train.

"So, it is safe to say that someone may have been down here before," Jenny said.

"Clearly," I began. I looked over at the other railroad tracks that ran parallel to ours. They stood empty, with no train car. "And seeing that those tracks don't have a matching car on them, I wonder if we are not alone."

It would be just our luck.

"Who do you think built all this?" Jenny asked.

"I don't know, but it sure does look expensive."

Jenny stared off at the disappearing tracks. "And, I wonder why," she thought.

Jeremy added to the conversation. "My educated guess is that this river acts as a loop through the bowels of the Old City of David.

Boats must have taken the treasures through the channel to the vault. And now, modern technology helped craft a faster route."

"Yeah, but look at the river J.J. Those rapids would tear boats apart," I said.

"Yes, but thousands of years ago, it may have been a steady stream."

"Whatever the case, the important question still remains. Who built it?" I asked.

There were no insignias or distinct markings on the train car. All the elements were clean and simple. A single protective guardrail ran around the rectangular platform. A number of openings signaled the boarding areas. Front and rear headlights, and respective bumpers, added protective measures.

This wasn't a ragtag construction. Whoever built the hovering train spent a lot of time and energy to fabricate all the complexities. They also exhausted a lot of money in the process.

Our mystery suddenly grew. Our questions multiplied. Our fears returned. I tried thinking about who could have done all this.

Jenny was the first to draw a conclusion. "Charlie, maybe these are the same people who attacked us in China—the hooded assassins."

Oh I remembered those guys.

"The *Men Shen*? I don't know. They looked a little behind in the times. Based on their primitive weapons, you think they had the manpower and money to do this?"

Jenny added, "They were the protectors of the tomb. The same scenario could be playing out here. This group of protectors could just be more advanced."

Jeremy spoke up, "Or maybe these are all the same group." J.J. came up close. "When Jennifer read Homer's tale, she commented on a society of people who carried the Oracle's epitaph across many lands."

"The Sons of Apollo," Jenny said.

"Correct. Maybe these *Sons* are guarding the three pieces of stone. Think about it, years of legends can morph a story. After a few centuries, it takes a life of its own. The *Men Shen* could just as easily be the Chinese transformation of these original protectors."

"And, the Sun symbolism used at Xi Wangmu's temple tied directly to the Sun god, Apollo," I added.

Jenny piggybacked off this theory. "The sun markings in this cave continue the trend."

J.J. said, "AND, I am sure that these same protectors must have existed in India when they found the first tablet. If this is one sect of people, then their numbers could be much larger than the group living in the Chinese mountains."

"If history serves me correctly, and we're dealing with the same group of men, then there is a good chance that they are nearby," I pointed out.

Seconds after making my comment, all of our flashlights were turned on. We searched the immediate surroundings, checking every crevice. We scanned the ceilings. We even checked the waters below.

We found nothing.

My hands shook uncontrollably. Thoughts brought me back to my near death experience with my hooded attackers. I needed to calm myself. Taking a few deep breaths, my pulse slowly reduced back to normal.

I turned back to the others. "Okay, so now we may actually be in some real danger. I've asked a lot out of you two up to this point. I understand if—"

"If you think we should speed it along a little?" Jenny asked, smiling.

J.J. added, "Charles, Jenny and I are the ones already on the train car. As always, we're waiting on you."

"I was going to say, *turn back.*" I shook my head. Climbing on board, I added, "You know how to drive that thing, old man?"

Jeremy was already at the rear engine. He flipped a few switches. The engine came to life, chugging away.

"I think I can manage," J.J. said. He headed back to the front controls.

The entire platform vibrated while the engine rumbled along. At the front controls, Jeremy turned a few knobs, and flipped a number of switches.

The front and rear headlights lit up with force. The bright spotlights illuminated the cave ahead, nearly drowning the entire area in fluorescence.

Jenny and I instinctively huddled up near J.J. There were a lot of unknowns about this train car. First and foremost, was our question of safety.

I hoped that the train could stay together for the next part of our journey. I also hoped that there was enough power to return.

J.J. didn't seem to worry much. He released the braking mechanism, saying, "You may want to hold onto something."

My pride told me to not move, but my fear won the battle. I latched onto one of the guardrails. Jenny followed suit.

Jeremy pulled the throttle back, and the train lurched forward. It was slow at first, inching along at a snail's pace. After a few feet, the vehicle picked up steam.

The magnetic rocks locked the car in line with the bronze railroad. The train started to glide along the predetermined route.

J.J. pulled the throttle back some more. The train continued to speed up, reaching twenty miles an hour.

Moist air rushed past our faces. Mist from the waters below sprinkled our bodies, instantly cooling us off. The headlights clearly lit the road ahead.

The path remained simple and straight. Soon, the cave opened up wide. Dripping wet stone walls surrounded us. We embarked deeper into mysterious territory.

J.J. was exceptionally excited. He felt like a train conductor. All he was missing was a horn to tug on. "How are you two doing back there?" he asked with his eyes locked on the road.

"Is this as fast as it goes?" I asked.

"No, but I don't want to push our luck."

He was right. It was better to play it safe than sorry.

The train continued through the ancient subway system. As it glided along the track, we noticed that there weren't any other stops.

This was an express train.

I glanced over at Jenny. She admired the passing walls. A smile spread across her face. Even with the risk of peril, and the prospect of the unknown, she looked fearless. It was the true sign of a treasure hunter. It was also a dangerous foreshadowing of a life she seemed to love.

Her face shimmered in the darkness. A faint glow radiated off her skin.

That was odd.

Her face got brighter, yet the only lights came from the front and rear headlights of our train.

As her complexion brightened, I looked behind to see where the light source came from. That's when I saw it.

On the neighboring set of tracks ran another train car. Its headlights shined right at us. The two blinding lights made it difficult to see its passengers.

But, the most important fact was that the other train was speeding toward us at an alarming rate.

My guess was right, we weren't alone down here.

I hated it when I was right.

The train zoomed, closing in fast.

"J.J. I think it's about time we push our luck and see how fast this baby goes."

CHAPTER THIRTY TWO

"You think they may be friendly, Charles?" J.J. asked, looking back at the encroaching train car.

An arrow sizzled past his head.

"I think not," I rebutted.

I barely made out the black hooded figures that filled the train. What I could clearly see, were the bows in their hands, armed and ready. I grabbed Jenny, yanking her to the ground. More arrows cut through the air.

"Looks like we can never catch a break," I said slyly. "These guys follow us wherever we go."

"You have some groupies," Jenny said in an effort to lighten the mood.

"It would be nicer if they were at least cute," I said.

More arrows bounced off our train car.

"I thought these men assisted in your escape back in China?" J.J. exclaimed.

"I guess they had a change in heart." We crawled up toward my old friend.

Jeremy flipped the throttle to a hundred percent, and the train car lurched forward. He stumbled to the ground, joining us on the floor. More arrows missed their mark. "Charles, what if these aren't the same assassins?" he asked.

I peeked over the railing and saw that the pursuing car was only twenty feet behind. I counted five attackers and one pilot. Ducking back down, I said, "Same or not, they want us dead."

J.J. said, "Yes, they do. We are keeping the same pace, but eventually we will have to stop."

Looking forward, I saw the shimmer of other headlights up ahead. Squinting, I made out another train traveling on our same tracks. It was not going nearly as fast. Our train sped on a collision course toward it.

With the way things usually went for me, I wasn't surprised. "Our stop may be sooner than you think," I commented.

J.J. reached up to slow us down, but I held his arm back. If we slowed down, the train behind us would catch up. If we maintained speed, we'd reach the one in front of us. Either way, we were in trouble.

But, our speed could be our advantage. "Let's ram them," I stated.

"Are you crazy?" both Jenkinses said in unison.

"We're defenseless. The only weapon we have is this train. Let's use it."

"What if..." J.J.'s voice trailed off. Ahead, we saw eight hooded assassins perched along the rear of the other train ahead. They were ready to board us.

We were definitely goners.

The roaring rapids crashed below. The cavernous walls screamed by.

We needed a strategy. Thinking fast, I reached up and flicked our headlights off. Our entire train blinked into darkness. We were suddenly camouflaged. This made us a harder target, and it gave us some element of surprise.

Our platform rattled as our speed reached forty miles an hour. The chugging engine grew louder, kicking our train forward.

My pupils adjusted to the dark. The car ahead quickly grew in size. "Now, YOU best hold onto something," I said, latching onto the railing.

With our headlights off, all we saw were faint silhouettes of our incoming attackers. The eight figures held their positions even as we rocketed toward them.

I clenched my eyes shut right at the moment of impact.

Our train barreled into the rear of the other one with enormous force. Our front end screeched, kicking upward. A loud snap dislodged our front rock clamps free from the railroad tracks. The car continued to lift upward as it mowed over the rear of the attacking train.

The impact shuttered through the entire platform. Massive vibrations rattled through the metal railing, shaking my flimsy body.

Amongst the darkness, I heard the screams of random voices drown out the chaos. I could only assume a number of our assailants fell to the water below.

This was a stupid idea.

Suddenly, our front end came crashing back down on the bronze rails. Without our front clamps, the metal car smashed onto the thin rails. Sparks flew.

The shift from back to forth jolted the side guardrail loose. My lifeline bent away from the train…

…Taking me with it.

I had little time to react to the crash. My grip was so tight around the railing, that when the tubular metal pulled outward, away from the train, I didn't let go.

My body flung over the ledge of the train and instantly dropped. The railing buckled under my weight.

I panicked.

I wrapped my full body around the downward falling rail. My legs circled the pole, and my arms tightened. The rail bent a full ninety degrees.

Wind flapped against my frame. The water splattered at my feet, but I didn't fall to my death. The railing may have bent down the middle, but it still remained connected to the train car. As if holding onto a fireman's pole, I was dragged along the speeding train.

Up above, craziness unfolded. In the dark, all I could hear were various screams. Our car dug its nose under the rear bumper of the front train. The platform strained, struggling to stay on the track.

"Charlie!" Jenny's voice rang out above. Her flashlight aimed down at me.

"I'm still here," I said in a trembled voice.

"Thank God." Her light still bounced off the top of my head.

I was terrified, but I was alive.

Hand over hand, I started to climb up the pole.

An arrow whizzed by my head. The other pursuing train was now nearly upon us. I had forgotten about them. Of course, Jenny's light painted them a perfect target.

"Turn your light off," I yelled.

No response.

"I said, turn—" The flashlight fell out of the sky banging me in the top of the head. The crack nearly knocked me unconscious.

It rolled off and fell to the raging river below. Throbbing in pain, I looked up.

Two dark figures rolled around. I heard Jenny's frantic panting. She was in trouble.

Adrenaline surged me forward. Climbing quickly, I scrambled back to the top of the train. Another arrow flew by, cutting at my exposed arm.

It barely broke skin.

Reaching the top, I pulled my head over the ledge. Jenny was flattened to the ground. A hooded attacker choked her.

J.J. was nowhere to be seen.

I needed to help.

Before I could lift myself up any further, the knelt attacker kicked my head with the heel of his shoe. I launched back. Instinctively, I reached forward, latching onto the man's ankle.

I fell.

My bear claw took the man's leg with me as I smashed the extended ankle into the corner of the metal platform. It broke instantly. My sudden weight also caused the man to lose his balance.

His body ripped off of Jenny's and came rolling over the ledge. I pulled him down with me like a ship's anchor. The assassin grabbed hold of the ledge, stopping our rapid descent.

I dangled through the air, back in the original position I started. This time, my saving grace was my assailant's body.

The black robe above swayed in the rushing wind. I prayed that the man had pants on under that thing.

Luckily, the man's broken leg made it difficult for him to kick me off. He was also a little preoccupied, holding on for his dear life—and unintentionally mine. I used this opportunity to quickly climb up the man's back.

Planting my hands on his shoulder, I lifted myself high up. The man screamed in pain. I kept on going. I was nearly there.

The rear engine of our train erupted in flames. The bright light illuminated our entire train car. I saw Jenny right above me, reaching out to help. The hooded assassin's hands clenched around the metal ledge. He thankfully clung for his survival.

My vision shifted across the underside of our train, to the other speeding car. I made out two figures armed with bows.

They fired.

The arrows dug into the chest of my bulletproof vest, a.k.a. the hooded assassin. The man's fingers went limp, letting go of the ledge.

I shoved off the assassin's body just as he dropped to the river. I grabbed onto the hanging rail to my right.

With a sudden burst of energy, I monkey climbed back up to the top of the train car. Jenny helped me over the ledge as I sprawled onto the platform.

My muscles ached in exhaustion, but my moment to relax was short-lived.

The flames of our rear engine grew. Jenny knelt beside me. Sparks flickered all around. And—

Where was J.J.?

Alarmed, I jumped to my feet. Two unconscious bodies lay on the floor nearby. I rolled them over. Neither was my old friend.

A fight rang out ahead. Flipping a switch on our cockpit controls, our train's headlights came back to life. J.J. stood in the front train tussling with two hooded men.

My body didn't move.

I watched, dumbfounded by the sight. My old friend was never one for fighting. Still, he threw hooks left and right as if he'd been doing it for years. This was evidenced by the two bodies he single-handedly knocked out on our train.

"A little help here, Charles," J.J. managed as one of the attackers got the better of him.

I bolted over the cockpit of our cart, and jumped onto the front train. Sparks spattered around me as I crashed onto the hard metal deck.

Rushing into the fight, I peeled one of the men off J.J. I landed a hit square in the man's jaw. The bones in my fist nearly shattered with the impact.

Was this guy's face made of steel?

The bullish figure in the robe barely stumbled back. Getting a good view of him, I saw that the threads of the black fabric draped over the man's body were bristling—ready to burst.

Of course, I decided to challenge the bigger of the two adversaries into a fight.

J.J. gave me a thankful glance.

"You did pretty well for yourself," I said to my friend while dodging a few of my attacker's blows.

"Somebody had to. You jumped ship at first sign of battle," J.J. responded. He tackled his man to the ground.

Meanwhile, our old train car screamed. It skidded along the railroad tracks. The engine still blew flames and smoke. But the trains managed to maintain their speed.

All three of them.

In the heat of our battle, the parallel car caught up to our old train. The five hooded men on board jumped over the narrow gap and onto the fragile platform.

This lit a fire under Jenny. She followed my footsteps and climbed onto the front train car with us.

I watched all this unfold easy enough. Mainly because I was clenched in a bear hug by my monstrous attacker. As he squeezed my helpless body, I faced the back of the train.

All I could do was watch.

Straining every muscle, I struggled to break free. There was no way to unclasp the man's massive forearms.

I felt my head getting dizzy. I knew I had to do something. So I cheated. I mean, it wasn't like I was in a fair fight or anything. No rules really applied here. It was a fight to survive.

I arched my neck, knocking my assailant's hood back. In the same motion, I attacked the man's exposed ear. With an open mouth, I bit down hard onto the flesh.

The pain was enough to cause him to let go.

I stumbled to the ground, and rolled away. The taste of blood still salivated in my mouth.

Getting to my feet, I found myself beside Jenny at the rear of our train. Jeremy, had broken free from his quarry and came beside us as well.

Now, we stood in between two oncoming threats. Behind us, five assassins boarded our old train which jammed into the undercarriage of the one we now stood on.

In front of us, two other hooded men readied themselves for a final attack.

And to our left, the third train ran alongside us, a spectator to our battle.

"Any ideas?" Jenny wondered.

"I'll take the five behind us, while you two take the other two," J.J. ordered.

I glanced over at my old friend. "Easy there, Rambo. I've got a better idea. When I say jump, you two make a leap to the train next to us."

Our attackers inched closer from all directions.

I had an idea. It was a long shot, but it could work. The only problem was that there was a good part, and a bad part to the plan.

"What about you?" Jenny worried.

I smiled. "I'll be fine. Trust me. Now go!"

J.J. grabbed his daughter and darted to the edge of the train. They leapt onto the other speeding vehicle.

Meanwhile, I charged the two buffoons in front of me. They planted their legs, ready to greet me. Just as I was about to reach the first man, I juked, dodging to his left. In the same succession, I dove to the ground, just out of reach of my larger adversary's open arms.

I surprised myself at how limber my body was. I slid along the metal platform. I disappeared between the big man's legs, and through the open part of his robe.

In a flash, I passed the two men. The bigger of the two bent over, searching for where I had gone.

I didn't give myself a chance to relish the moment. I sped up to the front cockpit and yanked hard on the brake.

The train car instantly screeched, trying to halt. I grabbed hold of the railings as the momentum quickly shifted. The beast of a machine cried in a continuous effort to stop.

Behind me, the old train car that followed, jammed under our rear bumper. Its engine propelled it forward. The force pushed its front end down, while lifting its own rear. A tremendous snap tore the rear clamps free, and lifted the entire butt of the train up into the air.

The platform flung at such speed, it catapulted the five men on board through the sky and into the water.

I simply watched as the train rose a full ninety degrees. It looked like a large black wall, with an enormous ball of fire at the top.

That was the good part of my plan.

My train continued to stop as the last two assassins regained their balance. Their attention was not on me anymore. Instead, they looked up at the flaming car.

That's when the bad part of my plan came into effect.

With the sudden stop of the front train, the now vertical rear platform tipped over. As it sustained its course, it came rushing onto us.

I dove to the ground and covered my face.

The towering inferno of metal crashed down on my train.

Yup, when I said *bad part*, I wasn't kidding.

CHAPTER THIRTY THREE

My two unwelcome guests didn't stand a chance. The flipping rear train car slammed down onto ours, squishing the two men instantly.

I, on the other hand, was still in one piece. Flattened against the front cockpit, the collapsing train car landed only a few feet from my body. The heat from the ball of fire washed over me, making my hair feel like it singed right off.

As the other train landed like a flat pancake, the flipping motion caused it to pivot back and land half of its frame onto our stopped train. The impact caused the heavy metal to slide and roll off the side of my platform, dragging the two dead bodies with it.

I was alive!

It worked!

Getting to my feet, I couldn't help but smile.

In that same moment, the parallel train car came reversing back to my position. It arrived beside me, hissing to a stop. J.J. and Jenny waved me over.

I jumped the gap.

"I'm surprised you are in one piece, Charles," J.J. commented.

"Are you crazy?" Jenny hit me. "What kind of plan was that?"

Before I could respond, J.J. did for me. "Honey, haven't you learned by now that Charles doesn't come up with the brightest of plans."

"It worked, didn't it?" I replied.

"I never refuted that," J.J. said, smiling.

As I approached the cockpit, I added, "Where's the driver?"

"Oh, that poor fellow decided it was time for a little swim," J.J. said snidely. He adjusted the manual controls, and the train kickstarted forward once again.

"We still going to pursue this?" Jenny asked.

"We've made it this far," her father said. "We might as well see what all the fuss is about."

I glanced back at the damage we left behind. "Hopefully that was the last of them," I wished aloud.

"I hope that this train ride is over soon," Jenny added.

Thankfully, it was.

A few minutes into the ride we reached a docking platform. It looked similar to the first one. A carved out stone protruded from the wall, leading into a dark tunnel. We parked the train and hopped off. Down below, the river continued to roar and wash off into a black abyss. I wondered how much farther these subway tunnels ran. Did they loop back to the beginning? Was this just a pit stop?

I didn't know.

Quietly, we headed down the next tunnel in hopes of finding the *Holiest of Holies.*

The tunnel here was much smoother than before. The three of us cautiously made our way through the narrow space. Soon, the cave opened up into a much larger chamber.

The room was perfectly square. The smooth walls ran fifteen feet high before dying into a stone ceiling. No markings of any kind lined the walls. No magnificent treasures covered the floors.

It was a spitting image of our previous chamber, except for one small difference.

A single pedestal positioned itself in the center of room. Resting on top, sat a circular tablet—the last piece of our puzzle.

"I can't believe it," J.J. whispered, approaching the pedestal. We followed.

"A lot simpler than I imagined," I commented.

"I know," Jenny added. "We had these extravagant trains, built on elaborate railways, take us through a network of tunnels, to this little chamber?"

"Your friends may be disappointed by the fact that there is no treasure, Charles," J.J. said.

They would.

J.J. pointed to the ground. Clearly defined scratches carved into the rock. "There did seem to be other items stored here. Look at the markings."

"It looks as if some heavy objects were dragged across the floor," I observed.

"You are correct."

It made sense. Why else would someone build these massive trains if not to carry loads of cargo out of this chamber?

"There goes your Arc of the Covenant," I said to Jenny, pointing at a few more track marks.

"Charlie, forget about the treasures, look at the pedestal. The tablet." Jenny walked up alongside her father.

I joined in.

We all gaped at the circular object. Like the previous two, Ancient Greek letters covered the entire face. I watched as J.J. mouthed the words aloud.

As they read the tablet, my attention shifted though. In the darkness beyond, my flashlight fell upon something else. On the far wall, a massive doorway was cut out of the rock. But the opening was blocked by rugged stone.

Where did that lead? I approached the opening and felt the rock. It was warm. The stone wasn't loose though. There was no cave-in here. The compactness of the rock indicated that it was man-made.

Looking at the exposed edges, I saw a hint of marble protruding from the stone. It looked familiar. "J.J. you see this?" I asked.

He was entranced in his reading though. I could tell he didn't want to be bothered. I felt the marble. Why did it look so familiar?

Then I realized why.

"Guys, based on our fun little train ride, where would you say we are?" I asked.

Jenny looked my way. "I don't know, why?" She sounded annoyed, as if I interrupted her.

"Because look at this opening. It's been blocked. You see this marble? Does it look familiar to you?"

Jenny followed my gaze. "Is that—"

"Yes it is," I cut her off. "We are right beside the Well of Souls, under the dome."

The marble matched the stairs that led down into the room beneath Foundation Stone at the *Dome of the Rock*. This is what the crusaders must have been covering when they built the stairs all those years ago. It made sense.

And, if we were here thousands of years ago, we could have saved ourselves the train rides and dark tunnels.

That would have been too easy.

At least we knew that we were close to the surface.

Jenny resumed reading the tablet, but J.J. had already finished. His face gave a ponderous look.

Jenny soon finished as well and simply looked up at her father.

"And?" I asked as I stared at both Jenkinses' faces.

"This is another breadcrumb, Charles. It details the next stop," J.J. said.

Great.

Jenny chimed in, "It looks as if the *next stop* is the final location though. Luckily, it's not that far. See here..."

Jenny translated an excerpt from the tablet. From the looks of it, the tablet detailed the final stretch of Homer's journey. The Oracle was taken across the sandy desert, to her resting place deep inside the bowel of a mountain. That mountain was called out by name.

Mount Horeb.

"Very impressive, Jennifer," J.J. complimented his daughter. He said it in such a 'pat on his own back' tone, as if her translation was thanks to all his successful teachings. (If only he knew.)

"You mean, Mount Sinai? The mountain range south of here?" I asked. Mount Horeb, was the Hebrew name for the largest mountain range in Egypt. The more popular label, which was also the Arab term for the mountain, was Mount Sinai.

"Exactly. It mentions a temple that leads to the entrance of Pythia's burial chamber," she added.

"You know how many temples and churches are built along that mountain range? It's like finding a needle in a haystack," I said.

"Yes, but within that temple is the final gate," J.J. said.

"How do you know it's the *final* one?"

"Because it says so right here. Unfortunately, to unlock the gate, we need the three tablets," J.J. added.

Puzzled, I looked at the tablet as if I understood how to read Ancient Greek.

J.J. continued, "Charles, as you know, the Greeks believed in the Holy Trinity. The number three harnesses the power of the circle of life. As inscribed within this tablet, all three tablets are required to be placed onto some mechanism to open the gate."

"Okay, so A. We don't have the keys to reach Pythia's chamber, and B. We have an entire mountain range that needs to be searched in order to find the right temple. Am I missing anything?" I asked.

"You mustn't rule out the possibility that we will have another obstacle of hooded assassins waiting to greet us, wherever that location may be," J.J. added.

Jeremy Jenkins, always the voice of optimism.

"Wait," Jenny said. She read the last line of the tablet. "The tablet mentions a map…"

Jenny kept reading.

"…On the back of the tablet. It shows the location of the final temple. The Temple of Apollo."

Of all the known structures discovered along Mount Sinai, none of them were named after the Greek god. I tried jogging my memory as Jenny went for the tablet. My eyes widened. Before she could grab it, I knocked her hands away.

"Don't touch it," I exclaimed.

Surprised, she stepped back. "Why?"

"Nothing good has come from us picking up these tablets. Remember China?"

J.J. laughed it off. "Nonsense Charles. Your point does not hold any validity. What of the second half of the tablet?"

"I didn't touch it."

"But someone did." J.J. reached out and grabbed the tablet. He removed it from the pedestal.

I held my breath.

Nothing happened.

"See?" he said. "You worry too much."

J.J. flipped the tablet over. Along the entire back, carved out of the stone, was a painted map. Richly detailed geography spread across the entire face. The desert hills and landscapes seemed accurately drawn. Even Mount Sinai was shown extending along the bottom portion of the map. Finally, a single marking between two rock formations called out the temple entrance.

"That was easy," I said.

"It looks like you can check the temple whereabouts off our list," Jenny smiled.

That's when the chamber started to shake. The walls viciously pulsated. Our beams of light scanned the room. Everything rumbled.

"I told you not to pick it up," I called out.

Behind us, a large stone slab slid down, blocking the entrance to our chamber. Another noise echoed around the room. A number of metal grated holes appeared in the floor.

"Charles, I concede. You were correct," J.J. said, slightly panicked.

The rattling stopped, abruptly. Everything calmed down. My heart beat frantically, but I hoped the others couldn't hear it.

My eyes searched the room. We found ourselves in a large coffin with no way out. I scrambled for the entrance. The stone slab perfectly sealed the opening. I ran to the other wall, where the marble stair blocked our way. There was no way we were getting out of here.

The others followed suit. Why would the chamber lock us in here? Did it want the tablet back?

I grabbed the stone and placed it back on the pedestal. Nothing.

I slid the object into my pack and continued to search.

"We are right below the *Dome of the Rock*," Jenny said. "There has to be an easy path out of here."

I scanned the ceiling to no avail.

"Charles, any bright ideas?" J.J. asked.

"I'm all out."

That's when I heard it.

A familiar sound flushed through my ears. I paused. It sounded like wind, blowing hard. Soon the whistling noise grew. Whatever it was, my gut told me it wasn't going to be good.

And my gut was right.

Out of the grated holes, water surged into the square room. It exploded into the tall space with the pressure of a fire hose. The streaming water fell like geysers, splashing onto the stone floor.

"This is something new," I said. More water came pouring into the room.

Within seconds the entire floor was covered in a pool of water. The geysers didn't let up, and the water level rose quickly.

High stepping through the water, we searched for an escape. Every avenue was a dead end.

"This answers why the chamber below the foundation stone was so smooth. It truly was a well," J.J. said, as if he had a major revelation about a burning question in his mind. He pushed against the marble. It didn't give.

The water reached our wastes.

I dove under, grabbing hold of one of the metal grates. With all my might, I pulled on the bars. I tried to break them free. The hose of water slapped me in the face.

It didn't budge.

Water continued to pour in. Within minutes we were treading water. Countless times, I dove under, searching for some miracle.

It was no use. The entire room had no latches, no hidden levers. I searched the ceiling. Our trajectory was rushing us upward at a maddening pace.

"Charlie?" Jenny pleaded. Her eyes scanned around for help.

I looked back at her, then J.J. I brought them here. It was all my fault.

The water filled the chamber even higher. We were nearly at the ceiling now. We swam in a human fish tank, and we were losing breathing room fast.

We were a foot from the ceiling. I swam back and forth feeling the stone slab for any hope. In my haste, I nearly glossed past some text written on the surface above.

I stopped and turned back to the text. Water splattered across my face, blinding me. The blaring sound of rushing water drowned out my friends' voices.

Rubbing my eyes I looked at the letters inscribed on the stone. It was written in Ancient Greek. I yelled for J.J. to come over. Amongst the flooding water, he did.

The waterline approached the ceiling. Our heads angled, trying to remain afloat. We inhaled taking in one of our last remaining breaths. I tried to tell J.J. what I found, but water gurgled into my open mouth. Coughing, I saw that I was out of time. I found the text too late.

I pointed, but my flashlight flickered off. We were engulfed by darkness.

My lungs filled with oxygen one last time as the water finished filling the room.

CHAPTER THIRTY FOUR

When I was younger, I always took pride in how long I could hold my breath. One minute and forty two seconds was my record. I hadn't tried doing that in a long time, but at the moment, fully submerged underwater, that limit was fast approaching.

My surroundings were pitch black. I couldn't see a darn thing. I couldn't even see J.J.'s floating frame under the water. I reached out, desperately trying to save myself. My arms and legs flailed helplessly.

Dizziness ensued.

The lack of oxygen was affecting my brain. Every nerve in my body urged me to open my mouth and suck in fresh air, but there was none to be had. All I'd get was a mouth full of water. It would have been a sad way to go.

But then something happened.

The water began to drain. A whirlpool of pressure siphoned downward into the depths of the chamber. The pressure acted like a vacuum, sucking the water toward some magical drain.

I burst above the surface, splashing around violently. I took in a deep breath. Both Jenny and Jeremy exploded out of the water screaming for air.

Somehow, the water continued to drain out of the room. "What's going on?" I managed to ask. No one was given an opportunity to respond.

The pressure strengthened.

As the water vacuumed out of the room, it pulled us back under the surface. The dark chamber made it impossible to see what was going on. Was it something we did? Did J.J. get the chance to read that text on the ceiling? Did he unlock something?

My eyes strained to see under the bubbling water. A crack of bright light emerged in the distance. It looked larger than a standard flashlight, and it had an irregular shape.

Fighting hard, I broke back to the surface. My lungs thanked me once again.

I yelled for the others.

No response.

The sloshing whirlwind of water drowned out any other sounds.

I yelled again.

Still nothing.

Where was everyone?

I dove under, blindly searching for my friends. The bright light at the far end of the room had gotten larger.

I swam toward it.

Surprisingly, it was easier than I thought. I was following the current. Apparently, that light was an opening of sorts, and that was where the water was siphoning into. If so, that would be a cave to somewhere. J.J. and Jenny may have gone through it.

I hoped.

The chaos disoriented me. I had no idea which way I was heading. I just focused on the single beacon as my guide. In seconds, I would know if that was a good idea.

The light was a three foot rectangular opening. Feeling the edges, its walls were rugged and sharp. Where did it come from? Why hadn't I seen it before?

I squeezed through the hole in the wall and into the adjoining space. Once through, I saw where the light was coming from.

Above me, a large circular hole cut through the ceiling of my new chamber. Daylight flooded through it, and two silhouettes blotted out certain parts. The Jenkins family was treading water at the surface.

I swam to the top.

I surfaced into the hole of a small opening.

"Thanks for the directions," I said, seeing my friends.

"You're welcome," Jenny said.

My surroundings became instantly recognizable. Still catching my breath, I panted, "Are we in the Well of Souls?"

"You are correct, Charles," J.J. said.

The Foundation Stone in the *Dome of the Rock* was our ceiling—the opening at its center, our breathing hole. "But how? Was it the words written on the ceiling?" I asked.

"No, that was gibberish. It wasn't even text. Those were just shadows and cracks in the ceiling," J.J. responded.

I felt like an idiot.

"Jenny is our hero," J.J. added.

When the water pressure filled the room, Jenny dove down to the blocked opening that led into the Well of Souls. Yes, concrete and marble blocked our path, but marble was a brittle material. She anchored herself and pushed against the exposed marble faces. Her strength, compounded by the pressure of the water, dislodged part of the stone. Once one of the steps loosened, the others followed.

Soon, the water took charge. It forced the marble stair blocking our path to break away and create an opening.

Jenny saved us.

"Amazing," I said.

Jenny's blue eyes glistened in the spotlight. The warm daylight accentuated her beauty. I couldn't help but stare.

"It was nothing," she smiled. "You and my dad had done most of the heavy lifting. I figured it was my turn to contribute."

The water simmered down. The three of us dove under and swam to the remains of the stair opening at the south end of the Foundation Stone. We climbed out of the pool and into the central chamber of the *Dome of the Rock*.

We were right back where we started.

Drenched, we sat down on a nearby bench. Exhaustion took over every muscle in my body. "Well, that was fun," I commented.

Jenny laughed. "Dad, I'm sorry to say this, but I don't know how you two have lasted this long."

"Charles believes it's his charm and good looks, but I have my own thoughts," J.J. said, plopping down next to me.

Jenny turned to me, ready with a snide comment, but she didn't say a word. Her eyes weren't even looking at me. They looked beyond the two of us.

Her smile was gone.

A half dozen hooded assassins stood between the colonnades that held up the central dome of the temple. Swords and bows aimed our way.

Wonderful.

Raising our arms, we stood up. "I'm sorry about the mess," I said.

There was no response. None of them moved.

I tried again. "Look, if you want the tablet…" I reached into my bag slowly. "…Here, you can take it."

The bows tightened.

"I believe, this is a time for fewer words, Charles," J.J. whispered.

I quieted and set down my backpack. For a long moment we all stood in silence. No one moved a muscle.

Finally, one of the hooded men spoke. He said, "Charlie Morgan, you lied to us."

He knew my name?

"What exactly did I lie about?" I asked, confused.

The one hooded man peeled back his hood to reveal his face. "You told me you had no desire in continuing this journey." That voice belonged to Lei-Phong.

The bald monk looked much different than I last remembered. His face was covered in white paint.

"Lei? What are you doing here?" I stepped forward, but the armed bows urged me otherwise. "You're one of them?"

Lei motioned the others to put down their weapons. "I'm sorry I was late getting here, Charlie Morgan. All I was told was that someone had entered our sanctuary. I only now see that it was you." My friend stepped in closer.

Jenny held my arm, but I continued forward. "We meant no disrespect, but why didn't you tell me you were one of them?"

Lei explained, "*Men Shen* warriors have two sides to themselves. Much like the yin and yang, we balance one another out. We are a peaceful people, dressed in red, and living a secluded life. When we are called upon to fight, we transform ourselves for battle. We are brothers, ordered to protect the buried secrets of Pythia, the Oracle of Delphi."

Lei wasn't alone. He acknowledged that there were protectors at every temple. Each swore to guard their goddesses with their lives. In Jeruselum, Asherah was the Queen Goddess that held the final tablet.

They were the Sons of Apollo.

Not all protectors were monks. Many were regular folk, hiding in plain sight. Some were even rich entrepreneurs. The rich men helped fund the transports in the tunnels below.

They all shared the same belief though. No one was allowed to find Pythia's final resting place for fear of what could happen.

"But what could happen?" I asked. "It's just a tomb."

"No, Charlie Morgan, it is not just a tomb. It is a source of power. If one harnessed the power of Pythia, then they would be able to see the future, and control the world." Lei said all this with a straight face.

"Lei, those are just myths," I assured.

"No, it is true. I have seen it with my own eyes. This is why we must protect the temple. Why have you pursued our goddess, Charlie Morgan?"

I explained my reasoning. I told him about the Baron's daughter, and about the sacrifice that was being required of her. I explained how the Baron was crazy, thinking that he could harness the power to see the future. But Lei's determined look said otherwise. He believed that it really was possible.

"I do not plan to use her power. My goal was only to prevent the Baron from achieving it himself. I was trying to protect the young girl."

It was true. Every word I said. I handed my backpack over to Lei, adding, "If this power truly exists, then no one should be allowed to enter the temple. I did not wish to disrespect you, my friend. Take the tablet. We will find another way."

Lei accepted my offering. "Why are you not wearing the dragon medallion?" he asked.

I blankly stared at him then realized he spoke of the gift he gave me. I shrugged.

"That medallion was a symbol for my fellow warriors not to harm you. It would have saved you much trouble in the caverns."

Was he joking? Of course, if I had known this, it might have made my trek down below a little easier. "A simple 'wear this to protect you from armed warriors' was asking for too much?"

"I told you that the dragon was a symbol for protection." Lei cracked a smirk. It was the first time I had seen him smile. He had always been so serious.

Lei took the tablet out of the bag. My only bargaining chip was being taken away. From the looks of it, it provided the *Men Shen* warriors a sense of relief.

Lei-Phong handed the tablet to his fellow brother. He then added, "Charlie Morgan, we thank you. I have given all my years to defending the—"

Lei jolted forward—his speech cut short.

He fell into my arms.

Surprised, I held onto him. Looking beyond, the other five hooded men collapsed to the ground silently.

What was happening?

Lei's eyes looked up at me, pleadingly. His white face tightened in sadness. A tear watered down his cheek.

Lei-Phong's body went limp, and his full weight fell upon my arms. I dropped to the ground, confused.

As I pulled my hands away, blood covered them. A bullet wound dug through my friend's back.

Before I knew what was happening, a new group of men stormed the scene. Dressed in black and armed with silenced weapons, they circled us on all sides.

"Charlie, what's going on?" Jenny asked.

I didn't speak. I was still stunned that my friend, Lei-Phong, just died right in front of me.

Slowly getting to my feet, I felt defeated. What could happen next?

A few of the armed men parted, and in came Burt Traijan. Sweat bled down his body. "Charlie! You are okay," he said, approaching.

"You killed all these men?" I demanded. "What were you thinking?"

Insulted, Burt said, "You should be thanking me, Charlie. Those men were going to kill you."

"I had it under control, Burt."

"It didn't seem like it a few hours ago," Burt said.

I stared confusingly.

"Charlie, I returned to the site earlier, only to find all my men dead. Arrows stuck out of each of their torsos. These men killed them. I quickly called in back-up. When we didn't find you, I got worried."

Knowing Burt, he was probably more worried about our treasure than our lives. I couldn't blame him though. Honestly, as sad as I was, I saw where the burly man was coming from.

"I'm sorry Burt. I really am. And I'm grateful, but this was my friend." I looked down at Lei.

"And those men out there were mine," Burt said.

J.J. and Jenny stood beside me. Neither of them said a word.

"Charlie, I hope it was all worth it. What valuables have you brought back?" Burt said. He stepped forward. His moment of sympathy flipped to excitement like an on/off switch.

Shaking my head, I said, "Nothing. The vault was cleared out."

A moment of silence passed.

"That's a shame," Burt responded. "But not all is lost. You are much more *valuable* than any treasure."

That was unlike Burt. I was expecting flames to fume out of his head. "That's sweet," I mocked.

"Much more valuable," a voice rang out behind me—a female voice.

Something whacked my head.

The blow surprised me. It smacked me with such blunt force, I fell to the ground.

My ears rang.

My head throbbed.

My vision faded.

I couldn't even hear Jenny's scream. Looking up, all I saw was the tall, slender figure of Berta Traijan. She towered over me. A large crowbar extended from her clenched fists.

Berta double-crossed me again, but why? I knew I shouldn't have trusted the Traijan twins. Jenny warned me.

I didn't get a chance to think about it further.

I blacked out.

CHAPTER THIRTY FIVE

As I opened my eyes, I found my world flipped upside down. Literally.

Everything around me was turned around. The floor was my ceiling. And from that ceiling clung boxes, barrels, and tables.

I swayed back and forth.

Light headedness clouded my brain.

That's when I realized, it wasn't the room that was upside down, it was me.

I hung by my legs. My hands bound behind my back. Blood rushed to my face, causing my dizziness. That, and the fact that the back of my head was still sore from Berta's crowbar attack. I was in some sort of dungeon. Cobwebs, dust, and filth covered every surface of the room.

"Welcome back," a voice said.

Arching my body, I saw my friend J.J. bound to a chair beside me. Rope wrapped around his entire chest, locking him in place.

"What did I miss?" I asked. I searched my other side. Jenny was bound in the same manner to another chair.

"Nothing of interest. Your friends escorted us to this fine little room," J.J. said calmly.

"You really have nice friends, Charlie," Jenny added.

My throbbing head proved her sarcastic point. Analyzing my new predicament, I saw that I hung from a wooden beam, framed out by two wooden posts. The entire contraption looked flimsy but man-made. "Did they run out of chairs, or something?" I asked.

"I'm not sure, Charles. Maybe they liked us better than you. Or maybe they thought you'd have a more difficult time escaping," J.J. observed.

"Well, I like this escape idea." If I dangled from this position much longer, my head would explode.

"We are open to suggestions," J.J. said.

I scanned the room. Our only two options were a small window at one end, or the heavy timber door at the opposite. I had no idea where either option led, let alone where we found ourselves exactly.

First step was figuring a way out of my bindings.

The timber door unlatched and opened wide. In came our wonderful captures, Burt and Berta.

"You are finally awake," Burt said in a cheerful mood.

"This is how you treat your friend?" I replied.

"Charlie, I should be saying the same to you. Why didn't you tell us the truth about what you were doing here?" Berta asked.

I glared at her. It was twice that this woman backstabbed me.

She pet my bruised scalp. "I'm sorry for damaging that pretty little head of yours."

I shook her away. "What part of my story did I leave out?"

"The part where you had a ransom on your head," Berta said.

That was the first I heard of it.

Burt explained, "Soon after you two arrived, we received a message. It was sent from one, William Ruthford. Apparently, you stole something of great value from this man, and he was willing to pay handsomely for anyone who knew of your whereabouts."

"So you sold me out?"

"Charles, I am a business man, but I am also your friend. What kind would I be if I gave you up so easily? I did look into it a bit further though." Burt knelt down by my bright red head. "This Ruthford man has quite a bit of power."

"You can't trust him," I said.

"But, I can trust you?" Burt refuted. "You promised me a treasure, but all you found was a rock. I gave you the benefit of doubt. You gave me no choice."

"That *rock* is a map, Burt. It leads to treasure. More treasure than your sweaty paws can handle," I said.

Berta spoke up. "We know Charlie. We contacted Mr. Ruthford. He told us of the full extents of the treasure. We now know the full truth. The man is on his way here."

"Guys, you need to let us go. You don't understand. Baron William Ruthford is not a character you should be dealing with."

Burt stood up. "Charlie, this Baron of yours is coming to MY city. I have more men under my control than anyone. We have nothing to fear. He offered us five million dollars for you, alive. It says something if he does not want you dead."

The burly man walked over to Jenny. "Your friends were not part of that offer. You should be thankful that we are the ones who are cutting the deal. We will not harm them."

Thanks, I thought.

Burt's phone came to life. Before I could plead for our safety, he answered. The good Baron had arrived at the airport.

Burt hung up the phone and came back up to me. "Charlie, it has been a good run. We will see you soon." In haste, he left the room.

Berta leaned in and kissed my cheek. I veered away. "Don't be like this, Charlie. It's nothing against you." She got up and followed her brother out the dungeon. The door closed and locked behind them.

For a moment, none of us spoke.

J.J. broke the silence. "Charles, I believe I've had enough of this place."

"I agree," I said. "Jenny, don't worry. We've been in situations like these many times before."

It was true. J.J. and I had escaped from far worse scenarios. "You remember the time in Mexico?" I said, looking over at my friend.

"I am already ahead of you." J.J. hopped to his left. Still bound to the wooden chair, it bounced, inch by inch. I began swaying back and forth.

The wooden columns on either side of my support beam were flimsy enough. They bolted to the concrete floor, but they were not anchored at the ceiling. J.J. reached the first support. He lifted his legs up and kicked at the solid timber. The frame shook. He thrust his legs again, making contact.

The post splintered.

Meanwhile, I swung back and forth like a swing set. Rocking forward, J.J. whacked the wood member at the peak of my swing.

I heard Jenny fumbling in a corner. I assured her once again, "Jenny, a few more hits and we're in business."

The wood cracked under the tension. It bent forward. Only a fraction remained. One more hit and I'd tumble free.

J.J. put all his might into his legs. He thrust the heel of his foot deep into the wooden post. The member didn't break. He kept pushing on the wood, arching his body back in the process. Blood vessels seemed to erupt all over his bald head as he flexed harder.

"Almost, Charles!" he strained and pushed.

The wood split some more. The upper half bowed outward, ready to topple over.

J.J. tried harder, and in the process, the front legs of his chair rose. He teetered, while his legs extended outward. Still bound to the chair, the rope dug into his chest. He fully spread himself and pushed mightily.

The post was about to give.

J.J. gave one last shove. As he exerted his last burst of energy, his chair tipped backward. I heard his yelp as my good friend fell to his back with a loud thump.

The column remained.

My friend lay helpless on the floor.

And I still dangled upside down.

"Charles, I'm okay, in case you were concerned," J.J. said sarcastically.

We were so close. I couldn't give up. I angled my body once again into a full swing. I pushed myself forward. The momentum rocketed me onward like a pendulum, and I swung away from the floor.

The support post broke free from its base. My unbalanced weight caused the beam above me to collapse under the pressure. I smashed onto the ground.

It worked.

My dizziness instantly faded away, and blood naturally flowed back into my body. I laughed as I lay on the floor. "J.J. I'm free!"

"Well done, Charles," he acknowledged. "But, I think we may differ on our definitions of *free?*"

We both lay opposite one another, still fully bound.

My chest flattened against the concrete slab. A heavy wooden post rested on top of me. Struggling, I tried to slither free. The post prevented any movement.

I tried again.

I failed again.

I wasn't going to give up though. With all my will I shoved against the ground to lift up. Panting, I inched my back upward. I continued pushing.

Sweat dripped down my face. Pain shuttered through every muscle.

Then suddenly, the beam rolled off me. The pressure disappeared. How did I do it?

"Jenny, J.J., we're good, I'm almost there!" I yelled.

"You may be almost there Charlie, but I already am." It was Jenny's voice.

Rolling over, I saw Jenny's beautiful face hover over me. She was free from her bindings and armed with a pocket knife. Jenny bent down, cutting me free.

"How did you escape?" I said, astonished.

"I took a deep breath when they tied me to the chair. It inflated my chest enough to make me appear larger. Once they were gone, I exhaled and shimmied out of my bindings."

I was impressed.

Then she added, "Plus, men usually get a little uncomfortable when it comes to a woman's private area."

"Where did you learn that? The cop you dated?" I asked as the last of my bindings came off.

"No, a magician I used to see. He taught me a lot of nifty tricks," Jenny said with a smirk.

Another guy she used to date? I could only imagine what the other *tricks* she hinted were.

Jenny read my mind. "The magician and the Greek guy were one and the same, Charlie." She smiled.

"Anytime now, sweetheart," J.J. interrupted, still lying on the ground.

We got to our feet, and quickly freed J.J. Then we searched for a means of escape.

The front door was locked from the outside. That left only one option—the small window at the other end of the room.

The window was eight feet up in the air and could barely fit one person.

But *barely* was enough for us.

We ran to the wall. "J.J. bend over. Let me climb up for a better view."

"Charles, you're going to use an old man as a stepping stool?" my friend whined.

"Now you're an old man?"

"How about you get on all fours," J.J. said.

Reluctantly, I followed orders. I dropped down while J.J. stood on my back. "You really need to lay off those sweets," I joked.

J.J. didn't acknowledge my bad joke. He was too busy peering out the window. "It looks as though this window exits out into an alley. We may still be in the heart of the city."

"Well move along then," I said. His weight started to dig into my back.

J.J. pried the window open and pulled himself through. Once outside, he did a quick scan to make sure it was safe. Then he told us to follow.

Jenny was next.

She stepped onto my back.

Just then the door to our dungeon started to unlock.

The Traijans were back.

Jenny jumped off.

"What are you doing?" I said.

"There's not enough time," she said. "I'm not leaving you behind."

I grabbed one of the chairs on the ground and glued myself to the wall.

The door opened and in came the familiar round figure of my once friend, Burt.

I swung with all my might, cracking the chair over the Armenian's head. The impact instantly knocked him out. He fell to the floor.

He wasn't alone though. Berta entered the room, confused about what just happened. She saw me and the wooden chair in my hands.

Panic flashed across her face, but it instantly disappeared. "Charlie, you can't hit a woman," she stated, in a matter-of-fact tone.

"But I can," Jenny said, holding the other chair.

The chair crashed over Berta's head, dropping her right on top of her brother.

I looked at the window. J.J. waited for us outside.

Then I looked back at the doorway. Another figure stood right at the center of the arched opening.

Lynea Ruthford.

A second later, a another figure stepped to her side.

Her father.

"Mr. Morgan, here we are once again," Baron William Ruthford bellowed in delight. "It is so good to see you."

I stood still, with Jenny by my side.

The Baron entered the dungeon, a shiny revolver in his hand.

Jenny and I cautiously backpedaled toward the window. My mind scrambled for a way out.

"Mr. Morgan, why do you look so frightened? You have nothing to fear from me...," Ruthford said. "...Even if you did destroy my home."

"The burning of your house was not my fault. Your goons did most of the work," I snipped back, but then thought about it for a second. "Okay, well technically, we may have caused the avalanche that ultimately demolished your house, so I take that back."

"Do I look upset?"

"There are a lot of things you look like," I retorted.

"Please, Mr. Morgan. There is no need for such childish insults. I am just here to talk."

Lynea stood silently next to her father.

"I don't believe we have much to talk about," I said.

"Oh but we do. We have plenty to talk about." The Baron pulled out the tablet from his bag. "You have once again helped me come closer to my final goal."

Ruthford handed the tablet to his daughter. "And, you have done all this in the hopes of saving my daughter's life." He paused a moment. He put his arm around his daughter. "It is an honorable cause, but Mr. Morgan, my daughter does not need saving. I knew, based on your history, that you have a soft spot for rescuing people—especially young damsels in distress."

The Baron poked a stare at Jenny, who was now pressed up against my side.

"After seeing what you did back in China, I had high hopes for you. I simply needed to provide you with the proper motivation. What better than a young girl pleading for her life?"

I looked at Lynea. She smiled as if she just won an award for best actress. This was the second time in one day that I had been duped.

"Sorry Charlie," was all she said.

"How did you know about my parents?" I directed that question to Ruthford.

"Mr. Morgan, I did extensive research on all prospective treasure hunters. I like to do proper background checks on people before doing business with them. This is something you should strive to do. It may prevent you from getting into such messes."

I still searched for a way out. On the floor, the Traijan twins remained unconscious. Maybe, if one of their soldiers were to see them in that state, it would be cause for alarm.

That could work.

I spoke loudly, "Well now you've got what you needed. Why don't you and your happy little family go claim your prize?"

"No need to raise your voice, Mr. Morgan. There isn't anyone nearby. Even your precious friend, Jeremy, won't make it far." Ruthford pointed to the open window.

"You'd be surprised. My father is a lot smarter than any of your men," Jenny said proudly.

"Ms. Jenkins, I admire your strength."

Alvin Mitchell suddenly ran into the room. Dressed in his trusty safari gear, he turned to the Baron. "I lost him. The old Jenkins *mate* escaped."

My veins flooded with blood at the sight of Mitchell.

"It is not important," the Baron said. He then turned his attention back to me. "Two out of three is good enough. Now why don't you make yourself useful, Mr. Mitchell? Wake our kind hosts and please escort our new guests to the vehicles. It's time to finish our journey."

It was time alright. One way or another, our journey was coming to an end.

PART IV

The Day I Saved the World

CHAPTER THIRTY SIX

Sinai Desert, Egypt

I sat in one of Burt's monstrous SUVs. Outside the window, the Sinai desert spread as far as the eye could see. I watched the sand rush by as we progressed to our final destination.

The car ride was quiet. It wasn't because I was alone. No, it was just that my company was lousy. Baron William Ruthford and his daughter, Lynea, sat in the opposite seats. Their chairs rotated to have direct view of me. As the Baron put it, 'it promoted better conversation.'

It was more like, *non-existent* conversation.

Two goons sat in the front.

I stared out the window. Dozens of black SUVs flanked around us, and a neighboring vehicle ran directly alongside ours. Tinted windows blocked out its passengers, but I knew Jenny, Alvin, Burt and Berta rode inside.

I could only imagine what Jenny was going through right now. She was alone with a group of scumbags. If they laid a hand on her, I'd—

Thinking was painful.

My head ached. I'd say it was from my short stint upside down, but the massive agony that rang through my temples was thanks to Burt. He slugged me with a bat after returning to consciousness. (Retaliation for me hitting him with a chair.)

Still, I didn't want to think. I just dazed out the glass at the endless sand. Somewhere out there was our only hope. Jeremy Jenkins was on the loose, and I knew my friend. He was deep into planning some sort of rescue.

I just needed to last long enough for him to execute it.

"This is the quietest I have ever seen you, Mr. Morgan," the Baron said from across the way.

"There's not much to say," I returned.

"Come on, you should be overjoyed. We are on the brink of mankind's greatest discovery. All of this was greatly influenced by you."

I rolled my eyes. It was true. I more or less paved the way for the entire journey. Admitting it meant I also led to the death of a friend of mine; Jenny being held captive; and having a crazed lunatic on the verge of harnessing the power to see the future.

"Why do you want to find this tomb so badly?" I asked.

The Baron thought a moment, then said, "We all have our reasons. You jumped to preemptive conclusions about me, Mr. Morgan."

This bullish billionaire killed people without a blink of an eye. He dealt with mercenaries and pirates. He was loaded, yet still craved power and would do anything to achieve it. "I don't think I am too far off," I mumbled.

"Oh, but you are wrong. You believed that I killed poor Mr. Blake in India. You are incorrect in that assumption. We found him in his hotel room with an arrow through his chest."

Lynea spoke up, "We were attacked by those hooded assassins, Charlie. We barely escaped with our lives."

"That was why I hired mercenaries, and THAT was why I was armed when we went to China. We were not going to be caught off guard once again."

"Still, you threatened my friend's life," I refuted.

"Incentive, Mr. Morgan. Your old friend didn't share the same *tell* as you. You were much easier to influence."

I glared at young Lynea who sat comfortably beside her father. She still had the same innocent face and petite figure, but all I saw was a vulture.

Her shy demeanor had faded away. This new version of the girl I had met months ago was much more authoritative— like her father.

"Since you're pulling back the curtain," I began. "If I was so valuable, why have Alvin try and kill me back in China?"

Ruthford held a puzzled stare. "Those words never left my mouth. Why would I want my most prized hunter dead? Especially when we had such a long road ahead of us?" he stated.

I didn't understand. What would Alvin have gained from my death? Was it simple jealousy? Or was the Baron just spinning a good lie? I shook it off. I'd have time for that answer later.

Shifting gears, I asked, "Why did you need investors to fund your little excursion? If it was a ruse just to lure me out, then you went to some exhaustive lengths."

"Like I said, we all have our reasons for this adventure. Mine isn't power like you assume. True, I wish to harness the ability to see the future, but it is simply for personal goals."

"Uh huh," I said, looking back out the window.

"He's not lying, Charlie. We have been searching for this miracle for ten years," Lynea said, annoyed.

"And you're going to be searching for another ten. Do you really believe that you will find some mystical power to turn you into a fortune teller? Are you looking to join a traveling circus?" I asked.

The Baron paused another moment. When he finally spoke, I couldn't have ever expected what came out of his mouth. Not in a million years.

He said, "We have to believe this power truly exists. It is our last hope to save someone very dear to me—my wife, Mr. Morgan. Lynea's mother. Without this miracle, she will die. You should understand our desire to help her more than anyone."

The news hit me like a brick wall. I didn't believe it. I couldn't understand it. Nevertheless, the man told me his tale.

Ten years ago, William Ruthford's wife, Lauren, was diagnosed with breast cancer. She was lucky in that they caught the disease in its infant stages. Hiring the best doctors money could buy, the Baron spared no expense to treat her.

The tumors dispersed, and Lauren fell into full remission. All was good until a few years later, when more spots emerged—this time on her lungs and liver. The cancer spread with a vengeance. Again, the Baron spent a fortune to cure his wife.

No one could have foreseen what happened afterwards. Lauren was a tough woman. She went through surgeries, radiations, and chemo therapies, all in an effort to fight the parasitic disease. She finally began to win the battle. Just as the tides turned, Lauren was struck with a new disease.

Paraneoplastic Neurologic Syndrome.

It was a mouthful, but basically, her immune system kickstarted to fight the cancer. Only it, revved its engines a little too much, and began attacking her body. Soon her immune system reversed its effects, and instead of being a natural defense for her body, it started causing damage to her muscles and bones. The doctors couldn't stop it.

The attack was so sudden.

Lauren was subjected to tremendous pains. Her body bruised from the inside out. The Baron was helpless to stop the outbreaks.

Her newfound disease was rare. Only a limited number of cases existed.

Still, William Ruthford did not give up hope. He scoured the globe and spoke to hundreds of doctors. None of them had answers. All they could do was calm her pain and slow the spread of the attacks.

And so, the Baron found a treatment that slowed his wife's heart rate and put her into a coma. In the rested state, her immune system remained dormant. This slowed down the cancer.

But this was only a Band-Aid. It was not a cure. The one thing that stood out in William's mind was that all the doctors had the same response. They would need years to come up with the technologies to cure his wife. Even with all the money in the world, William couldn't speed the process along.

His wife didn't have years though. All Ruthford could do was slowly watch Lauren wither away.

It was happenstance that someone discovered Homer's poem in Greece. When it was brought to Ruthford, it reignited his hope. If he could potentially see the future, then he could help speed up the present.

In turn, save his wife.

Ruthford could have been full of it. I'd seen it before. But for some reason, I believed the guy.

Maybe it was the redness in his eyes as he told the story. Or maybe it was the medical room I discovered when I was trying to escape his mansion. Oxygen tanks, beds, and medicine filled the walls of that room.

I remembered the shattered blood vials that Jenny found. Each had the same label—LR. I thought it was intended for Lynea, but maybe I was wrong. Maybe it was meant for Lauren Ruthford.

My mind detoured. I couldn't help but wonder if the Baron had the same fetish with matching initials that Jeremy did. Or maybe it was just coincidence that mother and daughter shared the same initials.

Seeing the sad faces across from me, I realized it was an inappropriate time to ask about it.

Either way, everything started to make sense.

It didn't excuse Ruthford for what he had done. Nor did it abolish the lengths he had gone to in order to reach his goal.

I didn't know what to say. Thankfully, the Baron wasn't expecting a response. I glanced over at Lynea. She sat quietly in her chair.

Then I looked out at the passing terrain. I thought of Jenny and her father. There was no limit to what I would do for them.

Sadly, I wasn't much different than the man who I called my enemy.

The desert passed by in silence. The caravan of vehicles created their own sandstorm as the tires kicked up a whirlwind of powder.

Soon we found ourselves following along the base of a steep rocky mountain. We sat quietly and waited for the car to reach its destination.

The map was simple enough. It clearly marked the final location along the Sinai Mountain. Thank God too, because the entire range of rock was littered with countless temples and churches.

On our trek, we zoomed past dozens of these religious structures. Each carved directly out of the stone.

It wasn't long before we reached our final stop. As we neared the mark on the map, we noticed two large stone pillars punched out of the sand.

The army of SUVs and Hummers reached the pillars and came to a complete stop.

I went to open the door when the Baron grabbed my arm. "Mr. Morgan," he started. "I want to make one thing clear to you. I did not tell you my story for your sympathy. I just wanted you to understand why I am doing what I am."

"I got it," I replied.

"I don't think you do. I am a desperate man, Mr. Morgan. I do not have much time left. I will go to extreme measures to see this all through. With that being said, it will greatly suit you and your friend to assist us on this final stretch."

I pulled my arm away from the Baron's iron grip. "In other words, be part of the solution, not the problem. You won't hesitate to kill us."

I exited the vehicle.

The heat hit me hard. The high sun felt like it was right on top of us, baking us in its rays. Squinting, I searched the other cars. A miniature army of mercenaries spread out like ants over the sand. I continued to scan the site until I found Jenny.

She stood beside the other Hummer. A party of angry individuals flanked her. Burt and Berta were to her left while Alvin was close by her other side.

We all regrouped at the two pillars.

"You hurt?" I asked as we neared one another.

"I'm okay. Long ride," Jenny frowned. "How about you?"

"Mine wasn't much better."

As we huddled around our latest discovery, everyone stared up at the pillars with questionable faces. Other than these two elements, there was no other sign of an entrance. The stone columns stood erect roughly thirty feet from the base of the rocky mountain. Looking at the surface of the towering peak, all one saw was a continuous stone face.

No cave.

No entrance.

Not even engravings or decorations.

It looked like a dead end.

The two stone pillars, on the other hand, were clear signs that we were on the right track.

Each had a smooth tubular surface, and each extended out like candlesticks. They were similar to the totems of our previous destinations.

The only difference was the fact that painted across each pillar was a female figure. On the left, a tall, slender woman carried a bag of fruit. Her face resembled a tiger.

Xi Wangmu.

The image to the right differed significantly. A portly woman was drawn with her legs crossed. She matched typical Buddhist iconography. It could only be one person.

Sanskirt, the Indian shamaness.

I stepped away from the pillars.

The Baron was already in deep conversation with the others. He turned to me saying, "Mr. Morgan? Ms. Jenkins? Please come over here." Ruthford then pointed to some henchmen. "And you three, set up a perimeter around the site."

We obliged. With all the men and guns around us, how could we not?

I passed Burt and his sister. Neither said a word. If it was up to them, we'd have been dead right now. I knew Burt all too well. No one got the better of him and lived to tell about it.

The Traijans thought that they owned this city, but it looked as if now they were taking orders from the good old Baron. How the tables turned.

Especially since it was their men the Baron was commanding. I swore I could see fumes venting out of the twins' heads.

Nearing the Ruthford family, I asked, "How may we serve, master?"

William's harsh look acknowledged my sarcasm.

"We found something," Lynea inserted.

Lynea and Alvin held two of the Trinity tablets in their hands. (Ducktape held the two halves of the *Xi Wangmu* tablet together.) They flipped the two circular objects over, revealing little cogs protruding out of each stone.

I never had much of a chance to look at the back of these tablets. I mean, with all the volcanos, earthquakes, avalanches, and bullets being shot at us, there was never an opportune time.

"You see these nubs, *mate*? They are bloody keys," Alvin said. He then pointed to the base of the stone pillars. "Look there? Matching marks. These must unlock the gate."

It was hard to listen to the Australian. All I wanted to do was choke the man. I wanted to ask him why he tried killing me.

Instead, I asked, "And where might this *gate* be?"

Everyone shrugged.

We were about to find out.

Alvin and Lynea marched to their respective pillars. They inserted each of the stone tablets into the key holes. With a soft *thump*, the circular objects slid into place.

Then they spun each tablet. Slowly, the stones turned until finally, they stopped.

A thunderous bong, roared from under the surface of the ground. The earth trembled.

Here we went again!

But the earthquake settled down just as quickly as it began. For a second, nothing happened. Then, the sand around us began to depress. Instinctively, we all stepped back.

The beads of earth sucked downward into a funnel. As if quicksand, the ground slowly disappeared.

Soon a vortex of sand dropped like an hour glass into some drain down below.

The earth around the base of the Sinai Mountain lowered while more sand dispersed. More and more of the rock that was once buried underground, became exposed.

The whirlwind of action caused a sandstorm to fog up the area. The surge of sand flowing around us sounded like the rush of an ocean current. We all shielded our faces from the debris. The roar grew louder until finally quieting down.

The sand stopped moving.

The dust settled.

As the clouds of smoke disappeared, all that was left was a direct stone path down to the base of the mountain. Walls of sand framed out two sides while a monumental stairway led down to a lower landing.

Along the edges of this lower platform, a series of metal grates seemed to act like drains, siphoning all the sand away.

Beyond the landing, carved out of the rock of the mountain was a twenty foot tall opening.

We were here.

We had arrived at the Temple of Apollo.

CHAPTER THIRTY SEVEN

It may have taken awhile, but we finally learned our lesson. Instead of storming into the great unknown and enter the dark cave that led God knows where, Ruthford ordered a few of the Traijans' mercenaries to go make sure things were clear.

Everyone waited anxiously.

Well, everyone except Jenny and me. True, it was in our nature to seek out treasure and explore long lost sites, but it never felt quite as good when you were forced to do so against your will.

At least I had a friend by my side. Jenny looked radiant, even after all that we had been through.

The thing is, I thought she liked being in our company a little too much. She had a sparkle in her eyes during all of our half dozen scrapes with death. I feared that she would follow in our footsteps.

I would never tell J.J., but secretly, I might not mind having her around.

We made a great team. (Though our track record wasn't all that wonderful.)

My thoughts dwindled away as the armed men returned. Even in this tremendous heat, these men still wore black from head to toe. It was as if this was a uniform requirement for all thugs to abide by. The mercenaries gave the signal that the coast ahead was clear.

"Shall we enter?" Ruthford grinned, already heading down the steps.

That broke me from my daze. I started down the monumental staircase. Stone walls flanked each side of the stair. The walls held back the remainder of earth. Straight ahead, a large cavernous tunnel led into the room beyond.

Jenny clasped my hand.

With our flashlights in tow, we all entered into the dark crevice.

It was odd.

As we passed through the tunnel, we walked a short stint through a small cavern. Natural rock formations roughed out the edges. Sand and rugged terrain was our floor.

But then it opened up into a large room.

We were transported to a very different space. Gone were the rock and earth forms; the dirt path; the patches of sand.

In its place was a giant temple. Walls made out of smooth stone blocks and a floor of marble framed out the room. Large tubular columns rose to hold up a finished stone ceiling.

The rectangular chamber fell in line with typical Greek architecture. The belly of the mountain hid behind these perfectly framed walls.

"How did they do all this?" Jenny thought aloud, marveling at the ceiling.

The ceiling extended at least forty feet above us.

"I don't know," was all I could say.

Smiles lit up Burt's and Berta's faces. Their dismay for the Baron seemed to disappear. They marched down the long stretch of a room.

William, on the other hand, came up beside me. He placed his hand on my shoulder, saying, "Mr. Morgan, I must sincerely thank you. I never imagined we'd find this place."

"Before you get ahead of yourself, Baron, you better make sure that we ARE in the right place. It's never this easy."

I looked at all four walls of the chamber. There didn't seem to be any signs to progress further. The room was simple, minus three enormous statues that stood in plain sight.

Each statue mounted in the center of each respective wall. As we walked down the promenade, we were flanked by a statue on either side, while the last one rested at the far end.

The carved marble figures were colossal in scale, and the detail in each one was astounding.

The mercenaries brought in a series of battery spotlights and quickly illuminated the full interior. With the harsh fluorescent lights in full effect, we got a better gander at the so-called *Temple of Apollo*.

"They're bloody *beauts*," Alvin said, investigating the first two statues.

Both figures were female. On the left, the sculpture depicted an elderly woman dressed in a long flowing robe. In her arms, she held a bronze harp. Her fingers posed as if ready to play a melody.

On the right, the statue was of a much younger woman. Dressed in military armor, she held a bronze bow pointed up at the ceiling.

In both cases, every little muscle and every wrinkle in their clothing and armor was carved in immaculate detail. Even the hair on each figure looked real.

As my luck would have it, these statues would probably magically come to life and kill us.

The Baron and his daughter passed these two statues and already reached the far end of the chamber. There, they stared at the final figure.

This statue was larger than the rest. It was of a masculine figure—one which held a large circular bronze disc above his head. The disc was perfectly round.

I instantly recognized what all the statues were. So did William Ruthford.

"Mr. Morgan, we truly are here," the bullish man began. "Look at this statue. Do you know who this is?"

I opened my mouth to answer, but the Baron cut me off. Apparently, it was a rhetorical question.

"The Greek god, Apollo," he said. "Look at the round object above his head. The bronze reflects our light, causing it to shimmer. The man is holding up the sun."

Nice job, I thought.

Burt spoke up. "What of these others?"

Hearing the voice of my *once* friend caused my muscles to tense up. I knew the answer, but chose against speaking. I didn't want to give the man the luxury.

The Baron knew this answer too, though. "The older woman to the one side is Leto, the mother of Apollo. Opposite her is obviously Apollo's sister, Artemis. In Greek mythology, she was known as a great warrior, and is always shown with a bow in her hand."

Berta stood under Leto's statue. "Apollo's mother? I'm unfamiliar with the majority of Greek lore, but I do know a few facts. Am I mistaken, or didn't all the gods descend from Zeus and his wife Hera."

Of all the twelve Greek gods, Zeus was the most powerful. He sat on his throne with his wife, Hera. Many of their offspring earned god status. Berta was right on that.

But not all of them.

Ruthford explained, "Ms. Traijan, you are correct to an extent. Unfortunately, the gods shared many similar traits with us humans. They were not above infidelity. You see, Zeus was married to Hera. Only he was an adulterer, much like other male gods. Leto was one of his mistresses.

"She birthed him twins, Artemis and Apollo. Now, like any wife, Hera was very displeased at news of this, and she sentenced Leto to be executed."

We all examined Leto's statue.

Ruthford continued, "There were multiple assassination attempts, but Leto's children protected their mother. They then hid her in a far off place where no one would find her—or so the legend states."

J.J. told me that he and William Ruthford shared the same passion for Ancient Greek mythology. Hearing the Baron now, I realized that it was true. He did know his material.

I knew my material as well.

One of the aforementioned assassins that wanted Leto dead was Tityos, a giant who was slain by the arrows of Artemis.

The other assassin that wanted Leto dead was the dragon, Pytho—the very dragon that Apollo killed to protect his mother and in turn, create Pythia, the Oracle of Delphi.

I found it ironic that during our entire journey, we had been focused on female prophets. Legends expressed each as *Queen Mothers* of their respective cultures. In each case, our search for these women led to attempts on our lives. Here, again, we were brought face to face with another *mother*. I found a new reason to be afraid of women.

Statistically speaking, this wasn't going to end well.

I crossed the room, away from the others. Giving a glance back toward the front entrance, I wondered where J.J. was with our rescue. I was ready to get out of here, and he was sure taking his sweet time.

Lynea approached. "Charlie?" she said.

I looked at her without saying a word.

"I just wanted to apologize for our little trickery. I find it sweet that you wanted to save me."

"Save it, Lynea. What's done is done. You fooled me once. It won't happen again," I said and walked away.

She silently crept back to her father's side.

Meanwhile, the others continued to analyze the room. Burt and Berta quickly got antsy. "What are we looking for exactly?" Burt asked.

Alvin answered, "We may be in the Temple of Apollo, *mate*, but there needs to be some passage to the tomb of Pythia. Look for a doorway."

I noticed Jenny admiring the Apollo statue. She was away from the others. It was an opportune moment to talk to her one on one. I marched toward her, but I was stopped.

"Mr. Morgan." It was William. "Your assistance would be greatly appreciated."

I glanced back, seeing the Baron in the center of the room. His giant shadow covered the rear wall of the temple.

"I'm as lost as you are," I said. It was true. I had no idea where to start. I had no desire either. Thankfully, I didn't have to. Alvin made the first discovery for me.

"Mr. Ruthford, come here," the Australian said. He stood next to the Apollo statue. Feeling the wall beside the large figure, Mitchell added, "There is a breeze coming through here. I think the statue is covering a bloody passageway."

Everyone huddled around the stone base of Apollo. Alvin was right. A steady warm breeze filtered out though the crease between the wall and the back of the statue.

The Baron commanded us to push the monstrous stone carving. We complied, but the heavy object did not move. More mercenaries entered the fray, and again we all failed.

It was no use.

Sweating bullets, I stepped away from the group. There had to be another clue. Returning back to the female statues, I found Jenny in deep concentration. I asked, "Hey, you onto something?"

Without looking away from the base of Artemis's sculpture, she said, "I think so. Charlie, look here."

She pointed at the cap of the stone base, right under the feet of Artemis.

"Something is written there in Ancient Greek."

"What's it say?"

Jenny mouthed the words, and then translated, "*The Powers of Apollo.*"

"That's it?" I asked.

"Yes."

I checked the sides of the statue, but there was no other text. Then I switched gears to Leto's figure. Scanning the same area, I noticed similar markings. "Jen, look over here."

She was already at my side reading. "*Shall open the path.*"

What did that mean?

The others soon surrounded us. Jenny re-read the translation. Meanwhile I investigated the statues some more.

The *Powers* of Apollo.

The Greek god, Apollo, was known to possess many attributes. It was almost as if every power that wasn't taken by the other gods was given to him. He harnessed the power of light, and the sun. He possessed the power to heal, and even the power to see the future. Countless other traits tied to him.

The riddle could have meant any number of things.

"Mr. Morgan, any suggestions?" Ruthford asked.

I turned to him to reply when something caught my eye. A reflection blinded me.

Looking up at its source, I realized what the clue meant.

Throughout my years of treasure hunting, I found that everything was designed for a reason. From a vase being placed in a certain location of a room, to the way a statue's hand was pointed, there was always an explanation for it. Nothing was done purely for the heck of it.

Looking up at Leto's statue, a glaringly large detail spoke out to me. In her hands was a large bronze harp. It glistened off our fluorescent lights.

One of Apollo's minor attributes was his love for music. Greek myths always talked of him playing some sort of instrument.

Why else would the harp be so prominently positioned?

I solved the puzzle, I think. The Baron realized it too. He anxiously followed my movements. "Indulge us," he said.

I didn't say a word. I'd let the man sweat it out for a few more seconds. I could have just told him the answer. I could have had one of his mercenaries test out my theory. Instead, I decided to show him myself.

I marched up to the statue and scaled onto its base.

"What do you think you're doing?" Ruthford asked.

"You'll see," I said.

No one tried to stop me. Much like three months ago, at the base of the Wanda Mountains, I was about to go for another climb.

The marble statue was smooth and slippery. It didn't provide many good footholds. But I had climbed worse. I planted my feet against the extended marble thigh, and I lunged upward.

The statue was only twenty feet tall. My climb was short and quick. Within seconds I had already reached the torso. Using Leto's right arm, I pulled myself up to her shoulders.

Propped between her shoulder blade and her bent arm, I sat comfortably on the makeshift chair. The strings of the bronze harp were only a few feet away.

The others, down below, watched in silence.

With my left arm bracing my body around Leto's head, I reached out with my free hand. I angled myself forward. My extended fingers neared the frame of the harp. Soon they glossed past it and touched the strings.

The strings were taut. I flicked one, and a soft hymn resonated through the room.

Nothing.

"Nice try, *mate*," Alvin chimed in down below.

With all eyes on me, it would be embarrassing if I was wrong. I couldn't be wrong.

It needed more.

I reached past all of the strings and, in one swooping motion, ran my fingers over all of them. A beautiful melody echoed through the room as each strings vibrated in harmony.

The sound continued to bounce off all the temple walls. Music permeated through the room. Right on its heels, a series of vibrations followed.

The pulsating was soft, but I really felt it in the arm of the statue. Dust and debris fell from the ceiling with each and every rumble.

Great!

Leto's arm suddenly cracked at the bicep. My makeshift chair dipped a fraction of an inch.

It cracked some more.

"Charlie, you better get down from there," Jenny yelled out.

I straddled the breaking marble forearm and quickly lowered myself down.

Before I could grab onto anything else, the arm broke free.

I fell.

The angled body of the robed marbled figure caught me. Like a slide, I slid down the legs of the statue and flung off the raised pedestal. I bounced off some large balloon-type object, and crashed onto the floor. Looking up, I realized that the large *balloon* was actually Burt's bulbous body. I had to give it to the man, his round shape created a soft cushion…

…For me. Unfortunately for him, he tumbled like Humpty Dumpty.

Dusting myself off, I got to my feet. "Sorry about that," I said.

Burt leapt to his feet. "You think you're funny! How dare you…"

Burt's voice stopped mid-sentence. His eyes widened. His mouth dropped. I swore I could see all the hair on his body straighten and poke through his suit. His expression had flipped from anger to fear like a flick of a light switch. He wasn't looking at me anymore. His gaze fell upon the large statue behind me.

The statue of Artemis.

I realized why he was so afraid.

The sculpture had suddenly come to life.

CHAPTER THIRTY EIGHT

I may have exaggerated a bit. The Artemis statue didn't really come to life, *per se*. In actuality, all that moved was its one arm. The arm bent at its joints and reached into the quiver strapped over the statue's shoulder.

It pulled an arrow out, and brought it to the bow string. The other arm remained still, aiming the bow toward the ceiling.

As if by magic, the moving arm pulled back on the arrow, tensioning the string. The fingers of the stone hand uncurled and released the arrow.

The tightened chord slingshot forward, launching the arrow upward with ferocious velocity.

Perfectly aimed, the arrow tip sunk into a crevice in the stone ceiling. It lodged itself there. Seconds later, a series of cracks radiated from that point. The cracks rapidly grew in size.

Soon they covered the majority of a square ceiling tile.

"What have you done?" Burt asked.

Before I could respond, the entire stone tile crumbled and fell.

My eyes followed the tile's trajectory. Jenny stood right under the collapsing stone. In a heartbeat I dove toward her. I tackled her out of the way just as the stone crashed onto the ground.

More fragments fell around us. Everyone scrambled to the sides of the room.

Seconds later, it all stopped.

The music stopped.

The falling rock stopped.

Even my heart felt like it stopped.

The dust settled, and I found myself lying on top of Jenny's small frame.

"How come we keep ending up like this?" I asked, smiling.

Jenny pushed me up, saying, "Because you keep causing trouble."

We got to our feet, as did the others.

"Mr. Morgan, next time it may be fruitful to inform us of your plan prior acting on it," Ruthford said.

"You asked for suggestions," I pointed out.

As everyone regrouped, we looked back up at the ceiling. A gaping hole now stood where the one stone tile previously rested. Behind it, the deep hole pierced through the rock of the Sinai Mountain. It ran like a small tunnel and punctured through to the sky beyond.

Of course we couldn't see this. But we knew it, mainly due to the fact that a beam of sunlight flooded through the hole and into the chamber.

The light focused its ray right on the large circular bronze element held by the statue of Apollo. The bronze object blindingly reflected all the sunlight making it near impossible to look at.

The Powers of Apollo.

The statue of the god of the Sun was holding a literal interpretation of the giant star. The bronze circle illuminated the entire room.

I covered my eyes to block the bright light. Squinting, I could barely see the statue start to shift. Somehow, it slid to one side. As it did, the bronze sun in his arms began to lose its glimmer.

Shortly, the full statue and its base had relocated over to one side, while the beam of light now fell on the far wall of the room.

Where the statue once stood, an opening revealed itself. And through the opening, a sea of blackness awaited us.

"Told you guys I had the answer," I said.

We all stepped forward. As we neared the tunnel, everyone cautiously came to a halt. No one entered. Our flashlights shined into the dark passageway. We saw no end in sight.

A gust of wind howled out through the tunnel sending a shiver up my spine. Looking down at the ground, I saw that the marble floor switched to stone. Small holes covered the top of each tile.

That seemed strange.

Burt and Berta stepped forward, saying in unison, "What are we waiting for?"

The Baron's massive paws grabbed the siblings and pulled them back. "Wait," Ruthford said. "Let us have your soldiers investigate what lies ahead."

They nodded.

Four of the mercenaries were ordered forward. They followed the directive without question. In unison, the four men entered the tunnel. They made it a few steps when one of the men stepped on something. A loud click snapped as the stone floor depressed.

"What was that?" Jenny asked.

Her answer came unexpectedly. A black cloud of smoke shot out from the perforated floor. The dark cloud instantly filled the entire tunnel. It made it impossible to see the four men inside.

We all stepped back.

Coughs rang out through the smoke. Then choking could be heard. Suddenly, the men burst out of the cloud and back into the temple.

Each held onto his throat, choking violently.

"Breathe," the Baron ordered, trying to calm the men. Their eyes were wide though, and panic enveloped them.

The soldiers collapsed to the ground, still choking. It was as if they were screaming for air. Their eyes watered. Blood oozed out of their noses.

One man coughed, and more blood spat out to the ground.

We all watched, helpless to act. The four men continued to keel over, desperate for air.

Moments later, all four men fell to the ground…

…Dead.

No one said a word. No one even moved. We all simply stared at the horrific scene.

I told the Baron it was never that easy.

Jenny turned to me. "Charlie, I can't look anymore. We need to get out of here."

"Nonsense," Ruthford bellowed. "We can't let these men die for nothing. We are so close."

"How do you know that?" I asked. "There could be dozens more traps beyond this point."

"Mr. Morgan," William said calmly. "Do you remember our conversation? We must see this through. If you do not have anything helpful to say, I'd suggest you do not say anything at all."

I turned back to the dead men on the floor. I thought about the riddle written on the two statues.

The Powers of Apollo.

Apollo was known as a healer. He was also known to be the god of death—more specifically, the plague. How he possessed the power to cure and kill, I didn't know.

That clue had many hidden meanings. Right now, we had to pass through Apollo's worst power.

The cloud of smoke in the tunnel dissipated. Ruthford looked at the stone floor saying, "It looks as if every tile is triggered to exhaust that black smoke."

Alvin added, "And whatever that stuff is, it killed those poor fellas."

"It's the plague," I said. I explained my theory.

"Do you think it will set off again?" Lynea asked.

"I have no idea." I looked at Ruthford. "Why don't you head on through to find out."

He smiled at me. Ruthford turned to Burt. "Mr. Traijan, please order another one of your men to proceed through the tunnel once again."

Two of Burt's men ran away. In a flash, they disappeared out the rear exit. I guess the Baron didn't have as much control as he thought. This thought was reinforced by Burt's response.

The Armenian refuted the request. "Mr. Ruthford, these are my soldiers. I will not knowingly send them off to their deaths."

Ruthford obliged, saying, "I understand." He then looked to me again. "Well Mr. Morgan it looks as if we find ourselves in a stalemate."

"You can all try and draw straws," I said.

Ruthford added, "Or we can press your luck. You're a lucky man, aren't you? The trigger mechanism might have been a one-time shot. The tunnel may be clear now. How about you and Ms. Jenkins do us the honors? You two have miraculously overcome all the obstacles thus far."

"We'll pass this time. Next time though," I said.

"It wasn't a question," Ruthford added.

A rifle jabbed into my back. Two mercenaries stood behind us, a gun aimed at both Jenny and me. Oh, this was wonderful.

Jenny grabbed my hand. "What are we going to do?" she asked.

I looked at the dead men. Each seemed to choke on whatever the black smoke was. I turned my attention to the tunnel. I couldn't tell how deep it ran.

Another jab pushed us forward. "Hey buddy, we get it," I snarled back at the man.

Jenny and I marched forward toward the opening.

Leaning close to her, I said, "It looks like it might be an airborne toxin. If we keep our eyes and mouths shut, maybe we can pass through it unharmed."

"That's it? That's your plan?" Jenny asked. "Close our eyes and hold our breath?"

"You have a better option?"

She shook her head.

"We can always hope it doesn't trigger a second time," I added. That would mean luck would truly be on our side. The way things were going for us, I doubted we'd have that luxury.

We reached the opening. Glancing back one last time, I saw our audience watch anxiously. They all stood far back.

Looking forward once again, I said, "Are you ready?"

"Ready as I can be," Jenny said. Her voice rattled.

Hand in hand, we stepped forward into the tunnel. We didn't even make it two steps when I felt the stone tile depress under my foot.

Black smoke hissed out of the floor and rushed over our bodies. Our figures disappeared in darkness.

CHAPTER THIRTY NINE

My eyes and mouth clenched as tight as they could. My fingers plugged my nose, and my heart sped rapidly. For a moment I didn't move as the burst of cloud rushed over me like a gust of wind.

Holding my breath, I finally took a step forward. Then another. Jenny's hand tightened around mine. Her strength cut at my blood circulation, but I didn't mind. The pain meant that I was still alive. It also meant that she was too.

We continued to walk forward. The hissing from the floor stopped, and the tunnel drowned in silence. Not a word was uttered from the rest of the party behind us. I was dizzy, terrified, and wondered if I was right.

The good sign was that we were still standing.

Our pace quickened as we moved on through the tunnel. I couldn't tell how far we had gone. My lungs screamed for oxygen. I walked faster as my chest ached. I needed to keep going. I started to feel light headed. Were we clear of the smoke?

I knew I couldn't last much longer. My body needed fresh air. I fought as hard as I could to hold my breath, but I had pushed beyond my limit.

I had to find out if we were clear, so I risked a glance.

I opened my eyes.

The black smoke was gone. The tunnel was gone. We had passed through to the next chamber and all looked clear.

Thank God.

I inhaled, taking in my first deep breath of oxygen. Jenny followed suit.

We survived.

Taking in the life-giving air, we sucked in more. I almost laughed in excitement. We quickly scanned one another for any signs of the plague. Breathing was normal, and no pain rocked through our bodies like those poor mercenaries.

"It actually worked," Jenny said, surprised.

"You doubted me?" I asked. Secretly, *I* doubted myself.

"Not at all," she said.

A voice rang out from the tunnel behind us. "How are things looking, Mr. Morgan?" It was Ruthford.

Glancing back, I saw the tunnel was still covered in black smoke. For a second, we were shielded from our adversaries. It was our first moment alone. I turned to Jenny and whispered, "Jen, you won't believe what I found out on my car ride here."

"It's probably not better than what I learned," she said, leaning in. "Charlie, Alvin is not what he pretends to be."

"What?"

"On our ride here, your *friends* bickered most of the time. Secretly, Alvin told me what was going on. You're not going to believe it."

I cut Jenny off, "I know. Ruthford is looking for a cure for his wife."

Jenny looked dumbfounded. "What?" she asked.

Apparently, that wasn't what Alvin told her. Before she could say anymore, we heard another hiss come from the tunnel.

The trap was sprung.

Seconds later, a monstrous figure broke through the black cloud. William Ruthford marched out of the tunnel. Lynea followed right behind.

There went our moment of privacy. I was surprised that they had gone without us confirming we were okay. That is, until I saw what was strapped over both of their faces.

They each wore gas masks.

"Where did you get those?" I asked.

Ruthford pulled his off, saying, "The Traijans kindly informed us that there were a number of masks stored in the vehicles outside. The two soldiers who ran off, retrieved them. They returned while you two entered the tunnel."

More figures emerged through the clouded tunnel. Each wore a similar mask.

"Thanks for giving us the heads up," I said angrily.

Burt pulled off his mask, laughing. "Charlie, I just wanted to see if you were as lucky as you say." He tapped me on my shoulder.

Berta added, "Don't look so sad, Charlie. I had forgotten about these masks. We only have them for emergencies. You would be surprised how many times we've been attacked with toxic bombs. These come in quite handy, but they wreak havoc with my hair."

She adjusted herself, walking past us. Everyone else did the same. Jenny and I just stood there stunned. It was a miracle we were alive.

Now I worried about what was next.

Our new surroundings were extremely vague, mainly because we couldn't see much of them. Our flashlights disappeared into darkness every which way we pointed.

It was near pitch black. From what I could gather, sand extended in every direction. Our echoes hinted that whatever space we now stood in was a large volume.

Those were the only signs.

That is, until one of our lights hit a black, shadowy object protruding out of the ground. We all marched up to the circular pole. As we neared, we saw that the pole matched the designs of the two totems outside of the Temple of Apollo.

Inscribed over the main face of the column was an image of another woman. It could only be one person...

...*Asherah*.

We had found the final shamaness. The same lock mechanism recessed into the base of the totem.

The Greek philosophy of the Holy Trinity was in full effect. Life was a circle, which was represented by the number three. This was the third key to bring everything around. Homer took those symbols quite literally in the creation of his fable. Three different religions all connected to one. It was something we had never seen before.

Whatever lay beyond, we were on the brink of seeing it.

"We are finally here," the Baron whispered.

"I hope so," Burt said. The twins were eager to get out of the cavern. They didn't like getting dirty, and sitting in this filthy dark chamber was probably making them sick.

William Ruthford pulled the last circular tablet out of his bag. He inserted it into the totem, and the object locked in place.

"Are you sure you want to do this, *mate?*" Alvin asked.

"Yes, I am," William stated. He turned the tablet until it clicked in place.

The ground trembled. This time no one was afraid. The trick had occurred enough times to diminish our fears.

Nevertheless, as the vibrations increased, a number of the mercenaries, including the Traijan siblings, instinctively stepped back toward the exit.

A rumble stabbed through the walls. Up above, rock clambered, but we saw nothing in the darkness. Soon, a beam of daylight pierced through the ceiling.

The beam grew in size as more light bathed into the room. The rock ceiling way up above parted, allowing for the sun to shine into the space.

As the chamber illuminated, our new location fully revealed itself.

We found ourselves in the belly of the mountain. To call the area a room was an understatement. In all actuality, it was more of a large circular arena. It was five times the size of a football stadium. The ceiling domed up around us.

The dome was a natural form in ancient times. Using compression, it allowed ceilings to span great distances, all while holding back the weight above them. This dome was the largest I had ever seen. It was perfectly carved out of the rock, meeting at a central circular ring at the top of the arch.

That circle was now open allowing massive amounts of light to bathe the arena. We stood at one end of the gigantic space. A perfectly flat bed of sand covered the floor.

"I feel like an ant," I said.

No one else spoke.

The ground continued to pulsate. Suddenly, the smooth nature of the sand changed. At the center of the arena, the ground started to sink.

A whirlpool of sand began to vacuum toward the center of the arena. The vortex grew, and the ground lowered in the middle.

Much like it occurred outside the mountain, the sand siphoned like an hourglass to some magical drain. This time, it was on a much grander scale.

Alert, we all moved toward the edge of the domed arena. The earth spiraled out of the room at an alarming rate.

Clouds of sand fogged up the chamber. Squinting, I could barely see the ground lower.

Then something stuck out.

As the sand disappeared, I noticed a structure project out from the ground. The more sand that sucked away, the more of the structure I noticed. Soon, a full building emerged from the ground. Then another. Then another. They continued to appear in various sizes and shapes.

Whatever was happening, it seemed that the earth had buried these structures underground. Our key triggered a drain to exhaust all the sand and reveal them.

But it wasn't just a few structures.

As the last of the sand dispersed, and the dust settled, we were left with the full image of our discovery—an entire city of stone buildings.

Streets needled between the structures. Their arrangement created a network of pedestrian passages throughout the enormous city. The field of brown buildings encompassed most of the arena. This wasn't just the tomb of Pythia, it was an entire civilization dedicated to her.

"I don't believe my eyes," The Baron said softly.

"I don't think any of us do," Jenny said.

We stood on a perched area. Stairs led down into the bowels of this buried city.

At its center, a bronze domed structure sparkled in the soft daylight. It wasn't the only thing shining. From our raised location, we could see many of the intertwined streets and buildings.

Window and door openings led to dark interiors, but what amazed us the most weren't the structures. Lining the roads and brimming out the dark crevices of the buildings were a bunch of glimmering objects.

As I looked closer, I realized why the objects reflected the sunlight. Berta did too. "Is that gold?"

"Yes, Ms. Traijan. Yes it is," the Baron said.

The streets were covered in treasure. Every pathway housed mounds of gold, silver, and other valuables. The entire city was blanketed in it. Even the buildings were stuffed with treasure.

In all my years in the business, I had never seen so much gold in one place. I never thought it possible.

"We're rich," Burt said.

"There are no words in our vocabulary that can describe what you are," Ruthford stated.

Legends said that kings from all over the world brought their treasures to the Oracle of Delphi as payment for reading their futures. For once, the legends were true. We found the vault that stored it all.

The Baron was the first to move. With the earthquakes settled, he began descending down the stairs and into the city. His daughter and Mitchell followed.

"Are you coming Mr. Morgan?" he asked.

"Where are we going now?" I asked.

"According to Homer's poem, Pythia's tomb rests in the center structure. The Traijans have their treasure. Now it is time for me to get mine."

Walking through the city felt like a dream. We followed the yellow brick road, but instead of brick, we walked on gold.

Ruthford didn't stop. He didn't investigate any of the glistening objects. He was a determined man.

We all trailed along. Burt and Berta fell behind, filling their pockets with treasure every step of the way.

I walked beside Jenny. Instead of looking at the treasures around us, she was staring up at the dome.

"What are you thinking?" I asked.

"Charlie, look at the far end of the roof above. You see that sculpture sticking out?"

I didn't notice it before. Carved out of the dome was a large figure. It almost looked like the upper torso of a man with its arms raised in the air. The figure grew out of the rock. Deeply defined facial features sunk the eyes and mouth of the head.

"Do you know what that is, Charlie?" Jenny asked.

"I'm assuming Tityos."

"I thought the same thing. Tityos was a giant. After his failed attempt at assassinating Leto, Artemis and Apollo buried the beast. You think that is his sculpture? Something to signify their victory?"

"If so, it's kind of creepy." The stone face looked deformed, as if Tityos was in agony. "I wouldn't want to have to look at that every day."

"If this is Pythia's treasure vault, and she is the Oracle to Apollo, then this could also house all of the god's spoils in victory. Dedicating a statue not only to the gods, but to the championing of an evil being kind of makes sense."

"True," I said. Then added, "If so, then Apollo's greatest victory was killing Pythos, the dragon." This deed in turn created the Oracle. "I don't see a dragon sculpture anywhere."

We continued through the streets. The roads widened as we approached the center structure. The building towered above the rest. As I scanned through the open windows of the side structures, I wondered who could have lived here?

Jenny wondered the same thing. "Why would they create all this, just to bury someone?" she asked.

"This is a full blown city. My only guess is that it must be the hidden island where Apollo and Artemis sent their mother to shield her from the gods. Legends said that the island didn't exist on land. People thought it to be some floating palace in the clouds, but no one thought about it being buried under the land."

"Very observant, Mr. Morgan," Ruthford chimed in as if he were part of our conversation. "What better place to bury such an important shamaness, than the one place hidden from the gods."

"Mr. Ruthford, I have to say, when someone goes to such great lengths to bury something in a place that was never meant to be found, it usually means something bad."

"You told me that once before, back in China."

"And you remember what happened?" I said matter-of-factly.

"Oh, I do, Mr. Morgan. I remember finding the second key to our journey. I remember coming one step closer to our discovery. How was that so bad?"

It was easy for him to say. I was the one stuck in the volcano. I was also the one who had hooded assassins try to kill me, and let's not forget the White Siberian Tigers that wanted me for dinner. I shrugged the conversation off.

The road was nearly twenty feet wide now. Straight ahead were the front gates to our final destination. The treasures that littered the ground faded away, revealing the stone walkway. As we progressed forward, a few of the mercenaries spread out to the outskirts of the road. They monitored the alleyways. I had to give it to them, they were methodical and alert. They scanned each and every crevice.

That's when I heard a soft thump.

One of the soldiers at the far end triggered a booby-trap. The stone tile on the floor depressed as he stepped on it. The click set off another gush of black smoke from the ground. The cloud engulfed the man, causing him to inhale the disease.

We all scrambled away from the cloud as the man went through the same frightful motions as his peers did back at the entrance. Seconds later, he collapsed to the ground, dead.

"What the heck was that?" Burt yelled.

"A warning for us to get out of here," I stated.

Ruthford brushed this off. "No, just a reminder for us to be cautious. Proceed Mr. Morgan."

The group, huddled close together. Our speed slowed down as we continued. Flashlights scanned the floor. A number of primed stones littered our way. Dodging them, we carefully trekked our way to the front gates of Pythia's burial temple.

Two massive bronze doors blocked our path. Icons of Apollo and Pythia engraved into each door leaf. They towered over fifteen feet up.

"Are you all ready?" Ruthford asked.

I was ready for this to be over.

Two of the mercenaries marched up to the double doors. They grabbed each handle and started to pry the doors open. Unlike *Xi Wangmu's* temple, these doors easily slid ajar.

The hinges groaned. The heavy doors scraped along the floor. A rush of stale air vented out of the opening. Straining, the two men continued to enlarge the doorway.

"Where are all the people who lived here?" Berta asked. She stared out at the city of gold behind us.

"I was wondering the same thing," Burt said.

I stared down a narrow stretch of alley. Buildings lined each side like a series of homes. I couldn't imagine anyone living down here. Still, the doorways and windows painted a different story. Someone did once live here.

"Do you think they all left before the city got buried?" Berta added.

The doors to Pythia's temple finally stopped moving. The large opening now revealed the full interior of the building. It also revealed what lay beyond. As if on cue, we were welcomed by the inhabitants of the long lost city.

Hundreds of them.

CHAPTER FORTY

The entire chamber of Pythia's temple was a sea of people—and they were all dead.

Skeletons filled the ground from wall to wall. All we saw was a field of bones.

"There's your answer," I said to Berta.

The bodies stacked over one another. Fragments of jewelry and clothing still draped some of the skeletons. Centuries of cobwebs and filth covered others.

None of this fazed Baron William Ruthford. He marched through the doorway, and into the temple. His boots crackled over the decayed bones. Skulls crumbled as he stomped on each one.

Cautiously, the rest of us followed.

Pythia's temple was another domed structure. The peak, much like the larger dome before it, had a circular skylight. It allowed daylight to naturally illuminate the interior. A series of simple columns ran along the perimeter to hold up the curved roof. A second series of columns supported a balcony that circled around the chamber like a running track.

Smack dab in the center of the large space was a raised landing. A rectangular tomb rested on top of the stone.

The tomb of the Oracle of Delphi.

I kicked a few fragile bones aside as I respectfully dodged the dead bodies sprawled along our path. Jenny remained close. "Are you okay?" I asked.

She nodded.

I glanced beyond Jenny. Alvin Mitchell silently followed in our shadow. He was extremely quiet. I was expecting him to relish in this discovery.

Everyone else scanned the surroundings. Worried looks spread across their faces. Well, all faces except the Baron's. His eyes locked on the tomb at the temple's center.

"What could have done all this?" Berta asked.

"Based on the arrangement of the bodies, it seems they willingly allowed themselves to die," the Baron said.

"How do you mean?" Burt asked.

"The skeletons are evenly spread around the chamber. There are no signs that any of these bodies struggled to escape. It's as if they sat down and welcomed their death," Ruthford answered.

Looking at the bodies, he was right. My guess was, when the city was going to be buried underground, the inhabitants all came to the center chamber and waited for their death.

That was dedication.

"This is so sad," Jenny mumbled.

"To them it could have been an honor," Alvin finally spoke. "Pythia was their goddess. Giving their lives for her was their bloody choice."

"Whatever their reason, it doesn't diminish the sorrow of it all," she said.

As we approached the tomb, a scent engulfed my nostrils. I recognized it. It was the same odor I smelled back in *Xi Wangmu's* temple. "Jen, do you smell that?"

"Ethylene gas," Jenny said.

"Yeah." As the Baron once mentioned, this gas was believed to be the source of a shaman's powers. Inhaling the fumes, they received hallucinations that gave them visions of the future. It was also a sign of something else. "Is Mount Sinai a volcano?"

"Not that I know of," Jenny replied. "But, it would make sense if this is where Pythia got her power."

My face expressed confusion.

"Charlie, why else would they have brought her here. Legends always said Pythia drank from the Castalian spring in Delphi. The spring that the priestess drank from was infused with the body of Python, the dragon. Maybe that wasn't the case. Maybe this was where she got her true power."

"Well if it is, do you remember the last time Ruthford defiled a tomb?" We triggered a dormant volcano. "Let's hope this doesn't happen again," I added.

Eavesdropping, the Baron chimed, "Mr. Morgan, do not fear. Come. Let's make history."

We arrived.

Following Ruthford up the stairs, we came face to face with the tomb of Pythia—the Oracle of Delphi.

Lynea brushed her hand over the stone cover of the tomb. "I can't believe we found it," she whispered.

The Baron put his arm around his daughter. "I told you we would." For the first time, the bullish man stopped to admire the ancient tomb.

The rectangular stone object had a number of glyphs and carvings engraved all over its surface. Each detail was unique, painting an image of the prophetic Oracle. Apollo's symbols flanked the walls of the casket.

That was the extent of it. The base of the tomb seemed to grow out of the stone floor. On top, a thick lid covered the casket.

"Help me with this," Ruthford said, trying to slide the lid off. The rest of us bent over to help. With all of us working together, the heavy stone slid off the tomb and crashed to the ground.

Peering into the casket we found something even more puzzling. There were no bodily remains inside. There was no treasure hidden within the tomb's walls. There wasn't even a sign that this really was a casket.

Instead, we were greeted with a pool of water. Bubbles fizzled at its surface. Gaseous vapors steamed up at us. The blackness of the water ran deep below the surface.

This wasn't a casket at all. It was a well.

"I don't get it," I said aloud.

"Mr. Morgan, what did you expect?"

"Maybe a body," I pointed at the obvious.

"Weren't you listening to Ms. Jenkins moments ago?" The Baron began. "She just recounted the tale of how Pythia received her power. The priestess drank from the Castalian Spring which contained the decayed remains of the mythical Python. The creature's remains were imbued into the spring. The same water that came from the abyss of the Earth's core."

The Baron put his hand in the water. "In theory this is that spring. When the last Oracle passed away, they brought her here, placed her body in the well, and let her decayed corpse soak up the waters. In turn, the next person to drink from this spring would obtain her power."

"You know, prophesies are typically vague and come sporadically," Jenny pointed out. "What do you hope to achieve with that type of power?"

"Ms. Jenkins, different writings express different beliefs. I believe that there is more control to this power than you think. We shall see momentarily."

Something ran over my foot. Looking down, I saw a white bone on the floor—another fragment of a skeleton. But then the bone moved.

I shined my light down. The bone slithered as it crossed over my foot and onto Jenny's. I realized it wasn't a bone at all. The shiny body curved and moved fluidly. It had soft skin. It was much longer than I first thought. Its body twisted and turned. It was much more dangerous than any bone.

I stared down at the body of a snake.

The striped lines running along the side of its jaws, and the triangular shape of its head only meant one thing. It was poisonous.

Before I could say a word, Jenny noticed the snake on her foot. She let out a soft yelp.

"Don't move," I muttered.

The others followed my gaze. The snake slithered around Jenny's ankle. Each full turn tightened its squeeze.

I needed to do something. I had no idea what, though. Any sudden movements and the snake could attack. It hissed as it wrapped more of its body around Jenny's leg.

I slowly bent toward the lethal animal, but it sensed my movement. It arched its head back to face me. The snake's jaws opened, revealing its fangs. Venom salivated along the tips of its two sharp teeth.

Crap!

"Charlie, what do I do?" Jenny whispered, terrified.

Someone else answered her question. A long knife slashed by Jen's leg, slicing head off the venomous snake. The body went limp, dropping to the floor.

Lynea held the knife in her hand. Her movement was fast like a ninja. I didn't even sense her by my side. How the heck did she do that?

"Thanks," I said.

She nodded.

We heard a scream. Turning around, I saw one of the mercenaries stumble to the ground and roll down the stairs. Another snake wrapped around his ankle. Its jaw clenched onto the man's thigh.

As he stumbled down the field of bones, the man panicked. He snapped the snake's neck with his bare hands, and threw the dead beast to the ground. Unfortunately, the snake's venom quickly took effect.

The man rolled over in pain. He screamed, clasping his leg. Convulsing, I watched foam froth out his mouth. In a blink of an eye, he was dead.

"What the heck is going on?" Burt yelled.

I shined my light out to the field of skeletons. Amongst the skulls and bones, random white objects slithered through them.

"We're not alone," I mumbled.

Dozens of snakes were hidden amongst the remains. It seemed that our actions of opening Pythia's tomb triggered them.

Another snake attacked. I stepped aside, dodging the animal. Picking up a random bone, I batted it away. The snake launched through the air, landing back in the field of dead bodies.

"Why is this happening?" Jenny asked.

"They don't want us here," I stated the obvious. "I should have known. Snakes are the animalistic symbols of Apollo. They are one of his protectors."

"Charlie," Berta interrupted. "Thanks for the history lesson, but how about we do something about this."

I didn't need to do anything. The Baron did it all for us.

In rapid succession, a series of gunshots rang out through the dome. The bangs deafened through the walls of the temple. One by one, each of the snakes fell to the ground, dead. Not a single shot missed its target.

I glanced over to see the Baron aiming his pistol. He quickly reloaded and fired again.

The mercenaries joined in on the action. I used my bone to bat a few more snakes away, while the others finished off all the slithering animals. In short time, all the snakes were dead.

My heart raced as I searched for any more lingering animals. Everyone spread across the field of bones. They scanned the area for movement.

First, I had tigers, then rats. Now I had poisonous snakes. I prayed that this was the end of my animal attacks.

As things settled down, I said, "Have we had enough of this place yet?"

The Baron was back at the base of the Oracle's casket. Lynea stood by his side. "Mr. Morgan, we have not completed our task." He pulled out a knife. "I must perform my sacrifice to harness Pythia's power. Only then shall we leave."

I couldn't believe it. Ruthford was truly going to sacrifice his daughter. Lynea was going to willingly allow this to happen.

The rest of us remained at the bottom of the landing. I didn't want to see this act up close.

Lynea held her hand out while the Baron pressed the knife blade against her palm. He made a precise incision and sliced a thin line across her hand. Blood instantly appeared.

That was it.

Ruthford smiled. "Mr. Morgan, did you believe I was going to kill my daughter?"

The thought didn't escape me.

The large man continued, "All I needed was some of her blood." The Baron pressed his hand over his daughter's. As he removed it, a red smear covered his own hand. He dunked his hand into the warm waters of Pythia's casket.

"The pure blood of a virgin is necessary to harness these prophetic powers. Drinking from this well shall grant me what I seek. This is why we have traveled all this way. I will finally show you what the years of searching was all for."

Baron William Ruthford scooped up a handful of water from the *spring*. He brought it to his mouth and drank. Ruthford closed his eyes. He waited for a sign. We all waited for sign. A minute passed as we stared in silence.

Finally, the Baron opened his eyes saying, "I don't see anything?"

It looked like his journey was in vain. I was about to tell him that he was crazy to think that it was all true. I mean who would honestly believe this non-sense?

"Why can't I see the future?" The Baron yelled. The aggravation in his voice shuddered through the walls.

Suddenly a knife pierced through Baron William Ruthford's back, and out his front chest. The blade tore through his shirt. Blood instantly soaked through his clothing. The Baron looked down at his chest, seeing the bloody blade protrude out.

"Because there is no future for you to see," a voice behind the Baron whispered.

William Ruthford's face paled quickly. His eyebrows trembled with terror, then sadness. The man collapsed to the ground, dead.

Behind him, stood his daughter, Lynea. Her hands both wrapped around the handle of the blade that still stuck in her father's back.

She looked down at all of us and grinned.

CHAPTER FORTY ONE

Over the years I had seen many different twists and turns. Enemies turned to allies—allies to enemies. I had been double crossed over and over again. It came to the point where I believed nothing could surprise me anymore. Then things like this happened. A daughter killing her own father.

Honestly, I didn't see it coming. It blew in out of left field.

Lynea stood over her dead father. The blood soaked blade still clasped in her hand. She didn't look angry. She didn't even look evil. She appeared just as she always had—a fragile young girl. Only, we knew better.

She stepped over her father's corpse and into full view. No one said a word.

What was her plan? I risked my life to protect this girl. I threatened my friends' lives to find a way to free her from her father's grasp. In the end, William Ruthford was the one that needed saving.

"I believe now is the time for a regime change," Lynea said, sticking her bloody hands into Pythia's open tomb.

"What are you doing?" I couldn't help but ask.

Lynea answered with a surge of confidence. "Charlie, my father was narrow-minded. He didn't see the big picture here. Do you understand what the power of the Oracle of Delphi means?"

"I thought you were here to save your mother?"

Jenny gave me a puzzled look.

"I'll explain later," I whispered.

Lynea said, "I didn't have a mom, Charlie. I lost her when I was a kid. For ten years, all she's been is a vegetable. My dad spent all his time trying to save her. He neglected me. I wasn't allowed to go out or have fun with anyone. I was a prisoner."

"He's still your father. Don't you think killing the man was a little overboard?" Jenny chimed in.

"He was no father. I was his tool. He only pretended to care about me because he needed my help. You think he was really concerned about me when we were in China? Charlie cared more for me than my *father* ever did."

Where was all this coming from? "So this is your way of getting back at good old dad?" I asked.

"Charlie, I'm not twelve years old. It's nothing that juvenile," Lynea said.

"Then what do you hope to achieve by all this?" I asked.

"There's nothing original in what I want, Charlie. There's no deep meaning to it all. It's pretty simple. I want power. I want to be free to do what I want. Free from my dad's shadow. Free from my mom's suffering."

"You're like a James Bond villain," I thought aloud. The voice that bellowed out of this small girl almost fell like it belonged to a totally different person. She was a good actor, I gave her that.

Lynea turned to Burt and Berta. "Mr. and Ms. Traijan, you have been a great help to me and my family. Feel free to depart with all the treasure you wish."

The twins nodded in appreciation.

"And what of us?" I asked.

"Aren't you intrigued to see what the power of Pythia can do? Let me show you what my dad was so adamant about finding."

Lynea scooped up a handful of water and took a sip. She closed her eyes for a moment and then opened them.

Nothing happened.

"Impressive," I said, sarcastically.

"You should be afraid, Charlie," Alvin Mitchell spoke up. "This is just the beginning," he mumbled.

Perplexed, I looked over at the man. He seemed sad—almost defeated. I went to speak, but Lynea interrupted.

"I see it now. I see it all!"

All I saw was a creepy grin spread across Lynea Ruthford's face. She locked eyes with me, then Jenny. Moving along, she scanned the room. Her gaze passed over Alvin and ended on Burt. That creepy smile suddenly faded away. "I suggest you duck down Mr. Traijan," she said.

"Pardon me?" he replied, confused.

"I said, duck, NOW!"

The thunder in her voice kicked Burt's body alive. He obliged, bending his round torso.

A flurry of arrows cut through the air barely missing Burt's head. They ripped over his shoulders, crashing into the stone floor with a snap. If he had waited a second longer, the arrows would have lodged right into his chest.

Up above, lining the perimeter balcony of the domed structure, a dozen hooded assassins appeared. The *Men Shen*, or the Sons of Apollo. (Whatever they wanted to be called.) Bows and arrows were armed and pointed directly at us.

How did Lynea know? Did she really possess the power to see the future? In all my time dealing with mystical legends, none of them had any truth. Lei-Phong told me that the power existed. He warned me about it, but I never really believed him.

Glancing back up at Lynea, I watched her step aside as an arrow flew past her. She sidestepped back as another missed its mark.

I didn't have much time to ponder the issue as Jenny tugged me to move. Lynea and the Traijans weren't the only targets the assassins were aiming at. We were too.

"Charlie we have to go!" Jenny yelled.

I turned away from Lynea and bolted for cover. Arrows ricochet all around us. A frenzy of gunshots and screams rattled through my head. My heartbeat instantly escalated. An arrow grazed my shoulder, slicing through my shirt.

That lit a fire to my step.

Jenny and I darted toward the main entrance. More gunfire erupted. The armed thugs defended themselves the only way they knew how. Alvin was a few steps in front of us. He motioned for us to follow.

I didn't dare look back. The sounds of battle pounded through the walls. Screams bounced off every surface. Casualties fell on both sides. I just focused on getting Jenny out alive.

Alvin waved us along toward the doorway. We were almost there when two hooded figures entered through the opening, blocking our path.

Great!

But Mitchell didn't stop. He barreled straight toward them. I was ready to scream for him to dive out of the way (even though I hated the man), but I didn't need to. The two hooded men stepped aside, allowing Alvin to pass right by.

They didn't intrude as we reached them. They stood aside, letting us continue as well.

In the chaos, I didn't question it.

I followed Alvin out the door and into the empty street. My pulse raced as we ran for our lives. Every step slid over the uneven placement of treasure. One wrong step and I'd tumble. We sprinted a few more blocks before turning a corner.

Giving ourselves a second to regroup, we paused against a wall. Panting, I said, "What was that back there, Mitchell?"

Still catching his breath, he simply shook his head. "Long story, *mate*."

Jenny had a better answer. "Charlie, I was trying to tell you earlier, Alvin's not one of the bad guys."

"Can you be a little more vague?" I said. Now wasn't the time for games.

As Jenny readied herself to speak, a figure stumbled into view. Then another. Two mercenaries were running for their lives. The men paused and looked at us. Stunned, we all stared at one another.

Then they attacked.

I wanted to ask why, but these ferocious beasts didn't look like the talking type. Adrenaline coursed through their veins. Their bloodshot eyes expressed their rage. In the heat of the battle, everyone was an enemy.

(Or they simply blamed us for what was happening.)

Whatever the case, my moment to relax was cut short. Diving aside, I barely dodged the first man's punch. Alvin wasn't so lucky. The other goon bullrushed Mitchell, tackling him to the ground.

I swung wide, clocking my assailant across the jaw. I then switched to the offensive and shoved him into the stone wall.

The man was much bigger than me though. As he hit the stone, he spun, elbowing me in the head. I lost balance and slammed into the wall myself.

We backed off one another.

Behind me, Jenny dove onto the other mercenary's back. She threw her arms around the man's face, trying to pry him off Alvin. The thug flung her over his shoulder and onto the floor.

Her scream distracted me. That was my first mistake. My attacker lunged forward. He lifted me off my feet and threw me to the ground.

As always, the first step in winning a fight was to get the upper hand. With the man propped on top of my body, he sure got it.

Punches drilled me in the face, then my stomach. I was in an instant daze. Gunshots pounded through my head. Shrieks rang out from every direction. My hands fought to block the flurry of blows.

Suddenly, my body stopped struggling. The mercenary stopped attacking. Both of us paused. We simultaneously heard the deadly sound—a loud hiss.

Less than a foot away sat a white snake.

Its body curled around itself while its neck rose up. Its face perched toward us. Its fangs exposed. It let out another blood curdling hiss.

Our quarrel instantly took a timeout. Both of us sat perfectly still. Even my panting chest stopped heaving. I held my breath.

The snake inched closer.

Another hiss came from the opposite direction. I didn't dare turn around. Any sudden movement could trigger them.

More hissing sounded, and more snakes circled us. My body tensed up, ready for the attack. I looked up at my assailant's petrified face. His eyes were wide. His mouth shut. He probably regretted stopping to fight us now.

Three arrows blurred by. They sunk into my attacker's exposed chest. The velocity of the arrows catapulted the man off my body. Upon impact, his scream sprung the snakes into action. All of them leapt through the air clenching their jaws all over the man's torso.

It happened in a flash. Their reaction was lightening quick. The mercenary flew through the air, with a dozen snakes dangling from his body. He landed on the ground just past my feet. He was dead before the snakes even sunk their teeth in him.

I didn't waste the opportunity. I didn't even care where the miraculous arrows came from. Quickly, I scrambled away from the scene, and back to Jenny and Mitchell.

I turned to the others…

…Only to come face to face with three hooded assassins. Their bows armed. Alvin Mitchell and Jenny stood beside them. A series of arrows protruded out of Alvin's foe.

I raised my hands in defeat.

"Put those down, Charlie," Mitchell said. "They're with us."

My puzzled expression allowed Mitchell to answer.

"These are my brothers. I am one of the Sons of Apollo," the Australian stated. The hooded men brought down their bows. "I'm sorry I didn't tell you sooner, *mate*."

Jenny approached. "I told you earlier. You weren't going to believe me."

Were they serious? How could Alvin Mitchell be one of them? The man's pearly whites sparkled as he smiled at me. "Surprise," he said, almost laughing.

The hissing snakes behind me jogged my body to move. I stepped forward. As I neared Alvin, I clenched my fist. With all my might I swung at the Australian's face. My knuckles drilled into the man's cheekbone.

Mitchell collapsed to the ground from the impact. The three hooded men quickly brought their bows back up. My anger took over. I had wanted to do that ever since I met the man. Now I had my chance, and I didn't care about the repercussions.

Alvin raised his hand up, ushering his brothers to step down. "It's okay. I deserved that," he said. I was ready to strike again, but Jenny stopped me.

"Charlie, we don't have time for this. Alvin just saved your life," she said.

"Really? Just like he did months ago?" I annoyingly said.

"I had to Charlie," Mitchell said, still on the ground. "I couldn't let you continue to help the Baron. I knew that after what you did, that bloke would have forced you to continue the journey. Or he would have killed you."

"So you figured to kill me first."

"Come on, Charlie. It wasn't that big of a drop. I figured you'd be able to keep afloat long enough for one of my brothers to get you out of there. We're not bad people." Alvin slowly got to his feet.

Jenny held me back. Her touch calmed me down. With my attention focused solely on Mitchell, I didn't realize that a few other hooded men surrounded us. Two of them tended to the deadly snakes.

More gunshots rattled in the distance. Alvin spoke again. "Charlie, I'm sorry for what happened. You're a nice fella. In reality though, you should be thanking me."

"Don't push your luck," Jenny whispered.

"There is more at stake here than our trivial rivalry," Alvin said.

Back at the entrance to our underground city, a slew of black figures appeared in the opening. About a dozen more mercenaries were entering the Oracle's city. Reinforcements had arrived.

"Yeah, our lives," I said. "We need to get out of here."

Bullets riddled the walls around us as the men locked onto our position. It probably didn't look good that we stood amongst a group of Apollo's warriors.

I yanked Jenny to move. We picked a direction and ran. Mitchell and his friends followed. More shots dug into the stone as we fled.

Dust clouded the streets after every impact. Debris collapsed around us. The narrow streets provided good cover, but the irregular floors made it hard to stay upright.

Bodies fell behind us.

We scrambled down an alley, then another. The gunfire was getting more accurate. Our new guests had good aim. We needed to find better protection.

In the distance I saw a small structure. A dark opening beckoned us to enter. We ran along the road and hurled ourselves into the darkness.

Falling to the floor, I heaved for air. My hands trembled. Jenny dropped to my side. We were out of breath. I saw the fear in her face. I needed to get her out of here, but I had no idea where to go.

Mitchell entered right behind us, along with two of his friends. "Watch your step," he said, pointing to the floor.

Less than a foot beside me, I saw a line of perforated stone tiles on the floor. I couldn't believe they even booby-trapped their own buildings. I sucked up my pride and asked, "Alvin, how do we get out of here?"

"We can't leave, Charlie," he said.

"The heck we can't," I retorted.

"Charlie, don't get me wrong, there is a way out, but we can't leave yet. Not without stopping Lynea."

"What are you talking about?"

"I can't let her leave this place. Do you know what will happen if she leaves here with Pythia's power?"

"Do I care?" I asked.

"She will destroy the world."

"That's a little exaggerated, don't you think?"

Mitchell explained. Anyone who harnessed Pythia's power did have the ability to see the future, but it also gave a person a vision of the past. More specifically, the Oracle's past. Every person who was imbued with her power also shared her memories.

Pythia's desire was to rule the world. The reason she was buried so deep in the mountain was so that no one could find her.

Homer's poem wasn't a celebration of her death. It was a warning for people to never follow in her footsteps.

This was why the *Sons of Apollo* were created. They were to prevent anyone from ever finding the tomb. Their lives were dedicated to stop people from discovering this power and using it.

"But you helped me solve the puzzle back in China," I said.

"I knew that beyond those doors were the nine tunnels leading through *Xi Wangmu's* temple. There was no stopping the Baron at that point, Charlie. I figured, I'd let my brothers take out our rich benefactor."

"Except the good Baron was a little smarter than you thought," I pointed out.

"Yeah," he said.

I didn't buy it. Alvin Mitchell was too sleazy to be one of these warriors. "Why aren't you robed up?"

"Every one of my brothers has a different role. My strength was not in fighting."

"What was it, annoying people?" Jenny gave me a stern look, but I couldn't help it.

"I was selected to be a public face. Certain treasures were given to me to strengthen my reputation. That's how I got famous."

My mind raced to catch up with all the information piling up. "So, you're really a Son of Apollo."

"Yes," Mitchell replied.

"And you're telling me that Pythia is going to take over Lynea's body. In the process, the girl is going to try and rule over the world?"

"You got it, *mate*."

"It doesn't sound as crazy as I thought it would, coming out of my mouth," I said aloud.

Jenny chimed in, "But we can't kill the girl."

Mitchell responded, "Jen, Lynea won't lose her mind. The Oracle only shows her what she can become. The girl has a lot of hate for this bloody world. She will twist the power for her own gain. I can't let that happen."

"How do we stop someone who can predict our every move?" I asked.

"Her powers haven't fully manifested. It will take a few hours before she can use it all. At first, she needs to concentrate. She needs to focus on something to see its future."

"How do you know all this?" Jenny asked.

"The waters running under this mountain feed into a number of springs. The other shamans in India, China, and Jerusalem all possessed a fraction of this power. My ancestors told stories of how difficult it was for them to defeat those ladies. I can only imagine what it will be like now."

Mitchell's eyes pleaded with us. "We need to find her and stop her, fast." His two hooded friends nodded in agreement.

I shook my head. Mitchell was full of it, but outside painted a different picture. Peering out one of the window openings, I watched the chaos unfold. Shrieks continued to ring off the walls of the caved city.

More directly, outside of our hideout, ten soldiers waited for us. Grenades strapped to their belts. Machine guns armed and ready. Bulletproof vests covered their torsos. These weren't Burt's and Berta's goons. They were much more organized. These reinforcements belonged to the Baron… or more accurately, Lynea.

"I hate to be the bearer of bad news, Alvin, but I don't think we're going to have a chance to find our *new* Oracle."

Turning back to the others, I saw another figure standing amongst the crowd. Lynea Ruthford entered through the doorway.

I was wrong.

CHAPTER FORTY TWO

Our hooded allies attacked.

Blades instantly emerged from under their cloaks. In a blink of an eye, they stormed Lynea Ruthford. They swung with extreme precision. Unfortunately, each slash cut through thin air.

With the fluidity of a ballerina, Lynea ducked under each blow. More strikes blurred by, but her body contorted just out of each strike's reach. She smiled. It was as if the young girl toyed with these men. A look of enjoyment stretched across her face.

The hooded men were good, I gave them that. Their agile skills anchored each of their attacks.

But, Lynea was better. A knife appeared in her hand. A few short strikes later, blood dribbled down her blade...and the two *Sons of Apollo* collapsed to the floor—dead.

The rest of us watched in silence.

Two of Lynea's thugs joined her side. Wiping her blade, the girl stated, "Why did you guys run away so quickly?"

"Not all of us have the power to see the future," I answered.

Lynea grinned. "So you believe me now, huh Charlie?"

"It's hard discounting what I just saw," I commented. Lynea dodged her attacker's strikes seconds before they even acted on them.

"I know, it's amazing right?" she said enthusiastically. "Charlie, being able to see everything before it happens is surreal. It's impossible to describe." She walked further into the room. "How do you think I found you three? I simply thought of you and was able to see where you'd be."

"I'm flattered that I'm on your mind," I said.

"Charlie, you're not on my mind for good reason." Lynea pocketed her blade. She glanced over to Jenny—then Mitchell. "You three are contemplating to stop me."

How did she know all this? If what Alvin said was true, her power was limited. I couldn't believe that I was entertaining the notion. How was all this even possible? My mind spun in circles trying to make sense of it all.

I played stupid. "I don't know what you're talking about. We just want to get out of this place."

Lynea silently marched back to the doorway. Her eyes remained fixated on me as she passed. It was as if she was envisioning her next words. "You're a horrible liar, Charlie," she finally said. "You will be convinced to try and stop me. I can see this clearly. I also know you will fail in the process. You will die."

She said it so sternly. Her voice sounded deep and hollow. Her eyes revealed a hint of evil behind them. That fragile girl I once saved from an erupting volcano was long gone. Did that girl ever really exist?

"Trust me, I don't want to hurt you," I said. "I'm simply tired of being shot at. Why don't you have some of your men escort us out of here?"

Lynea shook her head. "I'm sorry, Charlie. My visions don't lie. I can't do that."

"Your VISIONS?" I said. "You've only had these so-called visions for fifteen minutes. How would you know if they lie?"

Lynea's smile faded away. "I'm not going to risk it. I have more important matters to worry about."

"Like ruling the world," Alvin Mitchell said.

"Perhaps." Lynea motioned her mercenaries to take aim. She began a villainous monologue about all the things she could do with her new power. All the things she would do to this world. Honestly, I zoned her out. I had more important things to worry about—like my life.

My eyes scrambled for a way out. The mercenaries pulled out their machine guns. Quickly, I scanned the room. The doorway was blocked. A window opening was only a few feet away, but too far to run for without getting shot. Jenny and Mitchell remained by my side. I was out of options.

I didn't give up.

I searched the floor. The perforated stone trap was only a few inches to my left. Instantly, I got an idea. Looking back up to Jenny, her eyes were already staring back at me. She nodded, reading my mind. Mitchell did the same. If I triggered the stone, the black plague would launch into the room, creating a perfect distraction. It could also knock down some of our numbers.

I took a deep breath.

"Charlie," Lynea voiced. "I know what you're about to do," she started. "All its going to do is delay the inevitable."

"Delaying the inevitable is the story of my life." I stomped on the tile.

The depressed stone erupted in a cloud of smoke. The plague flooded the hut like a deadly gas.

I shut my eyes and plugged my nose. I hoped Jenny and Mitchell did the same. I heard panic, then coughs, followed by choking. It worked—except for the fact that I now stood blind in a smoke filled room.

Off memory, I turned and stumbled toward the window. I needed to get to some fresh air. My free hand felt around for a landmark. It found the stone surface of the wall. Using it as a guide, I followed the wall until it ended.

The window!

Quickly, I climbed through the opening and to the other side.

Crashing on the floor, I landed on top of a soft body. My impact caused the person to yelp. I recognized the voice. Jenny lay below me. My body covered hers. "Sorry," I smiled.

"You'll be even sorrier in a second," she quipped.

It didn't take long before I realized why. Alvin Mitchell smashed on top of me as he too climbed out the window. "My apologies, *mate*," he whined.

Pain surged through me. I didn't have time to acknowledge it. Pushing Mitchell aside, I got to my feet. We were in the clear. The black plague remained inside the small hut.

But we had bigger problems. The remainder of Lynea's army was waiting for us outside the building. We may have dodged one bullet, but we just found hundreds more.

The mercenaries were just as surprised at seeing us as we were of them. We used this opportunity. Springing to our feet, the three of us bolted off in the opposite direction.

It didn't take long for the brutes to react. Lynea's voice screaming in the distance didn't help the matter. With the shriek of a witch, we heard her order, "Kill them!"

In seconds, bullets grazed by. The whiz of each one screamed past my ears. Thumps drilled into the walls, missing their mark. The winding alley made us difficult targets.

My muscles tightened as I pushed faster. Jenny was by my side. We didn't utter a word. No innocent quips left our mouths. For the first time, we were legitimately scared.

Alvin Mitchell sped ahead. He motioned us to follow. We didn't have much choice. Sprinting down one road, the Australian suddenly cut left at an intersection. We shadowed.

We stormed down a much larger avenue. The pedestrian walkway widened. Gold covered the ground.

"I know a way to safety!" Alvin yelled.

We followed, zooming past the old buildings. Sweat blurred my vision. The shimmering treasures created a dizzying scene. It was like a crazy hallucination. I focused on Alvin.

Suddenly, an object flew past us. It landed on a bed of gold. Risking a glance, my eyes widened.

A grenade!

The explosion rocked our world—literally. Gold coins shot out like a barrage of bullets. The deafening noise shuttered through my head.

Diving to a side, I dodged the brunt of the force. Jenny collapsed with me. Up ahead, Mitchell continued to run.

"I always fantasized about money being thrown at me," I commented.

Jenny risked a nervous smile.

Behind us, our enemies closed in. They paused as the ground began to shake. One of the nearby buildings rocked back and forth. At its base, large cracks spiked up the surface.

The grenade weakened its foundation. Stone crumbled. More rock broke apart, teetering the large building our direction. Its weight was too much for the failing support.

The structure tipped over, directly toward us.

My heart skipped a beat.

Clamoring on all fours, we darted forward. We managed to get to our feet and sprinted as fast as we could. The building crashed behind us with a thunderous bang.

The road rumbled upon impact. A cloud of debris puffed out from the building.

We narrowly escaped.

"How about buildings?" Jenny asked, breathlessly. "You dream of those falling on you?"

"No, those are nightmares." I looked back at the rubble. "That will hold them off," I said. The good news was, the toppled building blocked the road behind us. It prevented our attackers from following suit.

The bad news was that the mini earthquake shook the foundations of the rest of the buildings that lined our road ahead. Fault lines cracked through the floor and up the sides of the other structures. Stones dislodged and fell to the ground.

The two story buildings started to sway back and forth as if they were dancing. Any second and they would all follow the same path as the first ancient structure. They would collapse onto the alley.

We just created our own gauntlet.

"What's going to hold those off?" Jenny retorted.

We sprung into action, bolting down the alley. Alvin was already at the far end waiting for us. His arms waved for us to move faster.

What did he think...we were taking in the sights? I pushed myself harder. Holding Jenny's hand we dodged the toppling structures. One by one they fell behind us like dominos. Each time the ground shook under our feet.

And each time, we remained one step ahead. The debris blanketed our surroundings in fog. Soon we couldn't see anything. All we knew was to keep heading forward.

Faster!

We scrambled onward. Finally, the chaos simmered behind us. The ground settled. Even the debris disappeared. We didn't stop running though.

We broke free from the fog. A dozen feet away stood Alvin Mitchell. He looked calm. With my pulse racing, I didn't slow down until I reached him.

Panting, I took a break.

"You've gotten a little out of shape there, Charlie," Mitchell said.

Hunched over, I said. "So your cockiness wasn't part of your act?" Behind me, the fragmented remains of a dozen buildings crumbled over the entire path.

One grenade did that much damage.

As if reading my mind, Alvin said, "These buildings are centuries old. They're pretty fragile."

"I see that."

Jenny stood up, saying, "So can we officially say that Lynea has gone over the deep end?"

"Mitchell, I thought you said she wouldn't have that much power yet?" I said standing up. The words out of my mouth sounded crazy.

"I don't know. It's not like I see this happen every bloody day."

Gunfire rang out in the distance. The Sons of Apollo were dropping like flies. "We can't stay here," I pointed out.

"I have a place. Follow me," Mitchell said.

Our break was over. We jogged down another alley. Alvin cut through the streets like he'd done so hundreds of times before. Not once did he pause to second guess himself. That is, until we reached a dead end.

"I was almost impressed," I said. Jenny pinched me.

Alvin brushed his hand over the dead end wall. It glossed over the stone until finally stopping on an irregular square. He pushed it. The stone triggered the wall to life. It trembled and slid to one side, revealing a dark opening.

These caves were beginning to be commonplace in my line of work. In silence, we entered. Moments later, the wall shut behind us, and we were lost in complete darkness.

We fled down a series of steps, finally reaching a lower landing.

"I can't see anything," Jenny chimed as we hustled through the dark.

"Don't worry. Just keep walking forward," Mitchell said.

Fifty feet later, we came to another stop. We stood in the dark while Alvin felt around for another switch. He found it, and pressed it in. Like before, the wall slid aside, and natural light bathed the tunnel.

With the tunnel illuminated, I saw that it wasn't a small little path. The walls, floor, and ceiling were all made of concrete. I also realized that this wasn't the only path. A number of dark passages veered off in different directions.

"What is all this?" I asked.

"Our underground tunnels," Mitchell said. "We built these under the city to move around unseen."

"This runs under the whole city?" Jenny wondered.

"No, only areas where the earth was sturdy enough." Alvin marched up the next flight of stairs.

We stepped out into the next area.

We were back to the ancient stone architecture. Our new chamber was bare. No gold lined the floor. No markings or engravings covered the walls. It was a simple square structure with a set of stairs on one end.

"Where are we now?" Jenny asked.

"One of our secret rooms," Alvin said. "It allows us to watch unwelcomed visitors from the shadows."

"How often does that happen?" I wondered aloud.

Mitchell didn't answer.

The tunnel door closed behind me. Still staring at the wall, I asked, "And do those tunnels lead out of here?"

"The north passage does. But—"

I cut Alvin off before his lecture. "I know, we can't leave yet."

Alvin disappeared up the stairwell.

The tunnels were impressive. I wondered what other surprises Mitchell had in store for us. I followed. The stairwell continued up another two flights. We reached the top floor and took another breather. I hated to admit it, but I was exhausted.

"What now, Mitchell? This is your show," I said.

Alvin approached one of the windows. He looked out at the ancient city beyond. "We need a plan," he said.

I peered through the opening. The battle had settled down. A mixture of mercenaries and hooded bodies spread out through the streets. The gunfire had ceased. In the distance, I thought I made out the Traijan twins still grabbing as much treasure as they could.

At the other end, standing at the steps that led out of the city was Lynea Rufthford. Her goons surrounded her like she was their goddess. I flashed back to earlier when she told me that I was going to die trying to stop her.

My friend, Lei-Phong warned me about the terrors that would come if someone attained Pythia's power. He died protecting that belief. I had seen Lynea dodge arrows like it was nothing. She killed her father without a blink of an eye. She just tried killing us.

I shook my head.

I looked at the rubble from the demolished buildings. They nearly became our tomb. I hated to admit it, but Alvin Mitchell was right. We needed to stop Lynea Ruthford.

I then saw the dead body of one of Lynea's mercenaries. Debris crushed half of the man's body. His armor and weapons strapped over his chest.

It dawned on me.

I smirked.

"Oh no," Jenny said, seeing my face.

Confused, Alvin Mitchell asked, "What?"

"Charlie's got a plan?" she said.

Jenny was right. I did.

CHAPTER FORTY THREE

The Sons of Apollo were dead. Well, all of them except for Alvin Mitchell. We were out of help.

The surviving mercenaries all huddled up toward the main entrance of the ancient city. They awaited direction from their new benefactor, Lynea Ruthford. She stood a few steps above them, looking out at the crowd.

That's when she saw me.

I marched down the street in plain view. My hands rose up over my head. My filthy shirt soaked in sweat. My shoes scraped past the glitter of gold. I walked a direct route toward the dozen soldiers.

This was my plan.

"Charlie," Lynea announced.

In a single motion, the mercenaries whipped out their guns and targeted me.

This was my *crazy* plan.

"I've come to talk," I yelled back, still walking. I tried to mask my trembling voice. I was sure my shaking hands gave me away.

Lynea smiled. She motioned her men to stand down. The young girl descended the flight of stairs to greet me. Her grin still stretched across her face. The shimmering treasure exuded a soft glow around her body. "No you didn't, Charlie. You've come here to stop me."

The soldiers stepped aside as I neared. "Well, that too," I added. A ring of men now surrounded me and Lynea.

"I told you, you would try."

I nodded.

"I also warned you that you'd die in the process," Lynea said sternly.

"I'm not much of a good listener," I said lowering my hands.

"And this was your great plan? March up here and kill me?" Lynea knew my answer.

"I'm not the sharpest tool."

The soldiers raised their guns once again, but Lynea talked them down. "There is no need for violence," she said. "Charlie won't lay a hand on me."

Lynea walked up close. Her hand fondled my hair. I didn't move. Her hand caressed my arm. She glided her fingers along the arch of my back and lifted my shirt. A small pocket knife wedged into my back pocket.

Taking it out, she flipped it open. "Was this what you were going to use on me?" she asked.

"Not anymore," I said.

"Come on, Charlie. This is silly. I can see every move you're going to make. Try and hit me."

What?

"Come on, give it a shot," Lynea demanded.

I didn't budge. This wasn't going the way I expected.

Swiftly, Lynea Ruthford swung her fist, smacking me across the face. The pain was sudden. I flipped my head back in shock.

I didn't see that coming. This definitely wasn't what I thought would happen. Regaining my balance, I said, "You pack quite a punch."

"My dad sent me off to martial arts classes when I was a kid. It was his way of getting rid of me. And it was my way of taking out my anger."

Lynea swung at me again. On instinct, I tried to dodge, but her punches quickly shifted to meet me at my new position. It was as if she swung at thin air, while I moved into every strike.

A flurry of hits later, I stumbled backward. For as skinny as the girl was, she really did pack a wallop. As my head got whacked again, I thought back to the volcano in China.

I remembered Lynea making a perfect gymnastic leap across an open chasm. I remembered her lift me off a ledge. She was a lot tougher than she led us to believe.

It made what I was about to do a little easier.

Lynea turned to her soldiers. "You see what I mean? Charlie has a heart of gold. He can't hit a woman."

I scrunched up my fist. "You're right Lynea, but you're not a woman. You're something else entirely." I swung.

My arm nearly tore out of its socket. I missed. The agile girl spun out of the way, and stabbed me in the throat with her open hand.

The air knocked out of me. Choking, I continued to flail my arms. Lynea stepped out of the way of each attack. In retaliation, she kicked me in the chest, knocking me to the ground.

She jumped on top of me, straddling my chest. "Charlie, I can't believe you did that?" Lynea flipped open the blade in her hand. "But this just got boring. The game's over. Your luck has run out." She raised the knife.

Suddenly, an explosion rocked the earth. Another followed. The ground rattled violently after each blast. The entire cave seemed to roar in anger.

The mercenaries jumped alert. Lynea dropped her knife. She stepped off my body. Buildings started to crumble around us. Rock broke away from the ceiling, smashing into the ground. A large fragment crashed a few feet from my head.

Everyone panicked.

Another explosion rang out. The impact shuddered through my entire body. A massive crack tore through the ground and up a nearby structure. The line vined all the way up the wall, crumbling the stone in the process. A second later, the building toppled over.

"What did you do?" Lynea said looking around. I could see her mind working. She stepped aside as a column crashed down.

I barely rolled out of the way. Unfortunately, I didn't have the power to see what was coming.

I struggled to get to my feet. The ground continued to vibrate.

The mercenaries ran for their lives. They didn't care about the gold. They didn't care about their boss. They scrambled up the stairs toward the exit.

Lynea remained. She stared off toward the sounds of the explosions. Her brows curled in concentration. "Your friends are doing this Charlie. I can see them!" she yelled while turning toward me.

Quickly, I lunged at the young girl. With the pocket knife firmly grasped in my fist, I sliced at Lynea Ruthford.

But I was too slow. Just before I reached her, her hand rose to block my thrust. The blade barely grazed her skin. I stumbled.

Lynea's furious expression meant I did my job. I was good at making people angry. Right now, I just pissed off one evil woman.

Before I could react, she kicked me. My back screamed in agony. The girl grabbed me by the collar and threw me back.

"Did you really think you could kill me?" Lynea screamed. Her voice vibrated off the hollow walls above us.

Getting to my feet, I held up the knife in my hand. "I never intended on killing you, Lynea." Blood dribbled down the tip of my blade. Lynea looked down at her hand. A thin line of red blood spread across her palm.

I wiped the blood on my fingers. "I just wanted to even the playing field."

I turned and bolted for Pythia's Temple. Lynea Ruthford wasn't far behind. Her scream sent a shiver up my spine.

This was MY plan.

Fifteen minutes earlier, I stared out the second floor window of Alvin Mitchell's secret hideout. I had a faint smirk as I turned to my two friends.

"Come on, Charlie. What's your plan?" Jenny asked.

I stepped away from the opening and huddled up with the others. "It's kind of a longshot, but I think it might work."

"It's not like we have any other ideas," Mitchell said.

So I began.

"Alvin said that Lynea's power isn't strong yet. She needs to concentrate to see one's future, right?" They nodded. "Well that makes it difficult for us to attack her head on. She might have the power to read our every move, but why don't we make her work for it."

"I'm not following," Jenny said.

"Look, Lynea can only see the future of whatever is front of her. When the assassin's attacked her, she dodged. When arrows flew at her, she saw them coming. If we can keep her focus on one person, then the other two can act freely."

"And what would you have the other two do, *mate*?" Mitchell asked. He didn't seem to have faith in my theory.

"Blow the place to kingdom come," I said.

Puzzled faces stared at me.

"Mitchell said that the buildings are fragile. We saw it first-hand a few minutes ago." I pointed at the rubble outside. "One grenade did that."

"And it nearly flattened us," Jenny said.

I then guided their gaze to the dead soldier nearby. "That guy has over ten of them. Imagine what that can do."

"Do you find it necessary to blow up every place you go to?" Jenny said.

My theory was simple. By causing the ancient city to crumble, we would probably cause all the mercenaries to flee. In turn, it would stretch Lynea's abilities. She would have much more to focus on than just one attacker. Making her try to use her powers with all the chaos going on might buy us a window of opportunity.

"Charlie, how will we get close to her?" Jenny asked.

"We, won't. I will."

Mitchell grabbed my arm. "Charlie, those men down there will kill you before you reach her. It's suicide."

"Lynea won't shoot me. I'll use my trusty old charm."

"Let me go, *mate*. I have more history with these men."

"Mitchell, I'll be fine. Plus, the girl likes me better than you. You focus on the explosion part. Let's go." I didn't give them time to refute my plan. I started down the steps.

We ran down the stairs and out the front door of the building. Back in the streets, we snuck our way toward the dead soldier. The road was quiet. It was terrifyingly silent. My thumping heart sounded like thunder against my chest.

We reached the corpse.

"Jenny, stay here," I told her. I didn't want her up close to the dead body. She didn't question me. Heading over to the mercenary, Mitchell and I hunched over to grab our prize.

Alvin took the belt full of grenades. I nabbed a small pocket knife. They were of no use to the dead man.

"Mitchell," I whispered.

He looked up at me.

"There's a second part to my plan, but you can't tell Jenny because she would never let me do it." I explained it to my new ally before walking back.

That was it.

All we had left to do was act out my plan.

Jenny approached. "Charlie, do you have to do this?" I sensed the concern in her voice.

"You have a better option?" I asked.

She didn't. She grabbed my hand. We had been through a lot together. Months ago, I promised her father, my best friend, that I would rescue her. Right now, I was going to finish that promise. In the process I was going to stop a crazed lunatic.

Jenny leaned in and kissed me on the cheek. Her soft lips felt warm on my skin.

She slowly pulled away.

"What was that for?" I asked.

"Luck," she whispered. I was going to need it.

I ran for my life.

The first part of my plan worked. I pissed off Lynea and got her blood. This second part was going to be tough. The mountain rattled around me. We angered the natural giant with our explosions. In retaliation, Mount Sinai shook at its core.

Lynea hounded after me. Her shriek bounced off the walls. I sprinted down the alley, dodging falling debris. Instead of running for an exit like any sane man, I headed deeper into the city. Zigzagging in and out of alleys, I finally broke out into the main boulevard. The road led straight toward Pythia's temple. The large dome called the building out like a beacon.

That was my next stop. My muscles were numb. Still, I pushed hard. I sprinted down the open street. I didn't have time to watch my step. My eyes simply locked on the open doorway terminating the end of the road.

It closed in fast. The side structures blurred by.

Within seconds, I burst through the doorway and into the massive chamber. Lynea was only a few steps behind.

The open tomb at the center of the room waited for me. I was almost there.

I tripped.

My foot rolled over one of the skulls. Twisting, I lost my balance and stumbled. I tried to brace myself. My leg sped to regain my stance, but I was too slow.

I crashed into the field of bones. A leg instantly pinned on top of me.

Lynea Ruthford was fast.

"Charlie, what are you doing!" she yelled. "I'm the only one who can have this power. Did you really think I'd let you share this ability with me?"

My body awkwardly flattened against the irregular floor. My limbs were forced behind my back. I couldn't believe this girl's strength.

"I never said I wanted your power," I managed to say.

Lynea crouched down. Her face moved only inches from mine. "Well you failed. I told you that you would..." Lynea's voice trailed off.

Her vision showed her what I was about to say. I saw it in her eyes. I opened my mouth. "You said *I* would fail. You didn't say anything about my friends."

A loud clank came out of nowhere. The sound echoed through the dome. It pinged again. Lynea and I turned to see a small round object clatter off the floor. It rolled to a stop right at the center of the open doorway—our way out.

We stared at the metal casing of a live grenade. It disappeared in a flash as it exploded into a ball of fire. The bones on the floor shook in the blast's repercussion. The entire chamber violently quaked. The columns holding up the building groaned in response. Vibrations crippled their stone composition causing veins of cracks to grow up the large piers.

This wasn't going to be good.

Columns buckled. The entire opening of Pythia's temple collapsed with a monstrous bang. Piers toppled over. Portions of the balcony caved under its own weight. Soon, the entire opening filled in with stone and rock.

Lynea leapt off me and ran for the doorway. The rubble blocked our way out.

I slowly got to my feet. Dusting myself off, I watched as more columns toppled over. Domes worked great in compression. They evenly distributed the load to span large distances. The explosion removed part of that compression. Now it was a matter of time before the rest of the roof collapsed. I didn't want to be around for that.

"Charlie, what did you do?" Lynea yelled. She turned to face me. Anger boiled in her eyes.

"It was actually Alvin who did that. And based on the look of things, he destroyed your way out of here."

"It looks like you didn't think this one through. You're stuck in here with me," Lynea said stomping my way. "And you're going to help me get out."

"No ma'am. I'm going to help myself."

I turned and ran once again. I sped for one of the far columns. The pier reminded me of the Tallow trees back in China. It had the same diameter. It rose straight up to the second floor balcony. Back then, I climbed the tree like a monkey.

Right now, I hoped to do the same. Jumping, my arms and legs wrapped around the circular stone. Clasping on tightly, I started to shimmy up the face of the column.

Lynea Ruthford screamed for me to stop. I didn't listen. I continued to rise.

I reached the upper balcony and pulled myself over. The cantilevered stone wobbled back and forth. With all the explosions going on, this wasn't going to hold much longer. But I needed to get up there. Glancing over at the far wall, I saw my reason why.

A small doorway led out the back of Pythia's dome. It was how the Sons of Apollo flanked us earlier. That was my way out. It was also a helpful tip from Alvin Mitchell.

"Charlie, you can't let me die!" Lynea yelled. "You save people. It's what you do!"

I leaned over the balcony. "I might be a slow learner, but your father taught me I don't have to save everyone."

Fragments of the dome crashed on the ground. "I'm going to get buried in here. Charlie, you're not a killer!" the girl pleaded. Her body trembled. Fear engulfed her. For a moment, I thought of climbing back down to help her, but I didn't.

I simply said, "I'm not going to kill you. I'm just not going to give you much of a future to watch."

With that, Lynea transformed. Her helpless expression shifted to demonic anger. Her body stiffened. "At least I'll enjoy watching your death," she uttered in a soft voice.

The balcony vibrated. Stone tiles snapped. I was out of time. Getting to my feet I bolted for the opening. The balcony crumbled behind me as I rushed through the door.

I left Lynea Ruthford in her own prison cell. I had won. I earned my relaxation.

A stairwell followed the curve of the building back down to the surface. Alvin and Jenny waited at the bottom. Exhausted, I made my way down. Jenny didn't look happy. Reaching the two of them, I smiled, "How about we get out of here."

"Well done, Charlie," Alvin complimented.

"You weren't too shabby with those grenades either," I conceded.

Mitchell pulled out his last one. He primed it, and chucked it up the stairs at the last opening to Pythia's temple. The detonation sealed the doorway quickly. "Now we can go," he said.

The cave growled above us. My plan worked all right, only it worked a little too well. As always, we were going to have to run our way out.

"Why didn't you tell me?" Jenny asked as we rounded the building.

"Honestly, I wasn't sure if it was going to work. I didn't want you to worry."

"Well I was terrified."

"I'm flattered," I said.

Mitchell turned back to us. "Why don't you two love birds save the bickering for the honeymoon." Mitchell grinned at us. Jenny and I both fell silent. Awkwardly, I didn't have any good comeback.

Neither did she.

Unfortunately, any line we came up with would have fallen on deaf ears. A shocking explosion erupted behind us as part of the mountain collapsed. Mitchell saw it first.

A stone column tumbled down. Jenny and I didn't have time to react. Frozen, we looked up just as the column came crashing down.

Great!

A hand shoved me hard. Another shoved Jenny. Alvin Mitchell pushed us aside just as the column smashed into the ground.

Falling over, the large stone landed inches away from my body. I had survived. As did Jenny.

I couldn't say the same for Alvin. Squished under the heavy debris, I saw my new ally trapped. In a heartbeat I was at the half buried man.

"Alvin!" Jenny yelled.

Most of Mitchell's body was sandwiched under the rock. I didn't know where to begin. I tried to lift some of the debris, but Mitchell screamed in pain.

"It's not working," I strained.

We tried again.

The cave around us continued to fall apart. We didn't care.

Mitchell was barely alive. Breathlessly, he said, "Charlie, get out of here."

"Sorry buddy, I'm not leaving you behind." I may not have liked the man. He may have tried to kill me, and he may have been cocky and annoying. But he just saved my life.

"I'm a goner, *mate*. Just go," Alvin coughed.

Jenny wouldn't let that happen. She started digging away. "You heard Charlie, we are not leaving!"

Planting my feet, I heaved a large rock upward. My back cracked in pain. Sweat soaked down my shirt. But the stone was moving. I made progress.

Suddenly a bullet bounced off the dirt nearby.

The impact startled me. I dropped the rock right on Alvin's shoulder. He screamed in agony. I didn't hear him though. I was distracted by the gunshot.

Turning around, I saw the shot's origin. Two new unwelcomed guests just joined our party.

Burt and Berta Traijan.

CHAPTER FORTY FOUR

Jenny Jenkins hunched over Alvin's dying body. Tears formed under her eyes, followed by droplets falling from her eyelashes. Everything seemed to slow down. The chaos of the mountain caving in on itself crawled to a pause. The constant drum of the collapsing boulders silenced.

I couldn't move. On one end, I needed to help free Jenny's friend from impending death. On the other end, I needed to save myself and Jenny from our own.

When was I going to catch a break?

Burt and Berta Traijan perched up on a crumbled rock. A bag full of treasure strapped over Burt's shoulder. A gun extended out of Berta's hand. Her tall figure towered on top of the raised platform.

"Don't move!" Berta yelled. Anger spread across her frowning brows.

Where the heck did they come from?

"Guys this is not a good time," I said. I went to help Alvin once again.

Another gunshot rang out.

Stopping in my tracks, I said, "Is that truly necessary?"

"This is all your fault, Charlie!" Berta Traijan's voice rang out. She dropped down to the walkway—her gun still aimed at us. "You caused all this. We haven't had time to gather all of our treasure."

A large rock crashed down nearby.

"Well I'm sorry, but you'll have to suffice with that bag your brother's got there." I motioned to Burt. He was still planted on top of the debris. He struggled to drag the heavy sack over the mound.

"Oh Charlie, that is not enough," Berta said. "Look how much more there is."

"No one's stopping you from getting your gold. I'm in the middle of something here."

"Not anymore," Berta said, nodding to the ground.

I looked down at Alvin and saw that he was not screaming anymore. The sand shifted, sucking down the debris. Alvin went along with it and disappeared under the earth.

Like quicksand, Alvin's body was sucked away.

Jenny dug at the sand. It was no use.

"That's sad," Berta commented. "The Australian was kind of cute."

Jenny came alive, lunging to her feet. I grabbed her before she could attack the Traijan twin. Berta fired a warning shot into the stone nearby. Dust kicked up off the ground.

"You better put a leash on your girlfriend, Charlie," Berta ordered.

I held Jenny back. She fought furiously to break free. "Easy, Jen," I calmed. "It won't bring him back."

Sense came back to Jenny, settling herself down. I was right. Alvin Mitchell was a lot of things. In his dying breath, he was a hero. The guy was full of surprises all the way to the end.

He saved our lives. Now we needed to make that sacrifice count. Jenny going all Rambo on Berta Traijan wouldn't end well for either of us.

"Berta, what do you want?" I asked.

The earth continued to rumble. "I want you to stop this," she demanded.

"This is a one-way ticket honey, and the train has already left the station."

"There must be a way, Charlie. Stop it, now! There is too much treasure to leave behind." Berta's eyes flared at the gold all around us.

"Anger doesn't suit your looks," I retorted.

Berta took another step forward. As she did, I noticed something resting by her feet. A small white rope twined around itself. But it wasn't a rope. It was one of the poisonous snakes—Apollo's last defenders. The snake's head rose higher after Berta's every step. As she stood next to the lethal animal, its fangs appeared out of its salivating jaws.

"Berta, I'd watch your step if I were you," I pointed out.

"I'm not going to fall for that, Charlie." Berta pushed my comment aside.

I warned again, "I'm not kidding. Don't move. There's a snake at your feet."

Berta hesitated. Looking down her skin paled instantly as she saw her tiny attacker.

The snake lunged.

Berta's reflexes were quick. In a flash, she leapt backward, dodging the airborne animal. The snake launched across the air, missing its mark. Berta fired her gun, killing the snake as it landed on the ground. She sidestepped away from the dead animal saying, "I guess I owe you my life, Charlie."

Berta's foot pressed down on the floor. The stone tile under her sole depressed a fraction of an inch. In the process, a soft click snapped. We were all familiar with that sound. Berta didn't have time to react. Black smoke shot out from the perforated vents in the floor. The plague enveloped Berta Traijan's body.

Jenny and I stepped back in alarm. Berta burst out of the dark cloud. She clasped her throat and coughed for air. She fell to her knees, panting. I didn't want to watch. Turning away, I shielded Jenny from the horrific sight. A few seconds later, the struggle for life was sucked out of our enemy.

Berta lay sprawled on the ground, dead.

The smoke dissipated. As we glanced back at Berta's lifeless body, we were brought face to face with another obstacle. Burt Traijan stood at the top of the mound.

His bulbous body still clenched onto the treasure bag. And he stared down at his sister.

No words came out of his mouth. His body fumed. I swear I saw veins bursting out of his forehead. Burt Traijan shifted his gaze from his sister to me. He let out a horrendous screech. The scream bellowed through the walls of the city.

As if on cue, the entire mountain began to pulsate more violently. The ground shook.

Not only did we piss off the heavy set Armenian, but we pissed off the mountain. Way up above, I saw a terror more frightening than Burt Traijan. It came in the form of the large statue of Tityon carved out of the rock. The statue covered most of our domed ceiling. Out of its mouth stormed the largest cloud of smoke I had ever seen.

The plague was flooding out into the area like a swarm of bees. The smoke moved with a mind of its own. It rushed down toward the city like a sandstorm. It covered everything in darkness. As it engulfed the city, it formed into a giant tidal wave...

...And it was plowing right for us.

Jenny and I darted.

With a screaming Armenian and a plague rushing after us, we sprinted to escape. My muscles ached. This entire journey was an endless scenario of 'running for my life'.

Mount Sinai's earthquakes didn't help. The vibrating ground rattled at each step. The ceiling crumbled left and right. Rocks shattered along our path.

My vision narrowed as I focused on the road ahead. We turned a corner and sped along an alley. Cracking foundations buckled around us. Entire buildings collapsed. I didn't have time to think. Every move was on instinct. For once I wished Alvin Mitchell was around to guide us through this maze of streets.

Of course I didn't get that luxury. We zigzagged along. Jenny held on tight. The whistling of the plague blew, catching up behind us. Burt's screams followed.

A few remaining mercenaries scrambled for freedom. No one seemed to care about us. Well, no one except Burt Traijan. Up ahead, I saw the stairwell leading to our exit.

"We're almost there!" I yelled over the craziness.

Jenny remained silent.

We WERE almost there.

Suddenly, the floor ahead of us heaved upward. It burst like a bubble of boiling water, only this was made of rock. As the stone exploded, a geyser of sand spurred up into the air. Another geyser erupted. More sand shot up into the sky. As it did, the ground at our feet caved downward. It was as if the sand holding up the floor deflated, and the stone sunk to some unknown abyss.

Stumbling, we came to a stop. Without thinking, I yanked Jenny on a ninety degree course. Our new route ran us into another alley. The mountain wasn't making this easy.

When was I going to catch a break?

More geysers exploded like broken fire hydrants. The sand whirlwinded around us, slapping at our faces.

"A simple earthquake would have been too easy," I thought aloud.

"Charlie, where are we going?" Jenny asked nervously.

I had no clue.

The ground behind us continued to drop away. Buildings sunk down—eaten up by the earth. As we sprinted along, I finally looked to my right. The plague blotted out the entire city. It rolled in fast. We were running out of time.

A gunshot bounced off a nearby wall. Burt was still in hot pursuit. Even with the natural disaster unfolding around us, he wanted me dead. Based on our current course, he wouldn't have to wait long to get his wish.

We cut into another alley. Heat oozed out of the floor. Déjà vu struck me. Jenny was right. Mount Sinai was another volcano. Seeing the heat radiate from the ground, it dawned on me that we had woken it up. Things kept getting better.

It didn't stop us though. My rubber soles stuck to the hot stone after every step. Blindly, I led us into another stretch of road. Straight ahead, a slew of dead soldiers blocked our way. We climbed over the bodies and ran. I didn't have time to feel sorry for the men. I was determined to get out.

On impulse, I turned at the next intersection. Luckily, the path was clear. More importantly, it led straight up a stair to the cave's exit.

Luck was back on my side.

We bolted up the stairs. The buildings around us washed away as the overflowing sand reclaimed them. My grip on Jenny's hand tightened. I was not going to lose her.

A few more steps.

I stumbled.

The ground pitched downward, sinking away. I collapsed, losing hold of Jenny. She screamed, sliding back the way we came. Her body rolled down the crumbling stairs.

Panic surged through my body. Turning back, I saw the large wall of darkness right behind us. There was no sign of Burt Traijan, but it didn't matter. The horrific black void devoured everything. I glanced down at Jenny, just as she disappeared into the cloud.

I lost her!

"Jen!" I yelled. Before I could move, the storm consumed me. Blackness took over. The plague sucked through my open mouth.

Inhaling, I swallowed the smoke. Instantly, I coughed. My lungs closed up. My eyes burned. Pain filled my insides.

Keeling over, I struggled for breath. Everything felt like it was tearing apart inside me. Then the ground disappeared, and I fell.

Luck wasn't on my side. Lynea was right. I was going to die trying to stop her. She warned me of my fate. It was over.

I blacked out.

CHAPTER FORTY FIVE

The scream was loud. Its roar screeched through my ears. Something clamped around my hand. Blood circulation stopped running through my fingers.

Everything was black.

I saw nothing.

Was I dead?

Musty air filled my nostrils. I recognized the scent.

What was going on? My senses ran on overload. I realized I knew that scream. The sensation in my hand was familiar.

The blackness disappeared, and my surroundings slowly came to focus. I found myself standing in front of Pythia's temple. Jenny stood at my side. Alvin Mitchell had disappeared below the sand. Berta's dead body was not much farther away.

It felt like I was in a wax museum and that I was part of a recreated scene of Berta Traijan's death from just moments ago. All the players stood in their exact positions.

None of this made sense. Why wasn't I dead?

It was as if I moved underwater. Sounds drowned out. Above me, the city collapsed in slow motion. An earthquake rhythmically pulsated under my feet.

Jenny gripped my hand. Confused, I looked at her. I lived this moment already. How did I get back here? Glancing down at my hand, I saw Lynea's blood still soaked into my skin.

Did I just see the future? Did the Oracle of Delphi give me a glimpse of what was to come? A vision of my death? Was this a side effect of touching Lynea's blood?

I couldn't believe it.

All I knew was that I was one of the luckiest men alive. I was given another shot to live, and this time, I was couldn't make the same mistake twice.

Burt, perched up on a raised platform with his mouth open. His thunderous scream roared. Behind him the tsunami of black plague rushed at us.

Maybe I wasn't that lucky.

"Charlie come on!" Jenny yanked me to life.

We bolted. Still, not believing my eyes, I followed Jenny's lead. We darted away from the chaos behind us. (Burt included.)

Heading down the street, buildings once again crumbled. Rock crashed all around. Everything happened just as I had seen it.

My dumbfounded look triggered Jenny to ask, "What's wrong with you, Charlie?"

I shook it off. As confused as I was, I knew I couldn't ruin this second chance. Jenny was alive. I was alive. I was going to do right this time.

Grabbing her hand I took charge. We weaved in and out of the rubble. We scrambled toward the exit. As if on cue, the geyser of sand bubbled up and exploded.

Jenny stopped in terror. I, on the other hand, wasn't fazed. I already shifted direction, pulling her with me. Determined, I ran forward.

The black smoke barreled toward us. We didn't have much time. Heat radiated through the ground. Lava was creeping up from the belly of Mount Sinai.

Straight ahead, a large group of dead bodies stacked over each other.

I was fast closing in on my *future.*

Jenny climbed over the bodies, but I stopped. I knew where this was heading. Was my mind playing tricks though? Glancing over, I saw the plague nearly upon us. Behind me, Burt was nowhere to be seen. The floor melted away.

I needed another way. I couldn't make the same mistake twice. That's when I remembered something. I looked forward, seeing a tall two story stone building still standing—one of the Sons of Apollo's secret hideouts. More importantly, the same one that we had entered with Alvin Mitchell.

"Charlie, why are you stopping?" Jenny screamed.

"We're going the wrong way."

"What are you talking about?" Panic trembled in her voice.

"Jen, we have to go toward the city center. That stairwell is going to collapse," I said. "Trust me."

I know, it sounded crazy. I could barely believe what I was saying. Jenny Jenkins stared back into my eyes. Without hesitating, she said, "Okay."

That was easy. I didn't even need to explain myself. I pulled her back over the mound of corpses. In the process, an object rolled off one of the dead mercenaries.

I caught a glimpse of it. Amongst all the terror, I smiled. Bending over, I picked up the object. It was a gas mask.

This was going to be our key out of here. "Put this on," I ordered.

"What about you?" Jenny asked. She already started strapping it on.

I reached into the pile. Searching through the bodies, I felt around for another mask. The black smoke bulldozed down our street. With urgent velocity, it rushed at us.

Suddenly, to our left, the stairwell we would have taken to escape crumbled. The earth ate it up. Jenny watched through her mask in astonishment. "How did you know?" I heard her voice mumble through the mask.

Jenny gripped at my shirt. Her nails dug through the cotton and into my skin. The plague was here.

My hand clasped another mask. In my small moment of victory, I yanked out the mask and strapped it over my face. Just as I finished, the black cloud engulfed our bodies. The smoke passed over like a gush of wind. It flapped at our clothes.

But we were alive.

Realizing this, I swung back to action. Small flickers of light bled through the dark fog. Jenny and I ran toward the two story hideout. The ground behind us continued to burn up and disappear.

The air howled. It was as if we were in some haunted house. The two of us entered the building and went straight for the false wall.

I felt around until one of the stones depressed. The wall slid aside and we entered the depths below.

The concrete tunnel was just as we left it.

Pitch black.

With the door shut, the last remaining beads of light disappeared with it. So did the whistling winds. The room instantly fell into silence. The black plague was nowhere in sight.

I peeled off my mask and took in a deep breath. Everything seemed fine. By fine, I meant that the same filthy stench that filled the room was still there.

I couldn't see a darn thing though. Jenny changed that with a snap—a snap from a lighter. The tiny flame barely lit our faces, but it was enough.

Jenny's blue eyes glowed under the warm light. I saw her hand shake. "Are you okay?" I asked.

Trying to calm herself, she said, "I've been better."

"Let's take a second," I said. "We're in no rush," I joked.

Jenny smiled. We sat still.

I saw the sorrow in Jenny's eyes. I knew how much it pained me when I lost my friend, Lei-Phong. I could only imagine what she was feeling with Alvin's death.

I wished I could help in some way. Only time would do that. I brushed my hand across her cheek. "It's almost romantic down here," I said.

"Almost," she retorted. Then Jenny asked, "Charlie? How did you know the stairwell was going to fall?"

"Lynea's blood...I think. This is going to sound every bit of crazy, but somehow I got glimpse of the future."

"And?"

"It wasn't a good one," I said.

Jenny came close. "Thanks for saving my life."

"How about you thank me when we get out of here."

"Which way do we go now?" she asked.

Mitchell said these tunnels ran throughout the city. He also mentioned one route that led to an exit—the north passage.

We followed Jenny's soft light as we walked down the dark tunnel. Paths led in every single direction. With the unfolding chaos, both of us had gotten twisted around. Our orientation turned upside down.

I reached into my pocket. Quickly, I pulled out my antique compass—Ferdinand Magellan's compass. My lucky rabbit's foot was going to save the day.

Flipping it open, I held the small object up. The arrow at its center teetered around in a circle and finally settled on a direction.

North was to our left, and so was a single doorway. It was our way out.

Jenny and I walked down the path. As we sped along, we were greeted by a number of intersections. Using our compass, we maintained our course and kept on.

Our tunnel started to heat up. The longer we walked, the hotter it became. Soon, the path had turned into a sauna. It only meant one thing. The lava below was catching up.

Concrete had a better heat index than rock. I knew that the walls would protect us for a short time, but I was hoping for longer.

"Charlie?" Jenny asked, pointing ahead.

Cracks appeared on the road. Beams of reddish light steamed into the corridor. Our path was getting ready to melt away.

The good news was that the glowing cracks acted like runway lights. They painted our path.

"Now it's about time to run," I yelled.

And so we did.

We scrambled down the hall. Behind us, the ground sunk away. Flames erupted as magma came rising up. We pressed on.

At the end of the hall, there was a solid black wall. We approached a dead end.

Getting there first, I slammed against the rock.

It didn't budge. Jenny joined in as we pushed as hard as we could. The wall didn't move. Lava came pouring our way. I didn't know what would be a worse death—the plague or lava. We were about to get an answer.

My pulse quickened once again. I looked back at the wall. How did we get out of here?

Jenny was the one to figure it out.

She felt along the wall until she touched a loose stone. Pressing it in, the rock slid aside. The outside light blinded us. Squinting, we ran out into the open desert while the concrete behind us fell away.

We didn't stop. We clawed at the hot sand, getting as far away from the mountain as we could. The sun beat down on us.

We kept on, full steam ahead.

After running for some time, we finally stopped. Jenny and I looked back at the doorway. It had disappeared. All that was left was a mound of earth. The towering rock wall of Mount Sinai blocked any remains of our exit.

We made it!

I couldn't help but cheer. Jenny couldn't either. I picked her up and twirled her around in joy.

"We survived!" I yelled. Jenny remained in my arms as I set her back down.

Our faces were inches apart. Everything quieted down. I glanced down at her lips. Her lower lip trembled with anticipation. Jenny leaned in.

What was I doing? J.J. would kill me if I...

"Excuse me?" a voice blurted.

Our moment suddenly ended. Looking over, I saw Burt Traijan standing before us. A few armed mercenaries stood on either side of him. Each of them had a gas mask dangling from their belts.

Crap!

"I'm sorry to interrupt Charlie, but I have my own moment I'd like to enjoy," Burt said. He pulled out his handgun. His friends did the same.

"Wait a second, Burt," I stalled. I raised my arms up. "You don't have to do this."

"Yes I do. Kill them," he ordered.

I lunged to Jenny, grabbing her back in my arms. I shielded her from our attackers. I held her tight, bracing myself for the firing squad. Then something came over me. In the face of death, I didn't care what my old friend would say.

Looking into Jenny's terrified face, I leaned in and caressed her lips with mine. Our lips pressed hard into one another. Our bodies gave into the moment.

The kiss rocked my Universe.

Suddenly, the rest of the world seemed to stop. Fireworks rattled around us. I could feel the ground tremble in passion. The warmth of her body grew as we both embraced the moment.

But then the warmth got hotter, and hotter. My back felt an enormous amount of heat. The earth shook more violently. I realized that it wasn't all in my head.

Pulling away, I looked at Jenny's face. Her eyes were still closed, waiting for another kiss. But my senses returned to reality.

I turned to look back at Burt Traijan and our attackers. Instead of a round Armenian, I saw a large crater in the sand where he and his friends once stood. Limbs and blood littered the ground. Flames and smoke dissipated up into the sky.

I turned my attention back out to the open desert and saw a lone military tank positioned on the ridge. The barrel of its cannon pointed our direction.

The tank just saved our lives...

...And Jenny and I had one explosive kiss.

Literally.

CHAPTER FORTY SIX

The hatch of the tank popped open and out emerged Jeremy Jenkins. I instantly recognized my old friend's shimmering bald head. He called out to us, "Your ride has arrived."

Jenny and I glanced at one another. Our wide eyes screamed the same thought. *I hope he didn't see that.* We jogged over to the tank.

"What took you so long?" I got to say to my friend for once.

"Speed is not a virtue of these transports," J.J. said, patting the tank.

I had to give it to the man. He did have a way with escape vehicles. "You missed the party," I commented, lifting Jenny onto the tank.

"What do you mean, I arrived right on time."

"Dad, we just escaped," Jenny said.

"Darling, you mean, I just rescued you." J.J. pulled me up onto the hull.

Behind us, smoke began to fissure out of the mountain.

"Charles, what did you two do in there?" J.J. asked.

"It's a long story. How fast does this thing go? I'd like to be far away from here before the place goes up," I answered.

"Very far," Jenny said. She stared at the mountain for a long moment.

J.J. looked back at his handy work. "Wasn't that your Armenian friend I blew up?"

I glanced over at the remains. "Yes, yes it was."

"Well then, there is no need for me to thank him for letting me borrow one of his vehicles."

"Out of all his cars, this was what you picked?" I knew Burt. He had a garage full of antique cars and trucks.

"Charles, this one had the most firepower. After witnessing the army heading out to the desert with you, I assumed I would need a little more muscle."

"You thought right, old man," I laughed. It was good to see my friend. As always, he arrived at the nick of time.

Jenny squinted in the sunlight. Her eye caught a glimpse of something out in the distance.

J.J. asked, "Did William find what he wanted?"

"And then some," I replied.

"We found something too!" Jenny commented. My heart skipped a beat. Was she about to tell J.J. what happened between us?

"And what might that be?" J.J. asked.

Jenny pointed at the sand next to the crater. A large bag rested half open. Objects glistened through the open top. J.J.'s eyes lit up at the sight of it.

He jumped off the tank. "Holy Mary Mother of God," he exhaled, running toward the sack.

Burt Triajan imparted one last gift upon us—a bag filled with all the treasure he had stolen from the temple. Treasure no one would miss.

"At least there's something good that came out of this," I said. I smiled back at Jenny.

We followed J.J. By the time we got there, my friend was shoulders deep into the open sack. He fumbled through all the gold. "I can't believe this, Charles."

We were rich.

"I'm sorry to burst your bubble there, *mate*, but that belongs to me," a voice rang out behind us.

Turning around, we saw Alvin Mitchell. One of the *Sons of Apollo* carried him over his shoulder. The black hooded man marched toward us like a machine—as if Alvin weighed nothing.

Where did they come from? We watched in awe as our two new guests made their way to us. The monk set Alvin down on the sand.

Jenny was the first to speak, if one could call it that. In her astonishment, she mumbled, "How?" (I think.)

"It was a bloody miracle," Mitchell began. "You two thought I was dead, but when the ground caved, I got sucked under. I dropped be into one of our underground tunnels. Amongst all the chaos, my friend here found me and carried me to safety. We escaped through one of our secret exits."

I still couldn't believe it.

Mitchell continued, "I imagine you two must have come pouring out of one of the other tunnels. Your friend's explosion helped lead us here to find you."

J.J. nodded in acknowledgement. He was still proud of his successful rescue.

"How did you know it was us?" I asked.

"*Mate,* Jenny told me that wherever there were explosions, you were never far behind—or in front of," Mitchell grinned.

Looking back at all the devastation, I had to give it to the Australian. He did have a point. Returning my attention to the injured Alvin Mitchell, I still couldn't believe he was alive.

"Charlie, you're not the only one who can come back from the dead," Mitchell chimed as if reading my mind.

I wanted to tell him that I one upped the man by cheating death twice, but I decided against it. Telling anyone that I saw the future sounded crazier than Alvin's unbelievable survival.

Jenny and I knelt down by the Australian's side. I said, "Now that you're alive Alvin, we can talk payment for my services."

"What?"

"I mean, I did just save the world."

Mitchell laughed. "By blowing up an entire ancient city? You just put my friend and me in unemployment, *mate*."

"It was about time you found a new field of work anyways. You weren't too good at the treasure hunting business. I believe that bag of gold over there should about cover my services."

Alvin conceded with a painful laugh.

"How's your shoulder?" Jenny asked, concerned.

"Hurts like bloody hell." Alvin strained to get up.

I reached down to help. Getting the man to his feet, I said, "You look like hell, too."

"Well, then that makes you look infinitely better, *mate*."

The other monk helped me carry Alvin to a nearby Hummer. We placed him in the back of the vehicle, while J.J. still filtered through the bag of Pythia's treasure. I motioned the other monk to hop in beside his fellow brother. Silently, he obliged.

I returned to my friend, saying, "J.J. it's time to go. We need to get Alvin to a hospital."

J.J. smirked. "Charles, a lot must have really happened in there. A few hours ago you were ready to kill the man. Now, you are concerned about his livelihood."

He didn't know the half of it.

"I'm just trying to prevent Alvin's little secret society from being a one man party." I glanced back at the two last remaining *Sons of Apollo*.

Jeremy lifted up the heavy bag. "I'll go load our prize in the tank."

I returned back to the Hummer. Jenny finished making Alvin comfortable. She caressed the injured man's head. "Charlie?" she said.

"Yeah?"

"You did good today," she added.

"I just finished the job I originally set out to do. Rescue you from the Baron."

"...And Alvin," she said.

Jenny's eyes stared at Mitchell's injured frame. I already began to resent helping him. Was it jealousy? "He got lucky," I finally muttered.

"I won't be so lucky if we don't make it to a hospital soon," Mitchell yelled out.

Nope. It was just his annoying personality.

Jenny circled the Hummer, and came up to me.

Behind us, J.J. had climbed up onto the tank and was trying to squeeze the large bag into the hatch. It looked like he was happier to have all the gold, rather than to see his daughter and me alive.

Jenny grabbed me. In a blink of an eye, she pulled her face to mine. Before I could react, our lips locked. We kissed just like before. And just like before, fireworks exploded in my head. I gave into the moment. When we pulled apart, I jokingly said, "Where did you learn that move?"

"From a guy," she whispered. "A cute brown haired guy who I'm hoping to date."

J.J.!

Looking over, I saw my friend still fighting to get the bag in through the narrow hatch. "What about J.J.? He'll kill me." That was an understatement. There was much worse my friend would do to me if he knew I liked his daughter.

"Charlie, he never knew about the other guys I dated. I'm pretty good at keeping secrets." Jenny leaned in again.

In the distance, J.J. strained, "Charles, why don't you come help me."

Saved by my friend.

I walked away as Jenny got into the Hummer.

The mountain continued to breathe smoke from pores in its rock. It was finally over. I wondered if Lynea was still alive deep in the bowels of the mountain. Did the plague end up killing her? I felt sorry for the Baron. Ultimately, he wanted nothing more than to save his wife. I thought of all the narrow escapes with death. It had been a whirlwind ride until the very end.

I was still one lucky guy. I had more gold than I could spend in a lifetime, a potential new love interest, and my old friend Jeremy Jenkins was alive and well. Climbing up onto the tank, I couldn't help but smile. I didn't do too badly for myself.

I pulled out my lucky compass. Maybe there was someone looking out for me up there.

Reaching my friend, I said, "Old man, I'm here to help."

Without looking back, J.J. said, "Charles, how about you help me understand why I saw you kissing my daughter."

Oh Crap!

It was going to be a long ride home.

Charlie Morgan shall return in…

A FATE UNCLAIMED

ABOUT THE AUTHOR

 George Demarakis was born and raised in Arlington Heights, Illinois. His love for history and creativity led him down the path to become a licensed architect. A graduate of the University of Illinois in Urbana/Champaign, George designs and builds educational facilities throughout the state of Illinois. He is always looking for different avenues to express his imagination. Writing has been one of his greatest desires, and he has finally put pen to paper. His first book, *A Fate Unknown,* started this journey. His love for the character, and the prospects of further tales, has triggered this into an ongoing series. New to the field of authorship, George looks to grow and continue this passion. He hopes that everyone enjoys reading the adventure as much as he enjoyed writing it.

To keep up to speed on Charlie Morgan's fate and see what's next for George Demarakis, follow him below:

Twitter: @gddemarakis

E-mail: gddemarakis@gmail.com

Made in the USA
Middletown, DE
06 June 2016